RAY VANDENBURG

DEADLY MEDICINE

A DETECTIVE KAPPAKAS MYSTERY NOVEL

Original Title: *Dodelijk Medicijn*

Translated by: *Jos Rijnders, the Netherlands*

Edited by: *James Temple, Michigan, USA*

Cover Design: *Shutterstock – Sheff*

ISBN: *9789462069077*

Dedicated to Susan

Introduction

'You don't need to put on your sunglasses, dear, it's dark outside,' he said, concerned. He knew she wouldn't react. It was a routine remark, made against his better judgment. But he refused to let matters rest as they were without making an effort. As frail seniors they were no longer able to fight back by themselves, so they'd more or less resigned themselves to their fate. To obtain justice, they clutched at straws.

Four years ago, Don and Suzie Atchison sold their simple house in St. Paul, Minnesota for an apartment in far-away Florida. Their apartment was in a forty-unit building, in a complex of twenty, mostly older buildings in Prosper Park, a quiet and dreamy district in Naples, on the southwest Gulf Coast of the Sunshine State. The population was old and gray; and most residents – like Don and Suzie – had sold their own houses before settling into the warm environment of their dreams.

Don had been a mechanic for Amtrak his whole working life. His job was to keep his trains in always in dependable running condition, and he fully applied himself to that task. But mismanagement and persistent declines in passenger numbers, drastic cutbacks were made in train schedules, maintenance and repairs, and, consequently, on personnel. At his farewell he didn't even get a 'gold' pen, the traditional retirement gift.

In 1955 he had married Suzanne, a flower arranger. They remained childless and had almost no other family. Like many retirees, they wanted to leave cold Minnesota to spend their days in a warmer region. Don had received a brochure from AARP, the American Association of Retired People, in which many retirement homes were offered in Florida. A nice new apartment building in a quiet location near the coast caught his eye.

Especially the words, *"We combine high-quality social accommodations with in-house mental and physical care to make you feel well and secure."* He also was reassured and comforted by, *"Our professional medical staff supports you day and night."*

When Don showed the brochure to his wife, she agreed that, if he really wanted to make the move, she would be happy with to go. Suzie wasn't very demanding by nature and usually let her husband deal with the more complicated affairs. After the rental agreement was signed, the couple looked forward to the moment they could say goodbye to the *'Bread and Butter State.'*

That great day had finally come, and now Don and Suzie were sitting in the communal garden eating slices of cake. Many new residents had been presented officially with the keys to their apartments. The Atchisons were allowed to store their furnishings temporarily in a shed near Prosper Park. As soon as they received their keys, they would get help to move their belongings into their new home. The owner was there to present information about the complex, and a few welcoming speeches were on the agenda. A small band, drinks and barbecue for all the new residents would complete the ceremonies.

Heart-warming! Such nice people here in Florida. And what a great reception! The Atchisons exchanged cheerful looks. This was exactly what they'd been looking for. They felt reborn. The speeches were positive, especially words from Mr. Peterson, Director of SocHom, and reinforced their confidence in their decision.

They got to know a couple from New Jersey. Stories were exchanged in which the grandchildren were the main topic of conversation. Don didn't much care for family talk, because they didn't have much family, and nothing to say about the family they had. He listened politely and nodded enthusiastically now and again. When they were alone, Don asked, 'What do you think Suzie? It feels good to me; these are all fine people.'

'Yes, I think so too, dear. We'll have a good time here in our old age. And thankfully, after all these years, we're away from the cold Minnesota winters. Oh, Don, I'm really going to enjoy it!' Suzie looked up at her husband with a blush of excitement on her white cheeks.

'Yeah, I think you're right, sweetheart. We're in for a great time here.' He smiled as he kissed his wife. 'Come on, let's collect our keys. It's time to settle in.'

Just then a man appeared at their table and introduced himself. 'Hello, how are you. I'm Mark Peterson. Welcome to our community. My staff and I will do anything we can to make your stay as pleasant as possible. I wish you great happiness in your new apartment.'

He smiled broadly, shook their hands and then moved on to another couple.

'Who was that?' Suzie asked eagerly.

'Well, that was one of the speakers, Mr. Peterson from SocHom.'

Chapter 1

SocHom! Don could no longer banish the name from his mind. Now, a few years later, the property's owner-operator was a millstone round his neck. It gave him sleepless nights. Six months after moving in, Suzie was diagnosed with Alzheimer's. She became increasingly stressed and even had some panic attacks. Their family doctor blamed it on the change of environment and prescribed medication. Suzie, who'd always been so loving and optimistic, had grown progressively demented and aged visibly.

Many residents from the older apartments, who only had small pensions, had complained for years about the bad state of repair of their apartments. SocHom was responsible for building maintenance but fobbed everyone off by saying the problems would be dealt with as soon as money was available. But the money never came.

Most residents – tired of complaining and waiting – took no action, resigned to tolerating bad plumbing, leaking gutters and overdue re-painting. They had no money for a lawyer to take their case.

Don decided to do light jobs himself and even began to enjoy it. It temporarily took his mind off of Suzie's illness. He even offered his services to other residents. The Erikssons from Maine were the first couple to ask for his help.

Brian Eriksson was a former garbage truck driver, and his wife Marcia gave reading lessons to children at an elementary school. In the evenings she'd served customers at Applebee's in Bangor. They'd lived in one of the oldest units of SocHom for about fifteen years. They also were childless. The Erikssons were not well off, so they needed Don's help.

'I don't have much to do anyway' Don explained. 'I'm a mechanic, heart and soul. Suzie will manage in the garden, but I'm not a stay-at-home, do-nothing kind of guy. Let me help you and see if I can fix a few things.'

The Erikssons had mixed feelings about this. They were glad someone would help, but they wanted SocHom to fulfill their responsibilities.

'Don, I know what you're saying; I can't sit still either. I've been taking the trash bags to the dumpsters for years. I also clean our garbage cans. Like you, the work I used to do became a habit I can't break,' Brian grinned.

'Well, in return you may clean my garbage can once in a while!'

The men laughed; they got along pretty well together. They relished eating Marcia's freshly baked cream puffs. It struck Don that the Erikssons acted unnaturally cheerful and lively. But then, Brian and Marcia often seemed near to tears. He also noticed they both lightly swayed their heads rhythmically. Did these people silently grieve over something?

'Did you hear what I just said?'

Suzie stared vacantly and didn't react to Don's loud voice.

'St. Paul..., St. Paul...,' she murmured softly, while she made slight, repetitive movements with her upper body. The words were like blows to Don. He saw a broken woman express feelings from a past that no longer offered her anything to hold on to. His eyes moistened. He took a deep emotional breath. Don Atchison removed her sunglasses. 'Here, these are the ones you need.'

With trembling hands Suzie put on her reading glasses. Don helped her into her wheelchair and pushed her to the front door to go outside into the sultry evening. 'Let's go. We have an appointment with our lawyer.'

Suzie became agitated when Don opened the door and began to lift her wheelchair over the threshold. They saw two large, dark figures standing by a large car at the curb.

Chapter 2

Mike Garcia drove his Ford Mustang into the garage, got out and pulled down the garage door. He put the key in his pocket. The cool interior of his car contrasted sharply with the heat in the garage. His leather pants and jacket felt oppressive, and drops of sweat broke out on his forehead.

The temperature in San Antonio was 98 F, hotter in the garage, and kept most folks inside their air-conditioned homes, cars and stores. The dusty back streets were deserted, except in the distance Mike noticed some Mexicans wearily smoking cigarettes outside a bar. A car drove by very slowly. The driver sang along with a Tex-Mex rap song and paid no attention to the world around him. Mike wasn't in the most fashionable neighborhood in town. He'd been here before and was used to it.

The BMW R 1200 GS, a fine road bike, was parked and locked up in the sun beside a freight container. Mike crossed the street, carefully looking around. He was alone. He took the motorcycle keys out of his leather jacket and released the crash-helmet attached to the bike. He turned the ignition key and the engine started to hum softly. So far, everything seemed OK. He looked at the BMW's shiny carrying cases behind him, one on each side of the rear wheel. Inside were packages for him to deliver. The cases were sealed, and the recipient would have the keys to remove the contents.

This was his seventh cross-country delivery run, and Mike reluctantly prepared to set out on the long ride in the Texas heat. He rolled off the kickstand and rode away quietly to avoid attention. As agreed, he flashed his hazard lights twice, a signal that all was well. Although the wind offered some relief, the sun burnt through the back of his leather jacket. He turned out of the street and headed for Interstate 10 eastbound to Houston. The two men on the lookout had seen his signal and drove off in the opposite direction. They could report to their boss that the pigeon was on its way home. Mike would make two overnight stops on the way before covering the 1,340 miles to Naples, Florida.

Chapter 3

The men politely smiled at the old residents.

'Mr. and Mrs. Atchison?'

'Yes?'

'We'll take you to your lawyer. Please follow us.'

Don looked suspiciously at the men. 'Who are you? Why doesn't the lawyer pick us up?'

'After the interview he has a plane to catch, sir. He's in a hurry. Mr. Seidner hires us for private limo services. We pick you up to save him time.'

Don was still doubtful, but he had to make a decision. He had to push ahead. 'Well, all right then.'

The conversation had gone right over Suzie's head. Don pushed her to the waiting car. One of the men helped her in. When Don was sitting next to Suzie in the back seat, one of the men firmly shut his door. The engine started and the doors locked automatically. The man beside the driver turned around to check on his passengers.

Mike Garcia had a couple of exhausting days behind him. He spent nights in motels, assigned to him by his client to provide good security for the errand. He was worn out. After eight hours on the BMW, he was relieved to arrive in Tallahassee, his second night on the road. He checked in at the Holiday Inn and sat down on his bed. He parked the bike right in front of his ground floor room's window, and he locked it to a downspout pipe with three solid padlocks. The alarm was on, so the bike's slightest movement would set off noise to wake him, and other guests, from the deepest sleep. He detached the sealed cases and put them in his room's closet. He lay down on the bed, needing sleep, but first pushed the buttons on his cell phone. He didn't have to wait to get through.

'Hello…,' Jennifer answered softly.

Chapter 4

Heavy clouds were gathering over the Gulf near Naples Beach. A breeze tried to drive away the afternoon heat. Now and then the sun disappeared behind a cloud, casting long shadows on the beach. Hundreds of mostly young people enjoyed the water, sun and sand, always an attractive combination for carefree recreation. The waves rolled steadily towards the shore to finally collapse lifelessly on the beach. Persistently, some surfers tried to ride the low waves with varying success. Sea gulls settled here and there, pecking in the sand for food.

From the high-water mark Jake Rodgers peered at the horizon, where the sun was setting effortlessly in its daily routine. He noticed the ocean was calming down and felt like walking through the water. A visit to the Florida beaches was a welcome break from his hectic office life. His consultancy job at PriceWaterhouseCoopers required long hours and demanding attention to his clients, seriously limiting his private life. So he always looked forward to a week without business contacts, phone calls, texts and e-mail. He'd just turned thirty-five and had given himself a present: a surfing week with his girlfriend, Ellis Henning.

'I think I'm going to cool my hot feet in the water for a while,' he said with anticipated pleasure. 'Come along?'

Ellis put her book down and turned around on her lounge chair, sat up straight and looked at the sky.

'Go ahead; I'll join you in a minute.'

Ellis smiled at her boyfriend and reached for the suntan oil.

'Would you first rub my back?' she asked, handing him the bottle. 'I feel the sun has been roasting me for a little too long.'

'As you wish,' Madam Journalist.'

His girlfriend, three years younger than he, was honored recognized and respected investigative reporter. During her early training in Orlando, her supervisor claimed she had what it takes for that job: a good nose for a story and dedicated pursuit of the facts, as well as solid writing skills. Soon she outshone many of her colleagues. She worked hard and was not easily put off in interviews. Ellis was tenacious if she thought she was on to something important. The recent murder of a prostitute by a rich entrepreneur had made headlines, dominating the front pages for some time. Then, when the businessman began stalking Ellis and harassed her with rude telephone calls, she didn't hesitate to call in one of her 'connections' to force the man to stop. She never told Jake what kind of 'connections' she was using. Ellis loved the attention Jake gave her. If he found out she hid things from him, she was afraid it might mean the end of their relationship. She quickly dropped that thought and said, 'Hmmm, this feels really good.'

'I'm sure it does. You still remember the first time?' he teased.

Jake had met Ellis during a beach volleyball tournament in Palm Coast. They both played on university teams. It struck him that she played doggedly and never gave up, not even when her team was down by several points. Once, she awkwardly landed with her face in the sand, swallowing a mouthful. For the first few minutes she did nothing but cough and snort, but she wouldn't hear of taking herself out of the match. Afterwards he'd approached her and asked, 'May I offer Miss Sandy Mouth a glass of wine to help her get rid of anything that shouldn't be there?' She'd laughed then, maybe at his expense, but he didn't care. To his amazement, she accepted his proposal, that is, for the glass of wine; and since then, their romantic relationship had bloomed.

'Of course,' she answered with pretended shyness. 'But that was a different kind of massage, or did you forget?'

'Yeah, sure,' he grinned. 'I'm off to get wet now. See you soon.'

She laughed as he slowly walked down to the high water mark. There were a couple of dozen other people on the beach, clearly intending to stay longer now that the sun had dropped below the horizon and the temperature was more bearable. Some simple beach cabins, where swimmers could change, stood against the range of dunes. Jake walked into the water and saw that the surf breaking along the offshore reef. A calm stretch of water lay inside the reef in front of him. Cautiously, he always judged the pros and cons of his actions. This had become a habit. So, he now carefully took in his surroundings and saw some kids playing with a skateboard. He smelled barbeque from a grill down the beach. On a dune top, he saw someone standing like a shadow against the twilight sky. He must be enjoying the view. Two kites had collided with each other and circled slowly downwards like two dying birds. A dog barked and repeatedly retrieved a stick thrown into the sea.

Jake watched it all, amused, and then continued his walk. He turned into the shallow water and stood with his back to the beach, slowly making his way into deeper water. It struck him that the water was so clear. He could see his feet on the bottom, even in the twilight. The water came to his waist, but he wanted to wade a little further. Then, a few yards ahead, he saw something floating under the surface. He supposed it was a crab and sidestepped away from it. He kept an eye on the thing. It changed color - from light grey to dark blue and back to grey. Then, surprised, his pulse picked up speed. Jake moved his hand under the water as he made out the floating object. He took it out, and stared in disbelief. He'd fished up a dripping roll of dollar bills constrained by a large elastic band.

'This is crazy!'

He was startled by his own voice and instinctively looked around, but saw no one near. He checked out the spot where he found the money and made a new discovery a little farther away. He picked up another bundle of bills, also with an elastic band around it.

'More money! Unbelievable!'

Jake decided to leave quickly. He could barely contain his excitement. It was like a successful treasure hunt. He wasn't sure if he was being watched, so he hid the rolls inside his trunks. He casually walked back to Ellis, carefully avoiding a few cuddling couples. She had put on a T-shirt and sat on her heels paring an apple. 'Why are you back so soon? I said I would join you.'

Jake flopped in the sand a little too hard, right in front of her.

'Now look what you've done, there's sand all over my apple!'

'El, listen. I've found some treasure, in the sea,' Jake stage-whispered.

'Yeah sure, and I just saw the Pope walk by.'

Jake nestled up against her. 'Look what I've got, money, money, money,' as he dug the two rolls out of his trunks. Ellis peered at the damp wads of bills with only moderate interest. Then her face brightened. 'But that's real money, maybe a lot of money!' she cried with increasing excitement.

'Hush, not so loud, people can hear you.'

She whispered, 'Hey! How much is it? It still looks good!'

'El, I think it hasn't been in the water too long. Someone must have lost it.'

'You mean, only just?'

'Yeah, look how perfect most of the bills are.'

Jake removed the band form one roll. They were hundred dollar bills, exclusively! In the center of one of the bundles was a scribbled note. While Ellis smoothed out the bills to count, Jake held his breath for a second. Written on the memo was, "WA 811– 10 PM"

'What's this?' Jake stammered.

'No less than two thousand dollars. That's what this is. Show me the paper.'

Jake handed it to her and softly whistled when he saw all the hundred dollar bills.

'I strongly suspect that this isn't just money somebody lost,' she said. 'All these hundreds, and the note's message is very creepy.'

Ellis stared in front of her, considering the possibilities and consequences. 'We can't just keep this money, Jake, no matter how much we'd like to. This would be a nice little vacation windfall for us, but I have a feeling there's a lot more behind this. Are you sure no one saw you when you fished this up?'

'I acted as casual as possible, El. What more could I do, I was only wearing swim trunks.'

'Yeah, okay. But we have to leave as soon as we can.'

Chapter 5

The man on the dune disappeared. At a safe distance he followed the couple, who stopped at a motel and entered a room. Mike Garcia parked his BMW on the opposite side of the road and studied the surroundings. The motel was about half a mile from the beach on a quiet back street. Nearby were a casino, some shops, a supermarket and a row of attached bungalows. Palm trees bordered the sidewalks and swayed gracefully in the evening breeze. He looked at the room where the couple from the beach had gone, the couple who not so long ago ran off with his money.

Jake dropped down on the bed and stared at the ceiling. Ellis sat down next to him and looked questioningly at him.

'Jake, I think we have something here that can cause us a lot of trouble. Someone must have lost this money, not long before you found it.'

Jake thought for a moment, eyes narrowed.

'Maybe they're already after us,' he worried.

Ellis startled, 'They? You suggest more than one person? Why?'

'Because it's so much money, found in one spot, and with a memo in it.'

'You mean this may be illegal or something?'

Ellis knew from her newspaper experience that payoffs were often handled this way. Concerned, Jake looked her straight in the eyes. For a second, the motel room was filled with deafening silence.

'It looks that way. Maybe they were listening in
on us at the beach. Technically that's a piece of cake nowadays.'

Various thoughts raced through her mind and she turned away from Jake. She sat down on a chair and bent forward, put her hands to her head, and was quiet for a while.

'Jake, you know that I've been in tight spots, and I want to know all
the ins and outs of the matters I come across. That's what I always do in my work, and that's what I want to do now.'

'You mean we should try and discover who's behind this?'

'Well, of course! You don't think they'll let you keep the money, just like that, do you? We can be sure they watched us on the beach. And then, we're not safe here anymore. The longer we stay here, the more dangerous it gets.'

'Yeah, I guess you're right. Listen, I trust your intuition and experience, but let's sleep first and get off to a fresh start tomorrow.'

Ellis breathed deeply. She grabbed his shoulders and said, 'Come on, Mister Accountant, we have work to do. We have to start right away. I can only sleep when I know whose money this is. We have a lead, so let's follow it.'

'Well, okay then,' he answered a little reluctantly. 'Here's the note. Let's see what it means: WA, 811 – 10 PM.'

Jake pronounced the words slowly and clearly.

'It's probably the name of a hotel and room number. Waldorf Astoria, room 811? What do you say?'

'Maybe. Let's find out.'

She opened her laptop and entered some words in the address bar.

Chapter 6

'Well, that hotel isn't so far away, about half an hour's drive, I think.' Ellis closed her laptop and looked at her boyfriend.

'What do you suggest?' Jake asked.

'I think we should go there first, it's eight-twenty now; so we'll arrive long before ten. I want to get rid of this money, and I want to know what we're dealing with. A good story during my vacation, I can't think of anything better!'

'Easily said. We don't know what's going on here. But alright, have it your way; I'm not against a little action; finally get my lazy butt moving again.'

'See, that's what I like to hear.'

She gasped when someone banged on the door. Startled, they looked at each other.

'Who could that be?' Jake whispered.

'No idea. Let's wait a minute.'

Again there was a bang on the door and this time a voice sounded, 'Please, open up! Your lives are in danger, and the money you found belongs to me.'

Ellis looked at Jake, scared.

'I told you; we've been followed,' Ellis snapped out. She pulled her suitcase from under the bed and took out her small Colt .380.

'What are you doing!?'

'You know I always carry that pocket gun with me, even during vacations. This is very serious. Open the door carefully.'

Jake positioned himself sideways behind the door, unlocked it, but left it on the door-chain. With the door ajar, Ellis called out to the man, 'We'll let you in, but if we find out you're pointing a gun at us, we will shoot first. Is that clear?'

Mike Garcia had no intention of harming the couple and put them at ease. 'I'll keep my hands up. Don't worry, I'm not carrying a gun.'

Ellis crouched behind the bed and kept her Colt aimed at the door. Jake stayed as far away from it as he could and reached out to unlatch the chain. Now the door was loose.

'Come in, with your arms up!'

That was just what Mike wanted, and much better than being pumped full of lead. He took a step forward and saw Ellis behind the bed with the Colt aimed at him.

'Keep your hands up, so we can search you.'

Jake stepped out from behind the door and stood behind Mike. 'Keep looking straight ahead; I'm going to check you now,' Jake said as he started to frisk him.

'Guys,' Mike said, 'I'm clean, I only want to warn you.'

Jake searched Mike's clothes and found nothing. 'OK, it's all right, El, no weapons.'

'Listen. Drop your hands and sit down on that chair. But I'm keeping an eye on you. We're not often bothered in hotel rooms by strangers banging on doors and coming after lost money.'

She looked him straight in the eye and felt the man was in trouble. 'All right, who are you and what are you here for?'

Mike sighed, looked at both of them, and told them his name. 'I'm an unemployed computer programmer from Houston. A few years ago someone approached me and asked if I wanted to do contract work for him.'

'Who were you working for when you lost your job?' Jake asked.

'For NASA, you can check this if you like. As you may know, many developing programs were canceled and I was laid off.'

Jake nodded and urged him to keep talking.

'I put an ad in the paper, offering myself for any service, preferably in computers. It didn't matter what it was. I wanted to find a job as soon as possible, so I could make a living. I couldn't afford to stay at home, bored out of my skull, for more than a couple of months. Then one night I was called by someone from San Antonio who said he might have a job for me.'

'Did that guy tell you right away what the job was?' Ellis asked, her gun still at the ready.

'No, he didn't want to say over the phone.'

Mike continued, 'Two days later I went to San Antonio and met two men, who introduced themselves as employees of a large law firm. They showed me their cards. First they asked all kinds of questions about my work and private life. At the end of the interview they wanted to know if I was willing to deliver packages now and then. It concerned important and confidential legal documents that could not be sent by regular mail. They needed a secure, private courier service.'

Jake and Ellis glanced at each other and then quickly looked back at their guest. Mike continued his story. Eight to nine times a year he would pick up packages in San Antonio and carry them by motorcycle to Naples. Every time, he was told it was a confidential delivery of sensitive documents. He wasn't allowed to talk about it with anyone, not even his girlfriend. If they found out he gave out information about his work to others, there was a risk of a breach in confidentiality, and his services would be terminated. Mike said he understood and told them he'd cooperate and carry out the assignments as he was told. He didn't need any more information about it, except for practical things like delivery address, motel stop-offs, money for food, fuel and his fee. The men looked at each other and nodded in agreement.

'They gave me the job. They only asked me to give some kind of security, so I wouldn't betray their confidence. I was eager to get the job, so I gave them the first thing that came to my mind; my girlfriend's address. Yeah, crazy, I know. They promised to leave the 'security' alone; it was just a precaution. You see, I'm not married and don't have children. I have a girlfriend, but we don't see each other a lot. She lives near Chicago. So anyway, I guess I looked like a good courier for their firm, but I had to give them something to remove any doubt. My girlfriend doesn't know anything about this, and I want to keep it that way, especially now.'

Jake and Ellis relaxed as they began to believe they were dealing with someone telling the truth. 'You said our lives were in danger. What do you mean by that?' Jake asked.

'I saw you found my money. I made a stupid mistake to go swimming first, before delivering packages here in Naples. I was so tired and hot after the long ride, I couldn't resist a refreshing dip in the Gulf. Maybe I got a little sunstroke as I seemed to forget all my instructions and just acted on my instincts. I'd tucked half my fee in my shorts - stupid of course.' Mike slapped his forehead.

'What makes you think we have your money?' Jake asked.

'When I realized I'd lost the money, I went looking for it. But then I saw others in the water near where I'd been swimming. All I could think of was waiting there on the top of the dune till it was found. I saw you stop in the water and look down. Then I focused on you and saw you pick something out of the water. I could see you were excited when you came back up on the beach.'

Ellis said firmly, 'We did find the money. If you can tell us how much it is, we'll give it back.'

'Two thousand dollars.'

Jake and Ellis exchanged looks of approval.

'Okay, we'll give it back,' Jake said. 'We believe you. By the way, have you already delivered the packages?'

Mike was silent for a moment and looked intently at them. 'I need to have the money back now,' he said forcefully.

'Why the hurry, Mike? Maybe you haven't told us everything. You said we were in danger, but you still haven't told us why. And besides, if you're in trouble, maybe we can help each other.'

When Ellis finished, she winked at Jake. He understood what she meant and already imagined the newspaper stories she would write.

Mike shifted in his chair. He felt he had to show his cards. After all, this would be his last ride: he would quit. He'd gradually come to the conclusion that he might be dealing with new friends here, instead of frightened victims. He also realized he was alone and couldn't lean on anyone else in case something went wrong.

'I think there's some kind of illegal organization behind all this. I'm not sure, but I can guess. Yes, probably illegal,' he repeated.

'Go on,' Ellis tried for more information.

Mike took a deep breath and said, 'At each delivery I have to show the rolls of bills, including the small note with the name of the hotel and the room number. I always receive the delivery instructions on the final day of my trip. For this expedition, I got my delivery instructions in Tallahassee.'

Chapter 7

Mike had just filled up his gas tank and entered a Taco Bell on West Tennessee Street. He wanted a cup of coffee and a breakfast burrito. He placed his order at the counter.

'Hello, how can I help you?' a friendly young blond asked with a heavy southern accent.

'Medium coffee, black please, and two burritos to go.'

She brought his drink in a covered hot cup and the food in a paper bag. She smiled and said, 'That's four fifty-eight, please.'

Mike nodded, paid, sat down for a few minutes, and emptied the cup. Then he went to the men's room where he checked the contents in the bag. There were the burritos. He broke them open and took out two plastic covered rolls. He removed the wrappers and quickly counted the money. Two thousand dollars in hundred dollar bills. In the middle of one roll he found the scribbled note. It was the address where he had to deliver the contents of the motorcycle cases this time. He tucked the rolls into his inside jacket pockets and zipped them up. He released some coffee into the urinal, walked outside to his bike, and set out on the final 440 miles.

'So you never knew before the pick up where you had to deliver the goods?' Jake asked.

'Exactly. They didn't want to take any risks. They don't trust their own wives, let alone hired couriers. I was sent to a different hotel for almost every delivery, and I delivered the packages to a different person every time.'

Jake looked at the rolls in his hand. The note had been partly damaged by the salt water, but was still legible. 'Do you know what you have to deliver?'

'They said it was important legal documents, which couldn't be sent by mail or ordinary courier service. That's all I know.'

Jake thoughtfully put a hand over his mouth. Ellis had put her pistol on the bed to reassure Mike, but she could reach it in seconds.

'Mike, all this sounds interesting,' Jake said.

Ellis agreed, nodding her head. She felt Mike was sincere and meant what he said. She also saw he was in trouble.

'It looks like you should make your delivery right away,' Jake said.

'You're late already, aren't you?'

'So you've never been in that Waldorf Astoria before?' Ellis asked.

'No, like I said, this is the first time. The delivery address is only given to me a few hours before I hand over the cases, like this morning at the Taco Bell. That's when I get the first half of my fee. The other half is paid when I complete the delivery.'

'So you'll get another two thousand dollars?' Jake asked flatly.

'Yes, that's how it always works. They use this method to make sure I make the delivery.'

'Wow, Mike,' Ellis sighed. 'This seems really fishy. Jake, let's give him back the money, we have no right to it.'

Jake handed Mike the rolls. He was about to leave. Ellis, looking serious, said, 'Mike, if you need help, you know how to find us, don't you?'

Mike hesitated for a moment before saying something. 'Be careful. I have to tie this up tonight and dream up a story to explain why the money got wet and I'm late. What they want most is the contents of the cases anyway. Well, I can give them that – no problem.'

Mike heard himself speak but couldn't put much conviction in his voice. He shook hands with Jake and Ellis and quickly left.

Chapter 8

Half an hour later Mike Garcia arrived at the Waldorf Astoria on Seagate Drive. The streetlamps were on now and cast their eerie light on the parking area. He was just north of downtown Naples in a nice area near the Outer Clam Bay on the coastline. There were few people on the streets this late in the evening. Mike parked the BMW in a well-lighted parking spot near the hotel entrance. He uncoupled the cases and entered the lobby. It was still busy with people coming in from dinner, the mood pleasant. Some late arrivals were standing at the check-in counter. As he walked past the closed breakfast room and arrived at the elevators, Mike looked over the waiting people with their luggage, while he held his two carrying cases.

The Waldorf was a four-star hotel and attempted to create a modern, eco-friendly atmosphere. The interior décor was colored in a sandy-yellow palette, and rooms were carpeted in earth tones. The target groups, 'families with kids and newly-weds,' would probably feel at home here. The elevator doors opened and Mike got in. He checked his note and pushed the button for the eighth floor. After twenty seconds or so, the elevator reached its destination. He got out and found the sign 'Rooms 801-811'. He walked down the long corridor, saw no one, and stopped at room 811.

Mike mustered up some courage by taking a couple of deep breaths, and then he knocked. He posted himself right in front of the door's peep-hole, so he could be seen and identified. The chain was unlatched, and the door opened slowly. Mike entered a large suite.

'Hello Mike,' a voice called from the far side of the room.

As soon as he was inside, the man who let him in gave him a quick professional pat-down.

'Clean, Boss.'

'Mike, come on in. Sit down,' the boss ordered.

Mike walked across the room to where the boss was sitting behind a desk. He was small and had a pot belly. His brown hollow-cheeked face was deeply furrowed. His grey hair lay like damp strands of grass across his head. A salmon-colored jacket hung around his shoulders. A bright red tie lay on the white silk shirt. Mike had always found his boss to possess a very 'personal' taste in clothing. A huge lout with a dull expression stood just to the boss's left. Mike sat down and looked blankly at his boss. The man who'd let him and frisked him, positioned himself behind the Mike's chair. Mike put his cases on the desk and waited.

From the kitchenette, a large, slightly hunchbacked man entered the sitting room, took the cases and returned to the kitchenette.

'Mike,' the boss suddenly broke the silence while looking at his large Rolex. 'You are late.'

Mike looked calmly at the man. However, his heart began to beat faster and his mouth went dry. He wasn't born yesterday. It was no surprise that he would get a different reception this time, considering his late arrival. Also, he suspected he'd been watched in both San Antonio and Naples. Mike knew he'd made a mistake and could only hope his shadows hadn't seen everything that had happened. He wasn't sitting opposite an errand boy: this was the boss. This was the seventh time they had met. The man never told him his name and Mike had no intention of asking.

'There were some delays.'

'Delays?'

'Yes, I went for a swim at the beach,' he answered apologetically shrugging his shoulders. 'The ride was hot and I wanted to cool off.'

Mike had decided to be honest about the reason for his late arrival. He heard the men snicker. The boss straightened himself in his chair and said, 'Listen Mike, you know this operation requires perfect timing. You carry important documents. We can't risk losing them, and we have to be absolutely sure everything is done right on time, according to plan.'

Mike tried to react seriously and contritely. 'I know, boss; I've always followed your orders. Only today things went a little differently and I'm sorry. It won't happen again.'

The boss studied his tawny hands. Then he looked sharply at the courier. 'Show me the rolls.'

Mike was surprised and didn't react right away. Now it's going to get difficult, he thought. After hesitating, he handed the money. His guess was the boss's goons hadn't followed him when he detoured from his expected route for his swim at the beach. Still, to be on the safe side he rode a few blocks around the neighborhood. He didn't see a suspicious car on his tail, so he parked his motorcycle by the secluded side of the seawall, out of sight.

The boss studied the contents of the rolls at length. 'What's happened to this?' he asked surprised.

Mike looked sheepish. 'During my swim I forgot the money was in my shorts. Fortunately, it wasn't in the water long and the bills look OK.'

The goons were amused and hoped to give him a beating. The boss saw the note was still legible and unrolled it. Then he gave the money back to Mike and asked him a few routine questions. 'Have you been in contact with other people during your trip?'

'No, only your people.'

'So you have spoken to no one about this operation?'

'Just like all the other times, I haven't spoken to anyone about it.'

'Are there things I need to know?'

'No, everything went by the book, except for my dive in the water of course.'

The boss waited a moment, drumming his fingers on the mahogany desk, and had a look in his eyes that showed he was uncomfortable.

'Billy,' the boss called. The man returned from the kitchenette with the cases. He nodded to his boss. Mike understood that the contents had been checked and approved. Another fresh load of "documents", drugs or money, he thought. The boss opened a desktop drawer and took out a brown envelope.

'The rest of your fee.'

Mike bent forward and accepted it. 'Again it's been a pleasure to work for you,' he lied and looked contentedly at the witless faces of the hired 'muscle' as he put the envelope in his inside pocket.

'You may go now. We'll be in touch with you again,' the boss said, waving him away. Mike knew there wouldn't be a next time. A day ago he'd had a pleasant phone conversation with his girlfriend, Jennifer Mattox. Afterwards, two things were perfectly clear to Mike: this was his last delivery, and he would try to pick up his normal life again.

He lifted the empty motorcycle cases and prepared to leave the suite. At the door one of the bodyguards barred his way. 'Telephone!' he barked. Mike stared blankly at the chunky man, took the borrowed phone out of his pocket and pushed it into the large open hand.

'Gee, you can talk,' Mike jibed. The man cocked his arm to punch Mike, but his boss ordered, 'Let him go, Sonny!'

Sonny reluctantly restrained himself and stepped aside. Mike left the room. He wished he'd been allowed to keep the hi-tech cell phone. But that was the least of his worries. He fastened the motorcycle carrying cases to the bike, started the BMW's engine, and rode away from the Waldorf towards a low-priced motel. His hair blew in the pleasantly warm evening breeze. He felt relieved, but also troubled; maybe the boss knew he'd lied and sent his goons after him. Or maybe he didn't have a clue about all Mike's thoughts and moves, so Mike could calmly ride back to his hotel, rest up, and set out for San Antonio tomorrow morning. Nevertheless, Mike Garcia decided to speed up.

Chapter 9

The car drove onto Gulf Shore Boulevard and in twenty minutes came to a halt on the driveway of a large house in one of Naples' most luxurious areas. Yellow light cast onto the grounds from the manor's windows, mostly compensating for the lack of street lighting near the building.

Suzie had dozed off and seemed to have no intention of waking up soon. Don studied the surroundings and saw some people walk from the house to their car. He suddenly wondered if this really was the lawyer's office. The doors were unlocked and a man in a white shirt and pants asked the couple to get out and follow him. Surprised, Don looked at the man and asked, 'is this our lawyer's office?'

'Mr. Atchison, please come in. Would you mind waking up your wife, she has to come along.'

Don was perplexed for a moment and stared ahead, motionless. He tried to figure out what kind of situation they'd landed in. However, he didn't get much time to think it over.

'Come on, sir, get out, please.'

It sounded less friendly now. Don woke up Suzie who began to mutter softly. He noticed a wheelchair standing ready for her. Who are these people, and what do they want from us? Don decided not to make a scene here, afraid he might upset Suzie. They were led inside the manor and then stopped in an entry hall. Don noticed a long hallway with a wide stairwell on the right. A slim young man slowly came down the stairs and inspected the visitors.

'Take them to the reception room,' he said to the man in white. 'The Doctor will be here any minute.'

Doctor? Reception room? Don's head started to spin. Had he ended up in the wrong movie? He could yell for help, but quickly thought better of it. He would be hoarse at once and start to cough, and wouldn't make much of an impression. Of course he thought of his wife, who had no idea at all about her situation. They were escorted to the end of the hallway and entered a large room furnished with some chairs, a cupboard, two long tables and a sofa. A computer, a number of books and files, and a kind of medicine cabinet completed the furnishings. Lace curtains hung in front of the windows, which made it impossible to look in from outside.

Don sat down in one of the chairs. He looked around and racked his brain, searching for answers. He tried to relax a little. Suzie was nodding off again. Don wanted to know right away where he was and who were standing opposite him. The door opened and a middle-aged woman entered. She was of normal build, had lightly graying hair, and was wearing a black suit. She wore half-frame reading glasses. She peered at them, looking concerned, took a file from the cabinet and sat down opposite Don and Suzie. The two men, who'd escorted them inside, also took seats. Before she started to speak, the woman inspected Don and Suzie a few moments.

'Mr. and Mrs. Atchison, first of all, I owe you an explanation.'

Don interrupted her. 'Why are we here? Who are you? Where is our lawyer?'

'Please Mr. Atchison, let me finish first. You'll get all the answers you want. I'm Dr. Santini, head of SocHom's medical service. That means you're not at your lawyer's and neither are you going to meet him. We have brought you here because we suspect you want to reveal sensitive information about SocHom.'

At first Don couldn't believe his ears. How did this woman know he had called in a lawyer?

Dr. Santini continued, 'Mr. Atchison, I'm sorry, but I will direct myself only to you, because I see your wife has fallen asleep. We have information that you intend to discredit our health program. You need to understand we take this matter very seriously.'

Finally it dawned on him: Brian Eriksson. 'Well, if that's so, I definitely need a lawyer.'

'Mr. Atchison, this is no time to make jokes. You really have no idea of the implications of your intended action. If you proceed with an attorney, you could harm the health of many older residents at SocHom.'

Don straightened his back and raised his voice, 'This is a disgrace! You say you look after the residents' interests. How do you think my wife feels? She is very ill and growing demented. Have you any idea how she will react to it? You should be ashamed of yourself. And right now I want you to call a taxi to take us back home. I'm serious!'

By speaking forcefully, Don Atchison lost his breath and started to wheeze. Dr. Santini wasn't impressed. She bent forward and spoke sternly to Don, 'Mr. Atchison, we're not going to order a taxi for you. You'll stay with us for a while.'

Don was dumbfounded. 'You're going to hold us hostage? How do you think you can get away with that? I promise, the press will soon get wind of this. It amounts to kidnapping!' He again needed to catch his breath.

'We've taken that into account, Mr. Atchison. We have already informed the local press about our program. They were very favorably impressed and even promised to devote an article to it very positive publicity.'

Don shook his head and stared at the floor. He let the Doctor's words sink in. Suzie woke up and muttered she wanted to go to bed. Don wondered how Brian and Marcia Eriksson were doing. He began to worry about them.

Chapter 10

Before arriving at his hotel, Mike had decided to see Jake and Ellis again and tell them about his visit with the boss. He also needed some company, largely inspired by the fact that he wanted to quit his exhausting courier job and start a new life with Jennifer.

Now, it bothered him that he'd never been told about the contents of the cases. It wouldn't have made any difference if he had known; at the time, he would have taken the job anyway, just for the money and for something to do. After many deliveries he'd now made a mistake. Against all the rules, he'd deviated from his itinerary by taking that swim before finishing the job. Stupid! What's more, he'd confided in two strangers. He noticed the boss was concerned, but didn't seem to mind his late arrival much. His instincts told him, however, his employer only pretended to play down the matter. He wondered about that. Why hadn't the boss pressed him for more details? Why had he asked pointedly about possible contacts with others?

Mike parked the BMW opposite his cheap motel. He waited five minutes and observed he hadn't been followed. If the boss's bully-boys had tried to follow him, he thought, they would've lost him by now because he'd been turning quickly up and down some streets along the way.

It was Jake who opened the door, and Mike soon put his lips to a cool glass of beer.

'How did it go?' Ellis asked.

'Guys, I'm going to quit. I broke their rules and I have a feeling the boss knows more than he showed.'

'Did you tell him you're quitting?'

'No, I didn't dare. I had no idea what the consequences could be, especially with a couple of thugs in the room.'

'Not that it's any of our business, but did they give you the other half of your money?' Jake asked.

'Yes.' Mike drew the envelope from his jacket and opened it. He got out the other half of his fee. His face showed a rigid look of disbelief. He held a bunch of Monopoly money in his hand.

'Well I'll be damned! What's this supposed to mean?' He gave Jake and Ellis a despairing look.

'They've figured you out after all, Mike,' Jake responded. 'Your boss's suspicions are stronger than you think.'

A white note had been stuck between the fake money. "Rules of the game broken. Don't do it again!" Mike looked shaken. 'After everything I've done for these guys, there is no appreciation. All those long hot stinking days on that damn motorcycle! Before now, I always did everything perfectly on time. This is the only time I deviated, even a little bit, from their schedule. Hell, they got their goods, didn't they?!'

Ellis said, 'Apparently they demand one hundred per cent compliance. You're not a toiletry dealer Mike; the goods you carry are obviously very valuable and it's all very hush-hush. They want to be absolutely sure the stuff is delivered according to a tight schedule. By the way, aren't you curious about what you've been carrying all this time?'

Mike reacted irritably. 'Of course! If I had the chance to find that out now, I would grab it with both hands!'

Ellis became serious. 'I think it's possible, Mike. We would also like to know what's behind all this, especially what you've been delivering. After all, I'm a research journalist, and I don't want to pass up a chance like this, even during a vacation. This is a shady affair, if you ask me. I wouldn't be surprised if we are dealing with drug distribution.'

'You mean heroin, or meth?' Jake asked.

'Yeah, think about it; Mike collects the goods in San Antonio, and where does he take them: south Florida, right? Both regions are drug-dealing hotbeds.' She was silent, and everyone thought for a moment. Ellis broke the short silence. 'Could you make one more trip, so we can find out what this organization is really up to?'

'What? I had just made up my mind to quit. I really don't want to do this anymore.'

'I understand, but don't you want to get some answers and know what's what?'

Mike emptied his glass and said, 'So you want me to make one more trip, open the motorcycle cases, and look at what's inside. Then I reseal the cases and deliver them to my boss. Is that what you want?'

'Partly, Mike,' Ellis replied calmly. She tried to sound reassuring. 'You are actually going to open the cases, but then you report to the FBI if it's about drugs or money. In our plan, no delivery takes place, but we'll ask the FBI to start an investigation. I'll write about it for the paper, so everybody can read what we've discovered and maybe prevented.'

Mike looked perplexed. 'Gee, that's really something. I don't know...'

'You don't have to decide now,' Jake interrupted him. 'If you can get up the courage to do this once more, then you'll do yourself and your girlfriend a big favor. And you could help Ellis expose a crime. But we realize this is mostly about you. You have to really want to do it. It's your call.'

'Yeah, right,' Mike said, extending his hands to indicate his new friends had to back off. 'Thanks for your commitment. It's important. I'll tell you my decision in the morning.'

'Fine, you can count on us, absolutely, whatever it is.'

'Thank you guys, I got to go. I could do with a good night's sleep.'

Chapter 11

It was three in the morning when Don Atchison woke up, startled. He popped up in his bed and anxiously looked around the dim room. 'I must have had a nightmare. Where the hell am I?' he wondered. The room he was in was about twelve by ten feet. The white stucco walls had flat yellow tiles at the bottom, with a light brown wooden edge at eye level. Above him were two neon light boxes in the drop ceiling. There was a door with a fire exit sign, a wash basin, a cupboard, three chairs and a wheelchair. Don suspected he was lying in some kind of hospital bed because there was a low rail around it to prevent a person from falling out.

On his left was a second bed where Suzie was sleeping. He heard her breathe softly. Don wracked his memory, trying to recall what happened yesterday. He remembered his discussion with a female doctor; at least that's what she appeared to be. He'd got angry and upset when she said he and his wife weren't allowed to return home soon. Next he saw two men coming towards him, but then the images faded. As his eyes got used to the dark, he thought his surroundings looked like a private hospital or clinic, very institutional. The door had a small window in it. A dim light was cast into the room from outside. He laid his head back again and stared at the ceiling. He needed to go to the bathroom. After unlatching the guard rail, he slowly slid out of bed and walked to the door. The handle yielded to his pressure. Don stuck his head out of the half-opened door and saw a wide corridor to the left. Then he looked to the right and saw a man sitting right next to the door.

'Can I can help you, sir?'

Chapter 12

Hot water dripped into the pot through a filter full of Arabic coffee. A delicious aroma rose to his nostrils. Mike Garcia filled a mug to the brim. After a fitful night he'd got up early with a light headache, and the caffeine should help. He took a few sips and felt better. Soon his head was clear again. He'd made up his mind and would make one last ride, not for the pay, but for the lack of appreciation he'd received for his past efforts. Jake and Ellis had opened his eyes by asking him if he could still square this "work" with his own conscience and his girlfriend. He picked up his phone and wondered if Jennifer was awake.

'Hello,' her voice sounded sleepy on the phone.

'Hi, honey, are you okay?'

'Yeah…' A long sigh followed. 'I'm just getting up. Is everything alright there?'

'Oh yes, I manage. I'm going to apply for work again today. I've got to land a new job sometime, don't you think?'

'Sure. It would keep you busy, wouldn't it? NASA should take you back, now that they've launched the new space program.'

'No way, Jen; they won't re-hire a fired programmer. What are you doing today?'

'Oh, this and that. And I've given some thought to your last call.'

'Have you?'

'I can't wait for the day we'll be together again, Mike. I'm beginning to feel more and more lonely in boring Joliet.'

'I know, sweetheart. I promise I'll find a job as soon as I can, and then you can move in with me. There's nothing I'd like better.'

'I know; I've waited so long, Mike.'

He stopped for a second. 'We both know, Jen, it's impossible right now. I want to be able provide you some security, a job, a house.'

'Where are you going to apply today?'

'Ah, let's see. At Sunlight Industries,' he lied. 'It's a small company, making solar panels. I'll tell you how it goes.'

'Alright, fine. Talk to you soon. Got to go now. I love you.'

'Love you too, Jen.'

'Kiss.'

'Kiss.'

He put the phone down and shook his head. He began hated to deceive his beloved. Most women would consider him a cheat. Men might think they could get away with this behavior by telling themselves they want to protect their partner from their troubles and worries. Women, however, would likely feel betrayed, because they want to be fully involved in their partner's life, helping in times of trouble.

Mike Garcia understood. That's why he jumped at the offer from Jake and Ellis. Exposing the shady organization could mean a big step towards a better future. He put on his motorcycle jacket and left the room.

Chapter 13

Dr. Margaret Santini furiously banged on the table. The sheer force of it toppled some empty coffee cups. Her staff were startled visibly and were afraid to say anything.

'Why haven't I received my supply?' she demanded through the phone. Eyes ablaze, she impatiently listened to the reply.

'I've had enough of your excuses, Peterson. Don't forget we have a deal. You're frustrating my treatment schedule. I won't have it!'

She cut off the call, took a deep breath and began to calm down. Her employees waited for her to speak again. Their small clinic specialized in combating dementia by giving patients a new revolutionary medicine, a hemp extract that could halt the much feared disease in its early stages.

The product had been used successfully for ages by natives of the Amazon forest. Eight years ago, a returning American missionary introduced the preparation to the modern world. The academic medical community rejected this "medication" because there was no research by independent laboratories or the Federal Drug Administration. There were no clinical test results to measure and analyze. Doctors and patients were warned of possible side effects and advised not to use the product. Nevertheless, Dr. Santini's team had enough faith in its beneficial effects to administer it to SocHom residents who exhibited symptoms of Alzheimer's disease.

Residents who applied for treatment were put through a careful selection process. First of all they had to be childless. If not, they were excluded from the program. If a couple was married or lived together, at least one of the partners had to show serious symptoms of dementia. The less affluent couples were given priority to participate in this unique health treatment program.

'Hello, everyone. According to Mr. Peterson we haven't received a new supply yet,' Santini informed her staff. 'I'm very sorry to say that we can't start treatment of any new patients.'

Her young staff, three men and two women in their thirties, listened attentively to their department head. When they were hired, they'd been carefully screened, and all five staff members had acceptable medical qualifications. Also, they had become loyal to Dr. Santini and the clinic. Their mission was to provide more bearable lives for people suffering from Alzheimer's. As they did their work, they demonstrated a great deal of dedication to their patients' welfare.

'Elaine and George, you're in charge of caring for our new guests, Mr. and Mrs. Atchison,' she said to two of her senior staff members. 'In view of the complexity of their complaints they've been quarantined for the time being. Take good care of them and make them feel at home, but be watchful; don't lose sight of them for a minute.'

Chapter 14

Mike had gone to their hotel, but Jake and Ellis weren't there. Probably went to the beach, he thought, so he decided go look for them. He recognized Ellis' Honda CR-Z parked near some shops on the promenade. He parked the BMW and walked straight to the beach, happy to see it wasn't too busy. Spotting his friends, he trudged through the sand, took a beach chair and sat down.

'Good morning,' he said cheerfully. 'You're lucky the weather is so nice.'

'Well, Ellis and I were just thinking you're going to ruin our easy-going lives,' Jake reacted seriously. 'You're about to tell us you like our little plan.'

Mike smiled, staring at the colorful design of his chair, while keeping his friends in suspense. 'Yes, I've decided to make one more ride. And I have very good reasons.'

The three of them moved to a quieter spot on the beach and discussed their scheme in detail.

Male nurse, George Broderick, returned with Suzie from the bathroom and pushed her wheelchair her room. He saw Elaine Iskander, a physical therapist, busily treating Don Atchison. He had a stiff neck and shoulder, probably from his stress over their involuntarily admission to the clinic.

'Hello dear,' Don said. 'Did George help you alright?'

Suzie looked up but didn't answer. Don smiled at the male nurse and then grimaced when Elaine manipulated a sore muscle, a little overzealously, he thought. 'Hey young lady, don't crush me!'

Elaine smiled and said, 'Mr. Atchison, you have such nice broad shoulders. I think you're sturdy enough to take it.'

Don chuckled to himself. Yes, miss therapist, I'm sturdy, he thought. After what Suzie and he had been through the past few days, Don had more or less resigned himself to the unexpected change in their situation. He'd had a long conversation with Elaine and George, who made it clear that the clinic meant no harm. Perhaps Dr. Santini had been abrupt with them, but he shouldn't draw any wrong conclusions from that.

Chapter 15

SocHom director, Mr. Peterson, had rejected Don's request for legal advice, because he said it might damage the residential and health program. Don and Suzie presumably didn't have the correct information about the causes for overdue maintenance and delayed repairs to their apartment. Further, although the nurses couldn't tell Don what the reasons were for their move to the clinic, they insisted that SocHom's first priority was to offer residents the best possible care. Don was beginning to believe that SocHom had the very best intentions for him and his wife. So, the couple's resolve to make their complaints public would not be helpful. They were told that a repair program had been started, and Don's and Suzie's apartment would soon be fixed up.

As Suzie's Alzheimer's got worse, SocHom decided to give the Atchisons a chance to join their new treatment program. Management suspected Don would resist, considering his earlier complaints about the condition of their apartment. His request for a lawyer was just what SocHom needed. It gave them a reason to pick up the Atchisons and take them by car to the clinic, instead of to their lawyer. All things considered, SocHom had done the couple a favor: their apartment was going to be repaired, and Suzie would soon join a treatment program to help diminish her dementia.

Don accepted the explanation, gradually beginning to believe that Suzie would someday be able to communicate normally and her short term memory would be restored. He'd do anything for her, and therefore set aside his objections. Don began to feel at home and stopped wondering what it was going to cost and who would pay for it. He rationalized the situation because they were receiving first-class service, including three proper meals a day, various therapies, escorted walks on the clinic grounds, and a variety of leisure activities, watching television and playing games. Don and Suzie were always accompanied by at least two staff, who gave them caring attention. Even a luxury cruise ship couldn't match such a service package.

Don had the opportunity to take a closer look at the clinic. It was a red brick, Victorian style building. 'St. Luke's Clinic', built in 1899, consisting of doctors' offices, twelve patient bedrooms, treatment rooms, storage areas and a large modern kitchen. The clinic was surrounded by a high fence. To comply with the latest security regulations, cameras were placed strategically in rooms and corridors. Although most staff members had their own homes, they lived on-site at St. Luke's during periods of two consecutive work weeks, so that patients could be monitored and assisted 24-7. Dr. Santini lived full-time at the clinic. During the evening and through the night, Santini had at least two nurses or therapists at her disposal. Don had thoroughly studied the interior during his walks through the building. He knew every corner of it but wondered why one particular door was always locked. He'd casually asked the staff about it, but was told they didn't know what the room was used for. Dr. Santini had snapped at him, stating that he should be more concerned about his wife instead of a locked room.

'Okay, Mike, that's how we're going to do it. Bueno!' Jake declared and gave him a high-five.

Ellis chuckled. 'Mike, this has got to work!' and hugged him.

Mike nodded and smiled broadly. 'This is a good plan, guys, I really think so. But, now I've got to get going, or I'll be late back in San Antonio. First, I have to deliver the BMW; then we'll wait for the phone call to line up my last ride.'

Mike said goodbye, rode back to his motel, picked up his bag, checked out and rode off on the first leg of his trip back to Texas.

Chapter 16

'Where you want this batch, Jefe?' Javier Rios shouted through the noisy factory. His boss pointed to the corner where he wanted his 28-year-old worker to pile up the boxes of medicines. The young driver obeyed and carefully stacked his cargo on three pallets. Javier had worked twelve years for Bioclon S.A., one of the largest pharmaceutical factories in Mexico. Starting as a porter, he'd worked his way up to be a fork-lift operator. This was the last workday of the week, which meant the logistics had to be in order, so that just before Sunday the trucks would have enough time to take their cargoes to the correct destinations.

The factory was located in Guadalupe, just east of Monterrey, and almost three hours' drive to Nuevo Laredo, a major transshipment point on the Texas border. Bioclon's primary markets were Mexico, the rest of Latin America, and the Caribbean. The company produced a whole range of medicines, from cheap aspirin, laxatives and diuretics to expensive drugs like those used in special dietary preparations, cancer treatments, and dementia inhibitors.

Bioclon had developed a dubious reputation for itself in recent years. The population was bombarded daily with advertisements for cheap popular drugs, which were consumed by millions of mostly poor people in the big cities. Many people suffered side-effects, which sometimes resulted in death. The more expensive pharmaceutical market sector also had problems because some preparations had contra-effects, which could aggravate the diseases they were supposed to treat.

The American Association of Pharmaceutical Scientists (AAPS) had already established that Bioclon had dumped on the market large amounts of drugs that were beyond their expiration dates. In some years, the company had enormous surpluses because demand had been overestimated. According to Bioclon, the unsold and expired medicines were destroyed. The company denied any allegations to the contrary and said that the preparation and sale of their products were always in accordance with national and international standards and rules.

Although Bioclon confirmed 'stale-dated' medicines still circulated on the market, it forcefully denied any responsibility for this phenomenon. The AAPS recently announced a thorough investigation in response to negative press reports about life-threatening medicines smuggled from Mexico for sale in the USA.

Javier Rios loaded his last pallet on the truck and saw, to his alarm, that it was already six-thirty. Without noticing, he'd kept working too long - again. Bioclon didn't pay for voluntary overtime, so he expected a stormy greeting at home, and swore, "Mierda!"

Chapter 17

Mike Garcia had three rough motorcycle days behind him. As he feared being late, he had managed to cut his journey from Naples to San Antonio short by half a day. It was crucial that he meet his employers at the agreed time and place. He rode into South Flores Street and parked the BMW near the dumpster. Down the street, Mike saw a dirty dark brown Chevy parked against the curb. Well boys, he thought, you can tell the boss I have arrived.

Mike walked to the garage and noticed the door was unlocked. He greeted his Ford Mustang, took off his leather bike gear and stowed it with the keys on a shelf. He opened his car door and grabbed his Wrangler jeans and a T-shirt from the backseat. After changing, he put the fake and the real money in a plastic bag. He put on his sunglasses, started the engine, and slowly backed out of the garage. He flashed his lights twice and was answered from the opposite side of the street. Mike looked left and right and joined the street traffic.

St. Luke's looked peaceful on this Sunday morning. The tops of the palm trees around the clinic waved gracefully in the wind. A few singing birds competed for "most melodious" vocal performance. The atmosphere was almost serene with the soft murmur of Gulf wavelets from the distance.

The fence's large gate swung open. A Cadillac drove into the garden courtyard and stopped in front of the main entrance. The driver got out and remained standing next to the car. Dr. Margaret Santini appeared in the clinic's doorway. She looked at the sky, nodded and descended the four steps. She appreciated the subdued morning mood in the open air. Santini was dressed in her Sunday best. She wore a gray suit with a medium V-neck. On her left shoulder she carried a Pampa handbag that elegantly matched her two-piece suit.

The driver held a door for her. She looked back to the clinic, waiting a few seconds, and then got into the back seat. The driver shut the door, drove the car down the driveway, and a moment later, they were out sight.

Don Atchison slowly closed the curtain. He knew Santini went to church. Only two staff members were still in the building. George and Elaine had started their shift early in the morning and were busy caring for patients. Don had heard that eight persons were now admitted to the clinic. A welcome opportunity presented itself for an investigation. He left the room with Suzie still asleep in bed. He cautiously descended the wide stairs. He entered the hall and looked into the long corridor into which several doors opened. Before walking down the corridor, he looked around once more and concluded he was alone.

Don couldn't subdue his curiosity: why was a locked room surrounded by so much secrecy? He carefully walked down the corridor, passing some offices, bathrooms and a storage room. He saw each door had a nameplate on it. The corridor ended at a T. On both sides the short halls both ended at a heavy brown door. Don turned left and could no longer see back down the long hallway. He reached for the door handle and slowly pushed it down.

To his surprise it yielded. He entered a room, and walked around but found nothing very interesting. It looked like a living room that hadn't been used for a long time. Don was standing in the middle when he heard a sound behind him. He turned around quickly and saw the door had swung shut. At once he decided to leave the room, without thinking why the door had suddenly closed. Don pushed the handle down, opened the door and looked tensely down the short hall. He saw no one. He waited a few moments before trying the door at the opposite end of the hall. Carefully he peered around the corner down the long corridor. Someone in a white uniform was climbing the first steps of the stairs. Rapidly, he pulled back and pressed himself against the wall. Don started to breathe faster. Had someone closed that door, not knowing he was in the room? Or had George paid a visit to the bathroom and then returned to his department?

Don's head was spinning. All he could do was guess, but it was important to remain unnoticed. He had to accomplish his mission, so he walked towards the second door. This room must be the mysterious one that Santini had hotly put off limits, when he asked her about it.

The door was locked. It didn't surprise him. It was what he expected. He would have been amazed if the room had been easily accessible. Then, something caught his attention. From behind the door came a slight buzzing noise. Don bent over and put his ear to the keyhole to get a better impression of the sound. The buzzing increased and got so loud that it frightened him.

The next moment, everything went black. A heavy object struck the back of his head. Don passed out as he collapsed. Blood trickled from his skull.

Chapter 18

'Why do I always have to find solutions for everything? You're a man; you should take care of us!' Amorita Rios kicked the clothes basket and furiously paced up and down the room. 'Javier, you have promised me so many times to bring home more money, but the last time was three years ago,' she said desperately, a little softer this time.

'Si, si,' Javier said. 'Calma, cariña. I will work on it, OK?'

'We only have food for a few more days. What can I say to the niños?'

'I told you, I am trying to get on the overtime list. It will happen, really. And don't talk so loud; you will wake the baby.'

Javier and Amorita Rios had three children, ages seven, six and one. Thanks to the support of Amorita's parents, the family was able to rent a good house in a decent neighborhood in Guadalupe. However, aside from that, they were left to their own devices. The children cost a lot of money, and recurring expenses were high. They had no car, only a moped they used for nearly everything. Amorita was in charge of the children's upbringing and the housekeeping. Javier felt the weight was on his shoulders to provide his children with the opportunity to go to school so they could find good jobs and start their own families someday, without being dependent on parents or in-laws. As a proud Mexican male, he was determined to take care of his family by himself, so he allowed no interference from others, however well-meant it might be. He and Amorita had argued often about this, but daughters were treated differently in his country than sons. His income was too low to pay for the house rent. She had frequently yelled at him that he might show more gratitude to her parents.

'Where are you going?' Amorita asked when Javier took the keys to the moped. He gave her an irritated look and said sharply, 'Where do you think? What are we talking about? I must bring in more money, right? Well, I will do that, because I've had enough!' Then Javier stormed out of the room.

'Javier!' Amorita shouted after him. 'Don't do something foolish…!'

But before she could finish her sentence, the door slammed. Her youngest child started to cry. 'Santa Maria,' she mumbled, shaking her head, and began to change the baby's diaper.

Chapter 19

Dr. Santini entered the room and walked to the bed where Don Atchison lay. Around his head was a large bandage, held together with small clips. She took a chair and looked at Don. His eyes were closed.

'Mr. Atchison, can you hear me?' she asked firmly. Don awoke from a light sleep, opened his eyes to slits and saw a hazy figure bending over him. 'How are you?'

Don didn't understand what she meant and asked, 'What are you doing at my bed?'

'You fell on your head yesterday morning. Can you remember that?'

Don thought for a moment. That woman must be crazy. 'I'm fine, you must be joking.'

Santini held up a mirror to his face. 'Hey! What's that on my head?'

'A bandage, Mr. Atchison, a large bandage to stop the bleeding after we sutured the wound on the back of your head. Do you still feel pain?'

'No, not really. What happened? I don't remember a fall.'

Santini looked at him pitifully. 'You were found in the corridor. The head wound from your fall explains why you don't remember it; the fall probably affected your short-term memory. But you'll regain that in a few weeks.'

'Will I?' Don asked in disbelief.

'Yes, and then you'll remember exactly what you were doing in that corridor,' Santini said a little slyly. She put a hand on his shoulder for a moment and then left the room. Don was quiet, looked around and saw George Broderick sitting at a table.

'Hallo George, you're here too? Do you know where Suzie is right now?'

'She's in the activity room, Mr. Atchison. She's trying her hand at flower arrangement.'

'"She's trying her hand at flower arrangement?" Wow, you know absolutely nothing about my wife. That's a favorite hobby.'

George Broderick came over to him. 'You should rest for the time being,' he said gently. 'Should I get you something to drink?'

'Can't I do that myself?'

'Not a good idea; you have a concussion.'

'Concussion?'

'Yes, not a heavy one, fortunately. But you must have fallen real hard.'

'I'm afraid so. Boy, and now I'm lying in bed. Well, George, it'll be your job to get me out of here fast,' Don smiled.

'I'm glad your spirits are up again, Mr. Atchison. We'll do everything we can to help you get better quickly.'

As George was about to get some water, Don asked conspiratorially, 'Hey George, listen. What do you know about the locked room here in the clinic?'

The nurse was caught by surprise. He filled a glass of water, turned around and stared at the floor. Then he took his chair, put it beside the bed and sat down.

'Here you are,' George said and handed the glass to Don. He continued, 'I know how you got here, Mr. Atchison, and I know you're still skeptical about the reason for your admission and the health program.' He paused and then said thoughtfully, 'Mr. Atchison, I like you very much, but I can only advise you to stop this, for your own good.'

'What exactly do you mean, George?'

'I…, I…'

'Well?'

George hesitated, looked at the door to see if it was still closed. He thought for a moment. 'I only want to warn you about the possible consequences of your actions. You're risking your life.'

'Well; risking my life? Strong words.'

'Sir, I mean it. That's all I can say about it.'

'But George, now you've made me even more curious. You know more, don't you?'

'You're wrong, Mr. Atchison. I only know that the room is locked. That's all.'

'Fine, young man,' Don said in a fatherly way. 'But have you ever considered finding out what's going on behind that door?'

'Going on? What do you mean? That it's a kind of Rosemary's Baby's room or something? Maybe there's just furniture in it, stored goods, or it may even be empty.'

'Yes George, that's exactly what I'm saying. Why should an empty room, or a storage room, be treated so secretly?'

He was silent and seemed lost in thought. Don ended the conversation abruptly.

'Listen, there's something I don't understand. First you tell me not to risk my life. But you also say you know nothing about the room. That's contradictory, isn't it?'

'Yes and no,' Broderick said, nearly at his wits end.

'George, if you know something, you must tell me. Suzie and I are being held here against our will. I was knocked unconscious. When I find out strange things are happening here, I think I'm entitled to know what's going on.'

George started to shift in his chair. He knew he wasn't allowed to give his patient any information about internal affairs. But he'd been honest with Don. Santini had forbidden him and all other staff members to enter the room in question, on threat of immediate dismissal without positive references. Every employee of St. Luke's had been obliged to sign a document when hired, which included the following clause: 'Certain rooms of St. Luke's Clinic are not accessible to employees; disobeying this rule will result in immediate dismissal without severance pay or continuation of benefits.'

All staff members had their own ideas about the locked room. Maybe there was a safe in it, or it was a private room for Dr. Santini. It might even be secured storage for expensive drugs. They could only guess. Nobody had ever been inside, except of course Santini, they supposed.

When Elaine Iskander asked Dr. Santini once about that room, she'd rebuffed very curtly. The therapist shouldn't meddle in internal affairs, but just focus on her work, said the head of the clinic. Elaine was surprised by the reply, but dropped the subject. She'd told George about the incident during a coffee break. He found it irrelevant and asked her not to bother with idle worries.

George thought back to this conversation and sat down in front of Don again. 'Mr. Atchison, I'm afraid I have to disappoint you. I can't help you.'

'I understand. You can't put your job at risk. I wouldn't want to have that on my conscience. It's alright; we'll manage.'

George was at a loss for words. He felt his stomach tighten, and it wouldn't loosen quickly.

Chapter 20

After returning from their extraordinary trip to Naples, Jake Rogers and Ellis Henning resumed their daily routines. Jake started a new and challenging assignment at Price Waterhouse Management Consultants. He was going to advise a can factory in California on sustainability and communications. This involved frequent travel, spending lots of nights in west coast hotel rooms.

Ellis took up the thread of her work where she had stopped. She had almost finished a major exposé about a garbage incineration facility in Tallahassee that was allegedly involved in illegal dumping, harmful to the health of nearby residents. She would check some of the facts she'd gathered and then offer the freelanced article to her newspaper.

They lived together on an idyllic site in Clearwater near the Old Tampa Bay. The house was decorated in a pleasantly modern style and was situated in an above-average neighborhood. In the ten days they'd been home, they'd often discussed their recent experiences in Naples. Every day Ellis grew more determined to start an investigation into the adventures surrounding Mike Garcia's mission to Naples. She was convinced it could be a big story and might give another boost to her career. For the time being, she had to wait. Nearly every day she called Mike, but so far, he hadn't received orders for a new delivery. But every time they talked, they went over the agreements they'd made during their meeting on the beach. Above all, Mike was to be as careful as possible.

Deftly and quickly Javier Rios rode his tuned-up moped through Guadalupe's busy traffic. After Amorita had given him hell, he'd furiously walked out of the house, bent on his own manly redemption. He felt humiliated and embarrassed and no longer wished to be called un mala hierba débil, a 'weak weed', by her family. He especially wanted to improve his reputation and maybe bring his in-laws down a peg or two. Respect was what he wanted, and that's what he was going to get.

Because Javier wasn't paying attention, he ran several traffic lights and nearly crashed into a lamp post on a sharp bend. Then he entered a poor neighborhood, un barrio, and had to slow down. Kids were playing in the street and grown-ups were drinking beer in front of their humble casitas. Javier stopped at a shabby wooden cottage. He sounded his horn. A man opened the screen door and stepped outside.

'Hola, amigo,' Javier called.

Shading his eyes against the blazing sunlight, Eberto Vargas casually walked through the mess that was supposed to be his front yard. He recognized Javier and lit a cigarette. He hadn't turned forty yet and had a tall, slim physique. He examined his unexpected visitor. 'Eh, qué pasa? What brought you all the way down here?'

'Hey man, good to see you again. I thought to myself, I should pay a visit to good old Eberto, long time no see.'

'Yeah, it has been a long time,' Vargas said casually.

'I want to ask if you can help me.'

'Like before?'

'Uh huh.'

'I don't know,' Vargas replied, uninterested and pulling on his cigarette.

'I need money very badly, man. My wife is about to kill me.'

'Maybe she should.'

'What?' Javier grinned uneasily. 'Very funny.'

Vargas said nothing and, laughing sarcastically, dealt him a teasing slap on the shoulder. Eight years ago in the factory, Javier had got to know the truck driver, who was five years his senior. Vargas worked in an outdoor department of the large company. He was in charge of transportation for the condemned and expired medicines. Whereas Javier's task was mainly to collect and pile up goods intended for burning, Vargas made sure these surplus products were trucked to the incinerators.

They had talked about it once or twice during breaks. Large quantities of mostly usable medicines were destroyed. If these goods could be diverted and sold, both men's futures would look much rosier. A few years ago Vargas had separated a small pallet upon Javier's request. Javier sold the drugs on the black market and his family had got some extra cash. It wasn't hard to get hold of some of the condemned products. The destruction wasn't supervised at all.

Mexico is less scrupulous about this than the USA. The foreman at the oven was paid for a so-called 'official delivery'. The man only had to fill out and sign a form that all delivered drugs were actually destroyed. Javier had no idea this process was profitable for many other employees at Bioclon. Some managers, even those in the higher echelons of the company, were happy to cooperate with this generally established way of earning something extra. Never a word was said among those involved, let alone shared with others. It was in nobody's best interests to spread around this information. If somebody exposed the practice, it was easy to guess the consequences. By looking the other way and remaining silent, a lucrative black market arose in expired medicines. Tons of drugs landed there, and usually the big Mexican Mafia guys ran the show.

'Will you help me again, Eberto?' Javier implored. 'You know you will get a good cut from me.'

Vargas laughed and ground his cigarette under his shoe. 'You know, I will do it for your wife and kids, comprende?' and added, 'Sixty percent.'

'Sesenta? Muy caro, amigo. Lo haremos a medias, fifty-fifty, like last time.'

Vargas turned around to walk away.

'De acuerdo, it's a deal,' Javier called after him. Vargas remained standing with his back to Javier.

'Monday evening a box will be ready for you. Payment by end of the month.'

'Si, comprendo, gracias! Say hello to Orlena from me.'

Vargas continued on his way to the porch where his wife waited for him. 'What are you doing here? Have you been listening? Go inside!'

Javier watched the couple disappear into the house. He raised his hand and waved. But this friendly gesture escaped their notice. Javier Rios started the engine of his moped and rode home, relieved.

Chapter 21

It was 9:45 in the morning. The temperature in San Antonio was not hot yet. Mike Garcia ran his laps in McAllister Park and now and then checked his heart rate monitor. Still five hundred yards to go. He passed some joggers and had to evade an off-leash dog. He felt a vibration on his chest. He stopped, took out his cell phone and pressed the answer key.

'Garcia …' he said breathing heavily.

He heard a click and suspected he was being put through. 'Tomorrow morning, six o'clock at the dumpster. New delivery. Be on time.'

He wanted to reply, but the connection was broken. It had been a hoarse, somewhat sinister male voice. Mike didn't recognize it. He abruptly ended his run and went to his Mustang. After wiping the sweat off his forehead and neck he got in, closed the door and dialed a number.

'Jen, it's me.'

'Hey honey, everything okay?'

'I've good news. We'll be together soon.'

'Really? You got a job?'

'Not yet, but I don't want to say much about it.'

'Why not?'

'Well, I want it to be a surprise.'

'Surprise? This isn't something you have to keep quiet, is it?'

'I promise, you'll be amazed. But I'm not allowed to say anything yet.'

'Oh, strange, but OK, never mind. When will you tell me?'

'Just a few days. But listen Jen, take good care of yourself. Check the door and windows before you go to bed.'

'Hey, what do you mean? You've never said that to me before. Why do I have to be careful all of a sudden?'

'Because I'm asking you, Jen. I love you. Please do it.'

'Well, if it makes you feel better.'

'Yes… and… thanks honey.'

'Are you hanging up already?'

'Sorry, hon, yes, got to go. Love you.'

Mike ended the call. How would Jennifer react if his plan failed? He sighed and quickly set aside the thought. He had to push on now.

Together with Jake and Ellis, he'd concluded they had a good chance of success. He would avoid risks, whenever possible, and make sure his opponents would discover as late as possible that there was something wrong with the supply. Then Mike would have enough time to get away, out of danger, and join Jake and Ellis. While he maneuvered his car through the traffic, he started to get excited. He felt the urgent need to go through the whole scenario at home once more. After that, he would call Jake and Ellis at the agreed time, take a shower and go to bed early. Mike hoped he'd be able to sleep.

Chapter 22

Dr. Santini sat relaxed behind her heavy mahogany desk. The office was tastefully decorated with large potted plants on the floor and some still-life paintings on the walls. Three armchairs stood around a low table in a corner. A fridge, sideboard and a sofa created a comfy atmosphere. Santini felt at home here. In her office she was be able to calm down and reflect on all matters concerning herself and the clinic.

Opening her laptop, she went to her bank's website. Every time she did her banking online, a funny feeling took hold of her as she opened her account. Today she also felt a little excited. She'd waited a long time for the money that should be in her account by now. Santini entered her username and password. The opening page of her bank account statement filled her screen. She clicked the 'check deposits' button. Her heart skipped a beat when she saw the figures.

'It's arrived!' she purred. Santini stared at the amounts for a long time. This was beyond her expectations. It still worked.

'And I'll make sure it keeps working,' she said to herself. After the adrenaline in her body dropped to a lower level, she walked to the sideboard and mixed a vodka tonic. Then she stood in front of the window and reflected on her accomplishments. A supercilious grin spread across her face. This is only the beginning, she thought. She had to get to work again. A new case in the clinic was getting problematic. It had to be dealt with.

Santini emptied her glass and took some old patient records from a drawer. She didn't want to risk keeping them on her laptop, which she only used for business matters. Hackers might gain access to the sensitive patient information and use it to blackmail her. She took a paper from the records with the summary of treatment. She arranged the papers next to each other on her desk. She kept one of them in her hand. Santini wondered why the Atchisons' treatment was, in some respects, different from that of former patients.

She took special notice of the dates when medicines had been delivered. Because only one couple could be treated at a time, there could be no overlaps in their schedules and treatment procedures. It struck her that between all previous admissions there had been a twenty-four-day interval between the requests for preparations and the actual delivery to the clinic. She looked at the paper she was holding and thought for a moment.

Forty-three days ago she had asked her business partner, Mark Peterson, to deliver the medications for the Atchisons. She began to worry. The recent phone call with the Director of SocHom had not yet produced the desired result. He had blown her off with a lame excuse about delays.

Time pressed. Mr. Atchison started to show deviant behavior. He'd snooped around and had been seen just outside the locked private room. Thanks to an attentive guard, Mr. Atchison couldn't remember the event, but that would soon change when he recovered his short-term memory.

She bit her lower lip and stared through the lace curtains. Atchison needed to get his medicines administered soon. Only then would the situation be under control. They needed to prevent the former train mechanic from remembering certain things that could result in unpleasant consequences for her. She decided to take action, took her beeper and pressed some buttons. Two minutes later there was a knock on the door.

'Come in,' Santini called.

George Broderick and Elaine Iskander entered and stood before her desk.

'Is someone guarding Mr. Atchison?' Santini asked directly.

'Yes, Doctor, there is always someone keeping an eye on him,' Broderick replied.

'Fine. Sit down please, I have something urgent to discuss.'

Both nurses glanced at each other and took a chair. Santini leaned forward across her desk, folded her hands together and said, 'We have a problem with Mr. Atchison.' Then she waited and carefully watched her assistants' expressions. 'It looks like he behaves differently from other patients. I think we should beware of his overzealous curiosity. I wonder what you think of it?'

The question surprised them. Elaine started to say something, but Santini interrupted her. 'George, what's your opinion?'

'Well, Mr. Atchison is very inquisitive and hasn't resigned himself to his forced admission to the clinic. But he stays reasonably calm and is cooperative because of his wife's condition.'

'Elaine?'

'Er…, I think I agree with George, Doctor. He is different from other patients. His brain functions well; he's on the ball. He makes jokes now and then during massages, probably to please himself. Like George indicated, he stays calm because he doesn't want to disturb his wife or cause problems for themselves.'

'George, Elaine; I'm not pleased with the fact that we've had to stop him twice when snooping around private rooms,' Santini said, curious how the nurses would react to that.

'Yes, so we heard. We're around him often and there are the guards. But we don't know how he manages to wander around on his own,' Elaine said.

'That's exactly the point,' Santini exclaimed. 'Why does he do that? Does he suspect something or is he just curious?' Santini thought for a moment. Then she broke the silence and said decidedly, 'We need the medical preparations fast. I can't take any risks. What use is security if someone still roams freely through the building?'

The nurses were surprised and startled by her tone. 'You mean we have to start the treatment now?' Broderick asked cautiously.

'Yes, that's what I mean. I don't want him to create a problem that puts us in a compromising situation.'

Elaine said with amazement, 'Compromising situation? I think our conscience is clear and we do good work. We improve the quality of life for people with dementia. But Mr. Atchison is still much too well for treatment. I don't understand you, Doctor.'

Santini now regretted being so open with her staff. She realized her remarks didn't always touch the right cord with others. It sometimes got her in trouble. She changed her tone to a more positive subject. 'You don't have to be afraid of anything. Peterson and I run this clinic in a responsible way. And it's true what you say, Elaine: we do give sick people some meaning to their lives. And we'll continue doing that.'

'Well, that's good,' Elaine said. George nodded in agreement.

Santini decided to end the meeting. 'Fine, that'll be all, you can go back to your work now.'

She watched her assistants leave the room and mentally digested the conversation. She had learned two things from it: Iskander and Broderick did not know what went on behind the closed doors in the clinic; and she wouldn't inform them when she personally started Atchison's special treatment.

Chapter 23

Mike left the Taco Bell; he had enjoyed the meal and received the usual envelope. He mounted his motorcycle and rode a few laps around a gas station. He wasn't followed, so Mike set out on the last few hours of his journey, a little ahead of schedule. If all went well he would deliver the goods on time. He left the monotony of Suncoast Parkway 589 and was glad to enter bustling Tampa. Crossing the Hillsborough River, he took an exit to Tampa Heights. He'd memorized the route to his destination.

After crossing a few of streets and making a couple of turns, he rode into East Oak Avenue and stopped at an optician's office. He parked the BMW at the back of the building and carried the cases to the back entrance. He knocked three times at short intervals on the frosted glass of the door. Jake showed him in. They welcomed each other with slaps on the shoulders. Mike followed Jake into a small windowless room. Ellis was waiting there, and after another warm welcome, she introduced him to two men.

'Mike, this is a good friend of mine, Sheldon Rosenberg. We've known each other for years and sometimes go on weekend trips. Sheldon is a surgeon and will help us solve the mystery.' Mike shook hands with Dr. Rosenberg, a man with a friendly smile.

'And this is our optician, Frank Salvin, who was kind enough to lend us this room.'

Mike nodded toward him and thanked him for his help.

'Mike,' Jake said, 'Sheldon has brought a mobile X-ray machine and will scan the cases. Within minutes we'll know what's inside.'

Mike looked inquisitively at Rosenberg. The surgeon noticed the look and tried to reassure Mike. 'You don't expect a surgeon to walk about with an X-ray machine, do you? Well, when I was a medical student I didn't know at first what specialty to choose. But radiology seemed interesting to me. I bought this machine with my own personal funds, so I could study undisturbed with it at home. Later, I finished my surgical studies, and as a surgeon, I've benefitted from my radiology knowledge.'

Jake and Ellis noticed Mike seemed to accept the explanation. Rosenberg continued, 'During scanning we must be careful to avoid breaking the seals. This is what I'm going to do,' he explained, and walked to a corner of the room. Behind a white screen was the machine that could turn 360 degrees on its axis.

'We put a case in the middle of the turning circle. As soon as it's working, X-rays are being made. The machine slowly scans all angles of the inside of the case. In fact, one large 3-D picture is created that way. If all goes well, we'll be able to recognize objects and even read handwritten or typed texts very clearly.'

'That's promising,' Ellis said.

'You should see the things we discover in the hospital.'

'I believe you.'

Rosenberg put one of the cases in the middle of the circle. 'We have to stay behind the screen, or the machine may also reveal our inner lives and that's not what we want,' the surgeon joked.

When everyone was standing safely behind the screen, Rosenberg turned a knob on the remote control. The machine slowly started to revolve around the plate. A soft buzzing sound filled the room. It seemed to take ages, but in ten minutes the cycle was completed. No one had said a word during the scanning. Mike broke the silence.

'Well, if anyone wants to know what I've been carrying all this time, it's me.' Everyone laughed.

'I'm going to develop the film now. It's a quick procedure because no chemicals are involved,' Rosenberg said. On the X-ray screen the pictures were built up pixel by pixel to a negative. They all watched from behind Rosenberg's back, anxious to know what secrets the case would reveal. The first negative was black. The next one, too.

'What's this?' Jake asked a little despairingly. Eventually, none of the twelve negatives showed anything.

'Hey, what's going on here? Something must have gone wrong in the process,' Mike declared, somewhat panicked.

Rosenberg looked dismayed.

'Let's do it again,' Ellis suggested.

'Maybe the machine is broken?' Jake asked.

Chapter 24

The surgeon shook his head but said nothing. He knew at once what was wrong. After twenty-four years of practice he knew what's what. He was convinced the machine worked well but feared his opinion wouldn't be shared by the others. So he also scanned the other case. The result was the same.

'I suggest we test something else. If it works, then something's the matter with the cases.'

'Yeah, right, Ellis. Otherwise we'll only keep guessing,' Jake agreed.

Rosenberg asked the optician to fetch a box and put some frames in it. The box was closed and wrapped in brown paper. The X-rays started to do their work. The negative appeared on the screen. Everyone stood still, amazed. They saw a mostly grey image with razor-sharp dark contours in the middle. Ellis said, 'Unbelievable, I've never seen an X-ray sharper than this one, and...'

Mike interrupted: 'Guys, these are special cases, designed to deflect X-ray images.'

They stared at each other. Rosenberg agreed. 'I think Mike's right. The cases have a metal lining, which the radiation can't penetrate. That must explain the black negatives.'

'Your boss takes good care of his stuff, Mike,' Jake said.

'But how do we move on from here?' Ellis asked.

Everyone paused, thinking how the cases' secrets might be revealed. Optician Frank Salvin picked up a case. The others watched with interest. Salvin closely inspected the locks. He was especially interested in the seals.

'What are you doing, Frank?' Ellis asked uneasily. Salvin looked pleased and his blue eyes sparkled.

'What's it going to be Frank? Let's hear it,' Mike implored.

'Very well, listen. This is my plan. First we scan the locks so we can read the combinations. Then we break the seals, open the cases and photograph the contents.'

Mike wanted to interrupt him but the optician didn't let him. 'Then we put the contents back and close the cases, enter the right codes and stick fake seals back on the locks. And that's that.' Salvin looked at the others one by one. They all looked skeptical.

'I'm afraid I don't follow you,' Ellis said.

'But I do!' Dr. Rosenberg exclaimed. 'This is brilliant. Listen guys;

I can scan the locks and read them out. Frank owns a printer that can make an exact copy of the seals. We don't need to force the locks and they remain sealed. Am I right, Frank?'

'Exactly,' Salvin answered, taking an eyeglass frame from his breast pocket. 'Look, I've made this frame myself, with a 3-D printer. I've been selling my own frames for a few months now.'

The others looked at the frame in astonishment. The optician asked them to go with him to another room. 'That piece of plastic was made with this printer. It's really not very difficult. First you make a CAD-drawing of the object. The software then sends the 3-D design of the drawing to the printer. In its funnel are synthetic grains. As soon as the printer starts to work, the nozzle moves as indicated in the CAD-drawing, and the object is built up from layer after layer of thin plastic. Just like building with tiny Lego-blocks.'

'Very impressive,' Jake said. The others agreed. Mike took a pair of glasses and asked, 'Did you make these with that printer?'

'Yes, and you can't see any difference from factory-made frames.'

'Well, what are we waiting for?' Ellis asked.

'Yes, let's get to work,' Rosenberg said and adjusted his machine to make X-rays of the locks.

Salvin took a case and inspected the locking strips. 'These are no ordinary clasps, as far as I can see. They look different and aren't manufactured in the U.S. Look here.'

He showed Mike the backside of the seal. 'Bloqueo de tira – Hecho en México' it said. 'That means the locking strip was made in Mexico. On the front side it says 'The Locking Strip'. That's the English brand name I suppose.'

When Rosenberg was done taking his X-rays, Salvin said, 'Now we're going to cut the strips.' With special clippers he cut through the hard plastic. Salvin took the two parts of the lock and arranged them exactly next to each other so the split was invisible.

'Wonderful material, this plastic, it always stays nicely in place.' Then he took some shots of the strips with a professional camera. In the meantime, Rosenberg had finished developing the X-rays and projected the negatives on the light box. Everybody looked at the combination of figures reproduced in whitish grey. Salvin was downloading the photographs to his computer. After selecting the best shot, he started the CAD-program. Five minutes later the complex calculation was ready and Salvin saved the result on a memory stick. Then he inserted the stick into the 3-D printer, switched on the machine and entered some instructions. What happened next had never been seen by anyone in the room, except Salvin and Rosenberg. The others' eyes followed the printing process in amazement. The 3-D printer was making a locking strip, identical to the original, including imprint and color. Mike startled the others with a victory cry, and slapped the startled optician on the shoulder. 'Man, that's great! Look how that strip was built up!'

Salvin said with some pride, 'Guys, this is going to be the production process of the future. Everybody will be able to make their own things. In the beginning, I was just as enthusiastic as Mike. Now it's almost routine for me.' He winked at the courier.

'I think manufacturers better prepare for the worst! This will be low-cost competition for them,' Jake said.

'Absolutely,' Rosenberg said. 'And my profession will also profit from it. Mass production of disposables for the medical implements will dwindle drastically.'

The printer stopped. On the work table, a plastic locking strip had appeared, made by a computer. Salvin picked up the strip, inspecting it closely. He compared it to the two original parts. 'Fantastic,' he said and handed the strip to Mike, who observed. 'Even the imprint is identical. This is a miracle machine.'

'Right,' Rosenberg said. 'Now comes the most exciting part of the operation. Mike, would you enter the codes and open the cases?'

'I'd like nothing better. That's the purpose of the exercise, isn't it?'

Ellis nodded affirmatively, thinking about a newspaper scoop.

Mike put one of the cases on the table, read the four numbers on the screen, and turned the dials of the code lock to the right positions. He pushed the bolt aside. Everyone held their breath. Snap! The lock sprang open. Mike looked at Rosenberg. The surgeon nodded; he could open the case now. He put it flat on the table and opened the top. They all leaned forward.

'What is it?' Ellis broke the silence.

'Papers,' Mike answered somewhat disappointed.

'Papers?'

Mike took a large sheaf of papers from the case. 'They look like stock records,' he said. 'They haven't put me through all this just for a heap of paper!'

Jake interrupted him and tried to assess what this was really about. 'Mike, we all expected something else: drugs, money, diamonds, you name it. But I think what we have here is just as valuable. You haven't been sent on your trips for nothing. These papers must be very valuable.'

Ellis agreed. She took a sheet from the pile and said, 'These look like product numbers for foodstuff.'

'Let me see,' Rosenberg said. He leafed through the papers. 'Yes, Ellis, these are product numbers, but not for foods.'

Chapter 25

SocHom Director Mark Peterson welcomed some new residents during the usual introduction meeting. It had become a routine affair, yet he still liked doing it. A band played light music. The delicious smell of hamburgers and roasting marshmallows wafted through the courtyard. After finishing his last drink, Peterson wished everyone a pleasant stay in their new homes.

The moment he walked back to his office, his day-to-day worries dispelled his festive mood. Mark Peterson had been worrying for weeks about his relationship with Medical Director Dr. Santini. She had treated him ungratefully and often put him on the spot. There were times he regretted having taken her on.

He had invited Dr. Santini to Naples a few years ago to run an important section of the institute. At St. Michael's Medical Center in Newark, Santini's former employer, she had been in charge of a nursing department for the senile elderly. The hospital management, Doctors and nurses praised her vision, devotion and treatments. They were quite disappointed when she decided to accept a new challenge in Florida. But, the hospital was also proud of the recognition her methods received and had wished her great success with her new job as Director of a specialized medical clinic.

They had met for the first time in a seafood restaurant in Fort Myers Beach. Peterson was impressed by her motivation and determination. He thought the position of medical director would suit her perfectly. 'Several years ago we bought St. Luke's to offer terminally ill patients improved quality of life in their final years. The group we aim at are Alzheimer's patients. I think you are perfect for the job.'

Santini didn't bat an eye. 'Thank you Mark. I will do anything that's in my power to transform St. Luke's into a renowned clinic for which financiers and benefactors will stand in line to provide support.'

They laughed in professional agreement. Santini knew dementia was a hot political and social subject. Various lobbying groups fought for the necessary donations to impress the voters with the intentions and accomplishments of their political parties. Thus the well-known Kelly S. Welsh Foundation in Orlando, a charitable Alzheimer's fund, was associated with the Republican Party. Rich party members and companies donated large sums of money. The foundation that offered help to demented patients left no stone unturned to praise its generous donors, so that both benefited.

'This will be an important part of your work, Margaret. You have to raise funds to keep things going.'

'No problem, I have my contacts. And you know, Alzheimer's is big business nowadays.'

Peterson nodded. 'There is something you must know. Our expensive medicines are no longer reimbursed by Medicare, but I'll personally make sure you'll have all the necessary medication at your disposal.'

Santini waited a moment before she responded. 'Thanks Mark, I appreciate this very much.'

Peterson frowned as he thought about that dinner. It had all turned out very differently than he'd anticipated, and now the whole scheme seemed on the verge of failure. But there was no turning back. Dr. Santini ran the show, even if she had no idea how he had organized everything.

Chapter 26

'What do these product codes refer to?' Ellis asked.

'Medications,' Dr. Rosenberg said.

'Medications?' Mike reacted, surprised. 'What kind of medications?'

'Well, you know, as a physician I recognize labels, codes and descriptions immediately. Let's scan a page and we'll know for sure what we're dealing with.'

Frank Salvin scanned a barcode with a tablet computer.

Reg. Nr.: ME/1/98/903/002-010
Brand: Prometax
Active ingredient: Rivastigmine
Group: Dementia medications

He then scanned another one.

Reg. Nr.: ME/01/107501-3
Brand: Reminyl
Active ingredient: Galantamine
Group: Dementia medications

'It seems these are medications to stop or slow down the progression of Alzheimer's disease,' Rosenberg said. Salvin made more random scans. Rosenberg inspected them closely. 'Looks suspicious.'

In the meantime, the second case had been opened. This one also contained itemized lists with product information. Some scans were made of these as well. They concerned the same type of medications. 'They are all acetyl cholinesterase inhibitors.. The inhibitors stop the degradation of brain impulses to the muscle cells,' Rosenberg explained.

'Understood, Doc,' Jake said. 'But if these are harmless lists, why all the trouble and secrecy...?' He didn't finish his sentence pointing at Mike.

Ellis wasn't sure about it. 'Guys, we must scan everything. There's a catch somewhere.'

'I agree,' Mike said. 'Otherwise they would've sent these lists by mail.'

'I have a camera with a scan option. Are there any more cameras around?' We can use everything,' Jake said. Within a few seconds, Jake and Frank started to make scans. Every shot was checked by Dr. Rosenberg. After ten minutes thirty papers had been done.

'This is going to take a while. How long have we got, Mike?' Ellis asked.

'An hour and a half. Then I gotta go. I absolutely cannot be late this time.'

Rosenberg was lost in thought. 'I don't understand,' he said, staring at the screen. 'These are all dementia inhibitors, so what could be wrong with that? I can only think these lists belong to a particular supply of medicines.'

He turned around and looked at Mike. 'Your boss needs this information for a special reason. Normally, nobody is interested in product codes to simply prescribe medications. The instruction leaflet is sufficient. Probably, his supply is contaminated and he needs detailed information about the production process.'

Chapter 27

Mike jumped up, talking fast. 'Wait a minute. When I pick up the cases, I always walk past a warehouse. I never paid any attention to it, but I'm sure I saw boxes there. Maybe this means the medicines are stored in that warehouse.'

'Maybe,' Ellis said. 'If we move ahead, step by step, I think we'll find the truth.'

'Sheldon just mentioned a contaminated supply. Perhaps they want to know what's good and what's not,' Jake said.

'If that's the case, these lists should give us a clue.'

Rosenberg gave an excited cry. 'Gotcha! This is something completely different!'

'What do you mean?!'

Rosenberg acted like he'd made a unique discovery. He held up the paper. 'Between all those dementia inhibitors I see a different drug here, a diuretic.'

'What's so special about that?' Jake asked.

'Well, not much, at least for now. But it's an exception here.'

After forty minutes, all documents had been scanned. Jake had five suspicious scans, Rosenberg two.

'Seven conflicting papers out of several hundreds. Makes you wonder, doesn't it?' Ellis suggested.

Rosenberg studied the seven documents carefully. 'Three of them have diuretic pills and four MPC-4 anti-rheumatic drugs. These are suspicious drugs. They are unbranded and in combination they can be lethal. I remember articles in the medical press warning about them. In my hospital, we're on the alert.'

'Mike, I strongly suspect this is a cover-up operation. Among the truckload of inhibitors seven boxes were hidden with condemned and expired diuretic and anti-rheumatic pills. The boxes probably appeared to have inhibitors inside. On the outside they were identical to the rest of the supply, with the intention to be misleading. That's what I think, but I'll happily trade it in for a more plausible explanation.'

'And I'll give it to you,' Ellis said. 'It's more and more obvious why Mike must deliver those lists separately. U.S. Customs has only seen the waybills. Information on specific medication is never asked for. Mostly Customs lets everything pass, but they do random checks. Don't forget there are hundreds of boxes in those trucks. The customs officers always check the front boxes. They don't have time to search the whole truck. Look at how long the lines at the border are, even then.'

'Exactly,' Mike said. 'Smugglers and other swindlers or con artists take advantage of that. My so-called 'boss' must know precisely what is delivered to him. But, he would have to open all the boxes to find the drugs he wants. That's an endless task and risky, too, if the DEA does random checks in the meantime.'

Jake nodded and said, 'That's why he hired you to bring the drugs' registrations on your motorcycle, with the documents of the deviating medications included.'

Rosenberg took the seven documents and held them in front of his chest. 'These are the seven code sheets that were hidden in this large pack of paper. They are the ones your boss wants to have. But why? Before Mike leaves, we should try and figure this out, folks.'

Ellis walked over to the whiteboard Salvin used for eye tests. 'May I, Frank?' The optician nodded. She took a felt-tip from the shelf and started to make a sketch. 'I always do this when working on an investigation. It helps me concentrate. I think this is what's going on.'

She described her ideas, mentioned some names, made connections, excluded possibilities, provided insight, asked questions, and came to a conclusion.

Rosenberg showed his admiration for her analysis. 'Ellis, we can see you're experienced at this. I share ninety percent of your thoughts and conclusions. However, there are still some information gaps. But we'll manage to discover the whole truth through our joint efforts.'

Everyone agreed. After the optician had copied the seven pages, he put the piles of paper back into the cases. He turned the lock dials back to the correct positions and applied the seals. Salvin was still amazed at the resemblance of the 3-D strips to the originals. Mike had already put on his motorcycle jacket.

Ellis said goodbye to Mike with a worried heart. 'Good luck, Mike. Take good care of yourself. We'll meet at the agreed place.'

Then Mike rode off on the last leg of his trip to Naples. Jake and Ellis thanked Frank Salvin and Sheldon Rosenberg for their help.

'If you need me, don't hesitate to call!' Rosenberg emphasized.

'We appreciate that Sheldon; you'll hear from us,' Jake said.

Ellis gave her friend a hug. 'I hope to see you again soon.'

When they walked out of the door, they saw Mike just turning the corner. Before they got into the car, Jake stopped. 'El, we won't see each other for a while. When we were inside, I got an e-mail from the office. They expect me in California next week.'

'Oh, so soon?'

'Yes, but you knew it was going to happen sooner or later, didn't you?'

She nodded. Jake opened the door for her. 'Now you can finish your investigation in peace and quiet.'

'Investigation, what do you mean?'

'The one into the incineration plant.'

'Oh, that investigation,' she said unenthusiastically.

Jake waited before driving away.. 'Er... is something the matter?'

'What do you mean?'

'Like I said, is something the matter?'

'Oh, sorry. I was thinking about Mike and how this will end. I'm a little worried, Jake.'

He started the engine and drove the car north. 'I'll come home as soon as I can. Then this case is sure to come up again.'

'Yeah, that's okay, honey.'

She leaned back against the head rest and thought about what was to come.

Chapter 28

Her cell phone buzzed. She grabbed it out of her pocket and saw the caller's name on the display. She pressed the answer key, 'Yes, it's me.'

On the other end of the line a hoarse voice spoke, 'Listen; leave our man alone for the time being. The chickens are close to home. They will lay eggs soon.'

'Okay.'

She heard the connection break, stared ahead and thought. A nasty smile appeared on Santini's face.

Mike tried to assess his boss's frame of mind. Was he serious, grouchy, irritated or cheerful? You couldn't tell from the look on his face. Mike had just greeted the little man with the stubbly beard and was waiting for a reaction. The bodyguards were standing in their usual positions and could hardly wait for a chance to rough him up. He had, of course, caused this himself when he had greeted the goons with a sarcastic jibe that he "looked forward to working with them again." If eyes could kill, he's be turning stone cold right now.

Mike didn't feel confident about the outcome. After all, the cases had been opened. Although everything had been double-checked in Frank Salvin's shop, this was his most risky delivery. If they discovered something out of the ordinary, he would play ignorant, even if he knew guys like these wouldn't appreciate him playing stupid.

'Sit down, Mike,' the boss ordered. 'Did all go well this time?'

'I think so. I've nothing special to report.'

'You're on time and everything seems okay,' the boss said.

One of the men came in from a side room with the cases under his arm and nodded to his superior.

'Good,' the boss said approvingly and straightened his back behind the large desktop. He bent forward a little and took a note from the desk. 'Anyway, Mike, now that you're here; I have a rush job for you.'

Mike was startled but tried to cover up his surprise. 'Rush job, boss?'

'Yeah, that's what I said. Here, this is the address. Billy and Sonny will give you further instructions. He handed an envelope to Mike. 'A double bonus. You took the fake money well. I appreciate that. When you've delivered this package, drop by again, alright?'

Mike agreed and walked out of the room with Billy and Sonny at his heels. He remembered Sonny from last time, when he had put the cell phone in his huge hand. Now he was allowed to keep the company phone until after the rush job. They walked through the long hallway of the hotel and reached the elevator. Sonny ordered Mike to get in. The gorilla pushed B for basement. The elevator descended. Mike's 'chaperones' were standing on both sides of him. They looked straight ahead. Their heads almost came to the ceiling. Mike decided to act nicely this time. 'Guys, I really appreciate that you're carrying my cases...' he said with a grin. Even before he'd finished his sentence he felt a sharp pain in his chest. Billy had just planted an elbow in it. Mike collapsed, after which Sonny hit him with the flat of his hand in the back of his neck. It felt like a hammer-blow. Groaning loudly he fell to the floor.

The pain came from two places in his body now. Before the elevator door opened, the goons gave him a little extra for the road. Two sturdy kicks in his belly made him gasp and spit.

The escorts got out and gave Mike a dirty look. He lay in a corner like a sack of garbage. He coughed wretchedly. Sonny searched him and found the brown envelope. He rustled the wad of hundred dollar bills through his fingers and took some out. 'This is for our health insurance, asshole,' he sneered. Sonny tucked the bills into his pocket. Billy looked on, snickering. 'And now come on.'

This was more easily said than done. His chest burned. Mike tried to get up.

'Come on, be quick about it!' Billy ordered.

He stumbled out of the elevator and regretted provoking the goons. They were in the hotel's underground service area. Various corridors led to closed rooms, both big and small. The men walked down one of the corridors. Mike moved like a drunk, his body aching all over. Billy opened a door and disappeared into the room while Sonny kept an eye on Mike. A moment later, Billy came out with the cases. 'Here, and fuck off now!'

Mike was barely able to manage the cases and staggered back to the elevator. The gorillas stayed behind. He put the cases on the elevator floor and pressed the ground floor button. Soon he made it into the parking garage. Mike walked over to his motorcycle, while looking for the keys in his pocket. Before attaching the cases to the BMW, he leaned forward on the seat for a few minutes, still gasping in pain. Slowly his strength returned. He prepared the bike for departure and was about to ride off. But first he made a call to a familiar number.

'Yes?'

'Mike here.' He coughed. 'Your goons have just beaten the shit out of me. What the hell is that supposed to mean? Next time you restrain them, dammit!'

'Don't take it so personally, Mike. Those guys are under stress. Just do your job and it won't happen again. See you soon.'

Just as he expected. This was the underworld, full of distrust, greed and death threats. Mike was beaten up because he'd belittled the boss's bodyguards. Big mistake, but he couldn't help himself. The best he could do now was to accept it and not be looking for revenge. He took out his own cell phone and looked up Ellis' number.

'Hi, Mike, how are things going?'

Mike fought back the pain in his chest and tried to sound as natural as possible. 'Ellis, things are not going according to plan. The boss asked me to deliver a package. I couldn't refuse, but I'd like your opinion. I was asked to take medications to a clinic here in Naples. On the box it says it contains dementia inhibitors, but it could be the suspicious drugs we discovered. What do you think?'

'Well, I don't know Mike, it's hard to say. All you can do is deliver the package. Hopefully, it will bring us a little closer to the swindle. Try and cooperate with them as long as you can.'

'I agree. They keep the drugs in a hotel, but we can't raid it. I found out when the bodyguards took me to the basement, although I wasn't allowed inside the actual storage room.'

'So you haven't actually seen any supplies?'

'No, well, I saw boxes in there, but the big boys blocked my view, I couldn't see what was in the boxes.'

'So all you can do is finish this trip, Mike. If it gets too risky, please call me again! Jake is in California for a couple of weeks and I'm on my own here. I hope I can help you; and there may be a good story for me in all this.'

He was silent.

'Mike?'

'Yes, sorry. I was just thinking about something. Yeah, that would be great, El. I'll call you as soon as I can.'

After they had said goodbye, Mike noticed he was now acting inappropriately toward Ellis. He shouldn't do that, he thought. Calling her 'El' should be reserved for her boyfriend, Jake, not for him. He hoped it hadn't bothered her. Then he looked around to make sure he wasn't followed or watched, and rode out of the garage with his face grimacing in pain.

After ten minutes Mike turned into Gulf Shore Boulevard. He followed the directions of the GPS and ended up in an area, almost on the Gulf, called Inner Doctors Bay. He found the driveway to the clinic, parked the motorcycle at the gate, and rang the bell. The imposing building was fifty yards away, bordered with trees and shrubs. A voice sounded through the intercom. 'Who is it?'

'The courier - to deliver a package.'

'Just a minute.'

It took a few minutes before Mike saw someone walking down the driveway. When the guard was close, he took out a remote control. 'Your I.D., please.'

Mike gave it to him. The guard looked a couple of times at the card and at Mike. 'You look kinda shabby compared to the picture.'

Mike kept his eyes on the guard and didn't react. The man returned the identity card to him. 'Alright, I'll open the gate and take the package.'

He pushed a button on the remote control. The door lock sprang open. 'Give it to me.'

Mike handed the package to the man.

'Leave now.'

The guard stood there until Mike walked to his bike. He put the key in the ignition and looked back. The guard was still at the gate. Mike rode off slowly and accelerated once he was on the road again.

Chapter 30

Mike decided to return to his hotel. On his way he made a stop. He felt a stabbing pain in his head, so he bought some Advil at a drug store and took out two tablets. He washed them down with a Diet Coke. He sat down on a bench at Pizza Hut. Clouds were gathering and in the distance it started to get dark. Forerunners of a thunderstorm, a normal event in Florida, he thought. He had to make a phone call. He hadn't been honest with Jennifer, and sooner or later, she would find out he hadn't applied for a new job. He got her answering machine, hesitated, and then broke the connection. He decided to head for his hotel, hoping she would answer his missed call.

Tears filled Don Atchison's eyes. He was sitting in his room opposite Suzie, who was knitting. Her head nodded rhythmically. She had hardly spoken since the day of their admission, didn't eat much, and forgot to undress before going to bed. These were signs of senile decay, and it made Don sad. Although he had recovered from the blow to his head, he still had no clear memory of the cause of his fall. Only fragments occasionally welled up in his mind; that was all. Don put a coffee cup back on a saucer and slowly walked to the window.

He started to wonder where the journey would end. For that's how he experienced life in the clinic: a journey to the unknown, without description, but with permanent care. In the meantime George Broderick was making the bed. After he finished, he went over to Don. 'Mr. Atchison?'

Don let go of his thoughts and looked sideways. 'Yes, George?'

'I have good news about your wife. Dr. Santini told me she could join the dementia program shortly. The special medications for her have arrived.'

'Is that so? That's good news, George.'

'You can join as well, if you like. Tests show that you suffer from amnesia, aggravated by your fall.'

'You don't expect me to leave my Suzie alone, do you?'

'No, of course not, Mr. Atchison. It would be great if both of you could follow the program. We're confident it will benefit you and your wife.'

'Well, it doesn't hurt to try.'

They both laughed.

It struck George that Don had become compliant and cooperative. Had he resigned himself to the rules of the house? Did he feel warned? It didn't matter much to him. He was happy to be able to help provide this couple with some quality of life in their final years. 'May I ask you something, Mr. Atchison?'

'Sure, George, go ahead.'

'Do you have any children or relatives?'

'No. Suzie and I wanted children very much, but God had other plans for us. We're Christians, from good-sized Catholic families. But we haven't heard anything from relatives for years now. That's really my fault; I don't care much for family, you know.'

Broderick smiled. 'I understand. Thanks for telling me.'

'Well, what difference does it make; we're spending our last years here. To be serous; I appreciate what you and Elaine do for Suzie. You're good people.'

'Thank you, sir.'

Don hesitated for a moment. 'I'd like to ask you, George, to call me Don from now on. Is that alright with you?'

His boss was pleased with the fast delivery of the package. 'Mike, you're my top courier. Well done.'

Mike laughed, still a little painfully. 'I'm just doing my job.'

'Come on, not so modest. What you do, those guys couldn't manage in a million years,' he said nodding his head towards Billy and Sonny.

Not a very smart move, boss, Mike thought, they may beat me up again.

'Here; a small bonus. I'll call you again for a new delivery from San Antonio. Goodbye for now.'

Mike accepted the envelope and pointed at the bodyguards.

'I see what you mean, Mike. Guys, stay here. This gentleman can show himself out.'

Mike imagined the two toughs grinding their teeth and decided to rub some salt in their wounds. 'Guys, you heard what the boss said. By the way, Sonny, do you always leave your fly open?'

Instinctively the bodyguard looked down. His pants were in perfect order. His face turned scarlet and he wanted to lash out.

'Sonny! Stay right there!' his boss barked. 'Mike, get out! I have enough on my mind without having to calm down these two.'

Mike grinned, put the company phone on the desk and walked out of the room. Outside he opened the envelope and counted two thousand dollars. He left the BMW in the garage and walked directly to the nearby Hertz Car Rental for a fast convertible. The manager showed him a Corvette. He paid four day's rent in full, with an option for another three days. 'I just spent my bonus,' he thought. Mike had a hunch that he needed a speedy and reliable vehicle. He sat down behind the wheel and examined the dashboard instruments. He smiled with pleasure and drove away. He parked the car just outside the hotel premises. He remembered his decision. He really wanted to quit right now, and he definitely owed that to Jennifer.

They'd discussed it in Salvin's shop. As soon as Mike had made the delivery, their plan would become operational. The unexpected extra delivery in Naples had taken him by surprise. Ellis was also surprised, but positive. In his mind he went back to the moment the package was delivered. At a hospital, or any institution for that matter, they would have been pleased to receive a high-priority delivery. Mike found the guard's behavior suspicious. The man had been surly, not showing even a little courtesy. Not that he'd taken it personally; what mattered was what lay behind that attitude. Now he could take action to find out what went on behind the clinic's walls and why the drug deliveries were surrounded by so much secrecy.

He felt like examining it all, down to the last detail. He still had a bone to pick with his boss, who'd allowed his toughs to beat him up. Mike decided not to return to San Antonio. Instead he drove to a low-priced motel just outside Naples, checked in and went to his room. He'd stay here for the time being. He called Jennifer, and this time she answered. A long conversation followed in which his girlfriend told him she was disappointed he couldn't join her soon, especially since she already had been waiting for such a long time. Something had come up, he had said. She hadn't accepted this explanation. He couldn't convince her that he had been looking for work or had already found a job. Finally she had ended the sometimes testy discussion, with a 'suit yourself!'

Mike stared at his cell phone, thinking that somehow it should have gone better. 'Damn.' Angry, he threw his phone on the floor, breaking the case. He collected the pieces and took out the SIM card. Later on, he would buy a new one.

Chapter 31

The Silver Airways Turboprop from Orlando landed exactly on time at Southwest International Airport in Ft. Myers. Businessmen hurried from the gate to the terminal's exit wanting to get home as soon as possible. Ellis took it easy, calmly pulling her small wheeled carry-on. She came from a meeting at her publisher's office where they talked over future subjects that should be investigated for interesting magazine articles. For the moment, she was hooked on Mike Garcia's case, which could be a hell of story. Since Jake was in California for a while, she took the opportunity to join Mike in his quest to discover the truth behind the suspected medicine packages.

Ellis walked into the main terminal, passed the airport police office and spotted Mike near the Information Desk. They greeted each other with enthusiasm.

'How was your flight?'

'Rather good, actually. I never used Silver Airways before. Maybe a little noisy, but the service was okay.'

'And your flight was right on time.'

'Yeah, I noticed. You can't say that about most other airlines.'

'Do you feel like a cup of coffee?'

'Would be great. Do you know a nice place here?'

'Yes, but it's no Starbucks. We'll go to Pete's Coffee Corner. It's pleasant and not too busy.'

'Sounds good to me.'

Ten minutes later they were enjoying cappuccinos.

'Do you know this place is run by a Dutchman? His name is Peter Hartsema, but he calls himself Pete because it sounds more casual. And what's more, his coffee comes all the way from Holland.'

'You're well-informed. I've read that many drinks and foods from Holland are very good, especially their beer and many varieties of bread and cheese.'

'Yes, but here we mostly drink weak-tasting beer, squidgy white bread and mild cheddar or processed American cheese.'

They laughed. They felt comfortable with each other. This was their first time together, just the two of them, and they had a mission.

'How did you get that bruise in your neck?'

'Oh well, just a little accident. It's nothing.'

'Mike, if we're going to work together on a risky mission, we have to trust each other, agreed?'

'Agreed.'

'So, how did you get that bruise?'

'Okay, you're right. The boss's goons said 'goodbye' to me a little too roughly.'

'Mike?! How bad was it, really?'

He laughed. 'You don't have your Colt pointed at me under the table to force a confession from me, do you?'

Ellis kept seriously silent, keeping a straight face.

'What I mean is they beat me up, even though I act nice. These guys are so stressed and full of adrenaline they took it out on me.'

Her face relaxed. 'Does it still hurt?' she asked compassionately.

'Not much, thanks to a bottle of Advil.'

'Good, so I don't have to worry about you?'

'Not at all; I'm a big boy. But how are you doing now Jake's gone?'

'Temporarily gone.'

'Of course, that's what I mean. Won't you miss him? What does he think of us working together on this investigation?'

Mike noticed her slight hesitation before she answered. 'Of course I miss him. But this is what we agreed on. And he knows that I'm away sometimes on a case. We both have interesting jobs. We respect how we organize our work and the assignments that cross our paths.' She finished the last of her coffee. 'Would you like another one? My treat.'

'Yes, please,' he replied. When she started to look around for a waiter in the Coffee Corner, Mike studied her with interest. She was a medium-sized, slim woman with regular features and big eyes. She used only light make-up on her face. Her mid-length blond hair hung loosely to her shoulders. She wore corduroy slacks and a casual jacket over her blouse. A broad leather belt was fastened around her waist. He had to admit that a very pretty woman was sitting opposite him, a clever, sprightly and interesting figure.

'And you? What about your relationship?'

The waiter placed fresh cups on the table. Mike thoughtlessly poured more milk into his cappuccino. 'With Jennifer? Well, we don't see much of each other, she lives at the other end of the world, so to speak, south of Chicago. We talk on the phone a lot. She wanted to move in with me, but that doesn't suit me very well right now. I first want to have a regular job again so I can offer her more security. That's what I keep telling her.'

'And what does she say to that?'

'Not much, really, sometimes she gets angry with me.' He looked at Ellis, a little embarrassed. 'But I must finish this first. I can't just drop it. It has given me so much pain and trouble, frightening moments, like the issue with the money. That's why I'm glad to have found someone to help me. I can't do this myself, and I don't have any connections here. But thanks to your contacts, we've already discovered a lot.'

'Don't get me wrong, Mike. I'm driven solely by self-interest. I have a gut feeling there's a great story in all of this. But it also could mean nothing. Hard luck for me then. You've got guts and aren't easily scared off. I appreciate that.'

'Thanks, El. Oh, sorry, may I call you El?'

She took his hand. 'Mike, all my friends call my El. So, please do.'

He felt a little surprised, but pleased, and withdrew his hand. 'I suggest we get going. As agreed, I booked two hotel rooms.'

'Alright. Let my pay for the coffee. Your turn next time.'

Chapter 32

Dr. Margaret Santini slit open the package with scissors. She counted thirty-six boxes of diuretic and anti-rheumatic pills past their expiration dates. Great! It was as if she'd won the lottery. For weeks she'd waited for them, and she'd had to muster all her patience. Like snow in summer, her animosity towards SocHom Director, Mark Peterson, evaporated. He'd used his influence to get the required goods. That's why she understood the short telephone message she had received from him recently. His message had been clear enough. To prevent problems, only Mark Peterson was allowed to contact his source. Santini needed to wait patiently until a suitable delivery was made again. As a doctor she was just a cog, a well-paid cog, in the machine. She counted her blessings.

Santini asked George Broderick and Elaine Iskander to come to her office. She told them the special health program medications were available and would be offered to one couple in the clinic. 'It's been a few months since any of our guests took part in the program. So I'm pleased the new medicines have arrived and we can continue our work to fulfill our vision.'

The therapist and nurse knew what they had to do. They would inform the couple they were in the program and explain the treatment to them.

'Next, you take Mr. and Mrs. Eriksson to the treatment room. That's when I take over and introduce them to our unique, first-class service. St. Luke's is the only clinic in the country that serves the wishes and needs of its guests in such a way.'

George reflected for a moment and thought he had made a mistake. It wasn't the Atchisons' but the Erikssons' turn. He wondered how he could explain this to Don and Suzie. George didn't show his concern to Dr. Santini and said, 'We'll inform Mr. and Mrs. Eriksson right away.'

Chapter 33

After checking in, Mike went to Ellis' room for a planning meeting.

'Come in,' she called after he had knocked three times.

Carefully, he put his head around the half-opened door. She was sitting at a small table.

'The last time I entered your hotel room I looked into the barrel of your Colt-38,' Mike teased.

'It still bothers you, doesn't it? By the way, do you carry a gun?'

He shook his head.

'Then we must buy one, for your own safety and mine. Do you know how to handle weapons?'

'I was in the army and you don't lose your touch easily. I prefer a Walther PPK 380.'

'Fine, we'll buy one. I suppose you have a credit card?'

He nodded.

'That's settled then. Now, let's discuss the case. What do we have so far? A few suspicious medicine lists and your express delivery to the clinic in Naples. It's possible this delivery was fishy. We can't be sure and it isn't much, but it gives us something to go on.'

'Some Googling may help us along. Let's have a look at that clinic.'

'Good idea. I'm going to make a call from the bedroom,' Ellis said, walking away.

'Who are you calling?'

'Our optician friend, Frank Salvin. He has such useful instruments in his shop. I'm sure he's willing to help us.'

She shut the door so as not to disturb Mike. He concentrated on his laptop and entered "St. Luke's Naples" on Google. The website appeared quickly on his computer screen. "Welcome to the homepage of St. Luke's Private Clinic". A large picture of the building and part of the surrounding grounds was featured on the page. He recognized it at once. The picture must have been taken near the gated entrance. Mike looked for "contact us" and "who are we?" links, but nothing. Funny, he thought, a website without contact information?

The website had just three pages with information about the clinic, treatments and staff. The text was written in a lofty style, intended to motivate people to contact "your Director of the Care Center."

He tried to find out who owned the website. On www.whois.net

he discovered that "St. Luke's Private Clinic" was registered under the name "SocHom Rentals Inc."

Bingo, Mike thought. But what or who is SocHom? He soon found out it's a residential community for senior citizens in Naples. The conclusion was obvious: SocHom and St. Luke's are connected to each other, communicating entities. This seemed to be a reasonable relationship, considering the needs of the elderly.

In the meantime, Ellis had returned to the room. 'Frank Salvin is prepared to lend us one of his instruments. He said we have to be careful with it. It's a very expensive piece of equipment. I also tried to contact Sheldon Rosenberg, but he didn't answer the phone.'

'Okay, I found a link. That clinic is connected to a residential care center, both in Naples. I suggest we pay a visit to the Director.'

'Yes. We can pose as FDA assistants. The cards Sheldon gave us will come in handy.'

'That surgeon of yours seems to have a lot of helpful contacts.'

'Hey, wait a minute,' Ellis tried to dampen his enthusiasm. 'We can't forget to be cautious with them. The more people we involve in our investigation, the greater the chance of mistakes. That's my experience at least.'

Mike nodded. He was convinced he had a terrific partner in Ellis Henning.

Chapter 34

The "officials of the U.S. Food and Drug Administration (FDA)" freely walked through the open gate of the walled residential community. Unlike most "gated communities" SocHom didn't have a gatekeeper and barrier at the entrance. This was an open community of forty buildings in Prosper Park, Naples. Residents walked free and easy across the grounds, an open lawn with footpaths. One group was lawn bowling. Some strolled with the help of walkers or drove themselves around in electric scooters or golf carts. Mike and Ellis looked at the signpost near the entrance:

Housing units   1-10
Housing units 11-20
Housing units 21-30
Housing units 31-40
Supermarket
Restaurant
Bar
Synagogue
Baptist Church
RC Church
First Aid Station
Library
Community Center
Physical Therapy
Hairdresser
Janitor
Offices

'The janitor would be well-informed about what goes on around here, wouldn't he?' Ellis asked.

'Yes, I think so. Not only would he know a lot about practical things and problems, but he may also pick up gossip from residents.'

'So, for a little undercover work, let's start with the janitor, okay?'

'Good idea.'

While walking to the janitor's office, a voice called from behind. 'Hello there! Where are you going?'

Mike turned around. They were accosted by a resident. He said,

'Hello ma'am, we're looking for the janitor?'

'Oh, then you're going the right way. What do you need him for? As far as I can tell, you're much too young to live here.'

'Yes, you're right about that. My parents live here. They complain about the heating. And now that we're here, we thought…'

'Yes, yes, very good. If only I had children, but I have to do everything myself.'

'How unpleasant for you,' Ellis said.

'So you're a single woman?' Mike asked.

'Yes, my husband died three years ago. Cancer.'

Mike shook his head. 'I'm sorry to hear that.'

Ellis thought this was the right moment to change the subject. 'How long have you lived here, if I may ask?'

'Oh, 25 years now. I was one of the first residents. I've seen many changes over the years.'

'So you probably know a lot of people here?'

'Well, knowing is a big word, let's say I keep myself informed,' the lady laughed.

Mike and Ellis looked at each other, realizing this could be a useful informant. 'Ma'am, we're looking for the restaurant too. Would you like to have some iced tea or a cup of coffee with a nice cream puff?' Ellis asked.

The woman looked a little suspiciously at them. 'I thought you we're visiting your parents? But never mind, that's not my business.' Then she smiled. 'Alright, you seem like nice young people, I accept your invitation.'

'Great. Then we can chat a little,' Ellis encouraged.

Chapter 35

The three of them were having coffee and chocolate cake (sadly the restaurant had no cream puffs). At this time of day the place wasn't busy and Mike and Ellis easily found a quiet spot where they wouldn't be overheard.

'That's nice,' the woman crowed, after putting a piece of cake into her mouth. 'To what do I owe this?'

'Well,' Mike said, winking at Ellis. 'We have something to celebrate.'

'Is that so?' the woman asked curiously.

'Today is our tenth wedding anniversary and,' he felt a kick in his shin, 'we're happy you're here to share a part of it.'

'Well, well, you youngsters have been married for ten years? That's great!' And then she whispered, 'Hey, would you like a fix? My treat.'

'Er, what kind of fix do you have in mind?' Mike asked.

'Fix! A dram. A blue ruin. A drink,' she called out.

'Mike, she means gin. Thank you ma'am , that's very kind of you.'

'Wait, I'll get it for you myself.'

The woman rose and cheerfully walked to the bar.

'What are you doing?' Mike asked covering his mouth with his hand. 'I don't drink alcohol.'

'Mike, this woman may be invaluable to us. We must try and keep her with us and find out what we can. I ask you, just once, to renounce your abstention from strong drink. And one more thing; refrain from telling people we're married, from now on.'

Mike felt her penetrating look. 'Alright. I'll cooperate. I agree we might get some useful information from this lady.'

The woman returned with the drinks. 'There you are, a drink in honor of your wedding anniversary. Enjoy!'

With her facial expression Ellis tried to prompt Mike to show his gratitude. 'Yes, thank you for the drink, we appreciate it very much,' he said with a slightly cynical undertone.

Ellis kicked him a little harder this time. Suddenly she looked startled at Mike and put her hand on her mouth. 'Oh, Mike, we haven't even introduced ourselves. Ma'am, this is Mike Johnson and I'm Ellis Harding.'

It was silent for a while. The woman's face froze. Mike laughed inwardly. Johnson? Harding? How did she come up with that?

'So… you're not Mrs. Johnson?' the woman asked carefully. Mike waited with a grin on his face for his wife's answer.

'No, we decided to use our own names, didn't we Mike?'

'Yeah, sure, quite true.'

The woman looked at them in disbelief, but decided to drop the subject. 'I'm Hannah Warakomski. My parents were from Poland. I was born in the U.S.'

'Warakomski. Sounds Jewish, is that right?' Ellis asked.

'Yes, I'm not orthodox, although I get a lot of support from the Jewish community here at SocHom.'

Ellis thought the moment had come for the real questions. She finished her gin and asked casually, 'Mrs. Warakomski, you say you know a lot of people around here. Have you ever met the management?'

'Management? You mean Mr. Peterson?'

Ellis nodded.

'Oh yes, he frequently visits the recreation room and has coffee with us. He always welcomes the new arrivals on welcoming day. I never go because it's really for the new residents. I've heard it's a very pleasant event with snacks and music. He always stays for a few hours to mingle with the people.'

'Do you know him personally?'

'Certainly! He's a fine man, very good for our residential community.'

'In what way?' Mike asked.

'How do you mean?'

'Socially. How can you tell?'

'Well, he helps with moving in, for instance. I mean, he makes sure people get settled and that packing boxes are removed. Things like that. He has a very pleasant manner and shows real interest in the people here. But he can't do everything on his own, of course; he has assistants. After all, he is the Director.'

Ellis thought this was the right moment to ask for more. 'And if anyone's ill, does he offer help?'

Warakomski reflected for a moment. 'You mean like at the first aid station?'

Ellis was cautious. She had to ask the right question now to prevent their guest from becoming suspicious. She knew from experience that if this happened to people, they were on their guard and evaded questions. If she beat about the bush, however, she wouldn't get to the heart of the matter. 'No, not at first aid, but perhaps he helps with referring people to hospitals or clinics outside the community.'

Ellis waited carefully for the woman's response. Now she either quits or answers.

'I don't quite get what you mean.' Warakomski leaned back and made a wry face.

There we go, Mike thought. He acted quickly, trying to help his partner. 'Mrs. Warakomski, please understand that our parents are not very healthy anymore. We need to check into the care available outside the community. Do you think Mr. Peterson will be able to help us with that?'

He heard Ellis give a sigh of relief. She winked gratefully at him.

'Oh, I'm sorry to hear that,' Warakomski said compassionately. 'Your parents aren't well? I think Mr. Peterson can certainly help you there.'

'You really think so?' Ellis asked, hoping the lady would be more specific.

'Absolutely. Recently he referred neighbors of mine to a clinic. According to the Doctor, they were very ill, although I never noticed anything unusual about them. But then they don't have to tell me anything. I'm just a neighbor.'

Mike looked at Ellis. 'Do you remember mother talking about Mr. and Mrs. Wainscott? I think Mrs. Warakomski has that couple in mind. They were just admitted to a clinic. Am I right, Mrs. Warakomski?'

She shook her head. 'No, I've never heard of that name, but that must be Brian and Marcia Eriksson. Nice people, originally from Sweden. They don't mix with others so much, but I don't mind.'

Mike and Ellis signaled each other that the conversation had to end.

'Ma'am, we enjoyed talking to you very much. But we have to speak with the janitor too. There's a big problem with Mike's parents' central heating.'

'Yes, of course.'

'We wish you all the best and thanks for the drinks.'

'Oh, you're welcome, give my regards to your parents.'

Mike and Ellis got up and quickly walked to the exit. At the door they heard a shrill voice, resonating through the whole restaurants. 'Hey, sir, what are your parents' names again?'

Chapter 36

Brian and Marcia Eriksson were amazed at what they heard. The offer to join a special health program was heaven-sent. Brian teared-up in gratitude. Marcia put her hands over her mouth and fell into her husband's arms. The couple's health had quickly deteriorated. Brian had suffered a slipped disk from lifting garbage bins at the SocHom apartments. He'd had a painful lower back for many years, so it hadn't been very wise to do any heavy lifting like that. Alzheimer's disease had changed Marcia. The dementia inhibitors didn't work for her. Under the expert guidance of Elaine Iskander, she'd followed psychotherapy and reality orientation training. Extensive practice courses on time determination, understanding signposts in the community and recognizing personal pictures hadn't produced the desired results. Elaine, who'd escorted the couple to Dr. Santini's office, watched them with mixed feelings. She felt responsible for the failure of the training sessions and therapies. She clutched at a straw: the 'Special Health Program'.

It was time to say goodbye. She wouldn't see her patients again. From now on, Brian and Marcia were in Dr. Santini's hands. Elaine's eyes moistened when she shook hands with the couple. Overcome by emotion, she embraced her patients and wished them good luck with the new treatment. Santini coolly watched the scene, regarding the couple with pity. She didn't care for this sentimental behavior, but she was elated to add some more patients to her list after a long wait.

Before leaving the office, Elaine stepped up to Santini. 'Doctor, I'm still curious about which preparations are given to my patients during the special program. I'm convinced it will improve my expertise.'

Santini looked irritated and made a gesture of dismissal. 'Ms. Iskander, please confine your curiosity to physical therapy and don't concern yourself with our medical treatments.' Santini looked sternly at her subordinate.

'Yes, Doctor, but I'm asking for professional reasons. I hope you understand.'

Santini began to get angry, while the Erikssons wondered what was going on in the corner of the room. 'Now, listen carefully,' Santini said with controlled annoyance. 'Go back to your ward and don't bother me again with such questions. Is that clear, Ms. Iskander?'

Elaine was amazed. She turned and hurried out of the room. In the corridor she leaned against the wall, needing some support. She tried to force back tears of frustration. 'I only wanted to know what medicines are administered to my patients, she thought, in some despair. Why did that woman have to treat me like that?'

A recent argument with George Broderick flashed through her mind. Elaine had been surprised about his point of view on the treatment of Mr. Atchison. George thought he should get the same medication as his wife, Suzie. Elaine had expressed her doubts about this, because Mr. Atchison's condition was clearly different from his wife's. But Broderick said Dr. Santini agreed. He accused Elaine of unprofessional insubordination if she acted against the medical director's will. Her job would be at stake. Elaine had blamed him for rejecting her valid concerns. She told him that he shouldn't hide behind the opinion of their superior, but should consider his own judgment.

'I'm not blindly following Santini, Elaine.'

'But why do you react so defensively when I make my own assessment of the case?'

'Listen, Elaine, we need to be helpful, both to our patients and the management of this clinic. Only with that attitude are we be able to achieve our goals and ideals. There's no room for self-satisfaction, second-guessing a qualified medical opinion, or argument.'

Elaine had listened patiently to him. She definitely wanted to avoid a scene and finally told him there was a patient waiting for physical therapy. 'Fine, we'll come back to it sometime, George. I have an appointment now.'

While she had calmly walked out of the staff room, George watched her closely. He wondered if he'd put her off with his last remark. He had no hold over his colleague, who was his equal, though they differed in function and profession. She was a specialist in therapy, while he was trained more in general care. Both provided medical services under direction of Dr. Santini.

As she left, Elaine felt George's eyes on her back, but that was the least of her worries. She went back to her ward and saw Don taking care of Suzie. She sat down behind the desk, took the Erikssons' treatment files and started to leaf through one. The contents of the file failed to interest her. She was thinking about one of George's remarks during the discussion a few days ago: 'Only with that attitude can we achieve our goals and ideals'. The statement kept going through her mind. What nurse speaks about achieving goals and ideals, if during the day he does his job as required and in the evening forgets about it and goes home to enjoy his family or friends? What kind of person talks about his job in such a lofty way? Nutcases and fanatics maybe. Such types are everywhere and can be recognized by their 'deviant' behavior and remarks. They often cherish peculiar ideas, which are used mostly for their own benefit. But professional nurses? They should stand by their patients, administer correct care, apply drips and check files, the basic work.

Chapter 37

Elaine closed the file, swept an unruly lock from her face and looked at a photo of herself with her father last Christmas. It gave her a warm feeling. With a tender smile, she remembered how her dad always encouraged her in the work she was doing. The photo reminded her to do her job as well as she could. That was her calling: helping dependent, frail fellow human beings, improving their mobility to make their lives more bearable.

She made up her mind. Santini's refusal to give her information about the medication in the health program was suspicious. In the medical profession, openness and honesty are requirements in a doctor-patient relationship. This view was taken for granted between most doctors and related practitioners. She got up, determined to find out what she felt she should know.

Elaine knew where the clinic's trash was collected. Outside, in the back, there was an open shed with dumpsters. One of them was for recyclable paper, boxes and packing materials. Because this part of the clinic wasn't covered by security cameras, she could do what she wanted without being observed. She knew the medical staff had no business there. The janitor and housekeeping staff were responsible for collecting and depositing the garbage. Twice a week the janitor accompanied the waste-disposal service and made sure everything was taken away. Elaine knew the janitor wouldn't be around the dumpsters at this time of day. The back wall of the clinic had no windows, so no one could watch her from the building. She'd never before set foot on this part of the premises. Why should she? She had no business at the dumpsters. But today was different.

When she got to the garbage area, she was disappointed. The contents of the shed were visible, but there was a locked gate in front of the dumpsters. Elaine swore softly to herself. A number was engraved on the lock. She thought for a moment. She knew where the janitor's office was, and because the man didn't work afternoons, she could try and get hold of the key. She walked to a wooden shed at the far corner of the grounds. She was completely out of sight from the clinic and annexes. Elaine hoped the shed's door would be unlocked. Janitors may be tidy for others, but not always for themselves. Besides, the clinic was fenced and what staff member would be interested in paying a visit to the janitor?

Yes, to her relief, the door was unlocked. She went in and looked around. What a mess, she thought, typical for some men. On the wall was a key box. Elaine opened the box door and found a lot of keys. Suddenly, she heard footsteps coming towards the shed. They seemed close, because the coral gravel path amplified the sound. She panicked, looked around quickly, and saw a large leather couch. Just in time she managed to hide behind it. Someone stepped inside.

Elaine held her breath and tried to peek from behind the couch. All she could see was a pair of men's black shoes. The man in the shoes stopped for a moment and then walked over to the key box. Elaine couldn't tell from the sound if a key was put back or taken out. The man coughed. Elaine got a shock. George Broderick? She was all too familiar with his coughs. He left the shed quickly and closed the door behind him. Quickly, Elaine rose to her feet, and over the edge of the couch looked through the dirty window.

'I'll be darned, it's George,' she muttered. She saw him heading towards the garbage dump. He opened the gate and entered the garbage shed. Only now did she notice he was carrying something. But he was too far away for her to see what it was. She saw George raise his hands and throw something. Or was he hiding it? Immediately George turned around, shut the gate and walked back to the janitor's shed. Oh my God, he's coming back. She dove back behind the couch, and a minute later heard George enter again. He hung the key back in the box and turned to walk away. He stopped. What's he doing now?

Chapter 38

She heard him sniffing air. He smelled something. A smell that didn't belong in that shed. But what was it? He inhaled once more, then left, quickly walked down the path, and turned the corner of the clinic building, out of sight now. Elaine was glad George was gone and hadn't noticed her. She didn't want to think about what may have happened if he'd discovered her. She stood up and took a couple of deep breaths. Nothing special. Yet George must have smelled something peculiar, something he hadn't noticed before. It worried her, and she hoped it meant nothing.

She went over to the key box and looked for the number that agreed with the lock on the gate. There it was, number 128. She took the key and carefully left the shed. She halted for a moment before crossing over to the garbage dump. Elaine made sure the area was still deserted and then moved on. She arrived at the gate and turned the key. The lock clicked open. She went in and left the gate ajar. The shed was open at the top. It was surrounded by three seven-foot-high walls and the gated fence. Here is where George must have thrown something away. There were five dumpsters, a barrel and a heap of compost, which was probably used in the flower beds.

Elaine came to the first dumpster and opened the lid. It just looked like a load of disposable plastic. This is not what I'm looking for, she thought. She opened another dumpster. This one was crammed with paper and cardboard. She was lucky, because she'd been looking for the packing material for the preparations and medicines used in the special health program. The cardboard boxes had been flattened and stacked in piles. She noticed most packages had contained dementia inhibitors. She picked up one and studied the text. She frowned when she read the expiration date on the short side of the box: 12-08-1996. She took another box and this one showed the same date. She started to check random piles and all had the same date. Do I understand this correctly? Do all our patients get sixteen-year-old medicines? She couldn't believe it! If this became known, all the news media would be at the doorstep, closely followed by Florida health officials and inspectors.

She checked some more cardboard boxes, but none showed an earlier date. As far as she could tell all products had been manufactured in Mexico by a pharmaceutical company named Bioclon. She remembered an article in a medical journal. This company had been discredited, but she couldn't quite remember the details. Then she stumbled on two big pieces of cardboard. No dementia inhibitors had been in these. The package had pictures and text on it. She read in Spanish: *Duretica diuretic y MPC-4*. Her heart skipped a beat. These are forbidden medicines. There had been news stories about this! Many people had died from taking a mix of these diuretic and anti-rheumatic pills. This is even worse than those inhibitor pills. She felt confused and wondered if she was dreaming. What is going on here at St. Luke's?

'If I were you, I wouldn't be bothered with some trash,' she heard someone say behind her. Elaine screamed, startled and frightened. She dropped the cardboard, turned around and saw her teammate pointing a gun at her.

'George?' she said in disbelief. She trembled and felt her heart beating in her throat.

'Don't pretend you didn't expect me. You saw me before, didn't you?'

'What's the meaning of this, George? I… I only threw away some old papers.'

'Ah, well, Mrs. Holmes has thrown away old papers. I have to say, Elaine, you're a bad liar. You know, I hate lying. It always makes me feel… you know… like a fool.'

George was about eight feet away from her. He came one step closer. Elaine had regained some of her self-control. 'Yes, I'm lying. That's not good. But tell me, George, what should I think of this?' She pointed at the piles of cardboard.

'Of what, Elaine? I don't understand what you mean,' he said fretfully.

'Look here. Packaging of fifteen or sixteen year-old medicines. And what about these forbidden drugs?' She held a box in her hand and showed it to him.

'Elaine, Elaine, I think your imagination has run away with you.'

'See for yourself then!' she shouted angrily. 'And what are you doing with that gun? Put it away. If these medicines have been administered here at St. Luke's, then that's…awful, dangerous and illegal.'

Elaine felt George was playing some dirty game. Pieces of the puzzle were coming together. Her brain was working at full speed now to find the right perspective on everything. 'George, what are you doing! What's St. Luke's doing?' she asked in desperation.

'Sorry, Elaine, but that's not for you to know. Now that you've found this, I'm forced to stop you.'

'George, no, don't do that!'

Broderick aimed his gun at Elaine's heart. A silencer was fixed to the barrel. 'What do you mean, Elaine?' He pursued grimly, 'You're going to ruin everything we are working to achieve here. Everything we've accomplished in a few years, you want to destroy. You won't do it!'

'Goals and ideals.' Elaine remembered those words. She could finally place everything, except she didn't know exactly what he meant by them. It was as if a veil was pulled over her eyes. But she had to keep her wits to dissuade George from his immediate purpose. 'You don't want this. You're not going to shoot me for some medicines.' She tried to give him an ego-boost. 'You're far too good-natured and responsible for that. You're a committed and devoted nurse.'

'Stop the chatter. Look at you standing there, Ms. Therapist. How naïve! You know nothing, but you could cross me. It's possible to 'know nothing' but prove to be a danger anyway. That danger is you!'

'George, please think. If you kill me it won't go unnoticed. You'll regret this, and I can help you. Please let me help.'

'George started to shake. Tears came to his eyes. 'Why did you have to discover this?' His voice trembled. 'I promised to take care of this project. I stuck out my neck, I trusted people, and they trust me. I can't disappoint them. Why did you have to spoil it?' He raised his gun and aimed at her head.

Elaine screamed. 'No, George. Don't do it, please!'

'You really think I have a choice? Do you? You know I can't let you go now. We both know that.'

Just as Elaine wanted to step aside to hide behind the dumpster, George said, 'Sorry.'

Overcome by emotions, he pulled the trigger. A muffled bang sounded. Pfft. Elaine staggered and collided with the dumpster and fell to the ground. Her body shook. She made a rattling sound. Her eyes dulled. George cautiously stepped towards her. He noticed Elaine tried to say something, but nothing coherent came from her mouth. He examined the body. The bullet had penetrated the left part of her chest. Blood gushed from the hole and spread across her blouse. Her head fell sideways. Glazed eyes stared at him. He was shocked by it. While he felt her neck with his fingers, he thought about his mission.

Chapter 39

Mike pretended not to hear Mrs. Warakomski. He shut the restaurant door behind him and showed Ellis the direction they had to go.

'That was close,' she said. 'I expect we're going to see Peterson now?'

'Yes, we have a name. Do you remember what the woman said about the Erikssons? "I've never noticed anything unusual about those people." Don't forget they're neighbors of hers. She noticed nothing unusual about them, but the Doctor apparently had a different opinion. I have some questions to ask Mr. Peterson.'

Ellis barely managed to keep up with his fast pace. 'And no more jokes, Mike, you're not going to tell Peterson we're married, understood? Sheer nonsense. Getting married, so conventional and old-fashioned.'

'Ellis, at least we have one thing in common.'

She looked at him suspiciously. 'Have we now? And what may that be?'

'We both think marriage is an outmoded, old-fashioned institution.'

'Well, that's a reassuring thought, but don't get any ideas. We work together out of self-interest. You, to find the answer to why you've worked so hard and taken risks. And I, because I'm looking for the scoop of the year.'

'Right, that's how it is. We have a strictly business relationship.'

But, if she believed his words, it remained to be seen. The mere word "relationship" was reason enough to be on her guard.

They arrived at the SocHom offices and followed the sign 'Director's Office' that lead to the door behind which they should find Peterson. Opening the door, they stepped into a large hall. Just inside, was a reception desk where a young secretary was plucking at her long hair.

'Yes, what can I do for you?' she asked in a sing-song cadence.

'That's what we're going to tell you,' Ellis said a little sharply. 'We have an appointment with Mr. Peterson.' She showed the young woman her FDA badge. Mike showed his. They tried to look intimidating to the secretary. However, she wasn't very impressed and picked up the phone to tell the person on the other end of the line there were two FDA agents at her desk. 'They say they have an appointment with you.'

Ellis and Mike expected that FDA officials should be allowed to enter a company or office unannounced, if necessary. And Mr. Peterson should know that too. 'Let them in,' they heard through the phone.

'You may enter that room,' the girl said bored.

'Thank you so much,' Mike said a little severely. She didn't seem to set a good example for a friendly and reliable retirement community. She appeared to be a foolish, dull type, with overdone make-up and hair spray.

Entering his office, Ellis and Mike stood face to face with the Director of SocHom. Again, they showed their badges and came to the point. 'You are Mr. Peterson, Director of SocHom?'

'Yes, I thought that would be clear. Who else would you think I am? But please, sit down. Would you like coffee, tea or maybe something else?'

'No thank you, Mr. Peterson. We don't have much time. You're aware of our regular inspections. Today we would like to see the surveys of the medicines the community prescribes for the residents.'

Peterson shifted in his chair. 'To tell you the truth, we've never had an inspection before. This is the first time. But I'm ready to give my full cooperation.'

'We appreciate that,' Ellis said. She saw Peterson was nervous. But I would be too, she thought, if the FDA descended on me unprepared.

'Then follow me, please. The information is in the next room.'

Mike hesitated to come along. 'Er…Ellis, you go with Mr. Peterson. I have to go to the bathroom. I'll be back soon.'

Peterson pressed the intercom button. 'Yes, Mr. Peterson?' a southern voice sounded.

'Amber, show this gentleman the way to the bathroom, will you?'

'Certainly, sir, no problem.'

While Mark Peterson and Ellis went into the next room, Mike left the office and stepped up to the young secretary. 'Hello, I'm Mike, and you are…?'

The secretary looked surprised. She wasn't used to visitors paying personal attention to her.

'Amber,' she replied quickly.

'Amber, that's a nice name. What does a beautiful girl like you do in a dull office like this?'

Amber began to blush a little and fidgeted in her chair. This hot guy thinks I'm beautiful, she thought. 'Well, ya have to earn a living somehow, don't ya?'

'But do you like it here?'

Amber shrugged her shoulders. 'It's okay.'

'You know, Amber, you're much too good to waste away here. Wouldn't you like to work for us?'

'What? Work for y'all? How?' she seemed anxious to hear more.

'Exciting investigation work, lots of traveling and of course a coke once in a while.'

The girl laughed. She scrutinized Mike's face for a few seconds. Wow, what a handsome young guy. 'I mean it,' Mike insisted.

'Really?' she responded, a little too loudly.

'Shh, not so loud. This is between you and me, right?'

'Yeah, fine with me.'

'Amber, I already need your help now. This is a computer, isn't it?'

'Yeah, sure it's a computer.' She gave him a curious look.

'I'm looking for a resident who was recently referred to some clinic by a doctor.'

'Yes?'

'That man may have been given the wrong medicines. And as an FDA agent I have to check out if this really took place, see?'

Amber looked hurt at Mike's remark. 'Yeah, I'm no fool.'

Mike knew she would cooperate now, as his psychological approach seemed to have the desired effect. 'Could you retrieve information about an individual with the surname Eriksson?' he asked and waited to see how Amber would react to his question.

'Eriksson? With a "ck"? Or, just a "k"? I'll check.'

'You're great, Amber.'

The secretary smiled. She sat up straight behind her computer, opened a resident's file and entered the surname. 'No data present.'

'Try with "k" only, Amber.'

She typed the name with a "k." 'Gotcha. Brian and Marcia Eriksson. What do y'all want to know?'

'I want to know if there's a note telling where these people are now.'

'Let's see.' Amber searched the file and came to the conclusion she couldn't find anything. 'No, there's nothing here about a different location. I do have their address here at SocHom.'

'Yes, that's okay.' Mike was disappointed, but he didn't show it to the secretary. Amber gave him the SocHom apartment's address and closed the program.

'Amber, thank you very much. Now, I need to rejoin Mr. Peterson and my colleague.'

She looked at him surprised. 'But you said you had to go to the bathroom?'

'Oh, not anymore. The urge left me, while being here with you.'

The girl laughed shyly.

'Bye,' Mike said and returned to the office. He saw no one, but heard the muffled voices from Ellis and Peterson in the adjacent room. It occurred to him that Ellis was distracting Peterson as long as she could, until he'd finished in the bathroom and joined them again. Shrewd lady, she is. There wasn't a second to lose. He moved quickly to Peterson's desk and searched the desktop and drawers. It has to be done fast, he thought. Curious Amber might just walk into the office at any moment.

Chapter 40

Mike madly leafed through booklets and notebooks, memos and a diary. If he wasn't mistaken, the sounds from the other room were getting closer. He wanted to get hold of something; if necessary, he'd take the diary. Once more he looked around quickly. Suddenly, the laptop caught his eye. A yellow note was stuck to it with a name and telephone number on it. Mike tore the note from the laptop and jumped sideways and fixed his gaze outside the window. At that moment the dividing door opened and Ellis and Peterson stepped into the office.

'Hey, what are you doing here?' Ellis asked in an attempt to head Peterson off. Peterson looked surprised at Mike, who was standing next to his desk.

'Oh, just enjoying the view. I must say, Mr. Peterson, you have an attractive residential community.'

Mark Peterson was feeling perturbed, but remained cordial. 'Er…, yes, thank you. I had expected you back in the other room, by the way.'

'My bathroom visit took a while, and your secretary held me up. Nice girl. She told me good things about SocHom, and she's happy with you as her boss.'

'Okay, good to hear that. I hope I've been helpful to you both. If you will excuse me now, I've more work to do.'

Ellis shook the Director's hand and said, 'Thank you for the inspection of your medical files. I can already say I haven't discovered anything objectionable. All seems to be in order. The FDA is satisfied about that.'

They rapidly left the office and in passing, Mike winked at Amber. The girl was visibly unnerved. As Mike closed the door behind him, he heard the Director call, 'Amber, come in here!'

The two FDA agents marched away from the building. 'Are we going to run again?' Ellis asked.

'If Peterson finds out what he's missing, he'll send security after us at once.'

'You're not telling me you found something, are you?'

'Maybe. I had to act fast. I didn't get anything interesting from Amber's computer.'

'Well, well, Amber's computer, hey?' she said mockingly.

Mike was surprised at her reaction. 'Yes, I persuaded her to search information about the Erikssons on her computer. But she had nothing useful about them. Uh, you sound a little jealous.'

Ellis stopped abruptly. She said indignantly, 'What did you just say? I already told you; don't get any ideas into your head.'

Mike didn't respond to that, but asked, 'Did you find out anything from Peterson?'

'More than you managed to get out of your secretary, anyway. Peterson works, or has others work with out-of-date medicines. This corresponds with the lists we scanned. Probably it concerns a dirt-cheap delivery. I saw bills for medicines that were far below the usual prices.'

'So Peterson showed you invoices for medicines that were at least fifteen years old?'

'Yes.'

'What did you have to do for that?'

'Hey, what do you mean?'

'I can't imagine Peterson showing you the bills just like that, knowing he could be exposed immediately. He might just as well have confessed and turned himself in.'

Ellis smiled secretively. 'It took me some trouble to get him to do it.'

'Come on, Ellis. Do I have to beg?'

She assured him. 'Let's say I employed my female charms to coax him into cooperating with me.'

Mike's mouth fell open. 'You did what?! How come I'm not allowed to get ideas into my head, but this bald old fellow…' Mike hesitated.

'Well, go on,' she teased. 'Do I detect some jealousy now?'

'Just tell me how you pulled it off. We don't keep any secrets from each other, remember?'

'Alright,' she said calmly. 'At a certain moment I said, "Mr. Peterson, I want to see the invoices for these medicine lists." He stammered, looking for a way out. Right away, I felt something was wrong. He suggested that we come to an agreement. Judging from his eyes, I understood what he meant by that. What could I do? I knew I wasn't an FDA agent, and he could check that if he wanted. I gave him my sweetest smile and a card from our hotel.'

Mike wanted to interrupt her, but Ellis raised her hand.

'Wait, don't say anything! I haven't finished yet. I told him you live around here and go home later, but that I'm from Austin and therefore will spend the night in a hotel. I didn't need to say anything else; that card and the looks we exchanged did the rest.'

Mike slapped his knee. He shook with laughter. 'Wow, your looks did the rest! Ellis, you amaze me. If these are your female charms, Peterson lucked into a sweet deal. And he didn't even have to do anything for it.'

'Come on now, be realistic,' she reacted a little angrily. 'That bald guy thinks he will get a long way with his advances. But, he isn't going to get anything, while I've already got what I want!'

'Yeah, yeah. You've done it again, Miss Henning. Another fellow's life is ruined because he's been cheated by a woman.'

'Do you want to know what else I've discovered, or not?'

'Sure, tell me!'

'Besides the suspicious invoices and the lists with outdated medicines, something else struck me. We've got the name of the general practitioner, a Dr. Bob Wheeler.'

'That's good. Maybe we should try and speak with him too.'

Ellis thought for a moment. 'Have you got something for me?'

'Oh, sorry, I almost forgot. The moment you and your new boyfriend...,' she punched him on the arm, '...came in, I just grabbed a sticky-note off his laptop. That was the only thing that intrigued me. Here it is.'

'2392958000, that's all? Looks like a telephone number?'

'Enough, I think. Phone numbers can lead to interesting people and information. We might try it.'

'What?'

'Dialing this number. Hey, are you a little distracted?'

'Mike, I'm thinking of tonight. Peterson has the card from my hotel, and you stole something from his laptop, which he probably has discovered by now. We must do something or we'll no longer have the situation under control.'

'Right you are, El,' and he looked at her sideways to see if she would accept his "El". There was no reaction, so it didn't bother her, he thought. She reflected on the way things went and wasn't aware they were already inside the residential area. Suddenly, she noticed and said, 'Let's have a cup of coffee here. I'm getting tired of all this walking around in the open. We can sit and continue talking quietly.'

'Good idea. I'd like a cup of coffee too.'

They crossed the road and ordered two latté macchiatos at Starbucks. They sat down outside to recover from the recent events.

Chapter 41

'I'm going to have a muffin with it. I'm getting hungry. Do you want one too?' Mike asked.

'Yeah, why not,' Ellis answered with her thoughts elsewhere. The coffee shop was situated at the edge of Naples. Mike and Ellis basked in the mild sunshine. Fortunately it wasn't as hot as during the past few days. 'Let's list all the points,' she said, while taking a pen and an old writer's contest announcement from her handbag. She made notes on the blank back of the paper. 'What have we got now? The medication lists from the motorbike cases correspond with some statements at SocHom. That delivery, or part of it, goes there directly. The question is, why did you have to deliver those lists separately? Let's look at that later on. Then, we have invoices that show questionable prices. Similar medications within the expiration dates are much more expensive. I suspect this is illegal trade. We have your memo with a phone number. Perhaps, it's from this clinic where you delivered the package.'

She put down her pen, read everything through once more and looked up at Mike thoughtfully. 'I almost forget something.'

'What?'

'Peterson is coming to our hotel tonight. We're supposed to have an amorous evening, remember?'

'Sure, I remember.' Mike tried not to laugh.

'How are we going to handle this?'

He looked at her with surprise. 'Oh, I have to help you out? With pleasure, Miss Henning.' Theatrically, he continued, 'I will throw myself as a shield between you two and put up a fight to prevent your virtue from being compromised.'

Ellis wasn't impressed by his acting. 'Mike, this isn't funny,' she said calmly but resolutely. 'We have to think of something, or he's going to spoil our little scheme.'

'Right, I have an idea.'

'Do you?' Her face brightened.

'We're going to be frank with Mr. Peterson. We'll let him come to the hotel and start a discussion with him.'

'Hey, start a talk with him? How, exactly?'

'Well, you know...What you've done to Peterson is great, a wonderful plan. Pretend you want to sleep with him and instead...'

'Alright, that's enough...'

'… instead we are going to put Mr. SocHom through the mill. In a word, fantastic.'

There were no visitors outside, so they could talk with each other in a normal tone of voice. But now they were silent. Ellis's brain worked like lightning. A smile appeared on her face that developed into a spontaneous cry of joy.

'Yes! I could never have thought of that myself. I was only thinking about how to keep this bald, fat creep off me.'

'Well, I'm glad I can be of some use.'

'Of course, Mikey, we're a good team, really. I'm getting another coffee for us while you think of how to go about it tonight.'

Ellis patted Mike on the shoulder and disappeared into Starbucks. He lost it for a moment. Had she really called him Mikey? She came back with two hot mugs of caffeinated coffee. He asked her, offhandedly, 'Hey, Ellis, did you just call me Mikey?'

'Er…, I think so. That's how someone named Mike is called – sometimes, right?' she asked a little edgy.

'Yeah, fine. It's okay. But, El, listen, about Peterson; this man is our key figure for the time being. He has a lot to explain to us. Wait and see; we're dealing with illegal medicine smuggling here. This is going to be a great story for your magazine.'

Chapter 42

George Broderick had carried Elaine Islander's body inside to the special treatment room. She was lying on a stretcher under a white sheet. An unnatural, tense silence prevailed. Dr. Santini looked at Broderick, and she wasn't happy. He looked away from her and stared at the floor. Santini walked over to the stretcher and lifted the sheet from the face, a white countenance with closed eyes. The cheeks were hollow and her once so wonderfully shiny hair had already lost some of its luster. Santini dropped the sheet. She sat down in one of the armchairs at the minibar and hid her face in her hands. Then she sighed, sat up straight and looked at Broderick.

'Come, sit down,' she said motherly, pointing at an armchair opposite her.

Broderick hesitated, then complied. He felt this was going to be one of the hardest moments of his life.

'George, I don't really know how to discuss this with you,' Santini said with concern. Broderick kept silent. He didn't dare look Santini in the eye.

'You've created great problems for me and the clinic. Shortly after the murder, I tried to talk to you, but you were unapproachable. I hope you've regained some self-control, so we can deal objectively with this nasty affair. Do you think you can do that?'

Broderick nodded. He flashed a look at the stretcher. She's lying there so peacefully, he thought, like an angel.

'Very well then. I'm not going to discuss the how and why. You've already told me about that, even if I could hardly understand you because of your crying fits. We must get the situation under control now and make sure no one's going to look into this over our shoulders.'

'Yes, sure, I'll cooperate,' Broderick said meekly.

'Fine,' she said bending forward. 'Within a few hours the next of kin will inquire if we know something about Iskander's disappearance. Then they will call in the police and send out a missing persons APB, looking for her. As this concerns a mature woman, they'll wait a little while before announcing she's missing. But the police will keep a sharp eye on the case if nothing is heard from Iskander within 48 hours. They'll come here to make inquiries.'

'Yes, I understand.'

Santini waited and looked seriously at Broderick. 'You fully realize, I hope, you're in the middle of this yourself. You're partly responsible for the health program. I've involved you in most things and have given you more information than other staff members, including Elaine Iskander. That's because I admire your loyalty and respect your ideals.'

Broderick blushed from so much praise.

'George, we'll do it this way: we won't tell the truth to police, her family or the press. It so happens we know nothing about the disappearance of Elaine Iskander. After her work shift she went home at the usual time. That's all we're going to say.'

Broderick's face brightened. He sat up in his chair and thought his reaction might surprise Santini. 'Yes, I absolutely agree, Doctor. This is what's best for the clinic, in view of the circumstances. I'll respect whatever you decide to do. And thank you for your help and confidence.'

You're a slime ball, Broderick, Santini thought. But she played along expertly, thanked the nurse for his cooperation, and told him he could leave the room. Broderick shook Santini's hand in grateful agreement, and went back to his ward. She opened the minibar and took out two small bottles. All of a sudden she felt like a drink. To calm down her troubled mind she mixed some tonic with a double shot of gin. The present circumstances could hardly be called promising. Broderick knew too much. He had sold his soul for the special health program. That's how he was. Therefore, she was convinced he wouldn't shoot off his mouth. His loyalty to the clinic was beyond doubt. To prevent her plans from being crossed-up again by external and internal incidents, she decided to act quickly. She took her cell phone from her bag, glanced through her contacts, and pressed a name on the screen,

'It's me; I need you here now.'

Chapter 43

Ellis nervously waited for what was to come. It was almost nine o'clock. She paced around the room, now and then cautiously looking through the slats of the blinds. She and Mike had gone over the rendezvous with Peterson in great detail, especially how her guest was likely to behave. Mike impressed on her to act as naturally as possible and not overtly ignore Peterson's advances. This had made her angry, and she demanded that Mike would immediately intervene if she gave a signal. The telephone rang.

'Should I answer it?' she asked tensely.

'Yes, go ahead,' Mike replied from the adjoining room.

She picked up the receiver and put it to her ear. 'Hello?'

'Ms. Henning? This is Mark Peterson. The plan has changed. I want you to come to my place. Right now.'

Ellis was surprised by his directness. 'Yes, but Mr. Peterson, I expected you to come over here, I'm waiting for you. I've put on music and lit a few candles.'

'Listen; if you want to find out things, you come to me. Or do you want me to call the FDA and ask them if you and your boyfriend are on their payroll?'

In the meantime Mike had entered the room and listened attentively to the conversation.

'I wouldn't do that, no,' Ellis said. 'What's the address?'

Peterson told her where he lived. 'Good girl. And Ms. Henning, leave your bodyguard at home. I expect you within half an hour.'

Peterson broke off the call.

Ellis frowned at Mike.

'You have no choice; you've got to go.'

'What are you saying? You want me to go to that creep's house? What are you thinking?'

He tried to persuade her. 'He knows. The FDA will send lawyers after us. Impersonating FDA officials won't be tolerated. If you refuse to see him, all we've accomplished so far will be wasted.'

'Nice guy you are! You know quite well he has plans for me. He definitely won't confess his sins and let me go home afterwards.'

'No, of course not. That's why I'm coming with you.'

'What do you mean? How can you do that without raising suspicion?'

'I'll be at a distance, but close enough. You carry your gun. You won't feel unsafe that way. If things get dangerous, you give the signal.'

'If I'd known beforehand what I'd have to go through, I would've chosen a different profession.'

'Yes, like that of a call girl. Very exciting too.'

Ellis's eyes flashed. But knowing that Mike was kidding, and that he would stand by her if the situation got tense, eased her mind, a little.

Ellis parked the Corvette near the address she'd been given. The house was in an upscale area of Naples and had front and side yards. At the back was a patio with a swimming pool. Although it was a detached house, it seemed to be linked to the adjacent ones. But that was an optical illusion; low fences enclosed the lots. Ellis sometimes wondered why houses were built so close together in America, the country being so vast. She got out and left the key in the ignition. She slowly crossed the street and checked the letter box for the house number. She looked back at the blanket on the passenger seat. Mike lay down as far as possible. It wasn't easy to hide in a car like this. As soon as Ellis was in the house, Mike could show himself and take the drivers' seat, waiting for events to unfold. The car was almost thirty yards from the house's front walk, outside the reach of streetlights. The street came to an end a little further on in a small cul-de-sac. Ellis rang the door-bell. After a few seconds she heard footsteps approach.

The door opened and Mark Peterson welcomed his visitor. 'Come in, Ms. Henning.' Looking past her he quickly scanned the outside area to be sure she was alone. Ellis stepped into the hall and waited till Peterson closed the door.

'I appreciate you complying with my request.'

Well, well, Ellis thought, request? Order, you mean. But to be honest, Peterson's attitude seemed to have changed in her favor. She was escorted to the living room. To her surprise it was tastefully decorated.

'Sit down, please. May I offer you a drink?'

'Yes, a diet-coke, please.'

'Alright then. Could you find my house easily?'

'This is a very nice place, Mr. Peterson. Is this the work of an interior designer or are you so skillful yourself?'

Peterson smiled but didn't answer. Ellis accepted her coke and took a pad from her purse. Peterson sat down and saw that his visitor was ready to take notes. 'I would appreciate it if you didn't write down anything about what we're discussing.'

Ellis looked surprised at him. 'Without notes I can't write a proper report. You understand that, I hope'

'Yes, but I'll tell you something first.' He took a sip from his whiskey. Ellis looked attentively at the man; she was all ears.

'Ms. Henning, I know you're not FDA.' He waited for a moment, bent forward a little and continued, 'Nevertheless, you know about our medicine policy. You've seen the files and I didn't mince words because I still believed you were an FDA agent. I've had you checked out and know your real identity. You're a research journalist for the Orlando Enquirer.' He waited for her reaction.

'By all means, continue,' Ellis said a little coolly and emptied her glass.

'Look, Ms. Henning.' He folded his hands and tried to look important. 'I run a splendid residential community that means the world to me. At SocHom, more than six hundred residents have found a wonderful final place to live. With all imaginable services, churches, relaxation programs and facilities, and personal health care. We've actually broken new ground in the area of care by offering a wide range of health programs to alleviate and sometimes cure diseases, disorders and mental deterioration.'

Ellis listened attentively to Peterson, but somehow his words sounded scripted and didn't sink in with her.

'That's why it's such a pity you found out about our medication lists and that you may intend to make everything public. If you prevent us from supplying free medication, this would be the end of SocHom. You would be damaging one of the pillars that form the foundation of our existence.'

Ellis missed the last sentence completely. The haziness in her head had disappeared. Instead her brain slowly spun in a vortex that gradually blurred her senses. Peterson stopped talking when he saw Ellis collapse in her chair. He arose and bent over her. He felt her pulse and lifted her eyelids.

'You can come in now,' Peterson called.

From the kitchen a small, potbellied man with gray uncombed hair entered the room. He had a tawny, hollow-cheeked face. The man looked at the drugged woman. 'She's a fine lady, just a little stupid to meddle in our affairs.'

Peterson kept silent and waited for the man to give a signal. 'Mr. Larkin, do you want to search her?'

Josh Larkin shook his head. 'My boys will do that later. They are dealing with my courier right now. He has betrayed my trust, and actually cheated me, if you want to know. I hadn't expected this from Mike Garcia, as he was a fine courier, and had made several trips for me. But, he and his girlfriend are getting too close now.' He stared expressionless at Ellis's drugged body.

'Mr. Larkin, do you want to wait until your assistants return?'

'Of course, Peterson. I don't go anywhere alone. Besides, you have a whiskey for me, right? I couldn't find anything in your kitchen.'

Chapter 44

Twenty-three minutes had passed. Mike was under the impression that all went well inside. He heard nothing special, and his beeper stayed silent. He had no reason to believe Ellis was in any great danger. The plan was she would leave Peterson's house after forty-five minutes. In his rear-view mirror Mike saw a car turn into the street. He managed to dive down just in time when the headlights shone into his car. The car stopped with screeching brakes right in front of Peterson's house. He heard the doors slam, followed by excited voices that broke the evening silence. Mike carefully sat up a little, just in time to see three men enter the house. Silhouetted against the bright light in the hall, he thought he recognized one of them. It was Sonny, the thug with the huge hands.

This isn't going according to plan. The front door was pulled shut and it was quiet again. But not for long. Mike suddenly heard someone shouting from inside the house. Someone had turned very angry. Then the front door was thrown open and the three men dashed out to the lawn. They looked around wildly. Mike hunkered down, but peeked over the edge of the dashboard. The men began looking into parked cars. They shouted to each other. It was obvious they would soon get to Mike's car. He didn't want to leave Ellis to fend for herself, but he thought it wouldn't be in their best interest to stay put. The men checked all of the vehicles on one side of the street, as far as the cul-de-sac, and were now coming in his direction.

Mike saw Sonny about twenty-five yards away, walking rapidly towards a car parked in front of him. Mike was sure it was his turn after that. He acted quickly. He turned the ignition key, shifted into reverse and accelerated backwards. Sonny looked up with a start and stood rooted to the ground for a moment. Then he swung into action, ran quickly and tried to catch up with the Corvette.

Sonny almost managed to grab the door handle, when Mike swung the car 180 degrees in the direction he wanted to go. The Corvette's tires screeched across the asphalt. Mike shifted to first and pressed the accelerator to the floor. A bullet smashed the rear window. The engine raced and up-shifted as Mike zigzagged the car down the street and swung around a corner. Sonny ordered the other two bodyguards to follow Mike. They jumped into their Chevy Suburban and sped down the street in pursuit.

Meanwhile, Mike had left the neighborhood at high speed and reached the lengthy Tamiami Trail. This road runs straight through the Big Cypress National Preserve Park north of the Everglades Park, an ideal road to shake off a pursuer. Mike knew the Corvette was a lot faster than the SUV. Mike decided to take it easy. He slowed down, and in his rear view mirror saw the lights of the SUV appear in the distance. They were still following him and getting closer. Mike wanted to prevent the men from returning to Peterson's house empty-handed. He knew for certain, Ellis was in danger. He thought about how he could trap the two guys.

When going over the plan, Ellis and Mike had studied the map of Florida. He knew a new bridge was being built on Marco Island, a half hour's drive from Naples. During the construction, drivers used the old bridge to cross Big Marco River. There he might have a chance to lose his pursuers. But he needed a two or three minute lead to create a trap. Mike stepped on the gas and the distance between him and the SUV increased again. He made sure the men kept seeing his tail lights. He turned right onto the unlit Collier Boulevard, which would lead straight to the bridge's construction zone. At this time of night there wasn't much traffic in this part of the Everglades.

Ten minutes later Mike caught the first warning signals in his headlight beams. Road signs ordered him to slow down for construction work. In the distance Mike saw the contours of the new bridge on the right-hand side of the road. Signs abruptly directed him to the adjacent old stretch to avoid the new road work. Access to the new cross-river connection was blocked off by a traffic barrier. Beyond that was new asphalt and a half-built bridge section.

Mike reacted quickly. He stopped, got out and shifted the red-white traffic barriers from the new bridge to just behind the Corvette. He looked down the road and estimated the SUV's headlights were about 500 yards down the road. He jumped back in his car, doused his lights, and slowly drove a short way across the old bridge. He watched the scene in his mirrors. The SUV tore towards the first warning signs. Then the driver saw two big traffic barriers flash past on the left side of the road. Before him was the brand new stretch of pavement. Too late, he saw the gaping hole in the new bridge. He hit his brakes hard; the SUV trembled and slid fifteen yards into space. Mike could hear the screams. The heavy Chevy landed upside down on the half dry river bed with a resounding impact. A moment later the gas tank exploded and the car was ablaze. Mike's car shook from the shockwave. He quickly reversed the car and put the traffic barriers back. He had no intention of giving innocent drivers the same surprise. The road before and behind him was empty. He turned the Corvette and drove away, knowing the sound of the explosion would have been noticed on the other side of the river.

Chapter 45

Mike was deeply worried about Ellis, who was probably at the mercy of a bunch of criminals. He rushed back to Peterson's house and didn't know what to expect there; but he knew for sure two of the three goons had been eliminated. Sonny would be a little harder to deal with. He could be a clever boy, who had others do most of the dirty work. Mike thought it all over once more as he drove onto Tamiami Trail. There would be Peterson, Ellis, and Sonny, three people. From Peterson he feared no physical resistance. Sonny was a different and dangerous case. Also, Mike had a bone to pick with him. He was determined to get Ellis out of the house. The only uncertainty bothering him was where the so-called boss might be. He hadn't seen him get out of the car when the thugs arrived at Peterson's house.

He steered his car onto Hawaii Boulevard and calmly drove towards Tudor Court, the street where Peterson lived. Mike parked the Corvette out of sight of the house. He took some handcuffs and the Walther from the glove compartment. He checked the pistol's clip and then opened the door. Silence prevailed, less than an hour after the hectic events, which sent the thugs tearing after him. It was near midnight, a time when most folks don't venture out in the streets. Mike locked the Corvette and walked along the street towards Peterson's house.

Getting close, he knelt down behind a little stone wall and scanned the surroundings. Suddenly the front door opened. Mike saw Sonny walk into the yard. He held a phone to his ear and spoke hurriedly. The only thing Mike could understand was 'hello, hello, answer the goddamn phone!' He concluded Sonny was trying to contact his two long-lost pals. The bodyguard then got into Peterson's car and tore out of the neighborhood. Mike couldn't be sure where Sonny was going, but the danger was over for Mike, at least for the time being.

He carefully crawled along the side of the house. The houses had no fences. You could just walk into a neighbor's yard. Light was cast from a window into the yard. Avoiding the light, Mike crept to the back of the house, where he found a large garden. He positioned himself with his back to the wall, moved his head sideways, and tried to look inside through the sliding doors of the sun room.

He saw Ellis slumped in a chair. Peterson was standing over her.

Peterson's mouth was moving, so he was talking to someone. From Mike's position this other person was invisible. The patio sliding door was ajar. He was lucky. Before Peterson realized what was happening, he heard someone say, 'Hands up, Peterson!'

Peterson was shocked by this uninvited guest and looked desperately to the kitchen door.

'Where's the person you were talking to?' Mike asked.

Peterson seemed confused and tried to walk away from Ellis.

'Stop there, Peterson, hands up now! This weapon's real. You don't want to test it.'

Peterson slowly raised his hands and took a step back. Mike squatted on the floor with his gun aimed at SocHom's director.

'For the last time, who were you talking to just now?' Mike asked raising his voice. 'If you don't answer, I'll shoot your kneecaps to pieces. Well?!'

Peterson nodded his head to the kitchen door. Mike got an idea to keep control of the situation. He threw a set of handcuffs to Peterson. 'Put them on,' he ordered.

Peterson hesitated.

'Put 'em on!' Mike growled.

Peterson looked frightened. Then he clicked the handcuffs shut while Mike lay down in a shooting position. All was silent. Peterson started to sweat.

'Listen, Peterson. This is what we're going to do. You open the door wide and go into the kitchen.'

The man started to tremble. He looked around nervously. 'Garcia,' he whispered. 'You're dealing with organized crime here. You have little chance of getting out of here alive. You never should have stuck your nose into this. That was a big mistake.'

'Peterson, I have two questions for you. What drug did you give Ellis, and why?'

The director of SocHom stammered. 'Er.., um.., well. It wasn't my idea. Word of honor! She was given a strong sleeping pill, GHB. But it's harmless. I was ordered to do it. That's the truth.'

Mike listened carefully to Peterson. 'We'll discuss that later. My first priority is to get Ellis out of here. Help me carry her to my car. You can do that with handcuffs on. Be sure of this, Peterson, I'm determined to get her out of here. Understand?'

Suddenly a voice sounded from the kitchen. 'Hey, Mike, what's with all the whispering? I'd like to hear you too.'

Chapter 46

Mike knew that voice. 'Boss, is that you?'

'Of course it's me. Not so smart, buddy, meddling in this. Hadn't expected that from you.'

Mike still didn't know his boss's name, but he decided to act civilized, like during their meetings at the Waldorf Astoria Hotel. 'Boss, I'm sorry to inform you that two of your bodyguards have crashed. I can't imagine you want to have more victims go down.'

Mike harbored no illusions that his former boss would be impressed by his words.

'You think you have to kill us, Mike? If I were you, I'd leave right away. If Sonny finds out you're not in your hotel room, he'll be right back. And you know how he is, don't you?'

Mike moved his Walther in the direction of the kitchen door. 'Peterson, open the door and go in.'

The man hesitated. Mike aimed his pistol at his right knee. 'Sorry, Peterson.'

Mike closed his left eye and lowered the barrel to the same height as the body part he wanted to hit.

'No, stop!' Peterson pleaded. 'I'll do what you want.'

The director slowly walked to the door. 'Larkin, I'm coming in.'

'Whatever you like, what objections could I make? You'd better do what Mike says.'

Peterson entered the kitchen and saw Larkin sitting at a small table.

'Welcome, Mr. Peterson, my name is Josh Larkin, pleased to meet you,' he said sarcastically.

Mike stepped forward and looked cautiously around the open door. Well, Mr. Larkin it is, he thought. 'Peterson, stand behind him,' Mike commanded.

The director was now ready to do everything he was told. Mike saw Larkin's hands were on the table, very relaxed.

'I'm going to toss you these handcuffs. Attach one to the oven handle and the other one around Larkin's right wrist.'

Larkin laughed. Mike was now standing opposite both men. He aimed his gun at the boss's forehead. 'I've always been polite with you because I didn't know what I was carrying for you. In a way, I even respected you. You always paid me correctly, except that once, and I thought that was very childish. I always did my job well for you, until I found out that I didn't carry money, drugs or diamonds. Then my conscience really started bothering me.'

Larkin interrupted: 'Your conscience? Are you getting a little righteous now? And why your sudden interest in medicines? Don't make me laugh.'

Mike didn't respond to Larkin and ordered Peterson to handcuff Larkin.

'I'd cooperate if I were you, Larkin. My finger's starting to itch.'

'Well, well, now you're threatening me,' Larkin sneered. 'What happened all of a sudden to your decency and respect, eh? Are you getting in over your head?'

Mike wasn't intimidated. 'Larkin, sit on the floor so Peterson can slap on the cuffs. Get this, I'm not afraid of Peterson, but maybe more of you.'

Peterson snapped a cuff around a solid looking handle on the oven. He waited 'til Larkin would rise from his chair and sit on the floor next to the oven.

'Peterson, wait. Before Mr. Larkin starts to move, I would like you to search him from behind.'

Larkin looked at Mike with mock cynicism. 'That's not something I would expect from Peterson.'

'Shut up. Peterson, go ahead. I've got him covered.'

Peterson stepped behind Larkin and started to frisk him. He didn't feel any special objects, only a pen, a calendar and some dollar bills. 'I think he's clean,' Peterson said.

Mike approached Larkin, still aiming the Walther at his head. He bent forward and said, 'Well, Mr. Larkin, you're not carrying a gun, are you? Just one question; where does this misplaced superior, unapproachable behavior of crime bosses come from? Is it because they always feel safe among their heavily armed bodyguards? And they don't set one foot outside the door without those morons around?'

Larkin gave Mike an icy glare. Suddenly he rose, gave Peterson a push and was about to attack Mike. But Mike had expected this and kicked Larkin in the shin. Wincing with pain, Larkin dropped to the floor.

'Peterson, cuffs!' Mike shouted.

A few seconds later Larkin's right wrist was attached to the oven. He began to swear and tried to pull loose. 'Sonny will be waiting for you, swine! He'll cut you to pieces. You won't escape.'

Mike looked sternly at him. 'Look here, Larkin, a big difference between you and me is you're sitting on the floor, cuffed, and I can move around freely.'

Larkin bit his lower lip, screwed up his eyes and said, 'Wait till Sonny says goodbye to you, bastard.' Then he looked at Peterson. 'And you, Peterson, I thought we had an agreement. Are you getting wobbly knees now? Can't you bear to see a woman get drugged? You don't expect any more of my help, do you?'

'Come on, Peterson,' Mike ordered. 'We don't have time for this bullshit. We've got to go. You grab Ellis by the ankles.'

Larkin stayed behind in the kitchen shouting. 'Hey, Peterson, you pity women, don't you, when they are in state like this, don't you? Man, you don't even know how to live with one.'

Mike noticed that Larkin began to rave, probably because he no longer had control of the situation. They carried Ellis outside through the back of the house. When they arrived at the neighbors' low fence, Mike said, 'Peterson, I want to take a look at the street first, because we don't want Sonny to appear in front of us all of a sudden.'

Peterson nodded.

'Don't do anything foolish,' Mike said, looking seriously at him. Mike left him alone with his unconscious partner. He moved towards the street and checked it out. All seemed quiet. Returning, he said to Peterson it wouldn't be wise to carry Ellis down the street to the end of Tudor Court. 'Let's take the path at the back. My car is at the corner of Hawaii, about a hundred yards from here.'

'Wow, Garcia, I love this job, let me know when you have another one for me. But never mind, I know now what Larkin is capable of. I won't have anything more to do with him. I promise I'll tell Ms. Henning the real story when she's fit to hear it.'

'Thanks for your help, Peterson, I appreciate it. But let's be quiet, people might hear us.'

Chapter 47

They cautiously walked through the dark alleyway between the houses. Ellis wasn't too heavy. But the men began to tire because she couldn't help; she still had no control of her muscles. They were at the end of the passage now. Mike could see his car. Before venturing into the lamplight, Mike stopped. There was a car coming. Mike let the car pass by and then stepped onto the sidewalk. He only saw vague contours of the driver.

'That was my car,' Peterson hissed astonished.

'It must have been Sonny, he's been looking for me or his pals. Wait 'til he stops at your house.'

Suddenly they heard coughing. Ellis slowly came to.

'Come on, Peterson, let's get to the car now. When she comes around she may be disoriented and start to yell.'

In the distance they saw Sonny leave the car and walk up the path to the house. At that moment the two men lifted Ellis again and quickly carried her to the Corvette. Ellis gave an unintelligible cry. Just when Sonny was about to enter the house, he stopped dead. Mike put a hand over Ellis's mouth. He took out the car keys, opened the door and tried to push her into the car. Sonny looked around and listened attentively. Finally, he disappeared between the houses.

'Watch her head, Peterson.'

Ellis hung back in the passenger seat and slowly regained consciousness. Mike sat down behind the wheel. He opened the window and said, 'Peterson, go back now as fast as you can. They won't hurt you, you're too important to their organization. Larkin knows I forced you to help me.'

Mark Peterson hesitated and looked suspicious.

'Go now, Peterson, be quick,' Mike snapped at him.

He started the engine and calmly drove out of the neighborhood. Once he was on the Tamiami Trail, he accelerated. Ellis was still lying dazed in her seat. She tried to open her eyes, but couldn't. Now and then she made strange noises. Mike trusted she would be her old self again before long. He drove into a gas station and parked at the back, out of sight from the road. He switched off the engine. Ellis had turned herself on her side, passed out again. Mike looked around, checking out the area, and thought about the past few hours. For the first time, he sighed deeply.

This was not every day business for him: two dead people, a hot pursuit and playing police detective. Images passed rapidly through his mind. What happened here? Mike leaned back in his seat, feeling stressed-out, even emotional.

He braced himself. He hated feeling sentimental. Only for his jazz favorite, Miles Davis, would he allow his emotions free reign. Fragments of the popular song "Summertime" flashed through his mind. After returning to reality, Mike looked at his watch and imagined what the evening – or rather, the rest of the night – would be like. Before sizing up the situation at his hotel, he would wait for an hour and a half, while consuming a hamburger and a coke at a nearby restaurant.

Around one-thirty, he decided to leave. Ellis was still in deep sleep. There was no longer any activity around the gas station. He quietly drove away towards the center of Naples.

Chapter 48

Mark Peterson tried to bring the glass of water to his mouth. He couldn't do it. He had no control over his muscles and was lying on the floor like a crumpled pile of laundry. With his sleeve he wiped a clot of blood from his face. His glasses were broken and his shirt was ripped. His hands were black and blue and grazed. He slumped against the oven. A splitting headache made it difficult for him to reconstruct what had happened. Peterson was greatly relieved that Josh Larkin and his bodyguard, Sonny, had left his house.

When he returned a few hours ago, Sonny had a surprise for him. And it didn't quite match what Mike suggested. True, Larkin didn't want to kill him. But that proved to be cold comfort. In retrospect, Sonny simply should have smashed his skull to pieces against the range; then he wouldn't be so miserable now, bathing in his own vomit and blood.

Larkin hadn't wanted Peterson to get away unscathed. After all, he'd helped Mike and left him, his boss, in the kitchen, cuffed and humiliated. Peterson was thinking that although Sonny had beaten him badly, it could have been worse. The goon also might have broken his hands or shattered his kneecaps. When Sonny was about to finish him off, Larkin had said that was enough.

Larkin knew Peterson was still valuable to him. For some time there wouldn't be a replacement for him. For many years now, Peterson had been familiar with the ins and outs of his community and was familiar with the methods of Larkin's organization. He tried to bring the glass to his lips once more. This time he managed to take a few sips. He crawled to the fridge and opened the bottom drawer. Here Peterson kept his small bottles of liqueur, whisky and gin. He had no one in the world to be considerate of, so he could take some booze now and again to temporarily forget his concerns about SocHom and his less desirable business contacts.

Chapter 49

It was ten o'clock in the morning. The sun spread its warm rays over Crest Lawn. The small burial ground on the edge of Naples was meant for homeless persons and vagrants. These people usually have no identity papers and are untraceable in municipal and national data banks; so they are interred anonymously in the presence of a priest or social worker. Sometimes an ad is placed in the local press with a message to people who may know the deceased or have information about family or friends. Seldom is there any response to these invitations, maybe because people are afraid they have to pay for any debts and funeral costs. Eventually the state pays for the simple coffin, the municipal gravedigger and the attendants. The interment is brief and sober, with only a few words from the priest or minister. There is no money for a memorial service followed by coffee and cake. There's nothing much to commemorate about the anonymous deceased.

This applied to the funeral that was due today. At nine-thirty, three cars drove into the burial area. Since St. Luke's Clinic had no hearses at its disposal, the deceased were transported in a large Ford van. The clinic's medical director was sitting in the second vehicle in the short procession with her closest assistant. They stopped near the grave sites. Dr. Margaret Santini and George Broderick stepped out of the Toyota Camry. Broderick opened an umbrella to protect his director from the blazing sun. A few moments later a much older car turned into the entrance of the cemetery. Father Raymond D'Angelico parked his Ford Escort behind the Camry. He got out and joined the others.

'Good morning ma'am, sir. Isn't Mr. Peterson coming?' Father D'Angelico asked.

Santini had expected that question and answered politely: 'Hello, Father. Mr. Peterson isn't feeling well today. He asked me to excuse him.'

'Please, send him regards from our parish. Who will we commend to the Lord today?'

'I don't think you know them, Father. They are Mr. and Ms. Eriksson.'

Santini looked at the big priest attentively. D'Angelico was shocked and said, 'Oh, but I know them very well, doctor. Mr. and Mrs. Eriksson. That's very sad. How did they die?' he asked, his face perspiring.

Broderick coughed. Santini placed herself right in front of the priest and looked into his pale eyes. 'Father, I find it hard to say this, but Mr. and Mrs. Eriksson took an overdose of medicine.'

Father D'Angelico looked astounded. 'You mean they committed suicide? I can hardly imagine such a thing!'

'We're very sorry, Father. At the clinic we call it voluntary euthanasia. Our ethical code requires us to respect deeds like these.'

'Yes, I understand. But you'll have to recognize the Church doesn't share your view at all.'

'Father, shall we continue this discussion at a more suitable time? I suggest we bury the couple now.'

Father Raymond D'Angelico nodded. He was still upset and could barely imagine the sad event of their deaths. 'Very well then, I'll offer them a few words of consolation and peace on behalf of Our Lord.'

Meanwhile, the attendants had placed the coffins on the ropes. Santini signaled the men to lower them into the graves. Father D'Angelico murmured some inaudible words, ending in "In nomine Patris, et Filii, et Spiritus Sancti."

Brian Eriksson disappeared into the deep hole, followed by Marcia Eriksson. Santini gazed with vacant eyes on the coffins. She seemed unmoved and was inwardly happy it had all ended favorably. When the attendants began to throw sand on the caskets, Santini turned around and said, 'Come on, Broderick; we're leaving. Father; it was a pleasure to meet you again and thank you, on behalf of the clinic for your cooperation and compassion.'

The priest said goodbye to the two and returned to his car. Santini nudged Broderick. 'Come George, we have to work on our next treatment. This one is going to be a lot more difficult.'

Chapter 50

When Mike returned to his motel, he saw what Sonny had done with his room. In sheer frustration the goon had torn up his clothes and irreparably damaged his rolling suitcase. All cabinets and drawers had been opened and the contents thrown on the floor. Mike didn't feel safe here, checked out and booked two rooms at the nearby Inn Place Hotel. He laid Ellis on the bed and tried to sleep on the couch. He didn't want to leave her.

When he woke up at six-thirty, he realized he'd slept only four hours, but he felt rested after the dramatic events of the past night. His right shoulder ached from sleeping on the couch. Maybe Ellis could give him a massage, if she'd fully recovered. He walked to the convenience store around the corner and picked up some food for a light breakfast. When she woke up a few hours later, Mike was browsing through the local morning paper.

'Hello there,' he greeted her.

Ellis rubbed her eyes, yawned and felt her forehead.

'You have a headache?'

'Where am I? Is this your bed?'

'Yes, but don't worry. I slept on the couch. Do you want a painkiller?'

'Please. Oh, my head,' she groaned softly. 'What time is it?'

'Ten-thirty.'

'Oh. What's happened to me? I was at Peterson's, and the next thing I know, I'm here.'

'We're in a different motel now. I moved us last night because Sonny trashed the other room and I was afraid he'd be back.'

Ellis nodded and looked around her new room. Mike gave her a glass of water and two pills. 'You were drugged, GHB, a dangerous medicine. It's lucky you hadn't taken any alcohol. That combination can be lethal.'

'Bastard, that Peterson,' she said angrily.

Mike sat down on the bed with her, giving her some food. 'El, it wasn't Peterson who gave you that stuff. There was someone else in the house too, my former boss. His name's Larkin.'

Ellis looked startled at him. 'I wasn't alone with Peterson?'

'Exactly; Larkin was hiding in the kitchen. He intended to take you someplace. I don't know where, but we may find out sooner or later.'

'Wait a minute, Mike, you're going too fast for me. I need to rest. Can we discuss this more, in the afternoon?'

'Fine, gladly. What I want most is for you to recover as soon as possible. Then I'll give you all the details about last night. You'll be surprised.'

Mike left Ellis alone and lay down on the couch in the next room. He took out his cell phone. He needed to speak to Jennifer.

Chapter 51

Detective Archibald L. Kappakas ("Kappa" or "Archie" to friends) in the Jacksonville Police Department shouted some instructions to his team in the next room through the glass wall of his enclosed office. The young police officers jumped up and were in their patrol cars in minutes. Next he again addressed the woman, who was suspected of car theft. 'We can keep you here for 24 hours, if you like. The choice is yours.'

The young woman seemed unimpressed by his threat.

'And hurry up, please, I don't have much time,' he tried. His phone started to ring. He sighed and grabbed the receiver. 'Listen,' he said to the person at the switchboard. 'I don't want to be disturbed now, I'm dealing with a suspect here…'

He interrupted his sentence, for a familiar name was mentioned by the operator. 'Oh, well, put him through,' he said and held the receiver against his stomach. He looked around and saw a policeman having a cup of coffee.

'Pete, come here!'

The woman jumped at the sound of his loud voice. The policeman put down his cup, entered the office, and asked, 'What's the matter, chief?'

'Pete, take care of this suspect,' Kappakas commanded. The policeman gestured the woman to follow him. When both had left the room, Kappakas put the receiver to his ear again. 'John, is that you?'

'Hey, Archie. Yes it's me. It's been a long time, hasn't it?'

'You can say that again! Well, John, you're not going to bother me about golf during working hours, are you?'

'No, listen.' John Iskander sounded serious now. 'There's something strange going on with my daughter, Elaine. She hasn't answered or responded to my phone calls for three days. I want to find out what's going on, and I can't wait.'

'Yes, I can see that. Do you know where she was last seen?'

'At work. She works for a private clinic. I tried calling there.'

'Which one? Where is it?'

'In Naples.'

'Naples? That's a long way from Jacksonville. I can't just go investigate in another county's jurisdiction.'

'I know. I would never bother you with this, if I didn't suspect something terrible has happened. I know, it's a hunch, but I want to be sure. And you've always said that....'

'Yes, yes, it's alright, John. I owe you. I know what you've done for me. Let me think first, then I'll call you back, in ten minutes, okay?'

'Fine, of course. Thanks a lot. I'll stay put, near the phone.'

'You do that, I'll call back soon.'

Kappakas put down the phone and stared at the wall. He was thinking. Although he had much on his mind, he couldn't say no to John Iskander. A missing person, even an adult, was always taken very seriously. Even though he didn't know much about the background, the whys and wherefores, Kappakas didn't want to bother him about that now. When a renowned lawyer, a good friend, asks you a favor for his own daughter, you're going to help him.

John Iskander was there for him, years ago, when he was falsely accused of sexual harassment. The press made a lot out of the case, and his marriage to Caroline suffered under great stress. Thanks to the efforts and perseverance of Iskander, the case was ultimately dismissed because of the false testimony by the woman in question.

Kappakas checked his diary, picked up the phone and called his commanding officer. After five minutes he had approval from his boss and was allowed to clear his desk immediately. He didn't even have to inform his temporary replacement about current, urgent affairs. He then called his friend, who answered at once and was very happy Kappakas was ready to investigate Elaine's disappearance. The men agreed to meet in the Dos Gatos bar in Forsyth Street.

Chapter 52

Thirty minutes later Kappakas and Iskander drank to their health. The bar – famous for performances from local bands and karaoke – had only just opened for the day. There weren't many visitors yet, so their conversation wasn't disturbed by noisy youngsters who'd had a drop too much.

Kappakas was in his late fifties, round bellied, a square tanned face with narrow dark eyes. He was of average height, about five foot nine. He had brown, wavy, combed back hair. Between his hooked nose and wide mouth was a neat mustache. Because of his Greek origins, he always was looking for the bright side of life, loved his family very much and cultivated lots of friendships. He liked a white wine now and then, but he preferred ouzo from his native country.

After half an hour, Kappakas said "yes, certainly" to his friend and was determined to find his missing daughter. There were no financial restrictions on taking the matter in hand. John Iskander had reserved a large amount to cover costs like hotels, rented cars and food.

'I trust you, Archie. I'm so glad you'll take this on.'

'Listen, John, I'm doing this with all my heart. You're like family. I hope to be just as successful as you were in my case. I feel obliged, buddy.' He slapped Iskander on the shoulder.

'When you're in Naples and you need anything, don't hesitate to call me. I'll take care of it. My daughter must be found.'

Kappakas took a flight to Fort Myers Airport three hours later. John had rented a car for him, so he could drive comfortably to his hotel in Naples. He slumped in his business class seat, closed his eyes and listened to the soft hum of the jet engines. The authorities in Naples had given him permission to start an investigation. In the belly of the plane, a suitcase was stored with standard arrest equipment: a Glock G23, the latest weapon of the US police, handcuffs, pepper spray and a bullet proof vest. He was thinking about Elaine Iskander. He opened her file, which John had put together for him. By the end of the flight, he knew how he would handle the matter.

Ellis heard the story with growing amazement. She'd become completely silent. The GHB was gone from her body and had left no traces. 'I almost can't believe this, Mike! You put your life at risk for me!' He looked at her brightened face with pleasure. 'El, I had no choice. I did almost everything automatically. If I'd thought about it, I probably wouldn't have dared do it, with all the consequences.'

Ellis smiled contentedly, bent forward and gave him a tender kiss on his cheek. He seemed a little unsettled for a moment and shut his eyes.

'I'm very grateful, Mike, but let's not get sentimental, okay? We have to go on.'

'Absolutely.'

'We're back where we started. All we know is Peterson works for an organization that deals in illegal medicines. Larkin runs it and is not afraid of threatening or even eliminating meddlers. Then there is the clinic where you delivered that package. But that's all we know. What's the destination for those medicines? Does the clinic play a role in it? You were working for a criminal organization. There's a lot more going on.'

'Yeah, seems so to me. I'll bet you a crate of wine that Larkin hasn't thanked Peterson because he was so kind to help me get you out of his house. And Peterson is scared to death now and won't give you a second chance to meet him.'

'Where have you got that yellow note with the number on it, you remember?'

'Oh, you're right. I almost forgot, here it is.'

She looked at the number and said, 'We have to try it.'

'Suppose it's that clinic, then it would be risky to make a phone call. What I would like very much, though, is to see the inside of the building,' Mike declared.

A mischievous smile appeared around Ellis's mouth. 'That means we must do something about it,' she said mysteriously.

Chapter 53

They were parked at a safe distance from St. Luke's Clinic. It was a new moon. The only light came from a few street lamps. A drizzle seemed to hang like a veil. The combination of the dim light and the weather was, literally, heaven-sent, because now they could enter the building unseen. Ellis and Mike watched the dashboard clock in the Corvette. Almost two o'clock. They checked if they had the necessary gear, a penlight, mini-camera, cell phone, two pair of gloves and their pistols. All were packed into a small canvas rucksack.

They got out of the car and crossed the street. The clinic was a hundred yards away. The building seemed to sleep peacefully in the darkness of rainy Naples. They entered the inner yard of an adjacent building and crossed into the back next to St. Luke's. There were no paved pathways, so they walked the last few yards through low bushes. They ended up at the eight-foot high fence. It looked solid and had spikes on top, meant to discourage any climbers. Mike put on gloves and pulled himself up, as Ellis gave him a boost. Carefully he avoided the sharp spikes and swung his legs to the other side. He jumped down, landing in a thorny bush. Although he'd covered his body pretty well, he scratched his neck. He cursed silently.

From inside the fence he helped Ellis climb up. When she wanted to throw her legs across the fence, her trouser-leg got caught on the spikes. 'Dammit,' she said softly. A dog started barking. Mike looked around uneasily. The barking stopped. Ellis managed to work her leg loose, but not without creating a large tear in her jeans. Mike raised his hands to signal her to drop down. He managed to break her fall partly, as they both tumbled to the ground.

'You'll never be a good catcher,' she whispered after getting up.

Mike signaled her to be silent. The slightest sound might betray their presence. They explored the dark backside of the clinic. Then they came to an open shed with containers inside. This was where the clinic had a blind wall. Right below the wall was a brick staircase, leading to a basement. Mike pointed at the door downstairs and indicated they should check it out. They went down the stairs and found themselves in front of a solid wooden door. He asked Ellis to light it for him. She took the penlight out of her pocket and shone it on the door. They saw it turned inward and looked at each other. Ellis nodded.

Mike stepped back, then lunged forward and threw his shoulder against the wood. The door opened with a bang. The noise startled them and, for a moment, they feared some response. Except for the sound of the steady rain, all remained silent. They entered the basement and softly shut the door behind them. They panned the area with the penlight. They couldn't see the whole room, but it looked like they were in a large space used for storing beds, cabinets, chairs and boxes. The air wasn't stale or damp. In the middle, a generator hummed softly. They heard another sound. Further down the basement they saw a large boiler against the wall. Flames inside caused the noise. The nights in Florida can be cool. Drainpipes and air ducting were attached to the ceiling. Ellis moved the sharp beam of her penlight across the basement walls. On the other side was a wooden staircase, leading up to the ground floor.

'This must go into the clinic,' Mike whispered.

Ellis didn't respond. She'd stopped near a large number of cardboard boxes. 'Come over here, Mike.'

'That's a lot of boxes. As far as I can see they're all unlabeled or unmarked. Do you know what I think?'

'Medicines,' she replied.

'Let's check.'

Mike opened his pocketknife and sliced open the tape on a box. Inside were smaller boxes, with brand names and text.

'Prometax. That's used for Alzheimer's patients with dementia.' He opened a box and took out a vial. There was no instruction leaflet. He checked the bottom of the box and asked Ellis to light it up.

'Aug. 1996. That must be the perishable date: to be used before August 1996. His heart started to beat faster. 'El, we've finally found the stuff that goes with the lists I took to Larkin.'

She was equally excited. 'Yes, this is probably illegal stuff,' she said. 'Giving people old, expired drugs to make money. Very clever.'

'Yes, and now we understand Peterson's role better. He got hold of cheap condemned drugs for his residents. Nevertheless, he will have paid a good price to the middle-men; that's how gangsters operate.'

'I wonder if these mysterious diuretic and anti-rheumatic pills are among them,' Ellis said.

'Maybe, but I suspect they're safely stored away somewhere else. They are more expensive. But why do they need them here? According to the website, in this clinic, SocHom residents are treated who suffer from dementia.'

'Shouldn't we call the police?'

'Maybe, but I want to wait a little more. First, let's go into the building. We may find stronger evidence.'

They left the basement, quietly climbing the wooden stairs. Mike pushed the door handle down. He wasn't surprised that it was unlocked. This part of the clinic was probably accessible only to management and staff. Locking doors wasn't likely in that case. They entered a short corridor, lit by soft nightlights. At both ends were doors, one of which had a sign with "Director" on it. The corridor was connected in the middle to a longer and wider one. Ellis looked around the corner. She estimated it was twenty feet long. This one was also lit by night lamps for safety reasons. It had several doors, both in the left and right walls. She beckoned Mike and put a finger to her lips. He understood that from here on they had to keep silent. Ellis pointed to the Director's door. He nodded and followed her. The office door was unlocked and they sneaked in. Ellis walked to the desk and started to search the drawers. Mike joined her. He took a diary from the desktop and opened it to the first page. In printed letters was written, "This diary belongs to" with a handwritten name underneath, "Dr. M. Santini". Ellis saw the office door was ajar.

'Mike, let me search. You stand by the door. We must be on our guard,' she said softly. Mike put the diary back and stood by the entry. Ellis shone her penlight on the books, papers, files and maps. She wasn't sure what she was looking for, but then something caught her attention, a large map with the letters "P.D." on the cover. She had always liked abbreviations. She opened the map and found case histories of patients. She took her camera to take some pictures.

Mike gave a muffled cry, 'Somebody's coming, let's get out of here!'

She shut the map, closed the drawer and was quickly beside Mike in a few big steps. They listened to the sound through the slightly opened door. Somewhere down the hall, they heard a door slam. Mike pointed to the entrance to the basement. They sneaked back out of the office and left the clinic's main floor the same way they'd come in. When they reached the brick steps outside, they noticed it was no longer raining.

They hurried to the fence, climbed over, and this time didn't land on the soft grass but on a concrete sidewalk. Mike landed badly. He hurt his ankle and yelped in pain. By reflex, they looked back to the clinic. A light went on in one of the rooms. Concealed in the dark, they saw a silhouette appear in the window. The shadow moved and disappeared from sight. The light in the room was turned off. Quickly they rushed to the Corvette. In the car they looked at each other and laughed uncomfortably, both heaving a sigh of relief. Mike saw Ellis held something in her hand.

'What have you got there?'

Ellis looked up surprised. 'Oh, a file, I think. I took it without thinking.' She winked at him.

'Come on; let's go back to the hotel first,' he said, and added with resolve, 'we can't stay here too long.'

They drove out of the neighborhood dying to read the file and then get some sleep.

Chapter 54

Furiously she grabbed the phone and ordered George Broderick to come to her office at once. 'And bring that record you've taken,' she snapped at him, while slamming down the receiver even before Broderick got a chance to react. As usual Dr. Margaret Santini was in her office early. Today she had to make preparations for some routine outpatients' treatments. On entering her office she got an unpleasant surprise, however. After opening one of her desk drawers to examine the patients' record, she couldn't find it. She was sure she'd put it in the drawer. After searching her whole office, it struck her that Broderick might have something to do with it. He was one of the few people who knew about that file.

Broderick politely knocked at the door, entered the room, and said good morning to his boss. Santini dispensed with formalities, raising her voice. 'Why haven't you got that patients' record with you? What makes you think you should get into my desk drawers?'

Broderick was dumbfounded. He looked at Santini in amazement. He didn't know what she was talking about.

'Well? Answer me!'

'I..., I....'

'Yes?'

Broderick braced himself and said, 'Doctor, I don't know what you mean. I don't have that record, absolutely not.'

However, he underestimated the force of his denial. Santini became more furious and banged her fist on the table. 'Are you calling me a liar? I'll....'

She was interrupted by her phone. With a fierce look in her eyes she picked up the receiver. With a catch in her voice she answered the call. 'Yes?'

A calm voice sounded through the phone. 'Good morning to you too, madam. Am I speaking to Dr. Margaret Santini of St. Luke's Clinic?'

'Speaking. Who is this?' she asked gruffly.

'I'm Detective Archibald Kappakas from the police force...'

Santini interrupted Kappakas. 'Detective? What are you calling me for?'

'I was just about to tell you that, Doctor. Please listen for a moment, I only have one question. Does Ms. Elaine Iskander work for you?'

'Er…, yes, no. I mean yes, of course. But she hasn't reported for work the last few days, and we don't know where she is.'

'Dr. Santini,' Kappakas said with a deep voice. 'I'd like to have a talk with you, in private, about her disappearance. Does ten-thirty suit you?'

His directness took her by surprise and she felt confused. 'Yes, of course.'

'Then I'll see you later. Thanks for your cooperation, Doctor.'

'Okay,' she replied, stunned.

Broderick saw that Santini was surprised, as well as upset. She absent-mindedly put the phone down again and stared ominously at her assistant.

'Is something wrong, Doctor?' he tried cautiously.

'You may go now George.'

'You look very …'

'Go now! That's an order.'

'What about the patients' record?'

'We'll discuss it later; I have more important things on my mind now.'

'Sure, you know where to find me.'

She seemed to have regained some control over the situation and said, 'Yes, I do. Please go now.'

Broderick walked out of her room, leaving behind an uncomfortable silence. Santini's brain worked at top speed. What a morning. She had prepared everything so well and taken the necessary measures. Before this police detective would come to question her, she called Josh Larkin.

'Yes?'

'It's me. We have some problems here.'

'What do you mean?'

'The police are coming to pester me with questions. They seem to have discovered something about Iskander.'

'And that surprises you?'

'No, of course not, but first, I want to discuss it with you.'

'We've been through this before, Santini. If you just do what you must do, you won't have any more trouble, right?'

'This is not the only thing. We've lost the patients' record. It's gone.'

Suddenly Larkin wasn't so calm and reserved anymore. He raised his voice and barked, 'Damn it! How can you be so stupid not to work with a computer? You should have backup files for everything. I told you several times, use a computer!'

Santini flinched at Larkin's remarks. She wasn't used to being bawled out. 'Sorry, we'll keep looking,' she said to avert Larkin's wrath.

'Find that record! If it falls into the wrong hands, we're finished. Whose turn was it anyway?'

'Mr. and Ms. Atchison.'

'I'll send a special delivery, with a different courier. You know, I'm under great pressure. There are customers who don't want to wait any longer.'

'I understand.'

Larkin was silent for a moment and then said, 'Another thing; Peterson has proved unreliable. He helped Mike's lady friend escape. Garcia killed two of my men. I want to put him out of action. He's put the organization at risk. But we won't be scared off by an unemployed courier. We're going on with our business. I'll make sure you get more supplies.'

Santini sank back in her chair. She heard everything, but it didn't all register. 'Thanks,' she said and hung up.

With trembling hands she opened the minibar. A drink was what she needed, before the police arrived and tried to make her say things she didn't want to say.

Chapter 55

Mike and Ellis had slept badly. The adrenaline had caused them to lie awake and frequently re-run the movie of their burglary and stolen patients' files through their minds. Early next morning they got back together. Both sensed something in the air, but they didn't quite know what to make of it. While Ellis was perusing the patients' record, Mike made coffee.

'There are a lot of patients in it. Over a hundred, I estimate. There are case history summaries with notations on treatments, medicine usage, Doctor's visits, therapies and lots of medical jargon. And many dates have hourly notations.'

'As far as I can tell it concerns case histories used in hospitals. You know, like those files that Doctors and nurses carry when they visit patients at their beds.'

'Yes, Mike, I'm familiar with that. I once had a Doctor at my bedside, not a handsome one unfortunately, who was scribbling away all the time. He apparently had little interest in talking with his patient.'

'Why were you in hospital?'

'Oh, appendicitis. Was supposed to be a routine job, but I was troubled by side effects. Nothing serious, but enough to keep me there for a few days. That's when I learned how to read a case history.'

'Coffee?'

'Yes, please.'

He saw her leaf through the thick record. 'That's a massive file. Are you looking for something special?'

'A name. Do you remember the name Mrs. Warakomski mentioned?'

'Sorry, I forgot.'

'See, that's what you need me for, to remember things. Eriksson, that was the name.'

'You're right, Eriksson. Is he in it?'

'I'm looking; it's not in alphabetical order.'

Mike looked at his partner scrutinizing the record. He felt his ankle, it was swollen.

'Bingo,' Ellis said calmly but triumphantly. 'Mr. B. Eriksson and Mrs. M. Eriksson. Wow, that's a big case history.' Her eyes danced across the paper looking for irregularities. Among the normal medicines she found two she had seen before: Duretica and MPC-4.

'They were both given dementia inhibitors. This explains the large amount of drugs we found in the basement. Probably the Erikssons were in some kind of treatment program for Alzheimer's. In this country there are several of these projects.'

As she read further, her mouth fell open in amazement. 'They passed away. There's a date after "Registro Mortuorum", their date of death.

'What's the date?'

'August 19. That's only two days ago!'

'Then they must be buried by now.'

Mike started to pace around. 'Let me think. We both know they've undergone treatment to inhibit dementia. You don't die from that. A combination of diuretic and anti-rheumatic pills can lead to death, however. Suppose the Erikssons took those pills and died from them. Why?'

Ellis looked at him and wanted to say something.

'In the case history the names of the Doctors or therapists treating them are also mentioned: G. Broderick and E. Iskander.'

'We could phone the clinic and ask if we can speak to one of them. We can pretend to be family.'

'Well, I don't think they're going to fall for that. Don't forget they're very alert now, assuming they've discovered the patients' record is missing.'

'Do you have a better idea?'

'Yes. Call some undertakers. The Erikssons would be buried here in Naples, right? That's what I hope at least. I'm going to Google the names of these therapists.'

Mike picked up a telephone directory from the reception desk. He found seven "Funeral Directors". He called the first one on the list. Ellis Googled the name, Iskander, first. She found no results concerning her address, and nothing on Facebook or LinkedIn. There were several people with the same name living in northeast Florida. She scrolled the page and saw the word "Iskander" at the bottom, followed by a vague text and a link to YouTube. That caught her attention. She clicked on the link.

Chapter 56

Detective Kappakas wasn't quite satisfied yet. He repeated the question. 'Dr. Santini, you just told me you know nothing about the disappearance of Elaine Iskander. That's correct, isn't it, Doctor?'

Kappakas was used to addressing professionals and public figures by their titles. He knew from experience that the persons questioned felt more at ease, more respected. It flattered their egos. Sometimes it benefited him. If it would work in this case depended on the person opposite him. Margaret Santini gave him a stern look.

'Detective, I already told you I know nothing about her disappearance. I wish I could help you. We're all very concerned about her. I think you'll understand that.'

'Oh yes, Doctor, absolutely. But maybe you can help me with the following.'

Kappakas deliberately kept silent for a few instants. Santini didn't react. As she wasn't sure what course Kappakas would follow, she began to feel uncomfortable and shifted her position.

'Was there anyone who worked closely with her? Except for you of course.'

Santini nodded. 'Yes, Detective, she worked with male nurse Broderick. George Broderick.'

'I'd like to speak with him.'

'I wish I could help you there, but Mr. Broderick went on vacation three days ago.'

'That's too bad. Can I reach him some way or other?'

'Of course; I can give you his phone number, and his address.'

'Yes, thank you; that would be great. Well then, that's all for now. You've given me a lot of information about the clinic and your methods. I would have liked to speak with some of your patients. Unfortunately I can't force you to allow this, unless, of course, I show you a court order.'

Santini gazed intently at the policeman. 'I'm really sorry, Detective, we have to maintain patient privacy, and they are quite ill. Is there anything else I can help you with?'

'No, Doctor, thank you very much for your time. If you think of anything at all that might be important, please let me know. Here's my card.'

Kappakas said goodbye and shook Santini's hand. Then he left her office. Outside a guard escorted him. Kappakas thought he'd give it a try. 'Sir, do you happen to know where Elaine Iskander is at the moment?'

The guard just shook his head and accompanied Kappakas to the exit. After the gate was shut, Kappakas turned around and let his eyes wander across the clinic. He had the impression Dr. Santini hadn't been candid with him. She'd been open about the clinic's programs and methods, and the relationship with SocHom. But he'd noticed she wasn't at ease when he asked if he could talk to Broderick. He didn't like the fact that Santini had avoided his request to speak with patients. Now he had to request a search warrant from local authorities. This meant he probably wouldn't get the required papers today.

Back in his car Kappakas checked his mailbox on his tablet. Six new e-mails had come in, two from John Iskander, three from his precinct and one from his wife. He opened the e-mail from his office, with the subject: Contact please! It read: "Dear Archie, someone responded to your video-message. Good luck. Pete."

This can't be true, Kappakas thought. He'd ordered Police Officer Pete Dykehouse to closely follow any response to the message about the disappearance of Iskander on YouTube. It exceeded his expectations to get a reaction so soon. He ignored the other e-mails for now and went to the YouTube channel of the Jacksonville Police Department and opened his video-message. In it John Iskander asked the public to look out for his daughter, Elaine Iskander, and give any information about her directly to the police or leave a comment below the video. The film took about forty seconds and featured Elaine's picture and some texts about her background and work. Kappakas couldn't suppress an exclamation when he read the latest comment on the video. "Urgent. E-mail us, please: migar3911@hotmail.com".

He opened the e-mail program and sent a reply. Then Kappakas drove back to his hotel, read the other messages and waited for any developments with his tablet and phone close at hand.

Chapter 57

Ellis looked surprised at her laptop screen. "You have a new message". After reading it she said, 'Well, the police lost no time reacting to my comment on that video-message.'

'Great,' Mike said.

'I'll send them another note. They may want to contact us.'

Two minutes later, the familiar –you-have-a-new-message- jingle sounded from her computer's speakers. Eagerly Ellis opened the e-mail and was pleased to see the police wished to contact them.

'A Detective Archibald Kappakas from Jacksonville wants to speak to us. He says it's urgent and can see us anytime we want.'

'Jacksonville?' Mike asked. 'You told me earlier the name Iskander is a familiar one in that area?'

'Yes, that's right. I've counted at least twelve people with that name. If the Jacksonville police are looking for her here, she must be from around that area.'

'Let's contact this policeman. We can't do very much ourselves anymore. He represents the law and can use his authority to force a breakthrough.'

'I'll send him an e-mail. Did you have any luck with the funeral directors?'

'No, none of them remember a burial or cremation of someone with the name of Eriksson. One of them said the church sometimes organizes a funeral, but usually only for vagrants, poor people or outcasts.'

'Well, Mike, you know what you have to do then.' She looked at him meaningfully.

'Are you kidding? You're comfortably surfing the internet while I have to speak with morticians and grave-diggers. And now I even have to deal with clergymen!'

She gave him a sweet smile. 'Mike, who else can say they've visited heaven and earth in such a short time?'

Mike wanted to make a one-fingered gesture but thought better of it. He left her alone and started calling churches and religious communities. Ellis received a reply from Kappakas. She read the e-mail aloud, "Appreciate your willingness to help. I prefer to come to you. Be there in thirty minutes. Bye, Archie Kappakas."

Ellis immediately sent a reply to say she agreed to meet and gave the name of the hotel. She told Mike that the Detective was on his way.

'Has the high clergy already made you any wiser?'

'Have you any idea how many denominations and churches there are here?' he asked rhetorically with some desperation. 'First I contacted the churches that are located at SocHom. Nothing. Then I started with the Catholic congregations. I'm halfway through my list. Would you like to take a few?'

'Sorry, Mike, religion and church mean nothing to me. I only believe in myself. That's hard enough as it is. I'm going to make a few sandwiches before the Detective arrives. I guess you'd like one too, after all your detective work.' She laughed and returned to her own room.

Kappakas parked his car in front of the hotel entrance. He went to the reception and showed his ID. Juan, the receptionist, looked startled and said, 'La policía, por qué? I do nothing, nada!'

'Take it easy, just give me the room number of Ms. Ellis Henning.'

'Oh, Dios. You see, una prostituta in my hotel. Mi Madré!'

Kappakas stayed calm for he wanted to avoid a scene. 'Calm down, please. She's not a hooker, why do you think that?'

'Por qué, she's with one hombré, pero habitaciones seperadas, separate rooms, yes?'

Kappakas laughed. He looked at the man's name tag on his shirt. 'Yes, I know, Juan. Nothing's wrong, nada. Now give me the room number, por favor.' Kappakas said it a little more emphatically this time, with immediate result.

'Si, señor policia. Numero vientetrés, twenty-three, señor.'

Kappakas took the elevator to the second floor, and a few moments later he knocked on the door of Ellis's room.

Chapter 58

The welcome was both professional and enthusiastic. After introducing each other, Mike invited Kappakas to sit down. The detective showed his badge and started to talk. 'I'm investigating for the police and the Iskander family in Jacksonville. The father of the missing woman, Mr. John Iskander, is a friend of mine. He's a lawyer and helped me out once, so now I'm returning a favor to him. I'm very curious about what you're going to tell me. Oh, and please call me Kappa; most people do.'

Ellis smiled and laughed a little. 'We'll try,' she said, 'and please call us Ellis and Mike. Would you like something to eat or drink?'

'I'd like that very much. And now tell me everything you know. As I said, I'm very curious.'

'Of course. It's a long story. It all started a couple of months ago on Naples Beach.'

Mike told him about his deliveries for Larkin, the discovery of the expired and suspicious medicines, the meeting with the director of SocHom, and the burglary in the clinic, where earlier he had delivered a package. 'Meanwhile, I was beaten up by a goon, and my partner Ellis was drugged by Larkin. Oh, and I almost forgot to mention two deaths, two of Larkin's henchmen who drove off an unfinished bridge. His other goon, Sonny, is still around and dangerous.'

Kappakas looked intently at the two younger adults. 'That's a long story, for sure. Sounds almost incredible to me. But...I'm only a simple police detective from a different area than southwest Florida. Maybe life is a little more intense here than I'd expect in retirement land. We'll have to use everything we know to find out where Elaine Iskander is, dead or alive. To the extent it's relevant, I'll include your account in my further investigations.'

Mike nodded. 'You can rely on us to tell the truth. We want to help.'

'Well, good to hear that. You just said you broke into the clinic. Did you take anything there?'

Mike looked at Ellis and pointed with his eyes to the table. Ellis took the patients' record and gave it to Kappakas. 'This is what we found in the director's office.'

Kappakas glanced through it and then spoke again. 'Before I continue, I should tell you something. If it's true what you said, you have committed several criminal offenses. I don't want to fool you, but when this case is over, an investigation could be made into your actions and involvement. I've already heard the Naples state troopers are looking for witnesses to the accident on that bridge, where they got two bodies out of the water. But you don't have to be afraid the state police or sheriff will knock on your door soon. As long as the investigation continues, I can make sure to keep you mostly free from their inquiries. I need your help too.'

Mike and Ellis felt some relief after hearing Kappakas' words.

'If we manage to bring this case to a favorable conclusion, and can expose Mr. Larkin's wheeling and dealing, I'll put in a good word for you with the other authorities.' He smiled at first, but then gave a loud laugh when he saw their astounded faces. 'Gosh, did I scare you?' Kappakas chuckled. 'It won't come to your arrest. After all, what evidence is there?'

'That's exactly what I was thinking. Nobody saw us, except for Peterson and Larkin, but they'll be wise enough to keep their mouths shut. They're up to their ears in this medicine swindle,' Ellis said.

'Wait a minute, take it easy,' Kappakas reacted. 'There's no proof of that either, remember? It's up to us – I specifically include you – to expose it. But let's discuss this record first. Is it important?'

His question made Ellis smile. 'It certainly is! I think it provides very valuable information. It's likely the medical director, Dr. Santini, doesn't work with a computer. At least, we didn't see one in her office. She may have a laptop, which she takes home, but then why maintain this sizable record?'

She showed Kappakas the pages for the Erikssons. 'Look, their therapist and nurse were E. Iskander and G. Broderick. And here, these drugs form a very questionable combination for demented people. My friend Sheldon Rosenberg says it may be lethal, certainly when administered to elderly people.'

'Is this friend of yours a doctor?' Kappakas asked.

'Yes, he's a surgeon in Oregon. We met through my work as a research journalist. He sometime helps me with medical issues and is now a good friend. He helped us evaluate the medicine lists.'

'Well, that's clear then.'

Mike pointed out the date of death of Mr. and Mrs. Eriksson. 'A married couple that dies on the same day; isn't it odd? I think the disappearance of Elaine Iskander has something to do with certain malpractices, but we can only guess what they might be.'

Kappakas ran his hands through his bushy hair and studied the Eriksson file. Next he took a notepad from his bag and started to scribble. 'Okay. What have we got so far? The Erikssons – both dead and buried – Iskander and Broderick – peculiar drugs – a reserved Dr. Santini – Larkin – Peterson – and you. Guys, what am I supposed to make of all this? There's a lot of circumstantial evidence. As a young policeman I learned to start with what comes last. Later in the investigation I'll get to earlier observations or discoveries.'

'You mean then, you find the source sooner?' Mike asked.

Kappakas straightened up in his chair and took a sandwich from the plate. 'Look; you must always stay in the here and now. Developments in a case are the consequences of accumulated events that eventually lead to established facts. This is pure textbook theory. If you follow this method, however, you sometimes have to take drastic measures to get answers about what you've already discovered. If I interpret this record and your stories in this way, I can only arrive at one conclusion…'

He took a bite from his sandwich. Mike and Ellis looked at him full of expectation.

'Which is…?' Ellis asked curiously.

Kappakas made a digging movement. 'Exhumation.'

'Exhume who?' they asked in unison.

'Mr. and Ms. Eriksson of course.'

Kappakas gave them a surprised look. As if he had come up with something he had only just realized himself.

Chapter 59

Eberto Vargas was eating arroz con pesca, his favorite food. An e-mail beep sounded from the dresser. He put the laptop on his knees. He read the message from Josh Larkin twice. "4 Boxes of Duretica and 6 boxes of MPC-4; Urgent – Must be delivered before next Friday 12.00 noon. Find new, reliable courier. Payment as usual. L."

He then deleted the message and shut the laptop. Tomorrow, Wednesday, he would send the delivery. Because Larkin had told him his courier had quit, Vargas had to organize the delivery himself. He knew someone who wanted to make a little extra money. He ignored Orlana's surly look. She hated this sort of activity during meals. He left the table without saying a word, put on his coat and walked to his car. He drove away, and twenty minutes later Vargas arrived at the house of Javier Rios. He parked his old Mercedes right in front of the door. He saw Amorita working in the kitchen. On a clothes line in the garden hung brightly colored laundry. He walked up the pathway to the screen door and knocked on the woodwork. Vargas looked inside through the wire screen. He heard Amorita's loud voice, 'Open up!'

Javier Rios appeared at the doorway. He opened the screen and said, 'Hola, Eberto, qué pasa? I told you not to come to my house.'

Javier took Vargas to a shed behind the house where they couldn't be overheard. 'Well, what are you doing here?'

Vargas came closer to him and whispered, 'The boss wants you to make a delivery. You must leave tomorrow. I'll report you sick at work; then no one will wonder where you are.'

'Okay.' Rios was perplexed.

'You get a car from me and have to be in Naples, Florida on Friday at noon at the latest. On your way you stay the night in motels. This is the chance of a lifetime, Javier. You will make good money; I will make sure of that.'

'Bueno, I am in. I trust you; you helped me out before. Only Amorita will not be happy about it.'

'Listen, I will talk to her, say you are going to work tomorrow. Do not tell her anything, okay? It will be fine.'

Javier Rios nodded and felt honored to get the job. Vargas slapped him on the back and gave him some instructions. Then Javier left the garden quickly and drove back to Orlana who had just finished the arroz. Javier went in and playfully patted Amorita's backside.

'Hey, what do you think you are doing?' she reacted indignantly.

But he said nothing and, whistling, went to his room where he started to put some clothes in a bag.

Chapter 60

Kappakas enjoyed seeing the astounded look on the faces opposite him. 'You find that odd? It happens more often than you'd think. Once we have a court order we can open graves and investigate anything. This may range from a visual examination in the coffin to taking out a body for a specific analysis, like an autopsy. Even from an almost completely decayed body, there's usually some useful tissue. Also, many conclusions can be drawn from hairs and bone marrow. Foreign substances are mostly found in the stomach, so it's possible to establish if someone was poisoned.'

'Nice job,' Ellis said, wrinkling her nose in disgust.

Kappakas pretended to apologize. 'Performing an autopsy is never pleasant, but it leads to many solved cases.'

'The bodies of Mr. and Mrs. Eriksson will be in reasonable condition, I suppose,' Ellis suggested.

'Then it's important to request a court order as soon as possible,' Mike said.

'This morning I'm going to request the exhumation order,' Kappakas replied.

'There's another thing,' Ellis said. 'How about family members? Shouldn't they give permission?'

'A court order transcends everything. In this case a crime is being investigated, so members of the family can't prevent an autopsy. But it's a matter of decency, of course, to inform any relatives.'

'It seems wise then to keep searching for the priest who conducted the Erikssons' funeral,' Mike said. While he took out his phone, Ellis browsed through the patients' record. Kappakas checked his incoming messages and was happy to discover his colleagues in Naples had found Broderick's home address.

'I'm going to pay a visit to this Mr. Broderick,' Kappakas said. 'I suspect Dr. Santini isn't telling us the truth and he's probably at home.'

'Seems like a good idea, Kappa. Should we meet again here?' Mike asked.

'I'll meet you at your hotel room. Then the receptionist can tell his children exciting stories about the frequent police visits to his work place.'

Kappakas first drove to the office of Judge Vincent Murphy in the courthouse on the Tamiami Trail. He informed the judge of the disappearance of Elaine Iskander and his doubts about the cause of death of Mr. and Mrs. Eriksson. Murphy considered it suspicious that the deaths of the couple weren't registered at the Department of Public Health. Doctors, undertakers and civil servants are required by law to report deceased persons to the Department within forty-eight hours after establishing their deaths. Murphy concluded there was legal cause for authorities to investigation.

A little later Kappakas collected the court order from a desk clerk. He left the building and drove to Broderick's home address.

Kappakas looked at the street signs and steered his rented Chevy Malibu into 103rd Street in Naples Park. He parked his car on the driveway of the address he'd been given. The house was smaller than others around it. He rang the doorbell. A man of about thirty, dressed in violet sportswear, opened the door. Kappakas showed his badge.

'Good afternoon, sir. My name is Kappakas, police. I'm looking for Mr. Broderick.'

The man stared at the badge and then said, 'Yes, what do you want from him?'

'I'll tell him myself, if you don't mind. And who are you, may I ask?'

'I'm George's friend, Guy Fisher.'

'Mr. Fisher, I'd like to speak with your friend for a moment.'

'Er…, well, he isn't at home right now. He's at work.'

'What's his job? Where does he work?'

'He's a nurse in a clinic here in Naples.'

'Do you think he's there now?'

'That's where he should be anyway. But I'd like to know what this is all about. I'm worried.'

'Sure, but Mr. Fisher, your friend is under no suspicion whatsoever. We only need him to clarify certain things. Don't worry.'

'Well, I can believe that. George is a sweet guy, who wouldn't hurt a fly, so to speak.'

'What's the name of the clinic?'

'St. Luke's, quite near the ocean, less than two miles from here.'

'Thank you, Mr. Fisher.'

Kappakas was about to walk away, when he said, 'Oh, and another thing; I would appreciate it if you don't call and inform Mr. Broderick that I'm coming. It's supposed to be a spontaneous visit.'

'Yes, yes, of course. I understand.'

'Good, we agree then. Good afternoon.'

Chapter 61

Kappakas reached the clinic in five minutes. He called at the gate and waited for a response.

'Yes, who is it?' an officious male voice sounded through the intercom.

'Detective Archibald Kappakas.'

It was silent for a few seconds; then the man said, 'You may come in.'

The gate was opened automatically and Kappakas walked up the driveway to the main entrance. Wide stone steps led to a massive wooden door. A guard opened it and asked why he had come. After Kappakas told him he wanted to see George Broderick, he was invited to come in and shown to a couch in the hall. He wondered if Dr. Santini was present. But right now he had no interest in her, although he had every reason to confront her about Broderick "being on vacation." All in good time, he thought. Then he heard voices in the corridor. The guard escorted a small, thin man, about thirty-five years old and dressed in a white uniform. He had bushy hair and looked tired. Kappakas noticed the man had tears in his eyes.

'Yes, and who are you?' Broderick asked defensively.

'Detective Archibald Kappakas. You are Mr. Broderick?'

'Yes.'

'I'd like to have a word with you.'

'What about?'

'I'll tell you in a minute. Can we sit somewhere quiet?'

'Sure, come along.'

They walked down the long corridor. Broderick opened the door into a conference room. He showed Kappakas to a chair. 'Sit down, please.'

'Thank you.'

Broderick started to talk. Now and then he sniffled and constantly ran his hands through his hair. 'My director told me you wanted to see me earlier. She didn't tell you the truth, Detective. She was confused and was surprised by your visit. Sorry, but I was at work as usual. If you want to know more about this, you must talk to Dr. Santini….'

Kappakas interrupted. 'Yes, it's alright Mr. Broderick.'

'Please, call me George.'

'Fine, George; I've just seen your friend at your house. I wanted to make sure you were at the clinic now. Have you spoken to him in the past fifteen minutes?'

'No.'

'Great. Well, I have an important question for you.' Kappakas started to speak slowly, bent forward and gave Broderick a stern look. 'Do you know where Elaine Iskander is?'

On hearing the name of Iskander something snapped inside Broderick. He started to shake and could no longer hold back his tears.

'Is everything okay?'

Broderick shook his head. 'I'm shattered. We miss her so much. She hasn't contacted us. We fear the worst,' he said haltingly.

'That's bad news. You think something happened to her?'

Broderick raised his head and gave the Detective an agonized look. 'Yes..., it seems crazy, but she's been kidnapped. Or....'

'Yes?'

'Or murdered.'

'Why do you think she's murdered, George?'

Broderick took a few moments to get his emotions under control. 'Just a hunch, I think. I'm a sensitive person, you know.'

'Who would want to harm Elaine Iskander?'

Broderick looked away. 'No idea. Not me anyway. I work closely together with her. She was, er…is a warm-hearted woman. The patients love her. I really miss her.'

'What's her relationship with Dr. Santini?'

'Professional. Dr. Santini may sometimes tells her off when she's done something wrong, according to her. Dr. Santini is a very passionate doctor. She wants the staff to respect the objectives of the clinic and perform flawlessly. Elaine has told me the Doctor doesn't always accept her views. Then they argue.'

'Are you ambitious in your work?'

Broderick hesitated for a moment and then said, 'When you work here, you endorse the aims of the clinic. I think one's personal view must be subservient to the general good and to the leadership that serves that good.'

Kappakas made notes in his notebook. 'Yes, George, one more question. Do you happen to know a Mr. and Mrs. Eriksson?'

'Yes, they were patients. Sadly, they passed away.'

'Any idea what caused their deaths?'

'No, I'm sorry. In general, nurses aren't informed about the causes of death.'

'So you haven't been told where they were buried or cremated?'

'No, we're not informed of that either. It's not our business.'

'Right. Do you think Doctor Santini can tell me more about it?'

'Sure. She handles all the details when someone dies here. You have to ask her about it.'

Kappakas stared at the nurse. He didn't quite know what to make of it. Either this young man knows nothing and is genuinely saddened, or he just pretends and has something to answer for. Kappakas knew from experience that you can't trust the cat to guard the cream. He was used to taking small steps, one at a time, allowing people to tell him what they wanted, without pressuring them, as many of his colleagues would do. At a certain point, people start to contradict themselves and stop cooperating. That point would come sooner or later in this case. He would work patiently to get the truth with as much help as he could coax from his inquiries.

'George, I appreciate your help. Please tell the Doctor I'd like to have a word with her later.'

'Okay, I will.'

Kappakas said goodbye to Broderick and quickly left St. Luke's to contact Mike and Ellis. As soon as he was out of sight, Dr. Santini entered the conference room. She walked to Broderick and smiled.

'Well done, George. You're a great actor. You'd do well in Hollywood. I told you; if you play it out like I say, we'll get through this.'

Chapter 62

While driving back to his hotel, Kappakas' phone started to ring. He tugged at the wheel and parked the car against the curb. He answered. 'Kappakas.'

'It's me, boss. We just received a call from a Dr. Santini. She says you saw her earlier. She wants to report a loss. She didn't say what was lost, but it is urgent, according to her. She'd like you come to St. Luke's Clinic and take her report.'

'Thanks, Pete, I'll go there right now and get back to you.'

He broke the connection and thought for a moment. Detective Pete Dykehouse was his contact in Jacksonville. Kappakas had chosen Dykehouse for this role so he wouldn't be dependent on the Naples police force, and could act quickly without troubling policemen he didn't know. He'd worked with Dykehouse before and respected him as a hard-working, loyal and very conscientious policeman. Kappakas knew what "loss" Santini wanted to report. He was lucky to have inspected the patients' record. Did Santini know Garcia and Henning had it? Or was she just guessing? He wouldn't take any risk and decided to play along with Santini. He wanted to leave the "queen" in peace in order to capture her later when the time was right. The chess match had just begun.

Back at St. Luke's, Kappakas was received respectfully this time. Dr. Santini was in a good mood. She welcomed him and asked him to take a seat.

'Detective, I heard you were here earlier.'

'That's right; I had a conversation with Mr. Broderick.'

'First, I must apologize to you for misleading you earlier. Contrary to what I said, George Broderick was around here when you asked about him. But I was a little confused. I was surprised and unsettled by the police dropping in on me. Once again, I'm sorry. I hope you'll forgive my error.'

Kappakas couldn't believe what he was hearing, but didn't show it. 'Doctor, it's better to breathe the truth than to drown in lies.'

'Detective,' she said pretending to be amazed. 'Do you mean to say: a fault confessed is half redressed?'

Kappakas grinned. She started to annoy him. It was best not to overdo things. Santini resumed speaking. 'Detective, I asked you to come because I want to report a loss.'

'Yes, I was called about it.'

'I'm glad the police are so considerate and responsive.'

'I have a form with me you can complete. You can describe the missing object and any further relevant information.'

Santini reacted surprised and said with some indignation, 'Object? Detective! It's a person that's missing.'

Kappakas swallowed. 'A person? I thought you were missing something – by theft.'

'Well right,' Santini said curtly. 'In any case, I want to report Ms. Elaine Iskander missing.'

'You want to report Ms. Iskander missing?'

'Yes sir, you've got that right. Now, what should be done?'

'But Dr. Santini, I don't understand. Why didn't you report when I asked you if you knew anything about Ms. Iskander's disappearance?'

'Disappearance, Detective Kappakas? That's different from missing.'

Kappakas, somewhat amused, let her go on. Santini continued, 'When you were here for the first time, we established the fact that Ms. Iskander was gone. But she wasn't considered missing yet. That's right, Detective, isn't it?'

Kappakas knew the woman was playing with words to make an excuse, but he maintained a friendly face. 'Legally speaking, you're absolutely right, Doctor.'

'So, Detective, I want to report Elaine Iskander missing,' she said seriously. 'We're very upset about it and expect you to do everything in your power to find her. We need her here, and we're worried about her.'

'Fine, fine. For that we need this form,' he said and took a missing persons form from his briefcase. 'As a matter of fact, we've been looking for her for a couple of days. We will do everything we can.'

'Good,' she said studying the paper.

'You can fill it in now or send it by mail, which ever you prefer.'

'I'll do it later. Thank you, Detective.'

Santini thought she was finished with the policeman, but he had another question up his sleeve. 'Er…, one more thing. What I'd like to know is, where are your deceased patients buried?'

To his surprise, Santini responded collectedly. 'That's up to the deceased's relatives. Interment or cremation, it can take place anywhere in the country. Most of our patients are from other states.'

'So the clinic, you, don't have a say in the matter?'

'That's how it is.'

'I see, yes.'

'Well Detective, that was all? I have things to do, including the missing persons form, if you don't mind.'

'One other thing. May I visit your patients and ask questions?'

Santini reacted coolly and professionally. 'Detective! How could you even think that? This is about personal privacy. You should know that.'

He slapped his head. 'Oh, how stupid; of course, privacy. Dr. Santini, please send in the form. Have a good day.'

'The same to you, sir. You can find your way out, can't you?'

He looked blankly at her and said a little cynically, 'Sure, I really feel at home here.' Then he left the office and suddenly wondered what Ellis and Mike would make of what had just happened in Dr. Margaret Santini's office.

Dr. Santini gave Broderick a call, directing him to keep an eye on the Detective until he was all the way out of the clinic and through the entry gate.

Chapter 63

Josh Larkin nervously pulled on his cigarette. He was alone in his office and thought about what had been going on the last few days. Things were getting out of hand. Something had to be done to prevent damage to his operations. In retrospect, it had been a capital error to hire someone from "outside" as courier for the San Antonio–Naples route. But Michael Garcia, young and fit, down and out, wanted to work, looked reliable, and had no wife and kids. In short, he looked like a perfect recruit.

Had he been too harsh on Garcia that one time, when he'd gone for a swim and made a late delivery? Or had he been beaten up too much by his bodyguards? After that, it was probably no coincidence that Garcia wanted to know what goods he was carrying. Obviously, the ample payment Garcia received had not been enough to guarantee his loyalty. It was all the more clear that power and money won't always keep people in line. But Larkin hadn't thought of that. He'd been humiliated when his business partner, Mike Peterson, cuffed him to the oven on Garcia's command. What's more, his former courier probably caused the deaths of two of his body guards. The men fortunately left no traces, so they couldn't be linked to him. And as if this wasn't enough, his other business partner, Margaret Santini, lost some patients' records. He still hoped she would find them, but it was more likely someone stole them.

He cursed when it occurred to him that this "damned Italian woman" didn't work with a computer and protected files. Larkin poured another large whiskey. He stubbed out his cigarette in the ashtray, and decided to take action. He started to work out some ideas, to protect his organization. An hour later he summoned two "associates" and gave them instructions.

Mike cheerfully stepped into Ellis's room. 'I've got him, the priest who was present at the Erikssons' funeral; a Father Raymond D'Angelico of St. Agnes Church.'

'Great. What did he say?'

'I posed as a local reporter - obituaries. He was surprised and, at first, didn't know what to say. Then he confirmed to have conducted the funeral for the Erikssons.'

'That's good. Where were they buried?'

'At Crest Lawn, not far from the clinic.'

'Really? That's a coincidence.'

'I wonder what Kappa will think when we tell him. I expect him any moment.'

Mike stretched out on the sofa. 'For the time being, our digging is over. I'm going to relax. I'm worn out from all those phone calls.'

She looked at him with mock concern. 'Yeah, you need to rest, so you can dig up dead bodies later on.'

Ellis disappeared into the kitchen to make dinner.

Twenty minutes later Kappakas arrived at the Inn Place Hotel. As usual he greeted Juan, the receptionist. Juan couldn't keep himself from mimicking a gun with his hand. They both laughed at it.

'Guys, what a hell of an afternoon,' was the first thing Kappakas said when he entered Ellis's room. Mike popped up on the sofa. Ellis came in from the kitchen and asked the Detective if he wanted to have a bite to eat with them.

'Love to.'

Mike rubbed his eyes, 'Did you have a successful day, Kappa?'

'Can't complain; and you? You tired?'

'Well, I don't like making so many phone calls, but I found our priest and the cemetery.'

'Great, I expected good work from my deputy sheriff.' Kappakas smiled and sat down at the table. Ellis poured him a drink and the three of them compared notes.

Chapter 64

Mrs. Warakomski pulled the door shut behind her and looked forward to speaking with the Director. She had a few things to discuss, and expected him to come up with solutions. While walking through SocHom, her thoughts returned to the nice couple she'd had a drink with. The meeting had been very pleasant and she hoped to see them again when they visited their parents. Her Jewish friends were well into their eighties and complained about nearly everything. Sometimes she got fed up with their wailings and even quit their bridge game, under the pretext of needing fresh air. She walked to the desk where Amber welcomed her.

'Hello, Mrs. Warakomski. Can I help you?'

'Yes Amber, I have an appointment with Mr. Peterson.'

'Yes, that's right; I'll tell him you're here.'

Amber spoke via intercom and waited for an answer. Peterson's voice was clearly audible. 'Mrs. Warakomski may come on in, Amber.'

Mark Peterson gave her a warm welcome. 'How nice to see you again. You look very well.'

Mrs. Warakomski almost blushed, but she was a little too old for that. She knew the standard pleasantries. Usually they didn't mean what they said at all. She'd almost rather Peterson honestly said she did not look so well, which is how she felt. She paid little attention to her hair and wasn't always dressed very well. And then there was her face; "old goat" fit better, and those funny colored spectacles on her nose. She looked at Peterson and thought: I don't need that "compliment," mister. I've only come here to get some help. She came to the point.

'Mr. Director, there are a number of things I want to discuss with you. I'm sure you can help me.'

'Just tell me what's on your mind?'

'First of all; I urgently need new pills. Can I get some now?'

'You know the procedure. You have to ask the Doctor. If he prescribes them, you can get them.'

'Yes, I know, but Dr. Wheeler is absent so often. I really need my pills.'

'Very well, I'll see him later today and then I'll bring some back with me. I'll deliver them to you at home this evening.'

Her face relaxed. Then she reminded him of a leak in the women's wing of the synagogue. She also had a complaint about the delivery of the evening paper. It was always put in the wrong mailbox. Would Mr. Peterson talk to the newspaper boy about it? And finally, there was something wrong with a burner on her old stove. Peterson promised to take care of everything quickly.

Later, in the evening, Mark Peterson walked to Ethel Warakomski's bungalow with a box of dementia inhibitors. He'd just met with SocHom's GP, Bob Wheeler. Wheeler had expressed his concern about the slow deliveries of the medicines lately. Peterson reassured him by pointing out that the manufacturer had had some problems, but these were solved now. He didn't want to tell Wheeler how SocHom got the drugs. The Doctor had patched up Peterson after he was beaten up by Larkin's thug. And Wheeler didn't ask questions about how or why it had happened.

It was already growing dark when Peterson rang Mrs. Warakomski's doorbell. She lived in one of the few low-rise buildings, consisting of attached bungalows with very small yards, called garden apartments these days. There was no answer. Peterson rang once more, a little longer this time, and still no answer. He peered in through a window, but there was nothing special to be seen. There was no light on in the living room. Sometimes single people died in their homes without anyone noticing. Peterson remembered two cases, where the front door had to be forced open to discover the occupant lay dead in his house. That flashed through his mind while he was standing in front of the closed door. He looked around and saw no one. It was dinner time.

Peterson walked around the bungalow and came to a gate in the narrow backyard. He went in and cautiously walked down the path to the backdoor. He saw one of the four windows in the door was broken. There was broken glass on the doorstep. The door was unlocked. He entered the small kitchen and looked around. 'Mrs. Warakomski, are you home?'

No response. Evening dusk darkened the interior. Peterson switched on the light in the kitchen so he could look around. 'Hello!' he called, stepping into the L-shaped living room. On the dining table he saw a dinner plate, some cutlery and a glass. A paper napkin lay in a ball next to the plate. Mrs. Warakomski had eaten a meal. Where is she? Peterson searched the room but found nothing of interest. To see better, he switched on another light. On the other side of the room was a second door, leading to the bedroom. It was ajar. He slowly pushed the door open, glanced quickly inside and stage-whispered, 'Mrs. Warakomski?'

He saw her lying on the bed, her head turned sideways. Her wide-open eyes stared aimlessly into the room. Her mouth was open. Peterson was shocked by the sight. He went to the bed and looked at the hole in her forehead. On her stomach was a silver menorah, a seven-branched Jewish candleholder. 'What's happened here, for God's sake?' he asked himself in despair.

Peterson observed Mrs. Warakomski must have been murdered only a short time ago. He decided to inform the GP at once and was about to call him. Just as Peterson took out his cell phone he noticed the light on the phone change. It was as if a shadow from behind him swept across the display. He quickly turned around. Before he could make another move or say anything, two bullets penetrated his brain. A third bullet entered his liver, knocking him to the floor. Blood gushed out of the back from his skull. He continued to shake for a few seconds and then a white glow appeared and faded before his eyes. Mark Peterson was dead.

Chapter 65

When Ellis switched on the news after getting up, she got a shock and cried out in dismay. She rushed to Mike's room, banged at his door, 'Mike, open up - quickly!'

Mike, who was still dozing in bed, popped up and called, 'I'm coming, just a moment!'

He put on his jeans and grabbed a shirt. What's all this about, he thought. He opened the door and Ellis stumbled into his room.

'What's wrong? What's happening?'

Ellis kept silent for a second, caught her breath, and said, 'Peterson's dead. Also that lady we met at SocHom.'

'You're kidding! Peterson and Warakomski, dead?'

'Yes, it was on the news. SocHom is sealed off and there are hordes of police around.'

Mike switched on the TV. Local news station NBC2 was speculating on the whys and wherefores of the murders of the director and a resident of the community.

'Unbelievable,' Mike said after they both followed the news for a while.

'Yes, that's what I thought when I first heard it. Obviously Peterson was too much of a threat to Larkin. But Mrs. Warakomski? Why was she killed?'

'The police will come up with ideas,' Mike suggested. 'I think Larkin is getting anxious and wants to get rid of disloyal assistants. But that still doesn't explain Mrs. Warakomski's death. In any case, things are moving now. I don't like this; we could be next on the victim list. If there's anyone who's threatening Larkin, it's me. And you, of course.'

'Oh, thank you very much. But you're right. Larkin is moving his pieces. He's going to deploy other people, who are loyal to him, and more importantly, who depend on him. But who are they? We need to find out as soon as possible.'

'El, we have to inform Kappa. Or would he already know?'

'Well, probably yes. I'll send him a text anyway and ask him to come over.'

'Okay, I'm going to take a shower, and as soon as Kappa's here, we'll work out an action plan. Mr. Larkin isn't done with us yet.' He gave her a confident look.

'Yeah, sure,' she sighed.

An hour later Kappakas, Ellis and Mike were having coffee and pastries. Kappakas took a bite from the sweet roll and said, 'Guys, we can't start digging until tomorrow. I wanted to do it today, but the authorities have to make arrangements first, like engaging grave diggers for the exhumation, deploying police personnel, and scheduling the presence of a forensic doctor. In short, it's a whole circus. We must try and keep the press and spectators away from the cemetery.'

Then he looked at Ellis and Mike. 'Unfortunately, that applies to you too.'

Ellis and Mike looked surprised at each other.

'Officially, civilians aren't allowed to be present at an exhumation. But more important is your safety. We don't want you to be involved in any kind of confrontation, although I don't expect Larkin will show himself. Nobody knows about the operation, not even the owner of Crest Lawn.'

'Not even St. Luke's Clinic?'

'No. We'll do this in secret. Santini and her staff will not be informed.'

'You just said "officially", Ellis said. 'I'm a journalist. So what if I watch the whole procedure from some distance? There's no harm in that, is there?'

'I'm sorry, Ellis, but I'm a guest here. If I allow you to be present, I could hurt my relationship with the local police, and this may impede the investigation. You can help me, however.'

Ellis looked up and waited.

'I would like you both to watch the clinic when we start digging. I want to prevent Santini or Broderick from showing up at Crest Lawn. If that happens, Larkin will know about everything right away.'

Ellis and Mike looked at each other.

'Very well,' Ellis said. 'Observing could be exciting too.'

Kappakas smiled, thinking this was best for all concerned.

Chapter 66

Jennifer Mattox was putting the dishes into the dish washer after dinner when her phone rang. 'Yes, who is it?'

'Are you Jennifer?'

'Yes, why? Who wants to know?'

'Are you Mike Garcia's girlfriend?'

'Er…, that's none of your business. Who are you?'

'Just listen to what I have to say. Don't ask any questions. Your friend Mike is meddling in things that are none of his business.'

'Oh, what kind of things?'

'If your friend doesn't stop, we can't guarantee your safety. You understand?'

'No, I don't. Who are you? What's this all about?'

'Just make sure your friend doesn't bother us anymore. Then we'll leave you alone. Got it?'

'You listen to me now…'

The man ended the call. Jennifer looked at her phone, bewildered, and had a hard time controlling her emotions. She phoned Mike.

'Hi Jen!'

'Mike! What business are you involved in? Someone just called who said you had to quit at once. Quit what? What are you doing?'

'Take it easy, Jen. Calm down. I can't say anything about it, it's complicated.'

Jennifer started to cry softly. 'Mike, what's going on? I have to know. The man threatened me. What's all this about?'

'I can explain, Jen, but I need time. I'm taking this threat very seriously. Let me think about it, and don't do anything foolish. I'll call you back in five minutes.'

'I don't know if I can still trust you, I really don't know….'

'Jen, keep your phone ready.' He raised his voice. 'I promise to call back.'

Jennifer sniffled and was barely able to speak.

'Sweetheart, did you hear what I said? Say something!' he begged.

'All right, I'll wait,' she stammered.

He broke off and looked at Ellis despairingly. 'Goddammit! Larkin has threatened Jennifer. I don't know how he got her phone number. This is going to be really serious.'

'Mike, Jennifer has to get away to a safe place immediately. Larkin is trying to clean up, damage control for him. You're his main stumbling block, but he's also taking revenge. He hasn't forgotten what you made Peterson do to him. Jennifer can no longer stay in her own house.'

'Yes, yes. I know. Maybe I should go and help her.'

'That's exactly what I mean. She needs you, Mike. You've already left her in the dark about what you're doing and why.'

'So it looks like I have to leave here and stand by her.'

Ellis gave him a penetrating stare. 'Listen, Mike, I'm not saying this to get rid of you. She's your girlfriend, dammit. Larkin has tracked her down. If you stay here and something happens to her, you'll regret it for the rest of your life. Kappa and I will manage here; we're going to solve the case and make sure it's going to be in the press.'

Mike wasn't fully convinced yet and resisted the idea of leaving the local arena. 'After all I've been through, now we're so close, with the exhumations and the investigation into Peterson's death… how can I let it all go?'

'I understand. But what's more important to you? Your work, the adventure, or your girlfriend? It may not be an easy choice, but under the circumstances I would choose my loved ones. If you care for her, you can't let her down. I hope you realize it.'

He looked at her. 'You're right, I care about Jen, so much that I promised her the world, which I can't live up to now. She wants me with her, to build a future together. Of course I take this threat seriously.'

Ellis pointed to the phone. 'The five minutes are over. Call her; she's waiting.'

Mike had a long conversation with his girlfriend, reassuring her with his promise to leave tonight to be with her.

Chapter 67

Mike landed at Chicago O'Hare the next day around noon. He took the shuttle bus to Alamo Car rental, rented a Chevy Impala and set out on the last leg of his journey to Joliet, where his girlfriend lived in a quiet suburb. More than an hour later a relieved Jennifer Mattox opened the front door of her small apartment.

'Mikey!' she shouted, full of enthusiasm and calling him by his pet name. She threw her arms around his neck and they kissed each other.

'Oh, how great to see you again! I've missed you so much. I'm so glad you came.'

'Of course, honey, absolutely. I came as fast as I could, and here I am.'

After embracing each other tightly for more than a few moments, they returned to reality. Jennifer's expression turned serious, and she spoke in a different tone. She looked concerned. 'I want to know everything, from beginning to end. Be honest, I only want to hear the truth.'

He smiled. 'So you want the truth?' he asked. 'Well, prepare yourself for an unbelievable story.'

She looked at him questioningly. 'What do you mean?'

'You're not going to believe what I've experienced in the last six months. But everything I say is the truth. Word of honor! You can call Ellis later on to verify it.'

'Just get started, I can't wait any longer.'

It took him almost an hour to give a detailed account of all the facts, events and experiences. Especially the "why-question" got a lot of attention. Sometimes the James Bond-like scenes made Jennifer's head spin. She frequently shook her head, and she winced at descriptions of the car accident and Mike's beating by underworld thugs. However, she reacted approvingly when confronted with his liberation of Ellis. She was pleasantly surprised by the outcome of the burglary at the clinic and the help of an experienced police detective. At the end of his account Mike brought up his relation with Ellis. He found it hard to assess how his girlfriend would react.

'You're expecting me to talk about Ellis. It's somewhat odd, of course, that recently I've been in the company of another woman almost every day.'

He looked her straight in her beautiful eyes. 'Before we have any misunderstandings about it, my relationship with her is purely professional. I already told you her boyfriend Jake moved temporarily to the west coast for his work. Ellis, however, wanted to continue the investigation. She's a research journalist and thinks it'll be a big story. I've Googled her of course. She works freelance for a publishing company in Orlando. We always stay in separate rooms, and we just have a friendly work relationship. She's a strong woman, very devoted to her work and with a good sense of humor.'

Jen's face showed some suspicion now. He knew what this meant. 'Jen, I'm only trying to describe Ellis. Let me put it like this; I have no special feelings for her. To me, she's like a colleague at work.'

She frowned and pursed her lips. At the same time she nodded.

'And don't forget, she wants to help us. She insisted I leave and get back to you.'

'Of course, dear, I appreciate it very much.' She bent forward and kissed him. 'You know what? I believe you. I believe everything you told me. You just can't make something like this all up, Mikey.'

He relaxed and laughed. 'No. You know, I'm not good at inventing stories or playing tricks on someone. I just don't have the talent.'

'Exactly! I know you well enough. But you must admit; it sounds like a wild story. I don't think our friends would believe it easily.'

'No, they wouldn't, but you do. That's because you're no ordinary friend, you hold a special place in my heart.'

She blushed. 'Come on, stop it.'

'No, no, I mean it. I've often let you down, promised you the world, and been untruthful about job applications and work. I'm sorry, but I didn't know what to do. Nothing worked and I felt stuck. That's why I took the courier job, to save some money and be with you. I made mistakes, but I did it for you, for us.'

Jennifer gazed tenderly at him.

'Jen, I love you. If you want, I'll stay with you, for good.'

She was shocked. 'You mean now?'

'Yes, from now on. I'm fed up with the life I've been living. I don't want it anymore. And you don't want it either, do you?'

She shook her head. 'Of course not, but... it's all so sudden. I'm not prepared for it. It's not as if we know each other so well.'

'That'll be much easier when we're together. No more skyping and long phone calls. That's what you always wanted, right?'

'Of course, I'd like nothing better. But are you going to drop everything just like that? Finally you're doing something useful, working with a respected journalist and a police detective. You're about to expose a bunch of criminals. That means, I think you're important to the investigation.'

Mike couldn't believe his ears. 'This is a side of you I didn't know. So what you're saying is, go back?'

'Not right away, silly. I'm so happy you're with me for once. Still I think you shouldn't let Ellis do all the work herself. Although she's working with that policeman, the relationship between you and her was different. You're close to each other all the time.' She added, 'In separate rooms, right?' She laughed slyly.

Mike took her little joke as a sign of trust and concluded Jennifer had accepted his working relationship with Ellis. 'So you don't want me to stay here from now on?'

'Only for a couple of days; I imagine Ellis could use your help. Without your intervention she probably would have done badly.'

He sighed. He softly caressed her hands. While looking for the right words, a smile appeared on his face. 'You know what, Jen? I couldn't agree more.'

Jennifer began to feel warm emotions rising within her. 'Good to hear that.'

She kissed him and said it was time to eat. She phoned a well-known restaurant and booked a table for two. Mike relaxed on the couch and felt the arrangement was okay. He would stay with her for two days, enough time to talk some more, getting to know Jennifer Mattox better and making plans to protect her from threatened harm.

Chapter 68

Kappakas was known for his high rate of solved crimes. Other detectives in his district envied his record. Kappakas had his own way of working, which wasn't always according to the book. He was determined to solve the Iskander case. In police terms this usually meant the case was closed when the perpetrator was traced and arrested. The victim's position or role was of minor importance. And if the victim could be liberated or saved from certain death, this was called a "welcome by-catch".

The text message he read on his phone, however, might indicate his solved crime rate would take a hit. He didn't easily doubt his capacities, judgment and strategic powers, but now he began to see he had made a severe error of judgment, an error which might not only harm his investigation but also the people he worked with. How could he have been so thoughtless? Or had he been too impressed by Dr. Santini? Anyway; he should never have allowed her to send in the missing-person's report by mail.

He was sitting opposite Naples Chief of Police Dick Matarazo to answer questions about his visit to the clinic. It would have surprised no one if he'd kept secret his meeting with Santini.

In twelve years' time Matarazo had worked his way up to the senior officer in the Naples police force. Superior to him, were only the Mayor and the City Council. He loved his job and didn't hesitate to participate directly in police operations. He kept in touch with the street and served as a model for other officers. He had just turned fifty-four and was in good health. Because of his handsome appearance and good taste in clothing, women were attracted to him. But there was one woman who always got his special attention. For a quarter of a century now he'd been married to Barbara. She was his anchor in the turbulent police world. They had three children.

Matarazo picked up the report and coughed softly. 'Let me see. We know you're working on the investigation into Elaine Iskander's disappearance.'

Kappakas nodded.

'Your name is mentioned, so I consider it wise to ask you to give me more information about this case. After all, you've been here for a couple of days now. What's more, I'd appreciate it if you'd fill me in regularly.'

'Of course; my focus is on clarifying, or solving the Iskander case. Everything related to it is relevant and can be shared with you.'

'What can you tell me about this report that I don't already know?'

'I questioned her. I had tried before, but she wasn't in. She later contacted us by phone. I was received very pleasantly and I understood she wanted to report a missing object. I mean, Elaine Iskander had been gone for a week then. I didn't expect her to report Iskander missing.'

'Why did you allow Santini to send in the report by mail? We usually take reports like this with us right away.'

'I should have taken it with me. It wasn't very clever to give her the impression I might not take her report more seriously. That's far from the truth, as you know. I was assigned to this case at the request of my friend, Elaine Iskander's father, John Iskander, and I will do anything in my power to solve the case.'

'Yes, so will we, of course. Er..., what further actions do you have in mind?'

'As you know, tomorrow the exhumation takes place and this should shed light on the death of the Erikssons. I appreciate you're going to block off the area, and it's good that the whole operation takes place in the evening. We don't want any onlookers from the clinic or elsewhere.'

'We'll provide plain-clothes men to avoid attention and ensure the work can be done without disturbance.' Matarazo paused for a moment, then said, 'One more thing Kappakas; you've probably heard the news about the murders of the SocHom director and a resident?'

'Yes, it was on the news this morning.'

'If you think I know something about these murders, Chief, I have to disappoint you.'

'You know, this is a small community. There're lots of elderly people here, and it's about the most boring place in Florida. There are people on the beaches and in their boats, but otherwise nothing much happens here. I mean, many people spend most of their time talking with each other about any little thing that's going on. Have you picked up anything?'

'Unfortunately, no. I'd like to know more myself.'

'Yes, me too. Well we're done for now, Kappakas, unless there's something else you want to say.'

'I'll contact you after the exhumation, okay?'

'That's fine. We'll keep in touch.'

Chapter 69

Kappakas said goodbye to Chief of Police Matarazo and was about to walk back to his car, when he saw a dark sedan parked opposite the police station with two men inside. His instincts told him he would be followed as soon as he drove away. Matarazo apparently didn't have much trust in an outsider on his turf. Kappakas had once followed a subordinate to find out who were his informers in a heroine case. Still, it was unusual and it was only done if it served the case, not out of distrust or to keep an eye on a colleague.

Kappakas realized he hadn't told Matarazo everything. He could only guess what information the Naples Police Chief had which he hadn't shared with his colleague from Jacksonville. In order not to hinder his own investigation there was only one course of action: to mislead and confront. Kappakas returned to his car without paying obvious attention to the surroundings. When driving to the end of the street, he saw the brown sedan accelerate.

Kappakas decided not to go to Ellis's hotel – although at first he had intended to. He drove calmly through fairly light traffic and noticed his pursuers stayed some distance behind. Exactly according to the book, he thought, and chuckled to himself. Fifteen minutes later, Kappakas reached his destination and parked his car in front his hotel's main entrance. He saw the car with the two men drive into the service station next to the hotel. When the car stopped at a pump, Kappakas was pleased to see that one of the brake lights wasn't working. He had a reason to talk to the men.

The driver pretended to fill up the car, while his partner kept an eye on Kappakas in the side mirror. Kappakas crossed the parking lot and calmly walked up to the car. The driver quickly hung up the nozzle to get back in the car and drive away. But Kappakas was quick enough and stood in front of the car blocking the way.

'Good morning, gentlemen - police.' He showed them his badge. 'Your left brake light is not functioning. You get a ticket for that. May I see your driver's license and registration, please?'

The men looked at each other. Then the wheels in their brains began to spin. How to get out of this? What's the sensible thing to do? They decided to play it safe.

'Sir, we're local police officers. We were ordered to follow you.'

Kappakas looked at them amused. 'Now is that so? How honest of you to tell me. Some cops would lie about it.'

The men gave him an apologetic look, glad to have told him the truth.

'Well, I have to let you go then. You know where I'm staying, so tell the Chief. And give him my regards.'

The policemen stammered "okay" and "thank you". They would be too ashamed to tell anyone all about the incident. Kappakas stepped aside and slapped the roof of the car, indicating the men could drive off. He watched the car disappear around the corner, enjoying his little victory.

Chapter 70

Javier Rios cursed. He had blown a tire and driven his fifteen year-old Buick into a ditch. He cursed Eberto Vargas who had saddled him with that old crate.

He had made good progress and was near Pensacola, between the Alabama-border and Tallahassee. There was little traffic on the divided highway, Interstate 10. A service station wasn't in sight. Rios decided to drive on slowly to the nearest area where he could change tires.

He arrived at a weigh station for trucks and parked to the side and a little behind the weigh station office. He took the spare tire from the trunk and jacked up the car. Changing the tire was easy. He realized he would be driving with a temporary donut spare, so he couldn't exceed forty miles an hour. Before closing the trunk, he looked under a blanket at the boxes of medicines. Of course they were still there, but seeing them reassured him.

Before turning into the road again, he looked in his side mirrors and saw a blue flashing light in the distance. He had to decide quickly. Forty miles an hour was the minimum allowed speed on I-10, and anything much under 65 would attract attention. Police would likely stop him to ask if something's the matter with him or the car. If they got suspicious, the gringo police would search the car. That was a big risk for a Mexican driving from Texas and maybe Mexico. He accelerated to 55. A moment later the police car overtook him. Rios didn't look to the side to avoid attracting attention. The police car quickly disappeared ahead of him, and Rios gave a sigh of relief. He slowed down, adjusting his speed to go easy on the temporary spare.

Chapter 71

It was 7:30 in the evening. Dusk was falling in Naples and the birds stopped singing. Silence fell over the city, which now lost its sunny outdoors attraction for visitors and residents. Only on the beaches was there still some early evening activity. In Naples North, everyone seemed to be on vacation, there was hardly anyone around, except in one place.

The police had sealed off Vanderbilt Drive and 11th Avenue, as well as adjacent streets, to all traffic. In between, lay Crest Lawn cemetery, near a golf course on the north side. No one was allowed to enter the area without authorization. Chief of Police Dick Matarazo had fulfilled Kappakas' request. Apparently he hadn't been offended by Kappakas stopping two of his plain-clothes officers earlier that day. In a way, Matarazo could even appreciate the Jacksonville detective's actions. He obviously had a good sense of humor, and sent the same two to pull "graveyard" duty to guard the exhumation.

Kappakas thought it was too bad Matarazo wouldn't be there this evening. They might have had a good laugh over the aborted police surveillance. He'd asked Ellis to come to his hotel and drive to the cemetery from there. She was excited to hear that Kappakas changed his mind, allowing her to join him. 'On second thought, I'll need you there.'

At 7:45, they reported to the policeman on duty at the entrance to the cemetery, showing their ID's and the court order with their names on it. After exchanging greetings, they moved on and came to an area that lay about five feet above street level. There were some trees surrounded by bushes. On either side of the pathways were badly-kept beds with low plants and ground cover. The burial place itself was situated at the highest point, surrounded by low ivy-clad trellis-work. There were only a few nice memorial stones, and simple markers identified most of the graves. Small crosses stood at the heads of most graves. The names, dates of birth and death of the deceased were engraved on each cross. In the middle of the cemetery there were wooden benches, so visitors and relatives could calmly rest and remember their loved ones.

Kappakas recognized Judge Vincent Murphy who was talking with forensic Doctor Alan Goldhaber. They were standing just outside the lamp-lit work area. The gravediggers had already removed most of the earth and were digging away the last of it from the coffins.

'Good evening, Your Honor,' Kappakas greeted Judge Murphy.

'Ah, hello, Detective. You're just in time. The men are about to lift the coffins. And who is this young lady?'

'May I introduce my assistant to you, Mrs. Henning. She's helping me with the investigation of Elaine Iskander's disappearance.'

'Are you in the police?' Murphy asked Henning.

'No, sir, I'm a research journalist. The Detective asked me to help him on this case.'

Murphy turned around and watched the men digging earth out of the hole. 'These guys don't have any problems with this. They see dead bodies and coffins every day. I prefer sitting behind a desk, don't you Detective?'

Kappakas kept silent and saw a small Bobcat earthmover drive into the cemetery. The gravediggers hit the first coffin with their spades and started to dig carefully around it.

'They're on top of each other, guys,' Dr. Goldhaber said.

The diggers didn't reply and continued their work. When the coffins were free, they put two canvas nooses with nylon eyeholes around the ends of the top casket. The Bobcat slowly drove up to the opened grave. A metal frame the size of a coffin was attached to the machine. The diggers hooked the nooses into the hooks of the frame. The driver was signaled to start moving the fork slowly upwards. A light creaking sound was heard when the upper coffin detached itself from the one underneath.

'Nothing wrong,' the judge assured Kappakas and Ellis. 'That sound is caused by the tension on the woodwork.'

Ellis hoped the coffin wouldn't burst apart and the body of one the Erikssons dropped into the half empty grave. The coffin was lifted inch by inch. The Bobcat made more noise now. Everyone around the grave looked on tensely. When the casket was hanging above ground level, the Bobcat's shovel swayed to the left and put it on a wooden pallet. The diggers unhooked the nooses and then pulled them away from under the coffin.

Cautiously the hoisting machine swung back to the grave, where it could lift up the second coffin. Five minutes later two coffins were lying next to each other on the pallet. Judge Murphy signaled the machine's engine could be turned off. An almost sinister silence filled Crest Lawn cemetery. The diggers sat down on a bench, had a cup of coffee and a sandwich, and watched the authorities at work.

Dr. Goldhaber asked the undertaker, who had buried the Erikssons, to open the coffins. Ellis watched the scene with mixed feelings. Opening coffins was not exactly her favorite pastime. She wasn't sure how she would react when the lids were removed.

Chapter 72

They both looked serene, Brian and Marcia Eriksson. White linen shrouds were wrapped around their bodies. The next step was their identification. It usually could only take place in the presence of relatives or employees of St. Luke's. Judge Murphy had made an exception, so the autopsy could be performed without the formal identification of the deceased. Dr. Goldhaber untied the cord of the shroud at the top and folded it back over the faces. The undertaker was asked to confirm he had recently buried these persons at Crest Lawn. After this, Goldhaber informed Kappakas that the identity of the bodies of the Erikssons had been established informally.

'Thank you, Doctor,' Kappakas said. 'The bodies must be examined now for any suspicious substances in the stomach, according to the court order. We will also check for any abnormalities on and in the bodies.'

Goldhaber nodded. 'Yes, I know. We'll only be able to examine the bodies after two days. The judge already mentioned that. We need a pathologist and toxicologist. We've made arrangements with these gentlemen and expect to begin the first post-mortem the day after tomorrow in the evening.'

Kappakas also wanted to know where the bodies would be kept in the meantime.

'In the mortuary. You can accompany him when they're moved, so you're assured the remains are stored in-tact. My job is done now.'

Goldhaber said goodbye to Kappakas and Ellis and then walked to the police barrier, where Judge Murphy was talking to the officer in charge. Kappakas took Ellis to a quiet section of Crest Lawn. When they were out of hearing range, he said, 'Ellis, I smell trouble.'

'What do you mean?'

'Did you notice the undertaker's reaction when he saw the Erikssons' faces?'

'Actually, no. He stood with his back to me. As we agreed, you were standing opposite me and could see his face.'

'Right, that was the plan, to watch everything closely.'

'But what did you see?'

'The undertaker looked surprised when he removed the shroud.'

'Surprised? How?'

'He seemed to be shocked by something. I've seen reactions like this before. He froze for a moment, and his pupils dilated. I was close enough to him to see it all clearly. It was like he saw different faces, faces he'd never seen before.'

'You must be kidding!'

'No, I trust my intuition. I have no reason to doubt it now, based on my observations.'

'Wow, Kappa, you're very sure of yourself, aren't you?'

'I don't like it. I want to know why he reacted the way he did. He identified the bodies informally, but that doesn't have to mean anything, officially. That's my experience.' He looked determined.

'I see what you mean,' Ellis said, 'you're saying we can't be sure we've exhumed the Erikssons.'

'Exactly! We need to be one-hundred percent sure. I think we've been misled. Someone obviously didn't want us to see the Erikssons, in order to throw off our investigation.'

'If it's true, do you have any inkling of who did this?'

He waited a moment before answering and then said decisively, 'Yes, Ellis, I'm sure I know who's behind this.'

'But I have a hunch you're not going to tell me.'

'Listen, I'm a policeman; first the proof, then the names. Come on, we should get out of here; they're about to lock up. I'm going to think about how to proceed. By the way, thanks very much for your ideas.'

Kappakas dropped Ellis off at her hotel.

'It's been an eventful evening. See you early in the morning. I'll come pick you up.'

'Fine. Good night, Kappa.'

He disappeared into the Naples' darkness and reflected on what he'd just discovered and how the pieces of the puzzle fit together.

Chapter 73

In the middle of the night Ellis found the answer. After pondering for a long time about who might be able to identify the Erikssons, a name suddenly crossed her mind. Amber. She didn't know her last name. Mike had talked to her during their visit to Peterson's office. Amber must have known the couple and should be able to identify them. If she was prepared to cooperate, they didn't have to call on residents of SocHom to find someone who would be willing to do the identification. Many of them would refuse because they were afraid to look at corpses. Ellis also expected a lot of gossip and turmoil if inquiries were made around the residential community. There was already plenty of that with the two recent murders at SocHom. It just wasn't in the best interest of the investigation.

Amber. She could speed up the case. On impulse Ellis called Kappakas. He'd told her she could contact him any time, if it was relevant. She let his phone ring eight times, but he didn't answer. Disappointed, she stopped the call and sent a text message. When he woke up he would know right away, she thought.

They left for SocHom around 9 a.m. Kappakas' expression was grave. He feared losing control over the case. While he calmly drove, Ellis tried to get a conversation going.

'Anyway, I'm glad you didn't hear your phone ring last night. But I was so excited that I'd thought of someone else to ask.'

'Never mind; thanks anyway. Without your idea, it could be difficult to confirm or refute the undertaker's identification. But we'll wait and see if Amber wants to cooperate. I hope so. It's important that we see the bodies again and get some answers to our questions.'

Kappakas drove his car into the SocHom premises. A gloomy atmosphere seemed to hang over the complex. He parked near the entrance of the late Mark Peterson's office. They went in and saw Amber sitting at her desk. The secretary looked up, surprised to see Ellis again.

'Hi,' she said, at a loss for any other words.

'Hello, Amber, here I am again. You remember me, don't you? This is Detective Kappakas. Oh, and please accept my condolences on the death of Mr. Peterson.'

Amber hesitated before responding; then said, 'Thanks, I'm already getting over it. A new Director has been appointed. He starts by month-end.'

'Okay, good,' Ellis said. 'Amber, the police would like your cooperation.'

'Cooperate with the police?' she asked tentatively.

Kappakas took over the conversation. 'Yes, Amber. May I call you that?'

She nodded.

'Did you know Mr. and Mrs. Eriksson?'

'Brian and Marcia? Well, yes, I knew them. Why?'

'We're investigating their deaths at St. Luke's Clinic.' Kappakas waited to see Amber's reaction.

'I think it's horrible. They still looked so healthy.'

'Amber, there is a problem. We need someone to personally identify them, other than the staff at St. Luke's and the undertaker.'

'Oh, I wouldn't mind doing that,' she suggested spontaneously.

Kappakas glanced at Ellis.

'We'll be very grateful to you, Amber. However, there could be a little problem.'

'Oh, what kind of problem?'

'It must be done now.'

'You mean right now? But I can't just leave the office.'

'Please come along with us to identify the Erikssons. We'll ask the janitor to keep an eye on things here. You'll be back in less than an hour.'

Kappakas waited for her to reply. Then she said, 'Alright, if there's no other way.'

Kappakas and Ellis were visibly relieved. It had been easier than they'd expected.

Chapter 74

After arriving at the mortuary, Amber said there had been quite a few deaths lately. She gave her thoughts free rein. 'I've never experienced this before. The murders of the Director and Mrs. Warakomski worry me a lot. How can something like that happen here at SocHom, where it's always so safe and quiet? That's why I want to help you.'

Kappakas said he was very grateful to her, encouraging her to make a careful identification of the deceased.

They rang the bell. Undertaker Jim Sykes opened the door. He was the one who had given the informal identification at the exhumation.

'Good morning, I'm Detective Kappakas. We met at the cemetery. I have a warrant from Police Chief Matarazo to view the bodies of Mr. and Mrs. Eriksson once more.'

Jim Sykes was a tall, thin man with not much hair on his head. He was slightly hunchbacked. With the hollow cheeks and pouches under his eyes he looked like a character in a vampire movie. He behaved a little nervously. He took the warrant and started to read. His fingers trembled. 'Seems okay,' he muttered. 'Is she with you?'

Sykes pointed at Amber, who quickly nodded yes.

'Yes, Mr. Sykes,' Kappakas answered. 'This is Amber, secretary of the late Mr. Peterson. She has been approved by the Police Chief to make a formal identification.'

Sykes muttered something inaudible and then told them to follow him. He led them into a very chilly chamber, where bodies were temporarily stored before burial or cremation. It reminded Ellis of her favorite TV-show "Grey's Anatomy." She saw two stainless steel tables, all kinds of instruments, some wash basins covered refuse bins, just like the TV show. The bodies were stored in long refrigerated drawers in the wall. The temperature inside was a constant 37.4 degrees Fahrenheit. The environment felt sterile and impersonal. Sykes showed his visitors where they should stand. Amber felt a shiver run down her spine.

'I've never done this before,' she said with a grimace. Ellis put a hand on her shoulder. 'But I'll recognize them right away,' the secretary added emphatically. Her remark reassured Kappakas and Ellis.

Sykes went over to one refrigerated drawer which was at eye level. He pushed the handle down and turned the metal locking device.

Everyone looked into the drawer and saw a body lying under a white sheet. A name tag was attached to one foot. Sykes grew visibly more nervous. But that might be his normal behavior. Maybe he didn't like people looking over his shoulder. He grabbed a bar at the end and pulled out the metal sled. 'Come and have a look,' the undertaker said softly.

The three others positioned themselves around the body. Kappakas looked at the tag. 'Amber, please confirm or deny this is Mr. Brian Eriksson.'

Amber made a step forward and looked at Kappakas and Ellis, then down at the body. Slowly Sykes pulled the sheet away from the head.

Chapter 75

Dr. Margaret Santini listened to what Larkin had to say. He was not used to calling her, but necessity knows no law, custom or precedent. If everyone followed his plan, the police would be kept in the dark, he thought. 'Peterson cheated me and was getting weak. He'll be replaced soon. Too bad, Santini, but I demand absolute loyalty and commitment. The death of the resident was an unfortunate coincidence. She happened to run into Garcia, and we didn't know what she was doing at Peterson's house later on. She may have talked and endangered our operations. I chose to be on the safe side. Sometimes things just go that way; we can't get nervous about it.'

Santini suppressed a critical question and instead asked when the new courier would deliver the next package.

'He's in Pensacola and can be here tomorrow. Then I'll tell him to deliver the goods to the clinic. We'll follow him, so nothing goes wrong.'

'Yes, that's okay. Then we can start two of our patients on a new program, Sunday afternoon at the earliest. It's about time too.'

Larkin didn't want to know who the lucky ones were. He didn't know them anyway. 'Is there anything else you want to say?' he asked curtly.

'Yesterday evening the whole area around Crest Lawn was blocked off. The traffic had to make a detour and no one could get through.'

'Any idea what that was all about?'

'There was a report in the papers about a gas leak in one of the main pipes, running underneath the cemetery. That was probably it, nothing to worry about.'

'Good.' Larkin broke off, leaving a bewildered Santini behind.

'Oaf,' she cursed out loud.

Chapter 76

Amber looked at the white hollow-cheeked face of an old man. The tension in the cooling room was palpable. She lifted her head and gave Kappakas a blank look. 'This is not Mr. Eriksson,' she said carefully.

Kappakas contained his surprise and asked, 'Are you absolutely sure, Amber?'

'Yes, one hundred percent. Mr. Eriksson was bald. This man has hair on his head. He looks different too.'

Kappakas saw Sykes had moved out of the circle. Kappakas wanted him back in their group, standing around the body of the now unidentified man. 'Mr. Sykes, do you have an explanation for this?'

The undertaker turned around quickly, to leave the room. Ellis saw what was happening. Like a cat she jumped towards the man and just managed to kick a leg from under him. Together they fell to the floor, Sykes hitting his head against the door handle.

Kappakas dove forward and grabbed Sykes. He said to him, 'Don't do anything foolish now or I'll arrest you. Come on, get up.' Jim Sykes lacked the power to resist.

'Ellis, are you alright?' Kappakas asked, still holding the undertaker.

'Yes, I'm fine,' she replied rubbing her knee and breathing hard.

'I want to see the body of Martha Eriksson as well,' Kappakas demanded. Sykes pulled out another metal drawer and removed the linen sheet. 'Amber, can you identify Mrs. Eriksson?' Kappakas asked. The secretary shook her head. 'No, it's not her either.'

Kappakas made a decision. 'Amber, would you mind waiting in the office next to this room? We want to ask Mr. Sykes a few questions.'

Amber looked shocked. She had no idea what was going on, but the undertaker's behavior was suspicious. She left the cooling room without asking anything.

Kappakas told Sykes to sit down on a chair. 'Now, please explain.' He stood in front of the man, while Ellis stood to the side. Sykes' face was anxious, his lips trembled, and there was fear in his eyes. He shook his head back and forth, and looked down at the floor.

'If you find it's hard to explain, maybe I can help you.' Kappakas' voice sounded firm and direct. 'Last night you confirmed at Crest Lawn that the exhumed persons, you had interred earlier, were Mr. and

Mrs. Eriksson. You saw their faces and nodded to confirm you recognized them. Are my observations correct so far?'

There was silence in the cooling chamber. Sykes still stared at the floor.

'Sykes?' Kappakas' voice threatened.

The man nodded.

'Is that a yes? Do you agree with me?'

As if Kappakas had just fired a gunshot, Sykes suddenly changed his attitude, rapidly spilling out an almost incoherent account. 'Yes, I did. But it wasn't them; I knew that. Why did they have to be buried? I suggested cremation. I felt this was going wrong. I don't know what's behind it, why they did this. I don't know what's going on here. What are they doing?'

Kappakas interrupted. 'Just take it easy now, calm down. Would you like some water?' Kappakas gave Ellis a sign. She filled a glass and handed it to the undertaker. He took a few sips and gave a sigh of relief.

'Yes, Mr. Sykes, feeling better now? I won't arrest you. I'm here to investigate the disappearance of Elaine Iskander. If you have something to tell to me about it, do it now.'

Sykes shook his head. 'I don't know anything about it; that's the absolute truth.' For the first time he looked the detective straight in the eye.

'Ms. Iskander worked at St. Luke's as a physical therapist,' Kappakas tried.

'No, Detective, the name doesn't mean anything to me.'

Kappakas looked inquiringly at the man and gave him the benefit of the doubt – for the time being. 'Back to last night; why did you lie about their identities?'

Sykes hesitated.

'Sykes?' Kappakas insisted.

'Yes, okay.' He paused. Then he continued, 'I was forced to do it.'

'By whom?'

'I can't tell you; they'll kill me.'

'Who's going to kill you?'

'No one, I hope.'

Ellis signaled Kappakas she also wanted to ask a question. He nodded. 'Are you under pressure? I mean, are you being paid for this?'

Sykes addressed her. 'They pay me to do things that aren't by the book.'

'So that's why you're uncomfortable with it, and you'd rather the bodies had been cremated? Is that it?' Kappakas asked.

'Yes, but I don't mean all the deceased that are brought here. Only particular ones.'

'Particular deceased people? Do you mean the ones from the clinic?'

'Yes, that's right.'

Kappakas shot Ellis an "ah-ha" look. He wanted to make an arrangement with Sykes. 'Listen. We're not interested in your dubious practices, or your business and professional licenses, right now. We want to see the real Mr. and Mrs. Eriksson. This is in the interest of our investigation of the disappearance of Ms. Iskander. If you cooperate with us and show us the graves of the Erikssons, then things will go easier for you.'

Chapter 77

Jim Sykes had been married for twenty-eight years and had four children. Like many middle-class families he had insufficient means to provide higher education for all his children. But with extra money received for swapping graves, a brighter future had presented itself to him. He'd realized that one day that money would no longer come in. But the day had come sooner than he'd expected. 'You can count on my cooperation.'

'That's very wise, Mr. Sykes,' Kappakas said.

'But on two conditions.'

Kappakas sighed audibly. 'And what are they?'

'That besides refraining from prosecution, you protect my family and give me a chance to start a funeral home somewhere else. My family and I will need witness protection.'

'Mr. Sykes, is it that bad?'

'I'm afraid so.'

Ellis asked him what kind of protection he had in mind.

'If I help you, I want to get a house well away from Naples, where I'm not known. You also must support me financially to start a new company.'

Kappakas shook his head. 'Come on, Mr. Sykes. A removal is okay, I can understand that, but if you want to continue in the same line of work, you'll be six feet under in no time.'

Sykes looked furiously at Kappakas. 'This happens to be a family business, Detective. It was established seventy-three years ago. You expect me to end the tradition?'

'Listen. They'll be able to trace you very quickly through the National Funeral Directors Association, the Chamber of Commerce, yellow pages, you name it. If they only try to discredit you, they'll demand records of deceased persons from the state. And, if your life is threatened, then what? I think it's time for a change, Mr. Sykes, something which doesn't involve so much death.'

Kappakas' words made an impression on the undertaker. Especially Ellis's nodding in assent the whole time made him uncertain. 'Come on, we don't have to come to a watertight agreement right now. First were going to perform a new autopsy, but this time without involving the judge or police chief. We're going to do it ourselves.'

There was a knock on the door. Amber appeared in the doorway and asked if she had to wait any longer. Kappakas decided to end the meeting and take Amber back to SocHom.

'I'll drop in on Sykes this afternoon,' he told Ellis who was checking her messages.

'Okay, but returning to your plan of action, Kappa. You want Sykes to open the graves of the Erikssons, but without permission of the authorities, correct?'

'Well, that's supported by the original exhumation order, but we won't ask the officials to attend, this time. Look; sometimes my methods are unorthodox, which not everyone appreciates. But I have solid arguments to keep things in my own hands.'

She gave Kappakas a conspiratorial look. 'And what would these arguments be?'

'Ellis! I can't give away all my secrets – not yet.'

They both laughed.

When Kappakas was serious again, he said, 'Our first priority is Elaine Iskander. To find out about the clinic's procedures, we need the Erikssons. We must know how they died. Then we'll draw our conclusions and hope to find out more about the disappearance of my friend's daughter.'

'Simple enough, right?' she teased.

'Well, Ellis, it will be quite a job to dig up the bodies. I could use your help.'

'Wow, Kappa, it's going to be thrilling, isn't it?'

He said nothing, mulling it over, as they drove Amber back to SocHom.

Chapter 78

Kappakas didn't waste time. He told Ellis he wanted to go back to visit Sykes. As soon as they pulled up in front, Ellis got out and quickly peered through the mortuary's windows.

'There's no sign of life.'

'Not surprising, considering the fact that you're standing on the undertaker's doorstep,' he said, grinning.

'Come on, let's ring the doorbell.'

Stumbling sounds came from inside. A young man in his thirties unlocked the door. 'Can I help you?'

Kappakas showed his badge and said he had an appointment with Mr. Sykes.

'Well, he isn't in. He left a letter for you. I'll go get it.'

Ellis and Kappakas looked surprised. The man handed Kappakas an envelope and said, 'That's all I can do for you. Now, if you'll excuse me.'

'I'd like to see your ID,' Kappakas said.

The young man took out his wallet, looking for his ID card. 'Here you are.'

'Joseph Keenan. Do you work here?'

'Yes, I'm an undertaker's assistant.'

'Did Mr. Sykes tell you anything about his departure?'

'No, but I'm sure it's all in the letter. I really have to go now, good bye.'

Joe Keenan shut the door, leaving slightly bewildered Henning and Kappakas behind.

'That guy was sure in a hurry,' Ellis said.

'Come on, let's read the letter in my car.'

Kappakas tore the envelope open and took out a note.

Dear Detective,

I have to disappoint you. I can't assist in illegally opening the other graves. Although I find your investigation important, I value my work, my family and the law above all else. Helping you more would be dangerous. I'm going away for a while to think over what you told me. Maybe I'll give up this line of work and start something else. But I don't want help from you or the state. I have to think of my family first. My working situation has been uncertain for too long. So, from now on, I no longer will do any work for so-called third parties. You'll understand what I mean. Don't try to find me. You won't succeed. Joe doesn't know where I am either.

Jim Sykes

Kappakas handed the letter to Ellis. He was thinking. 'We're facing a tricky situation here. Sykes changed his mind and ran away because he's afraid Larkin will think he's a rat. That guy eliminates anyone who's not loyal to him. How can he possibly know what we're doing? We just got started and our bird has already flown.'

'We should have taken him with us when we left. He thought over what we told him and, from his point of view, made the best of a risky situation.'

Kappakas looked a little aggrieved. 'You mean I made the wrong decision?' He saw his tone unnerved her a little. 'Oh, I'm sorry; I didn't mean it like that. We're in this together. But you're right, it looks like we should have taken Amber to SocHom with Sykes in our car.'

'I think he got scared, Kappa. He no longer had any idea what would happen to him.'

'Yes, Larkin's power could have a long reach. We're running out of options to do another exhumation without involving the authorities.'

Ellis laughed at this.

'You think this is funny, Ms. Henning?' he asked peevishly

She shook her head and said enthusiastically, 'Kappa, we do have one more option. Before Mike went to visit Jennifer, he'd traced the priest who had witnessed the Eriksson's interment, Raymond D'Angelico at St. Agnes Church.'

Kappakas' attitude changed immediately. His surliness was replaced by positive energy. 'Ellis, this is great. I can't remember you telling me this.'

'That's because I didn't,' she said matter-of-factly. 'Should we get going then?'

'To do what?'

'Pay the good father a visit.'

'Of course. I'm still thinking about letting Sykes get away. But, what's done is done. Let's go to see this priest. Where do we find him?'

'Mike gave me an address on Vanderbilt Beach Road. It shouldn't be too far from here..'

After a half hour's drive, they entered the grounds of St. Agnes Church. The impressive white building was the hub of an active parish that offered many activities, especially for the poor and homeless. Kappakas and Ellis walked to the entrance and heard singing coming from inside. A choir was rehearsing. At the altar, acolytes were setting out religious objects for the service. From a side door of the nave, a priest appeared with a Bible in his hand. Kappakas and Ellis walked across the aisle through the church and saw the clergyman say something to the youngsters. When he moved on to continue his work, he discovered two people standing near the altar.

'May I help you?' D'Angelico asked.

'Good morning, Father. I'm Detective Archibald Kappakas and this is my assistant Ellis Henning.'

'Hello, Detective, young lady. You want to speak with me?'

'Yes, please, Father. It's about two people from your congregation. Can we talk somewhere privately?'

'Of course; I hope it's not anything serious?'

Kappakas didn't reply and waited for the priest. After assigning the boys some tasks, D'Angelico lead the way to a meeting room. When they all were sitting around a simple table he asked, 'You said you wanted to talk about two of my fellow believers. What's going on, Detective?'

'Did you know a Mr. and Mrs. Eriksson from the SocHom community?'

'Yes, I knew them very well. Unfortunately they've passed away. I buried them two weeks ago.' Father D'Angelico gave Kappakas a curious look.

'We're investigating the circumstances of their deaths. We'd like to visit their grave.'

The priest looked startled. 'Investigation? Why? I thought they died of natural causes.'

'We hope so too, Father, but we have reason to believe there may be another cause for their deaths.'

'Oh, are you serious? What makes you think so?'

'Are you aware that the couple had been participating in a special health treatment program at St. Luke's Clinic?'

'Yes, I am. They told me about it. They were enthusiastic to be allowed to join it.'

Kappakas came to the point. 'There are strong indications that some wrong medications used in the program may have led to their deaths.'

Father D'Angelico seemed shaken and gave Kappakas a despairing look. 'If that is true, it's horrible. How can I help you?'

Kappakas hesitated. Then he bent forward and looked penetratingly at the priest. 'Father, we must open the grave to find out if our suspicions are correct or not.'

Father D'Angelico was somewhat taken aback by this direct approach.

'Oh, opening the grave? We Catholics don't do that easily. The bodies should rest in peace till their resurrection. That's our belief. On the other hand, we can't live with a disputable cause of death either.'

'Would you show us the grave?' Ellis asked.

'Yes, I could do that. But you can also ask Mr. Sykes, the undertaker. That's a more helpful course of action.'

Kappakas nodded. 'That's what we tried first. But according to one of his assistants Mr. Sykes left town and won't be back for a while.'

D'Angelico reacted, surprised. 'Please, forgive me, but this is getting stranger all the time.'

'Our thoughts exactly,' Kappakas said. 'But I'm sure the Church wants to have certainty in this matter. We definitely do.'

'Absolutely; you want to see the grave? Fine; if you like, I can show it to you now. The cemetery is a public place anyway.'

'We'd appreciate it very much, Father.'

D'Angelico looked seriously at his guests. 'After all that's been going on in our religious community, I sometimes feel ashamed of being associated with it at all. But please, continue calling me Father, even if you're not a member of our congregation.'

Kappakas and Ellis both nodded. 'Thanks for your permission, Father,' Ellis said.

D'Angelico smiled. 'Well that's settled then. Shall we go?'

The priest whispered something to the altar boys and then walked over to the choir conductor. Then he returned and said he was ready to go. 'I do have to be back at three o'clock to prepare for evening mass.'

'It won't take that long,' Ellis said.

Chapter 79

Crest Lawn looked almost deserted. There were only two people present, probably vagrants, sitting on one of the benches. Restfulness prevailed, only now and then disturbed by the twitter of sparrows hiding in the low bushes. In the distance the buzzing of tires could be heard on Immokalee Road.

Father D'Angelico led the two to the place where the Erikssons were supposed to be buried. 'This is their grave. Here they lie buried.' His words sounded steady, not a hint of doubt could be heard in them. 'Look, Detective, the earth around the tombstone is still fresh; it hasn't blended with the surrounding soil yet. Here you'll find the Erikssons.'

'Why don't most graves have tombstones, Father?' Ellis asked.

'These are mostly indigent people, often without ID or a permanent home and address. Almost all of them had no close family or other relatives. Even if they have relatives, they won't have anything to do with the deceased. It's sad, Detective, but they only come to funerals if there's money involved, when they are left an inheritance.'

Kappakas looked at the grave and stroked his chin. 'That is sad, but we're glad you've shown us the grave. Now, the most important thing is still to come. We need to exhume them and have them identified.'

'And your next question is: Father, would you identify them for us?'

Kappakas blushed a little. 'Yes, you got me there.'

'Of course, I would do this for Mr. and Mrs. Eriksson, so they can find peace. If you wish, I can ask members of our congregation to assist. The Erikssons were poor, but that didn't stop them from regularly attending mass. Some parishioners will remember the couple.'

Kappakas discussed the exhumation procedure with D'Angelico. He was glad the priest was open to his plan and his reasoning.

'To sum it all up; we'll do it tomorrow morning. You arrange diggers and a hearse. It should look like a funeral, so that passersby don't think something's the matter. We'll refrain from an operation with police and authorities. All of us know our plan is not according to regulations. But as the saying goes: necessity knows no law. I'm happy we're all convinced to let heavenly law prevail over earthly regulations, in this case.'

'Well said, Detective.'

'Yes, I think so too.'

They both smiled agreeably. Ellis reintroduced a serious tone into the conversation. 'We must be careful, however, that Father D'Angelico won't be put on the spot by difficult questions. I have an idea how to prevent that.'

'Boss; Rios is on his way. We can expect him in six hours.'

Larkin merely said, 'Okay,' and sent his informant away. He looked at Sonny, who was fidgeting with his telephone. 'Hey, Sonny, is Garcia keeping quiet?'

The boss's "guardian angel" put his cell phone quickly back into his pocket and said, 'I hear him. He's with his girlfriend now. He'll keep quiet for the time being.'

Larkin didn't respond to this. 'Listen. Sykes ran off. That cop from Jacksonville was after him. If I knew where he was, I'd....'

'You mean Sykes, boss?' Sonny asked.

'No, of course not. That cop! He's getting in our way more and more. And Garcia's little helper is also untraceable. Check every hotel. They must be somewhere.'

'You mean check all the hotels in Naples?'

Larkin glared. 'Is something wrong with your legs? Get going, now! When you find him, report to me first. Don't use your hands or gun this time. Is that clear?'

Two minutes later he heard Sonny's car tear out of the parking lot. Larkin was thinking. Two guards were still with him. He sent them out of the room. Then he took the phone and dialed a number. It took a while before it was answered. Then Larkin heard a click.

'Yes?'

'This is me. Things are getting out of hand. We have to talk, but not over the phone. Seven-thirty below the overpass on 5th.

'Fine, see you soon.'

Chapter 80

If Dr. Santini had arrived at St. Luke's on time, as usual, she never would have noticed the hearse. But on her way she had to do some shopping and handle a phone call from Larkin. As she was driving past Crest Lawn, the black Cadillac with the small purple flags on the front turned the corner and entered the cemetery. Another interment, she thought. She felt immediately sorry it wasn't one of her patients. She stopped her car at the roadside and watched, just out of curiosity. When the hearse had disappeared behind the cemetery's bushes, a vagrant on the sidewalk caught her attention.

The old man was dressed in faded old clothes, worn-out sandals on his feet. He walked with a stoop, and in one hand he held a cane, in the other a bottle. He went through the entrance of Crest Lawn to the cemetery. Another vagrant is being buried, Santini thought. His friend is going to pay him his last respects. How touching! She watched the man walk away, shook her head, and continued on her way to the clinic. She turned into the driveway, feeling this day would pass very successfully.

The old man had approached the hearse and saw people standing near the car. He walked on and, in front of the car, saw a stout man with a beard talking with a young woman. When the two noticed him, they stopped their conversation and greeted him. 'Unrecognizable. I almost took you for a real vagrant,' Ellis complimented him.

'Father, you could go on the stage, your disguise is perfect,' Kappakas said.

D'Angelico appreciated the humor of the situation and in a way was proud of his transformation. 'Well, can I be myself again here?'

'Yes, the coast is clear,' Ellis said, delighted the priest had followed her suggestion. Kappakas looked admiringly at the clergyman, who had straightened his back, obviously enjoying his role.

'Do you know who I saw opposite the cemetery?'

'The Grim Reaper?' Kappakas suggested.

D'Angelico ignored the feeble joke. 'Dr. Margaret Santini.'

'Really? You're serious?' Ellis said.

D'Angelico nodded. 'Yes, I recognized her car. I've met her a few times. The last time was at the Erikssons' burial. Some coincidence, don't you think?'

'Do you think she saw you?'

'Yes, she must have. When I arrived here, she watched the hearse drive into the cemetery. As I came closer I saw her look at me. I turned away from her, but I noticed from the corner of my eye that she drove away.'

Kappakas shook his head. 'Well, that proves we can't be too careful.'

'Yes,' D'Angelico said. 'It was a good idea, Miss Henning. If I had come here as a priest… well, that could have spoiled everything.'

'Exactly,' Ellis said. 'I'll give you an update, Father. After locating the Erikssons' grave with you last night, some of your parishioners removed the tombstone and the soil early this morning. We couldn't use shovels later in the day; it would be too conspicuous and noisy. Now there are eight people here, and I think together we can lift the coffins from the grave.'

D'Angelico nodded, walked to the hearse and asked some of the young men, all of them parishioners, to get the straps from the trunk of the car. The priest had borrowed the hearse and tools from an undertaker friend. 'I remember standing right here, a couple of weeks ago,' D'Angelico said. 'Mrs. Santini was talking about poisoning from medicines as a cause of death. She said Mr. and Mrs. Eriksson died from self-inflicted euthanasia by taking an overdose.'

Kappakas and Ellis were astounded. 'But why didn't you mention this before?' Kappakas demanded. Ellis also firmly stated, 'This is crucial to our investigation. If it's true, we'll get much closer to finding out what's going on.'

The priest apologized. 'When we met yesterday, I felt kind of overwhelmed and sad at the same time. I'm sorry, but now you know.'

Kappakas had recovered his composure and told the priest he hadn't meant to criticize him. 'I'm sorry if I was rude, but we're determined to establish their cause of death.'

D'Angelico brushed aside the apologies. 'It's alright, Detective. I understand your position. If there's poison involved, I also want to find the truth about the deaths of these amiable people.'

'Thank you very much, Father. I think your people are ready now to lift out the first coffin,' Kappakas said.

D'Angelico gave his assistants the signal to go ahead. The men had secured the straps around their shoulders to prevent them from slipping. Inch by inch the coffin rose from the grave. The men worked together very well, now and then correcting or warning each other.

When the coffin was placed on some planking, everyone was convinced the lifting operation would end well. Although the second coffin lay deeper in the grave, the parishioners had learned from their experience with the first one and had less difficulty getting it out. When both caskets were on the planking, D'Angelico broke the uneasy silence and noticed the serious faces of Kappakas and Ellis. With a smile he said, 'Just realize we're only here a short while before departing this life, prayerfully to a better one. It may give you some relief. I assure you of this as a Catholic and fellow human being.'

The others understood what he meant.

'Thank you, Father. It's not my usual daily business to deal with raising coffins,' Kappakas said. He addressed one of the parishioners. 'Would you open the coffins, please?'

The man asked someone to help him and together they removed the lids. Then the driver of the hearse, whose official business was laying out the deceased, opened the body bags. Ellis and Kappakas intently watched D'Angelico's face. He held a hand to his nose and took his time to identify the already slightly decayed faces. He turned around and said somewhat emotionally, 'Detective Kappakas, these are the bodies of Mr. and Mrs. Eriksson.' He again blessed them with prayer.

Kappakas and Ellis shivered, but at the same time, felt relief.

'I'm positive. These people visited my church regularly.'

'Then I consider this a reliable and official identification. Thank you very much, Father. We appreciate what you've done.'

'It was all for them, Detective, for their souls' repose. I hope you can complete your investigation soon, so they can return quickly to their place in the earth.'

Kappakas nodded. 'We're going to load the caskets now and take them to the mortuary you recommended.'

The priest walked along with the detective and the journalist, and they watched the bodies being placed into the black Cadillac. 'A weight has dropped from my shoulders, dear people. This is truly a wonderful day for me. I'm happy I've been able to make a contribution. I'm very grateful to our dear Lord.' Tears appeared in his pale eyes when he warmly and gently shook hands with Kappakas and Ellis.

'Good bye, Father. We'll let you know our findings; you can be sure of that,' Kappakas said.

'Well, I'll be off then. Play the poor vagrant a little longer, which suits me fine, by the way. No one recognizes me, not even my parishioners. God go with you both!' Then he thanked his own people, waved them goodbye and resumed his role. Everyone watched him go out through Crest Lawn's gate.

'I feel sorry for that man,' Ellis said. 'Did you notice the pain in his eyes when he recognized the Erikssons?'

'We owe a lot to D'Angelico, Ellis. If what he says is right – I mean poisoning as the cause of death – there's definitely a suspicious link with Mike's medicine racket.'

She agreed. 'Yes, we'll find that out soon. Come on, let's go. The bodies have to be put in cold storage.' They said goodbye to the priest's helpers and got into the hearse.

'His men have already filled up the grave again and put the tombstone back into place. Wonderful people, those Catholics; you can count on them,' Kappakas said.

They waited till everyone had left Crest Lawn and then gave the driver the signal to leave. When they drove onto Immokalee Road a little later, they didn't see any cars parked along the street. Kappakas looked out the window and reflected on the investigation. The car passed a lonely pedestrian, who went on his way, stooped and leaning on his cane. 'Look, Ellis, our vagrant.'

She smiled tenderly.

Chapter 81

Sonny leisurely walked into the Ramada hotel. This was number seven on his list. He hadn't found Kappakas at the other six hotels. Sonny was dressed in a floral tropical shirt and slacks. He carried a briefcase and set it on the floor at the check-in desk. He looked around the lobby and noticed there were just a few people around.

'Buenos dias, señor, how can I help you?' the receptionist asked.

'Hi, my name is Steve Zacker. I want to see Mr. Kappakas. Where can I find him?'

The receptionist looked at Sonny for a few moments, without speaking. His appearance was impressive.

Sonny was impatient. 'Well, you going to answer me, or what?'

'Ah, I will check…, Mr. Kappakas is not in his room now. I can leave a note …'

'Gotcha!' Sonny thought happily, as his pulse picked up. 'No, that's not necessary. I'll come back. Can you keep a secret?'

The man nodded convincingly. Sonny put a fifty-dollar bill on the counter, mostly covered by his big paw. These Mexican hotel employees earn shit, he thought. They're happy to take tips for any kind of service, even if privacy is an issue. Latinos can be bought; he was sure. Sonny leaned forward, speaking softly: 'Don't tell him I was here. It's a secret.'

The hotel employee quickly looked around, took the money. 'Sí, señor.'

'Fine, you know how it works, don't you?' Sonny said. 'When he returns, give me a call; then you get another fifty. Keep your mouth shut, com-pren-day?' he said with his forefinger threateningly pointed at the Mexican.

The young man anxiously nodded his head. He watched the big man leave the hotel.

When Sonny was in his car he phoned Larkin. 'Boss, it's me. I found that Krappy-ass cop at the Ramada.'

Chapter 82

The hearse drove to the Downtown Naples Hospital and stopped at the entrance of the mortuary. Kappakas and Ellis were welcomed by two assistants, who led them to the cooling room. Then the vehicle drove to the back of the building, where the bodies were carried inside. Kappakas had asked his boss in Jacksonville to help him find a suitable place for doing the autopsies. Kappakas had his doubts about the integrity of Police Chief Matarazo, so he tried to make contacts through his own office.

A pathologist, Kappakas knew, maintained relations with colleagues at various hospital laboratories in Florida. He was prepared to call a colleague in Naples to ask for his cooperation. The latter, however, agreed on the condition the local authorities would be kept out of these unofficial autopsies. Kappakas guaranteed this and said that in the unlikely event of a judicial inquiry, he would deny he had approached the pathologist with such a request. He had never let his colleagues and other contacts down, so people usually took Kappakas at his word, confidently willing to help the honest and reliable detective. Their confidence was not altered by his occasional deviations from official procedures to achieve his goals.

Dr. Robert Campbell didn't know Kappakas, but he trusted his colleague in Jacksonville when he was asked to examine tissue from the two bodies named in a police file concerning the disappearance of a physical therapist in Naples. The forty-nine-year-old pathologist loved his job. It gave him a lot of satisfaction when he could contribute to establishing a cause of death and solving crimes. Everybody in the hospital liked him, not only because of his amiable personality, but also because he never made sick jokes about cutting and examining body tissue. That couldn't be said of some of his colleagues. With his average height, splendid grey hair, steel blue eyes and square features, he was a welcome, somewhat handsome and much-praised specialist.

Campbell gave Kappakas and Ellis a warm welcome. 'Welcome to our splendid hospital. Please follow me. The bodies are in the cooling room.'

They passed through a few corridors and came to the back part of the building, to the department which handled the deceased, containing a mortuary, cool cells and an autopsy room.

'Just to be sure I have it all straight, Detective Kappakas, please refresh my memory as to why we've gathered here with these two bodies.'

'Of course, Doctor. Facts have come up in our investigation into the disappearance of Elaine Iskander that might – I emphasize "might" – mean this couple died under suspicious circumstances, and the cause of death may differ from the one that was officially established. We're thinking of some kind of poisoning, but we're not sure. A definite answer about this is important to the course of the investigation.'

Campbell nodded. Kappakas continued, 'I hope we've made clear to you why we don't wish to involve the Naples' authorities, and that the autopsy has only been approved by my superiors in Jacksonville.'

'Yes, I understand that you'll vouch for me if things come to light. I would like to add that I find the disappearance of the therapist strange. I promise I'll be thorough, using all professional care.'

'Good to hear that, Doctor. Thanks to your help. We may take a big step towards solving this case.'

Campbell nearly forgot to mention he had found a toxicologist in the hospital prepared to perform the toxicological analysis. 'He's a good friend of mine, Dr. Alan Schornstein. He's really one of the best experts in his field in Florida.'

Then he stepped to the caskets and removed the lids. He pulled back the sheets and looked at the disfigured faces. He touched the skin and noticed it was cold enough to perform an autopsy. 'Detective, I'll spare you the details. Both bodies are in the early stage of decomposition. Please wait in the next room, so I can start my work.'

Kappakas had seen many dead people and had steeled himself to keep his emotions in check. He had even witnessed the autopsy of a young man shot by a street gang member. He'd been dead for a couple of hours. His face was still intact. But it's a different story when someone has lain in the ground for ten days before an autopsy is performed. 'It's your job, Doctor; I'll wait in the other room.' He addressed Ellis. 'What about you? You don't want to see this, do you?'

'Uh, no thanks. I'm not that curious!'

'If there's something you need to know, I'll tell you as soon as possible,' Campbell called after them.

He looked at his two young assistants and said, 'Let's get started.' Campbell and his assistants put on surgical masks and gloves.

'First we take the best preserved body. If there's a significant concentration of a suspicious deadly substance in it, we won't look any further.'

The assistants pulled off the sheets.

At the sight of both upper bodies they reacted in horror. Campbell, who had turned away to pick up a marking pen and scalpel, abruptly turned his head, looked at the tormented faces of his helpers, and then glanced down at the bare torsos of the Erikssons. He too was appalled at what he saw. He shivered, as shocked as his assistants. Dr. Robert Campbell only needed a few minutes to make a gruesome discovery.

Chapter 83

The traffic on the Tamiami Trail swished in an uneven rhythm above their heads. They were standing under a low overpass of 5th Avenue near the Bayfront Inn and were surrounded by trees, so they couldn't be seen. This was a safe place to meet in secret, a place Josh Larkin favored. The gang boss knew Naples like the back of his hand. He was very much attached to the city and liked its splendid, pearly beaches and wonderful architecture. He could often be found on the pier watching frolicking dolphins. The attractions of the city and its surroundings compensated in a way for the hard world he lived in.

Standing out of the light of some streetlamps on the overpass, Police Chief Dick Matarazo worried that he was losing control of the situation.

'Josh, I can't just kill that cop from Jacksonville or that young woman, can I? Far too risky. I'm keeping an eye on him. That guy is too smart. He seems to have an extra sense for things out of the ordinary, like the case of Sykes, who we should've warned.'

Larkin's eyes flashed. 'Dammit, Dick, that Sykes was the turning point. That man should've known there were different people in those caskets. That was a mistake. Now he's gone. But the cop will figure out something, he's cleverer than all your people put together. Why haven't you stationed a patrol car at the Lawn?'

Matarazo reacted as if stung by a wasp. 'What? At the Lawn? Why? That's all over now, isn't it? No one can identify them anymore. Except Santini, of course, and that weirdo, Broderick. Hell, did that guy cause me some problems by shooting that woman. Stupid fool!'

Larkin, getting more annoyed, made sharp movements with his arms, punctuating his words. 'Yes, yes, that's all over now, Dick, everything's taken care of. We must think ahead. Why are you scrimping on personnel? Hire a couple of guys and pay them well for their services. We can't do everything on our own, can we? We need more muscle. Come on, put some men near the Lawn; you can't cover all the bases in this business.'

Matarazo sensed his own frustration rising too. But the worst thing was, this ugly gang boss was trying to scare the piss out of him. He stabbed Larkin's chest with his finger. 'Now listen carefully, Larkin. I'm the boss here in Naples, you understand. I run this business. Without me, no one is anyone around here. Without me, you get nothing done.

So, don't push me, buddy. This affair has already given me more problems than I like.'

It worked. Larkin seemed impressed; hard to imagine in a gangster of his caliber. He relaxed somewhat and tried to humor his business partner. 'Fine, I'm listening. Maybe we should give you more of a hand? You're the boss of a large organization.'

'As soon as we finish our business here, I'll move the whole lot to Texas.'

Matarazo looked as if he saw water burn. 'You're moving to Texas? I have no business there. Maybe you forgot, Larkin, but I happen to be Chief of Naples' police. That's in Florida.'

Larkin tried to calm him down. 'Yes, yes, you're right,' Larkin said, smiling deviously at Matarazo. 'I have a much better business in mind for the Texas market, but I want to run it from Naples. And I'll come knocking on your door again for protection and support.'

The policeman shrugged his shoulders. 'Well, my motto is: it doesn't matter how you earn your money, as long as you earn it.'

'Exactly, Dick. Now we understand each other again. We both know it's going to be risky here with the clinic and all. Tonight another package will be delivered, and Santini is going to help the last patients with it. She doesn't know that yet, but then it's all over. I don't want to shoot myself in the foot and neither do you, right?'

Dick Matarazo found what he heard convincing. The plan had logic to it. He hadn't expected that from Josh Larkin. But the man had prepared himself and was ahead of him in thinking about the cooperation, the chances and possibilities for success of the enterprise. 'Er, could you fill me in on the new plans? After all, I have to prepare and take necessary precautions.'

'Sure. Come on. Let's sit down on that stone wall. Too bad there are no dolphins here; I always enjoy watching them.'

'I didn't know you were so sensitive, Josh. Never thought you'd be interested in animals.'

Larkin gazed at the calm bay. Lights of moored boats and streetlamps on the overpass were reflected in the rippling water. 'Well, you know, Dick, you could call it my soft side and I'm not ashamed of it. You may laugh at me if you like. I don't care. Tomorrow I'm joining a tour, looking for dolphins in the open Gulf. Fantastic!'

'Yes, tourists love it. Enjoy yourself, but tell me about your plans now.'

Larkin chuckled softly and looked at Matarazo. 'Alright, we're going to make you richer. Listen.' Larkin kicked a small stone into the water and stood up. He hoped his partner would catch onto his ideas right away. So he explained them slowly and clearly. Later Matarazo told Larkin he thought he'd lost his mind. The plan was so extraordinary the Chief of Police could never have imagined anything like it.

Chapter 84

Javier Rios was hungry and stopped at a Pizza Hut somewhere near Fort Myers. He'd had it. Everything that could go wrong had gone wrong. A flat tire, a leaking radiator, and in the Taco Bell no one had paid any attention to him. Empty-handed he returned to his Buick, without an envelope, without further instructions. He'd lost faith in a successful outcome. What kept him going was the cargo he carried, which apparently was very important to some people. He would be paid, well paid, according to Eberto Vargas. But he wasn't pumped up about it anymore; the adrenaline was gone.

He ordered a pizza and a coke. Rios knew he was late, much too late. But he had an excuse. They would understand. After all, he'd been willing to leave his family temporarily in the dark to do this job for Vargas. When he was home again in a couple of days, he would have a lot to explain to Amorita. However, he was sure she'd accept what he'd tell her.

Rios paid, got into his car and began the final hour of the long journey. He entered the delivery address into his GPS: Prospect Avenue, Naples. To be precise, he was going to the office of a Mr. Larkin, manager of an import company, dealing in car parts. The company was in an industrial area on the eastside of the Naples Municipal Airport. He was thinking about the money and Amorita's nagging. Why was life in that other world so attractive and addictive?

Chapter 85

Dr. Campbell put down the scalpel and pen and remained staring at the bodies for a while. He didn't quite know how to deliver the news to Kappakas and Henning. He could hardly imagine the look of disbelief and amazement that would appear on their faces when confronted with this news. He asked one of his assistants to show them in. When they entered the autopsy room, Kappakas was the first to react.

'We've only waited five minutes. You're not going to tell me you already have results?'

When he saw the pathologist's grim expression, it became clear that he'd found something very unpleasant. 'Dr. Campbell, are you alright?' Kappakas asked.

'Detective,' Campbell began calmly. 'I have some surprising findings for you.'

Kappakas and Ellis Henning gave him their serious attention.

'For the time being, a toxicological examination will be impossible. Nearly all the organs of Mr. and Mrs. Eriksson have been removed.' Campbell looked at his guests with a mixture of disappointment and bewilderment.

'The organs have been removed?' Kappakas asked in disbelief. 'I don't understand. How did it happen?'

It was as though a bomb had exploded in the autopsy room. Ellis stared, confused, at the corpses that were hidden again under the sheets. Campbell regained his composure and adopted his professional attitude. 'That's a question I can't answer, Detective. I suspect this is a key point in your investigation.'

Kappakas nodded.

'And therefore, it's important you see for yourself what's happened.'

'What exactly do you mean, Doctor?'

'To fully understand what I've just told you, it's important for you to examine the bodies with your own eyes. I'm sure it's the best thing to do in the interest of your investigation.'

Silence hung for a moment in the autopsy room.

'Yes, you're right,' Kappakas said. He addressed Ellis. 'Would you like to have a closer look at the bodies too?'

Ellis didn't hesitate. 'Yes, of course. I'm still kind of upset, but the

Doctor is right; we have to see this for ourselves.'

'Okay, remove the sheets then,' Kappakas said.

Campbell nodded to his assistants. They positioned themselves at the head of the corpses and removed the wrappings. The sight was horrible. Kappakas made a wry face and Ellis put her hand to her mouth while at the same time turning away.

Campbell pointed to the areas of the bodies where the organs had been taken out, as well as the intestines. 'You see the chest and abdomen were opened and then sewn up again. Unless these people gave their permission to donate their organs, which I doubt on the basis of our preliminary talk, we're probably dealing with illegal removal of vital organs, the liver, kidneys, heart and the rest.'

Kappakas sighed. Finally the nasty truth of the situation dawned on him. 'Damn,' he said under his breath. Then he continued in a normal tone of voice. 'Doctor, this is about organ robbery, isn't it?'

Campbell gave Kappakas and Ellis a serious look. 'It looks like it, Detective. Countries like China, Guatemala and Bolivia are notorious for it. Especially, parentless children are victims. Criminals kidnap them and remove their corneas, which are then sold for a lot of money. These children are blind for the rest of their lives. This is an issue that's not much recognized, unfortunately. But what's happened here to the Erikssons goes a step further. Their livers, kidneys, lungs, pancreases and hearts can be sold to the highest bidder. And this bidder is not some good guy who is paying his children's school tuition by working on his computer. It concerns ruthless, hardened criminals, black market gangs, who find shady buyers for these coveted organs. It's a multimillion dollar business.'

Ellis listened with increasing disgust to Campbell's account. She said it all was too much for her and left the room. Kappakas clenched his fists and scowled. 'Doctor, this is unbelievable. And it happens right here, in Naples?'

'Detective, even your own neighbors may perform these inhuman practices, so to speak. Naples is no island in the United States. It looks friendly, with all the tourists, sea, sun and dolphins. But for illicit trafficking, this town occupies a strategic position between Central and South America and the rest of the U.S.'

'Yes, everyone in law enforcement is aware of Florida's geographic role in illegal trade. You seem to know a lot about it.'

'Sure, but I'm not proud of it. Pathologists deal with crime, and that's the way it is. Eighty percent of our work is done at the court's request. We play an important role in finding the truth for the sake of relatives, lawyers, judges and of course, juries. All in all, it's a satisfying job. Only in this case, my heart breaks. This is not what I'm after, Detective. This is organized crime and I'd rather stay out of it.'

Campbell was apologetic and helpless at the same time. He would much rather have made a different diagnosis, a more regular one. But a toxicological investigation into suspected traces of poisoning seemed superseded. The absence of most organs – the robbers had left the most wanted organ, the cornea, untouched because of the victims' old age – sufficed to establish a criminal offense.

'What's your opinion, Detective? Can you already draw some conclusions based on what you've seen?'

The policeman from Jacksonville gave Campbell a thoughtful look and answered decisively, 'This is a big breakthrough in my investigation. It's shocking but it also clarifies matters.'

What Kappakas didn't mention was the couple had been childless and without any relatives. In the patients' file the abbreviation N/A was written behind the question if a donor card had been drawn up. This might have been a reason for St. Luke's Clinic to cooperate in making the bodies of the deceased available to others. Kappakas couldn't imagine that the clinic itself was actively involved in illegal organ trade. He pushed the thought aside.

'I think we know enough now, Doctor. I'm going to check on my assistant, see how she is. She's not used to seeing corpses, and certainly not in this condition.'

'I can imagine.'

'Oh, and Doctor, there's one more question. Do you know Police Chief Matarazo?'

'Well, I don't really know him, but I have to contact him when autopsies need to be performed. I've met the man several times.'

'Has Matarazo been in the news in some negative way? I mean, has he been criticized for the way he works?'

'Well, you know, there have been rumors about him, but they've never been confirmed. Nothing has been heard about it lately, and I don't know anything about it. I'd prefer to keep it that way so I can do my work undisturbed, also my work for the Police Chief.'

Kappakas' face relaxed and he started to leave. He decided to let the matter rest for the time being and not ask Campbell about the nature of the rumors around the Naples' Police Chief. 'Thank you for your help, Doctor. I'm sorry to have provided you with surprisingly unpleasant subjects. The same applies to Ms. Henning, I'll see her now.'

Campbell responded professionally that it was all for a good cause. Kappakas shook his hand after they had agreed on when the Erikssons were to be transported back to Crest Lawn. Till then the bodies could remain in the hospital. He found Ellis sitting at a small table reading a magazine. 'Hello, have you recovered a little from the shock?'

She put the periodical aside and said, 'I'm okay now, but I couldn't face it any longer. Sorry, but I got a little squeamish, I think.'

'That's alright. You should have seen me when I was confronted with my first corpse, and she – it concerned a young woman – was not in such a bad state as the Erikssons.'

'What are your conclusions so far?'

'Come on; let's discuss it at the hotel.'

They took a cab to the Ramada. During the short trip they didn't say a word. Both were very tired and longed for a hot bath and bed. After Ellis paid the driver, Kappakas said, before entering the lobby, 'From now on things may get rough, Ellis. I think you should carry a weapon. Keep your eyes and ears open. The closer we get to the truth, the more motive our opponents will have to stop us.'

'She nodded. 'I always keep it in my purse. I wanted to keep up with you.'

He saw her wink. 'Great, that's a relief, believe me.'

'I do.'

They reached the lobby and Kappakas asked the clerk if there were any messages.

'Sí, señor. Here you are.'

Kappakas took the envelope. Then they rode the elevator to the 7th floor. He opened the envelope, read its contents and started to chuckle.

'What does it say?' Ellis asked.

Kappakas looked a little teasingly at her. 'I'll tell you in my room. You'll be surprised.'

Chapter 86

Kappakas dropped into his chair and, rereading the note, grinned again.

'Are you finally going to tell me what's in it?'

'Of course,' he said, standing again and taking a bottle of beer from the mini-bar. 'When I stay in hotels for an investigation, I always make an arrangement with the receptionists. When strangers ask for me, the receptionist says I'm out, even if I'm in my room. Then they make a note, which they hand me later; or when I'm in my room, they give me a ring.'

'Smart.'

'It says: "Mr. Steve Zacker said he needed to see you, but I told him you were out. He didn't want to leave a note and would come back later. I got fifty dollars to keep my mouth shut and would get another fifty if I'd call him when you'd returned. As agreed, I won't do that of course. Saludos cordiales, Felix."'

'Larkin?' Ellis asked.

'Probably, who else? Maybe he was notified by Matarazo, who sent two guys after me to see where I stayed. Matarazo and Larkin know each other, that's obvious.'

Ellis looked surprised and said, 'You reach conclusions quickly. Maybe he was worried and wanted to protect you.'

Kappakas suppressed a laugh. 'I see what you mean. But don't forget police and criminals often have connections with each other, which are usually hard to trace. I have a gut feeling we're dealing with such a connection here. So I'm going to try and draw Matarazo out. I've got to know where he stands. If you're right, I'll admit it.'

'How will you go about it?'

He paused to organize his thoughts. 'Today we've made a shocking discovery. Mr. and Mrs. Eriksson have, in all likelihood, been killed. Their organs were removed, so we couldn't perform a toxicological examination. But this won't keep us from finding out the truth about Elaine Iskander's disappearance.'

'I think you have enough clues now to nose around in the clinic. From the patients' file, we know a lot of people die there from obscure causes, mostly after they'd joined the so-called health program.'

Kappakas smiled. 'Ellis; it's a good thing you managed to get hold of that file. In a trial it will provide crucial evidence.'

'I've put it in a safe place. Would you like another beer?'

'No thanks, I have to be careful with alcohol during work. But have one yourself. Like to know what we're going to do now? We're going to call Matarazo and ask for help and protection.'

'Is that the way you want to draw him out'

'Exactly. He won't like it, but he'll have to give us his assistance. We have an agreement.'

Ellis returned to her hotel and stepped into the quiet lobby. She took the elevator to her floor and walked down a long corridor to her room. When she took the electronic key card from her purse, she saw the door was ajar. Quickly she pulled her Colt from her hand bag and slowly pushed the door open. She saw a huge mess. Cautiously, she stole through the room and checked the places where someone could hide. After checking out the whole place, including the closet and under the bed, she put the Colt back in her purse. The floor was littered with all of her things, clothing, linens, toiletry and magazines. She paid no more attention to the mess but went straight to the bed, lifted the mattress and looked at the slats. The patients' file was gone. She swore. Then she walked back to the door and locked it. Apparently the thief had been in a hurry and hadn't taken the time to shut the door completely. Ellis seemed to stay calm, but she couldn't suppress a second curse. That file would be strong evidence if this case came to trial, Kappakas had said. Clearly St. Luke's had illegally reclaimed what was rightfully theirs. She phoned Kappakas.

'Hi, it's me. I'm afraid I have bad news.'

'Let's hear it.'

'You're not going to believe this, but the patients' file is gone, stolen from my room.'

'Oh, hell!'

'Yes, someone's made a very big mess over here. Who's behind this? Larkin? Santini?'

'I wouldn't know anybody else who'd be interested.'

Kappakas quickly considered the situation and reached a remarkable conclusion, 'They probably don't realize it, but they're helping us. As soon as this file is back at the clinic, Santini will continue her special health program, which gives us a reason to search the clinic. She has no computer, as you know, just this one file with a wealth of information about her patients. Santini can start her program again, with a new couple that's probably been waiting a while.'

Shivers ran down her spine. Ellis hardly dared mention the names out loud. 'Don and Suzie Atchison?' she asked in a subdued voice.

'Right!'

'Oh yeah, that reminds me.'

'What's wrong?'

Her heart began to beat faster; then she said anxiously, 'Mike and I looked at the most recent patients' files. They show that the residents, who were admitted last, qualify for the program. And who were admitted to the clinic after the Erikssons? The Atchisons!'

'Yes, I see the connection. I agree, so we'll look into it tomorrow. I need Matarazo's permission, which he's going to give; you can bet on it.'

'Can't we do something now? I mean, Larkin and Santini could be working together. Now I understand what the condemned medicines are used for, they need them for their program. Kappa, we've got to stop this before things get even worse.'

'I know, but we can't do anything without a search warrant. The only thing I can do is stand guard at the clinic. I expect Santini is waiting for a new delivery. Since Mike quit, they must have hired another runner.'

Ellis tried to change Kappakas' mind to search the clinic with him right away, but she also understood that police work requires patience, and premature actions are likely to backfire.

'Ellis, go to bed now. Lock the door and get some rest, you've been through a lot today. I want you to be in good shape and ready tomorrow.'

She almost answered 'Yes, dad', but thought it was a little too much to be funny right now. 'You're right. Be careful when you're standing guard there. I'll meet you tomorrow.'

They hung up. Kappakas put on his bulletproof vest.

Chapter 87

Javier Rios turned into Prospect Avenue and looked left and right in search for the sign for Naples Autoparts Imports (NAI). He realized he was nearly half a day late, but it couldn't be helped. Anyway, the recipient of the packets would be very pleased when he finally got his delivery. Then he noticed the NAI logo and expelled a sigh of relief. The journey was over. Soon he'd get the money, lots of money. Rios entered an open gate and reached a dusty area, half the size of a 'futbol' field, with a low, two-story building in the far right corner. Next to it was a small portable, serving as an office. Spread across the area were crates, pallets and used tires. In another corner were two containers with the letters NAI. At the back stood a large shed, probably used for storing car parts, Rios thought. He stopped near the entrance of the office, got out of the car and walked to the door, feeling hopeful that his task was almost over. Even before he knocked, Rios saw the door open and a large man stepped out.

'Are you Rios?' Billy asked.

'Yes, sir.'

Billy was surprised by the Mexican, he couldn't remember anyone calling him 'sir'. 'You're delivering something?'

'Sí, from San Antonio.'

'Go inside, we'll take care of the rest. Give me your car keys.'

Rios handed Billy the keys, entered the small office and saw two men inside. One of them obviously was the boss; he was sitting behind a desk. The other, a large bald man, stood in a corner chewing gum. Josh Larkin ordered the Mexican to sit down.

'You're late.'

Rios hadn't expected such a curt welcome. 'The boxes, señor, they are in the car,' he said confidently.

Larkin looked at Sonny. They smiled. Then Larkin addressed Rios again. 'Maybe you didn't get it, but I expect an explanation. Why are you late?'

Rios was confused by the way the boss spoke to him. They have their packages; qué pasa? He shrugged his shoulders. 'Una llanta ponchada, one flat tire, jefe.'

Larkin looked at him in mock amusement. 'Oh, one flat tire?' Then he repeated to Sonny, 'One flat tire.'

Sonny gave a nasty laugh and spit his gum hard into a waste basket.

Rios now felt anxious, very uncomfortable. He had expected a warm welcome, not a chilling shower. He didn't even know who he was facing. Larkin chucked an envelope at Rios. 'Here's your money; now get out - fast!'

Rios hesitated. That was quick. 'Sí, señor, uh.., gr-gracias, va-vaya con Dios,' he stammered. He stood up and waved goodbye. Once outside, he saw his car had been parked near the dumpsters. First he found it strange, but then he realized it was easier to store the goods that way. To reach his car he had to walk between two large steel cargo containers. When he was halfway, a man suddenly appeared from behind one of the containers. Even if Rios was armed, he didn't stand a chance to defend himself against the attacker. When Billy turned the corner and saw Rios walk between the containers, he fired. Three bullets from his magnum silencer penetrated Rios' heart and skull. He was dead before he fell. Billy picked up the envelope, spit on the corpse, and then calmly walked back to the office. He made a gesture across his throat. Larkin and Sonny nodded.

'Good riddance,' Larkin said. 'Should have done that to Garcia.'

Larkin phoned Santini.

'St. Luke's Clinic, Dr. Santini speaking.'

'The blackbird has fed her young. They'll fly soon.'

'Thanks.'

Larkin looked at Sonny. 'Come on, deliver the packages tonight. Make sure no one sees you. Take Billy too.'

The bodyguards nodded; and a little later they dumped Rios' body.

Chapter 88

Kappakas parked his car at a safe distance from the clinic. It would be unwise to stop right in front of it. Larkin's boys weren't highly-educated, but they definitely had eyes and weren't stupid. From his vantage point, Kappakas had a perfect view of the whole complex. If someone came to make a delivery, he would see it. He adjusted his seat to a reclining position so he could just peer over the dashboard. Various vehicles passed the clinic, but they showed no sign of stopping, let alone turning in to deliver anything. An hour and a quarter passed before something happened. A small van stopped at the clinic's gate. A man in uniform dropped something into the mailbox. Later on, the Police Chief's car passed by. Kappakas just managed to see the license plate number and wrote it down in his notebook. Taking down plate numbers was an old habit and had proven useful many times - routine. Another half hour passed when a Cadillac stopped in front of St. Luke's.

A big, broad-shouldered man got out and looked around. Only someone on his guard does that, Kappakas thought. He lifted his small binoculars and saw the man push the entry buzzer. A man in a white uniform walked up to the gate. The two spoke to each other. Then the large man walked back to his Caddy and took out several boxes. He put them down behind the gate near the man in white. The driver had to walk back and forth four times before he'd delivered all the boxes. The men said goodbye and the driver started to drive away. Contrary to what Kappakas expected, the man reversed, turned his car and drove off in the opposite direction.

He wondered what that meant. He decided to follow the Caddy. The black car was conspicuous enough. Calmly it drove through moderate traffic. It was a little after nine and nightlife gradually began to occupy the streets of Naples. After almost thirty minutes, the Caddy passed the Naples regional airport and turned left into Prospect Avenue. Here Kappakas had to stay out of sight because the man had entered an industrial area. It was hard to find a place to park, only the road's shoulder could be used, but then he'd attract too much attention. When Kappakas passed the avenue, he quickly looked into the street to see where the Caddy was. The car had vanished. Kappakas knew enough for now, so he pressed the accelerator and returned to his hotel.

Chapter 89

'Suzie, listen. Can you hear me?' Don Atchison had been trying to tell his wife the news a number of times, but she hardly reacted to his attempts. The Alzheimer's had reached an advanced stage, in spite of the drugs the clinic had prescribed her. She couldn't walk on her own anymore and relied permanently on a wheelchair. Male nurse, George Broderick, and the new young physical therapist, Joan Bercich, had to help Suzie with eating, undressing and going to the bathroom. She was completely dependent on the care of her husband and the staff.

However, there was a ray of hope. She had been allowed to join the special health program St. Luke's had reserved for select patients to make their lives a little more bearable. Don had wanted to tell her she would be picked up any moment to move to another room. He'd told Broderick he didn't want to be a candidate for the program. 'I want to do this for Suzie; she needs it; but I don't.' Broderick had tried to persuade him to follow the program together with his wife, but he gave up his attempts when he realized Don was adamant. It was in an unexpected moment that Suzie moved her head in the direction of the voice and gave her husband a dazed look.

'You'll be picked up soon for a special treatment. It'll do you a world of good,' Don said, glad his wife responded to his words. Longer than usual, Suzie kept looking at Don, her eyes empty and sad. His wife's face moved him almost to tears; they hadn't been close in this way for a long time. Don realized nothing registered with her anymore; her mind had lost touch with reality. But it couldn't keep him from involving his wife in current affairs.

'I envy you; you'll get a first-class specialized treatment.' Did he detect a vague smile around her mouth? A tear ran down her cheek. She averted her eyes from Don and began to nod again. Don Atchison would give anything to be able to take a look into her soul. He didn't care about the rest of the world, only Suzie mattered to him. He loved her as much as always and refused to accept the illness that she'd already suffered so long. He took a magazine from the table and tried to read a little, when Broderick entered the room.

'Mr. Atchison, the moment has almost arrived for your wife. Tomorrow after breakfast we'll come and move her to the Doctor's treatment room. It's too bad you don't want to participate, but we respect your decision. However, you should know that our policy is only to allow admitted patients into the treatment room. Tomorrow, you'll have to say goodbye to your wife, at least for a while.'

Don already had resigned himself to it. He didn't want to hit a blank wall for a second time. He would cooperate, if only halfheartedly. His thoughts wandered back to the beginning of their stay at St. Luke's. He'd resisted the clinic's practices and restrictions, and he still did. Sometimes he argued with Broderick, but he had always been on good terms with Elaine Iskander. His obstinacy and curiosity almost got him killed when someone dealt him a hard blow on the head, and since then he kept quiet. He had decided to say no more about it. Musing over the lonely nights in the clinic, he remembered a remarkable incident.

On a rainy night, not so long ago, he was standing in front of the window and saw two people climb the fence, in the direction of the road. Apparently they'd already been inside, for they were carrying something and seemed to be in a hurry. Nevertheless, one of them waited for a second and looked at the lighted window where Don's dark silhouette was backlit. Then too, he'd decided not to inform the staff of what he'd seen. And now he was about to be separated from Suzie for a couple of weeks. He would be alone and was overwhelmed by melancholy. He had no children, Suzie was infertile. He was an only child and Suzie had just one brother, who had died; so they had no immediate relatives. Only a niece of Suzie's sometimes phoned and even visited them once in their old house in Minnesota. He tried to remember the niece's name, but couldn't recall. Don refused to accept this, however, and wondered out loud, 'What's the name of that niece again?' He swore and then gave up. His stream of thought halted abruptly when he noticed Broderick had left the room. Suzie was lying on the bed watching TV, probably without realizing what was on. In her lap was her favorite drawing book. Now and then she scribbled something on the paper. Don Atchison thought it best to follow her example and lay down to sleep.

'I'm going to turn in. You should go to sleep too. Tomorrow is an important day.'

For the last time that day Don rang for the nurse to help his wife prepare for the night.

Chapter 90

The clock showed 6:30. Ellis was still in deep sleep when the phone on her nightstand started to ring. She was dreaming she was a drum majorette marching in a brass band. Next to her someone played the same tune on a portable xylophone for the thousandth time. It was annoying, so she tried to make her stop, but the woman kept repeating the ditty. Ellis awoke and wanted to scream at the woman next to her to stop playing that ridiculous tune, when she noticed her phone's ringtone. She rubbed her eyes, yawned and reached for it. When she pushed the answering button, silence returned to her room and she said, sleepily, 'This must be very important....'

'Ellis, Kappa here....' he interrupted her quickly. 'Listen, Mike Garcia just called me. His girlfriend's name is Jennifer Mattox and....'

'I already know that.'

'Of course you do, but Jennifer has a distant uncle who has contacted her and....'

'What's wrong with that?' she yawned wearily.

'Ellis, let me finish,' he said indignantly. 'This uncle's last name is Atchison, and he says his wife....'

'What did you say his name was?'

'Atchison, Don and Suzie. Wake up, please! These people were admitted to St. Luke's. He said his wife is going to start some special health treatment program.'

Suddenly it was quiet on the other end of the line. But it wasn't long before Ellis realized what was going on. Instantly, she was wide awake. 'Atchison? Kappa, we've read his file. I told you so yesterday. I didn't know he had any relatives. What a coincidence Mike's girlfriend connected to this.'

'I'm going to Matarazo shortly to persuade him to give me the search warrant. This will be his first real test case. If he doesn't support me, it makes him suspect. So he'll cooperate, I'm sure. This is going to be police work, although I don't quite know what I'm up against. If you want to join me, wear a vest and bring your Colt.'

'Wait a minute Kappa, I want to go, witness it all first hand, and I won't let you go alone. I'll get ready and come meet you. Can you get a bulletproof vest for me from Matarazo?'

'Yes, I think I'll manage. Come quickly, I'm about to leave.'

An hour later, Kappakas and Ellis drove in the dense morning traffic to the central police station.

'You said you wanted to leave as soon as possible. Now, we're stuck in the rush hour traffic. You know how to give people the jitters, Kappa.'

'Sorry, but this case is urgent, and therefore I may seem impatient. If my intuition is right, we can make some headway today. First of all we should try and keep Mrs. Atchison out of that health program.'

'Any idea what you're going to find?'

'None whatsoever.'

She looked at him, surprised.

'No, really; it may not be so bad after all, or our worst suspicions may be confirmed. I'm not going to jump to conclusions; I want to keep an open mind.'

'I see.'

'Here it is.'

Kappakas parked his car in the visitor's space in front of the police station. Behind his windshield he placed a card that permitted him to park in any police parking lot anywhere in the country.

'I'll be right back. They won't like a civilian involved, and I want to avoid questions about your presence. I've only come to collect a search warrant, you see.'

'Sure, you're the cop, and I'm the journalist. Go do your job and I'll wait to do mine,' she said in good humor.

Kappakas looked at her with mock offense and got out. He entered the police station and reported at the desk. He asked the officer if the Police Chief was in, because he needed a search warrant.

The desk officer looked inquiringly at Kappakas. He accepted his badge and studied it thoroughly. He asked rhetorically, while pressing a key on his board, 'You're not from around here, are you?'

Kappakas looked straight back at the man but said nothing. He was allowed to go to the second floor. At the top of the stairs Dick Matarazo was waiting for him.

'Good morning, Detective. You must have an urgent reason to appear at our police station so early in the day.'

'Thank you, Chief. I won't keep you long.'

'Please tell me what you need.'

Kappakas gave the Chief a serious look. He'd decided on a direct approach, confiding in the police chief. This was the best way to find out if the man had a hidden agenda. But he had to proceed cautiously and not put all of his cards on the table.

'For St. Luke's Clinic, I'd like to have your permission to search the premises and question the Director.'

Kappakas was deliberately silent for a few moments to see how Matarazo would react.

'So you want to search the clinic,' Matarazo said calmly, without a trace of surprise on his face. He continued, 'You would need a search warrant from the courthouse, but for an interrogation you don't need permission.'

'I know, Chief. The point is I have reason to believe Dr. Santini is involved in the disappearance of Elaine Iskander. Besides questioning her, it's therefore necessary to search the clinic.'

Matarazo acted surprised. 'You say you have reasons to suspect Dr. Santini of being involved in a crime. Please tell me the basis for your suspicions. I have to be in charge of an investigation and any criminal charges in this jurisdiction.'

'I understand, but as policemen we both know we must protect our sources.'

Matarazo's expression was curious. 'Ah! You mean your suspicions are based on information from certain sources, and you don't want to compromise your informers, right?'

'Exactly. I'd much rather share everything with you, but just now that would be very unwise, even with the Chief of Police. I don't have sufficient certainty and proof to be completely frank now.'

'And you want to burst in at the clinic to gather that proof?'

He had no choice; there was nothing else to do but give an affirmative answer. 'Yes, Chief, if I don't do it and don't get your help, my investigation will come to an end. This is the only way to find out the truth about what happened to Ms. Iskander.'

Matarazo thought about it while tapping his pen on the desk. 'You know, we've already looked into this matter and found nothing illegal or suspect. We think Ms. Iskander left the clinic of her own free will. That leaves two things that may have happened to her. One, she's gone into hiding somewhere, maybe because of personal problems. Two, she's dead and her body hasn't been found. Sometimes, people just disappear, without leaving a trace.'

Matarazo gave Kappakas a pointed look to impress him. The detective wouldn't be drawn out and remained silent to see if Matarazo would continue his argument.

'Okay, if you think you have information that may clarify this matter, I won't stand in your way.'

'I appreciate that very much, Chief.'

'Alright. I'll support your request for a search warrant and assign two officers to go with you. Is that okay with you?'

Kappakas was amazed. These guys will certainly keep an eye on me and report back. 'Fine! Thank you very much for your cooperation.'

'Well, you know, it would make a very bad impression to read in the newspapers that a policeman from Jacksonville ran into trouble because he didn't get support from our department. We don't want that to happen.'

'Yes, I understand, we'd have done the same for you in a situation like this. Law-enforcement agencies should help each other out.'

'Detective, if this is all, I'll have the warrant drawn up and have our judge approve it at the courthouse.'

Kappakas waited a moment and then asked the question that he'd been burning to ask. 'Chief, one more thing. Do you happen to know a Mr. Larkin?'

Matarazo's eyes shifted side to side. He seemed to have not anticipated the question. He recovered quickly and replied, frowning. 'Larkin is a shady entrepreneur. We know him. Why do ask?'

Kappakas had to be careful now. He didn't want to spoil his relationship with the Chief. 'I have information that he plays a role in the supply of illegal medicines to St. Luke's.'

Matarazo shook his head. 'We don't know anything about that here. We do know he deals in shady secondhand goods, and we suspect him of certain illegal activities. We're investigating his operations and may have a case against him before long. If you have relevant information, I'd like to use it.'

Kappakas noticed Matarazo spoke in general terms, so he agreed, left it at that. Later, with the approved search warrant in his hand and two policemen behind him, he got back in his car, where Ellis waited for him.

'Glad you're back. Some annoying cops asked me several times what I'm doing here. Your police sticker wasn't enough to stop them.'

'Stop grumbling, we have permission to search the clinic, and some of your annoying cops will help us,' Kappakas responded with a twinkle in his eyes.

She turned around as two policemen got into another car. 'Are they coming with us?'

'Yep; Matarazo offered help, although I didn't ask for it. Just to back us up. We search the clinic, and they stay around to reinforce our authority and protect us if someone threatens us.'

She looked at Kappakas incredulously. 'And you buy that? Come on, I thought you mistrusted the Police Chief, and now you're happy with his helpers?'

'Ellis, you know how the saying goes: a friend in need is a friend indeed.'

He looked at her with a look of 'what do you have to say to that?' on his face. She just said, 'Let's drive.'

He started the engine and left the parking lot. Kappakas tried to imagine how Santini would react to his unannounced visit. He thought of the patients too, particularly Mr. and Mrs. Atchison. In his rearview mirror he saw Matarazo's cops following them. Kappakas wondered how the Chief had instructed them, but that was the least of his worries.

Chapter 91

Don Atchison was crying. He was standing near the door of his room and saw a couple of nurses place Suzie on a movable bed. He'd said goodbye to her and was happy she would undergo the special treatment. Don watched her until she was pushed into the elevator at the end of the corridor. That was the last he would see of her for the time being. However, she was in good hands and had a chance for an improved, more dignified existence, if the advanced dementia would release its stranglehold on her.

George Broderick had told him Suzie would be the first patient to receive the new drug, cannabidiol. It was an extract of the hemp plant, and in Australia had already produced promising results in people with Alzheimer's. He returned to his chair and looked at her empty bed. His excitement subsided, and he began to feel ambivalent. On one hand he was glad Suzie had a chance for a better life, but on the other hand, the emptiness in his room made it hard for him to feel optimistic about the future.

The night before, he'd taken a look at Suzie's drawing book. One particular scribble surprised him, "Jennifer". Don's breath stopped short. Suzie had been capable of communication after all. It was a miracle. How sensitive she was to have been able to understand that Don was wrestling with a problem, this problem! She had been aware and responded. Don considered it a gift from God that his whispering his mental search for their niece's name had fanned Suzie's dying inner flame. He took the phone and pushed zero for the operator to be connected with Jennifer Mattox in Joliet, Illinois. Luckily she was the only person with her name combination in the area, so he wasn't surprised when she answered the call.

Jennifer vaguely recalled her Uncle Don. He told her that he and Suzie had been admitted to a clinic of the Florida retirement community and that Suzie was getting special treatment to alleviate the effects of Alzheimer's disease. He added that he thought it was wonderful for her because he loved her very much. He wasn't a candidate for the treatment, because he didn't suffer from any degenerative disease. Don said he wanted to share this news with someone. He had very few relatives, but he remembered their distant niece. Only, he couldn't think of her name. Suzie had been the ministering angel. When she heard him whisper something about their niece, she'd scribbled Jennifer's name on her drawing paper. He felt this was one of the most moving moments in his life. Jennifer Mattox said she was glad to get such good news from her uncle. She wished him luck and hoped his wife would benefit from the treatments.

Thinking about that phone call, Don put the drawing book aside. He made himself a cup of coffee, and with the cup in his hand he walked to the window. He saw a police car stop in front of the clinic gate. He shoved his chair closer to the window to watch what was going on. Two policemen got out of the car and followed two others in civilian clothes. There must be something the matter, Don thought. A small stout man with a beard said something in the intercom. A minute later George Broderick came out and approached the foursome waiting at the gate. The stout man handed him a document, which was obviously important, for Broderick opened the gate immediately and everyone walked through. Don thought the scene was over much too quickly and was left with nothing more to look at but trees and bushes in the garden around St. Luke's.

Chapter 92

Kappakas and the others headed straight inside for Dr. Santini's office. He remembered the way from his two previous visits. Kappakas ignored questions from Broderick, who wanted to know why this apparent show of force was necessary. Without knocking, he entered the office. The policemen positioned themselves at the door, while Ellis followed Kappakas. He quickly looked around and saw Santini wasn't there.

'Where's the Doctor?' he asked looking sharply at Broderick.

'Uh..., I don't know.'

'Take us to her or you'll be arrested.'

Broderick winced and began to stammer. Kappakas impatiently ordered the officers to handcuff Broderick. 'Take him to the police station; he refuses to cooperate!'

When the male nurse realized he was cornered, he fluttered like a leaf on a tree. 'I believe she's in her treatment room,' he said timidly.

'Then take us to her.'

They left Santini's office and followed Broderick down the corridor. When they reached the stairwell, Broderick suddenly made a run towards the clinic's front door.

'Stop him!' Kappakas ordered.

Broderick didn't make it to the door. The policemen grabbed him and pushed him to the floor. Broderick gave up and cried out; he would cooperate. Kappakas watched the scene and even felt just a little sorry for the skinny male nurse. He stood next to Broderick and said, 'What is this supposed to mean?'

Broderick's expression was grim. He didn't know how to react but tried a feeble explanation for his thoughtless action. 'I..., I think I'm a little "allergic" to police. Sorry, I shouldn't have done that.'

'Mr. Broderick, your behavior makes you suspect. After questioning Dr. Santini, we're going to interrogate you too.'

Kappakas signaled to the policemen to handcuff Broderick, who wasn't happy that his excuse didn't help. He felt confused and feared his secret was no longer safe.

'No..., no. Why must I be cuffed? I don't understand.'

'I'll explain. Your behavior is suspicious. It may have to do with the Iskander case, or you're involved in illegal practices in this clinic. We'll discuss it later.'

Ellis gave Kappakas an admiring look. His interrogation and confrontation techniques were clever. Ellis wondered how Broderick would react. He began to stammer and refused to move.

'I…, er…, have nothing to hide. I've done nothing wrong.'

'Well, then you have nothing to worry about,' Kappakas said in a fatherly tone. 'Now, lead the way to Dr. Santini.'

Broderick started to walk into the long corridor, but then stopped. He was standing between Kappakas and Ellis and the two policemen. He was surrounded and it would be impossible for him to run away again. He panicked and began to sweat. 'It's her…'

Kappakas looked sharply at him. 'What do you mean, "It's her", Mr. Broderick?'

'She does it, she gives patients the wrong meds, she goes…'

Kappakas looked alarmed. 'What do you mean, who is she? Dr. Santini?'

The male nurse looked fearfully at him.

Kappakas demanded. 'Well, come on, let's hear it!'

'Yes, it's Santini. She's injecting a patient now. I've done nothing wrong. She does bad things.'

Kappakas looked at Ellis. They could tell from each other's expressions swift action was required.

'Broderick, walk, on the double! Where is she?'

Arriving at the end of the corridor, he said, trembling, 'This is where she is, in the treatment room.'

Kappakas quickly opened the door and entered. Dr. Margaret Santini stood bent forward at Suzie Atchison's bed. When she heard the door open she suddenly turned. She had a needle in her hand. She was astonished when she saw Kappakas.

'What are you doing here? You have no right to…'

'Put that needle down!' Kappakas interrupted.

'Okay, take it easy, I'll put it down. This patient has just had her dosage and…'

Chapter 93

Again Kappakas didn't let her finish and said to the policemen, 'Men, bag that syringe for evidence and take this woman to NCH Downtown Hospital. Ellis, call first aid and tell them to pump Mrs. Atchison's stomach. It's urgent. Go with her to the hospital.'

Santini protested. She stared fiercely at Kappakas and said, 'What are you doing? What gives you the right to kidnap one of my patients? I'm going to call Chief Matarazo, I'm sure he'll make mincemeat of you.'

Kappakas patiently heard her out this time, getting more and more tired of her theatrics. One of the policemen began to push Suzie's bed to the corridor. Ellis walked beside the bed looking at Suzie's pale and weary face. Santini stood rooted to the spot. Her eyes blazed and she was desperately trying to find a way to get control of the situation.

Kappakas said, 'I have a search warrant.' He handed her the document. 'I must ask you to give me your full cooperation to search the clinic and question the staff.'

Santini showed no inclination to comply and asked, 'Does Chief Matarazo know about this? How did you get this warrant? I'm not going to permit you to snoop around here.'

She tried to assert her authority and forceful personality, but Kappakas ignored her and watched Suzie Atchison being wheeled out of the room. One of the policemen kept an eye on Broderick and, as a precaution, kept his hand on his holstered pistol.

'Dr. Santini, let's stop playing games,' Kappakas said. 'We suspect you of administering illegal drugs to your patients. We should have proof of that within the hour.'

Santini scoffed. 'Detective, this is ridiculous. You have too much imagination. May come in handy at police parties, but it's certainly misplaced in this clinic.' She continued acidly, 'If you allow me, I'm calling Matarazo now.'

'Okay, Doctor, but before you pick up the phone, please read the warrant carefully. Just a hint; look at the bottom of page two.'

The blood drained from Santini's face when she saw Matarazo's signature. Kappakas gave her a steady, stern look. 'You see, Doctor, we don't just burst in somewhere without good reason and authorization, regardless of what you may think.' He asked the policeman to handcuff Santini. 'I'm arresting you on suspicion of murder and maltreatment of patients in your care. You have the right to remain silent, and anything you say may be used against you in a court of law. You have the right to an attorney, and if you cannot afford an attorney, the court will appoint one to represent you.'

Santini submitted very reluctantly to arrest, her eyes still flashing now and then.

'So we're going to wait here till Mrs. Atchison's stomach's been pumped?' Broderick asked. He pointed at the empty space where the bed had been. Everyone looked at him.

Santini was the first to open her mouth. 'Broderick! I've always thought you were an ignorant and pedantic little man. You, and your so-called "great thoughts", your unwarranted pride and smugness.'

Broderick was taken aback by this sudden attack by his ally. Santini's words embarrassed him. He looked perplexed. His face flushed with increasing resentment. Santini hadn't finished yet. With an exaggerated gesture, she pointed at Broderick and said contemptuously, 'Detective, this is the murderer of Elaine Iskander!'

Even Kappakas was surprised by the change in atmosphere. He imagined that if Broderick and Santini both had dirty hands, they would want to place the blame on each other to try to avoid responsibility. Broderick began to laugh uncertainly. He had to muster a lot of courage to take a stand against his employer, the clinic's Director.

'Why do you say that? It's absurd! I think you're afraid the police might find something inside Suzie Atchison.' He looked fiercely at Santini, who smiled condescendingly, ignored Broderick, and spoke to Kappakas. 'Detective, George Broderick murdered Ms. Iskander a few weeks ago. He shot her behind the clinic. I can – and I will – make a statement under oath.'

Kappakas looked at Broderick, whose mouth had dropped open with surprise as he looked around nervously.

'Separate these two. They're not allowed to speak with each other anymore. Officer, take Broderick to my car and wait for me.'

The policeman roused himself and firmly guided Broderick out of the office. The male nurse resisted at first, but thought better of it, as he was already handcuffed. He decided that, under the circumstances, it was best to stay calm and offer his cooperation, so the police would build a case against Santini. He began to think up a strategy to place the blame on her. By cooperating, maybe he'd receive leniency, even if he couldn't completely escape charges.

Chapter 94

Kappakas closely observed Santini. She was trying to play innocent while focusing blame on Broderick. She, in turn, watched Kappakas with more than average interest. It seemed like she even enjoyed the fact that he'd come to the clinic heavily armed with police backup.

'I'm amazed by your behavior, Detective. I didn't expect this. When you were here before, you seemed – to put it mildly – somewhat timid and even irresolute. But maybe you fooled me and those visits were just a soft prelude to this big spectacle.'

'Think what you like, Doctor. I'm dealing with a couple of serious crimes, and I advise you to match your tone with the seriousness of the situation.'

'Oh, Inspector, did I hurt your feelings? I promise I'll behave seriously.'

Kappakas had more than enough of the director's mockery and decided to question her right away. He hoped Ellis would call him soon with the results of the examination of Suzie Atchison's stomach contents. 'Please, sit down here. I want to ask a couple of questions, if you'll answer voluntarily without your lawyer present.'

She reacted surprised. 'Ask questions? I hope they're better than last time.'

But she did what Kappakas requested, took a seat and with a haughty look at him, decently crossed her legs.

'What were your intentions with Mrs. Atchison? You said you injected her dosage. What exactly did you give her?'

Santini thought for a second. 'Wouldn't you rather like to know more about the murder of our colleague, Elaine Iskander? It seems much more important to me. But then, you'll need to question Broderick.'

'I'd like some answers from you now.'

Santini shifted uneasily in her chair. She wasn't used to speaking openly to outsiders about her work in the clinic. She coughed lightly and looked seriously at Kappakas. 'Mrs. Atchison is suffering from advanced dementia, Detective. She may not have long to live. The services we provide at St. Luke's aim to make life as agreeable as is socially and medically possible for people with Alzheimer's. We have created a treatment program with special care and attention for these patients. I gave Mrs. Atchison a sedative to relax her before we start her medication.'

'What kind of medication does she get?'

'Mainly dementia-inhibitors, which are very expensive drugs. We work very cautiously.'

'Do you sometimes get packages delivered at the gate?'

'Yes, frequently. Couriers deliver all kinds of things, but especially medicines.'

'Like dementia-inhibitors?'

'Yes.'

'And others?

'What others?'

'Medicine.'

'Ah, diuretic pills, sedatives, blood diluents, cholesterol lowering pills… to name of few.'

Then Kappakas came to the heart of the matter. 'Well, Doctor Santini, who sends you those medicines?'

She hesitated before answering. 'I'm not going to answer any more questions before consulting with my lawyer.'

Kappakas looked intently at her. Santini had the right to legal advice and representation, and he wouldn't risk taking testimony that could be inadmissible in court. 'Certainly, you may call your lawyer.'

'Thank you,' she said artificially friendly. Then she took her phone and called her lawyer. 'Brett, hello, this is Margaret, I need your help right away. I'm being questioned by the police, but I'm not going to say anything until I know you'll represent me. Can you come to the clinic?' She listened to her lawyer's answer and then said, 'Yes, I've been arrested on suspicion and advised of my rights.' She gave Kappakas a confident look, while she heard Brett Hammond say he was available for her. 'I appreciate that very much, Brett. See you soon.' She put her cell phone back in her purse and said to Kappakas, 'My lawyer, Brett Hammond, is on his way here. Perhaps you would like some tea or coffee?'

'Tea, please,' he said and analyzed the Doctor's behavior. Santini was notably calm now and courteous. What struck him most was she'd lost her sarcastic, defiant tone. Kappakas would have to wait for the lawyer to arrive before asking more questions. Margaret Santini was an extraordinary personality, able to quickly "change gears."

'Here you are, Detective, a nice cup of tea. Chocolate?'

'No, thank you.'

She sighed. 'It does take a while, don't you think?'

Kappakas took a sip of his tea, lost in thought for a minute. Then he said, 'Sorry, I didn't hear you.'

'The results of the examination of my patient, Mrs. Atchison. It takes a long time.'

'Oh, yes. If they find something special, it may take a while. Extra tests would be run and a toxicologist consulted.'

Santini pretended to be shocked. 'Oh, but Detective, should I fear the worst now?'

'I don't know, Doctor. It all depends on the results of the tests and your replies to my questions.'

Kappakas' cell phone started to ring. He grabbed it quickly and pushed the answer key. Santini looked on, very interested.

'Kappakas here.' It took a few minutes before Ellis had told him all the facts. 'Thanks,' he said softly, but loud enough for Santini to hear it. He broke the connection and sensed Santini had followed the conversation with a self-satisfied look on her face. When he looked at her again, he saw the woman he'd met before - with the tight vicious smile. He coughed and said, 'Uh..., you know, I can't give you any information, this was a confidential conversation.'

Santini's eyes shone. She knew better. 'Doesn't matter, Detective. As you said yourself, in your work you can't just take things at face value. Well, now we can proceed with the patient's treatment. It's a good thing we gave her a sedative, or she might have become very upset by all this fuss.'

Kappakas kept silent and thought about continuing the interrogation in the presence of a lawyer. His reflections were interrupted when Santini held out her arms to him.

'You may unlock them now, they're starting to hurt.'

'As long as you stay here and don't do anything foolish.'

Santini looked indignant, but her smile betrayed her. 'Me? I'm content to wait here for my lawyer.'

Kappakas forced a smile and unlocked the cuffs.

'That's better; now all we can do is wait,' Santini said, and sat down calmly.

Half an hour later, Ellis returned to the clinic. Kappakas asked one of the policemen to keep an eye on Santini so he could consult his assistant in the corridor.

'Ellis, what's going on?'

She appeared downcast and pointed at an empty room diagonally across from Santini's office. 'Let's talk over there. I have some bad news, I'm afraid.'

They were barely inside the room when Kappakas asked, 'What's wrong? You look shaken.'

'Kappa,' she said urgently. 'There are foreign substances in Suzie's stomach. A toxicologist discovered two different ones, and a large dose of them could be deadly. She will stay in the hospital for observation for the time being.'

Before Kappakas could say anything, Ellis continued, 'I couldn't tell you on the phone. I was afraid your reaction might influence Santini.'

'What do you mean? I have her where I want her. She asked for a lawyer.'

'What? Then, I'm glad I didn't say anything. She would probably clam up and refuse to answer any more of your questions.'

'Okay, considering this case is so complex, I understand your choice not to tell me the facts. It was a smart move to leave me in the dark. Now I can convey your information to her later with better results. She behaved matter-of-factly, because earlier she'd told me she only gave a sedative to Mrs. Atchison.'

Ellis had a thought. 'This could also mean she doesn't know what meds Suzie got.'

'Possibly; I won't exclude anything at the moment. We haven't got a lot of evidence yet, but I think we've made progress. When I asked who supplied her with the medicines, she refused to say another word without her lawyer. By the way, according to Santini, he should be here any minute.'

'Can we handle all this here, Kappa?'

'Good thinking. We really should do the questioning at the police station. Don't forget Broderick has been waiting for me for some time now.'

'Where is he, by the way?'

'In the police car at the front gate. The other officer is keeping an eye on him.'

'When I arrived there was no police car there.'

Kappakas' jaw dropped in surprise. 'Has Broderick been taken to the station already?'

'Possibly, why not call Matarazo?' she asked.

Kappakas agreed and phoned the station. He got the officer at the desk. 'Detective Kappakas here. Has a handcuffed suspect been brought in? His name is Broderick.'

'Just checking; hold the line, please.'

Ellis gave Kappakas a curious look.

'He's checking,' he whispered.

After thirty seconds the officer was back on the line and said, 'We put this guy in a holding cell. He started to act up when he was driven to the station. Come on in and you'll hear all about it.'

After Kappakas had hung up, he couldn't suppress a smile. 'You know Ellis, I think Mr. Broderick is going to make a confession very soon.' He made another call. Matarazo promised to prepare two interrogation rooms. You never know where you stand with the Naples' Police Chief, he thought.

Chapter 96

Santini sat in an interrogation room on the third floor of the police station. She could be heard over the intercom in an observation room and watched through one-way glass. Matarazo wanted one of his detectives in the room, but Kappakas refused. He wanted to follow his own agenda, not Matarazo's. Instead, two plainclothes officers were assigned to him. If necessary, they could provide physical protection. Although Kappakas was eager to solve the Iskander case, he was also patient. He first let Broderick simmer in his cell and reflect on his situation.

'It's a nice room, Kappa. I guess the interviews are being recorded?' Ellis asked.

'Yes, also filmed. If necessary, I can use Santini's and her lawyer's facial expressions to confront them later.'

'Has Santini's lawyer arrived yet?'

'He's waiting downstairs in the reception room.'

'Should I go get him?'

'Let's both go.'

Brett Hammond was in his forties and appeared to be a successful lawyer; well dressed in a dark suit, leather briefcase, Rolex on his wrist, neatly combed-back black hair and a Texan accent. Of course this last characteristic is not typical of his profession, particularly in Florida, but it added a dimension to the relationship between client and attorney. Kappakas shook Hammond's hand, and was led to the interrogation room. The defense counsel whispered some legal advice into Santini's ear and then turned to Kappakas.

'Detective, I'd like to speak with my client in private first. I want to be fully informed, so we can proceed competently with this interview.'

'Of course, let me know when you're ready.'

Kappakas and Ellis left the room and stood before the one-way glass. Hammond had switched off the microphone and shut the blinds, so no one could hear or see him and Santini.

'Any careful lawyer would do that when they're alone with their clients. Privacy in the attorney-client privilege is a basic right,' Kappakas said.

'Do you already have an interview strategy?'

'First, I always wait and see what the lawyer has to say. But in this case I must learn the name of the supplier of the medicines. In general,

I prefer not to run ahead of things in an interrogation. It's better to go slow and leave open quiet spaces for the suspect or attorney to fill with comments. It's a mistake for police to be overconfident of the facts or prejudiced, thinking they know all the answers before the suspect has even reacted.'

'But you expect her to mention Larkin; who else could it be?'

'Yes, but interrogations sometimes take an unexpected turn. And it's usually not in the direction you want to go.'

Ellis checked her watch and said, 'They're taking a lot of time.' She was itching to witness her first official police questioning. It was especially exciting because so many interests were at stake. In Santini's case, she expected a breakthrough.

Hammond turned on the intercom, and said they were ready to begin. Ellis wasn't certain what was going to happen as she returned to the room with Kappakas. Hammond was the first to speak, exactly as Kappakas predicted. 'My client and I object to the presence of Ms. Henning during the interrogation.'

Ellis looked surprised but waited for Kappakas to reply. 'I understand that in some states journalists are not allowed to be present at interrogations. But Ms. Henning is not only a research journalist, she's also my assistant. Without her help, I can't do as much in this case.'

Hammond didn't feel like having a lengthy discussion on the subject and said firmly, 'Detective, I'm sorry, but I want my client's rights to be respected.' The lawyer gave Kappakas a stony look.

'Of course, I understand. Ellis, you'll have to leave.'

'Do I have to?'

'Yes, Mr. Hammond decided to assert his client's rights, and we must comply.'

Disappointed, she left the room and stood behind the one-way glass. Kappakas opened his notebook, turned on the loudspeaker, pushed the button of the microphone for the tape-recording and opened the blinds. The officers stood by in the corners.

'Start interrogation at 11:45 A.M. of Dr. Santini, Director of St. Luke's Clinic in Naples, Florida,' Kappakas spoke gravely in the microphone. 'Dr. Santini is represented by her legal counsel, Mr. Brett Hammond.'

Santini looked quietly confident as the introductory formalities were completed.

'Dr. Santini, we'll continue the questioning that we began at the clinic earlier today. The interrogation is now official, which means anything you say can be used against you in court. But I assume Mr. Hammond has already pointed this out to you.'

A slight nod of the head was all Santini was prepared to give.

'Dr. Santini, do you understand? I need a verbal response for the record.'

'Yes, I understand.'

Chapter 97

'Fine. My last question was, who is the supplier of your medicines? At that moment, you claimed your right to remain silent and first wanted to consult your lawyer. By now you've been able to ask his advice, so I'd like you to answer my question.'

Santini looked at her lawyer. Hammond said, 'Detective, my client claims her Fifth Amendment right to remain silent and won't answer your question.'

Kappakas sighed. He had more or less expected this. 'Well, that's too bad. You'd do yourself a favor by telling me his name.'

Santini didn't move a muscle and kept staring self-assuredly at Kappakas.

'Otherwise I can come up with a name of someone who delivered illegal drugs to you.'

'You're bluffing, Detective. You know nothing at all,' Santini said acidly.

'Does the name Josh Larkin mean anything to you?'

Santini answered stoically. 'Never heard of him. You're just making things up.'

'You maintain you never heard of a Mr. Larkin?'

'Yes; you should have your ears checked, Detective. I already told you I don't know that name.'

Kappakas kept silent for a few seconds, looking concerned. 'Doctor, have you ever heard the name Mike Garcia?'

Santini turned to her lawyer and said, 'Brett, this name game is annoying me. Could we stop it?' Hammond said nothing because he knew police detectives are usually well informed about names and facts about suspects, who themselves are usually in a phase of denying everything, hoping to get off the hook.

'Mike Garcia was a courier for Mr. Larkin. He made at least eight trips from San Antonio, Texas to Naples, transporting packages of illegal medicines to Mr. Larkin. Recently Garcia delivered medicine from Mr. Larkin directly to your clinic.'

Santini looked questioningly at her lawyer.

Kappakas continued, 'What were these medicines for?'

'Um…, for a special health program.'

'What's the purpose of this program?'

'Patients with advanced Alzheimer's disease receive individual care and special medication to make their lives more bearable.'

'How are these medicines administered, intravenously? I saw you using a needle on Mrs. Atchison this morning.'

'That's right; the pills are liquefied and injected into the brachial artery. But it's completely without risk. Your assistant already indicated that nothing suspicious was found in her stomach at the hospital.'

'Did my assistant tell you this?'

'No, not directly. She called you from the hospital when you were with me at the clinic, remember? I could tell from your face it was false alarm.'

Kappakas got down to business. Now it was his turn to give her some advice. 'Doctor Santini, you're not very good at reading faces. How about taking some lessons?' He saw Hammond couldn't suppress a twitch of a smile. Santini stayed motionless, looking in front of her. 'Mrs. Atchisons' stomach contained some poisonous substances. For the time being she's staying in the hospital for observation. You'll understand we take this matter very seriously, Doctor.'

Suddenly Santini became irritated and raised her voice. 'Where did you get this nonsense? You haven't got a shred of evidence against me. Brett, say something.' Hammond was surprised and agreed with his client. 'She's right, inspector. You must provide evidence to support your allegations.'

Lawyers, Kappakas thought. When their clients are in trouble, they push them in even further. Well done, "Mr. Lawyer." I'll give you the proof. 'Mr. Hammond; you must understand that a Jacksonville detective would never accuse someone without evidence.'

'What evidence then?' Hammond didn't know what specific evidence Kappakas was talking about. But the detective turned to his suspect again and said coolly, 'I've inspected your patients' file.'

'What? Inspected our patients' file?' Santini turned her face to her lawyer and grimaced 'hear him?' 'Yes, yes; and I've just won the lottery,' she laughed sardonically.

'A few weeks ago your clinic was burgled,' Kappakas proceeded undisturbed. He leaned back and looked sharply at his suspects. 'Unauthorized persons entered your clinic and stole the patients' file.'

Kappakas saw a condescending look appear on her face.

'Brett, do we have to listen to this nonsense any longer? I think your imagination has run away with you, Detective.'

Kappakas kept silent and looked her straight in the eye. Santini felt obliged to say something. 'Why are you playing games? I had the file in my hands this morning and made notes in it.' She looked triumphantly at her lawyer, who now was curious to hear what Kappakas had to say to this.

'Doctor, we only play games in our spare time,' he said as he pulled some photos from his inside pocket. He put them on the table and shoved them right under her eyes. 'Do you recognize these photographs?'

Santini's expression changed. Her mouth fell open, her pupils dilated and her face turned pale. 'How on earth did you get these?'

Kappakas said nothing and kept looking straight at her.

'Brett, these are shots from the patients' file. How is this possible?'

'Detective, I assume you can give us an explanation?' Hammond asked.

'Like I said, there was a break-in at your clinic, and the patients' file was stolen.'

Santini looked desperately at Kappakas. 'Yes, you told me, but I've written in that file this morning. So, again, how is this possible? When exactly was it stolen, and how did you get these photos?'

Brett Hammond touched his client's arm to indicate she should calm down and that he wanted to speak. 'I want to ask two questions, Detective. Why haven't you informed my client about this theft? And, we'd like to know who the thieves are.'

'These questions are easily answered, Mr. Hammond. When I had a conversation with your client at the clinic for the second time, the file had already been stolen. Your client, however, didn't report it to the police, but she did report that Ms. Iskander was missing. I can't judge what is important to someone and what isn't, but your client had the opportunity to mention the missing file. As to your second question; the file was taken by Mike Garcia and Ellis Henning.'

'Well, that's interesting,' Santini said indignantly. 'So you're working together with a thief?'

Kappakas shrugged his shoulders. 'You didn't report the missing file, so we can't hold Garcia and Henning responsible for a theft.'

'This is crazy! Hammond, say something!'

Kappakas maintained control. 'Now, listen good. The file is in your possession. Who gave it back to you?'

'Why ask me? You think you know everything,' Santini retorted.

'Absolutely. Our job, Doctor, is to find out things, learn relevant names and connect things. Is the name Larkin familiar to you?'

'You already asked. I'm not falling for that.'

'Okay. In any case, you can no longer administer that "special treatment program," or whatever you call it. We've taken measures to prevent that.'

Santini kept insisting on prosecuting the two thieves. The lawyer was somewhat confused, but as far as he knew, legal action against the thieves was not possible.

'Um..., Margaret, you have – as you stated yourself – the patients' file in your possession now and you didn't report it missing. There's nothing we can do about it now.'

Chapter 98

With a satisfied expression, Kappakas watched the two opposite him. This was a done deal. Now he could move on to phase two of his interrogation. There was a knock on the door. Ellis stuck her head in and said she had to speak to Kappakas. He apologized and left the room. Santini took the opportunity to lecture her lawyer.

'You must do something, dammit, Brett! My clinic gets burgled and you're simply going to accept that? That cop's little helpers should be charged, but I don't hear you say that. I get the feeling you're not worth your fat fee.'

Hammond didn't get the chance to defend himself because Kappakas returned. He looked gloomy. After sitting down, he folded his hands and seemed to think about what he was going to say. 'Doctor Santini, I've received some bad news from the hospital lab. The laboratory examination of Mrs. Atchison's stomach contents confirms the presence of poisonous substances. Those substances come from medicines documented in your patients' file, diuretic pills and MPC-4 anti-rheumatic drugs.'

'I don't know what you're talking about.'

'You have liquefied expired drugs, condemned pills, and administered them intravenously to Mrs. Atchison.'

'That's absolute nonsense. What are these assumptions based on?'

'This morning you were standing right in front of me with the needle in your hand. You lied when you said you had used it to inject a sedative.'

Brett Hammond began to shift uneasily in his chair. Santini had not given him all the facts. Kappakas increased the pressure and tried to break her down.

'Why did you give your patients these medicines? As I said, we've discovered the names of these drugs in your patients' file.'

Santini was taken aback. She looked straight ahead and shook her head. Kappakas went for the kill. 'I will tell you. You poisoned them so they died prematurely. Then you removed the unaffected and intact vital organs to sell them for a lot of money to the highest bidder.'

'No, no!' she insisted, on the verge of tears. 'What a horrible allegation!'

'You think so? How do you explain the fact that all useful organs were removed from the Erikssons?'

'What? Who?'

'Mr. and Mrs. Eriksson. You buried them yourself. Father Raymond D'Angelico was present and can confirm this.'

Santini's mind reeled. Her lawyer was at a loss what to say because he hadn't been aware of these terrible events. As the accusations against his client began to mount, he gave Santini some standard advice. 'Margaret, I advise you not to answer any more questions.'

Kappakas shifted his focus to Hammond. 'Mr. Hammond, I understand you want to protect your client, but I strongly advise you to allow her to be open about these accusations.'

'What? I've heard no formal accusation yet.'

Lawyers always want everything to be formalized precisely, Kappakas thought. 'How about poisoning patients and removing their organs? Also, she murdered or was an accomplice to the murder of Elaine Iskander. If you want me to express these charges even more concretely, I'll do it for you. But I seriously doubt if it will help your client.'

Santini looked dismayed and seemed no more than a shadow of the former proud and confident Director of St. Luke's Clinic. Kappakas began to pressure her again.

'I urge you to speak up now. You will make things worse for yourself if you don't.'

She shrugged her shoulders. Inside her a battle was going on between her character traits and the deeper layers of her soul. Was she capable of surrendering to humility and humanity? Could she help herself by stepping into a different world and adopting a vulnerable attitude?

'If you say nothing, you'll be charged with murder and illegal harvesting and sale of human organs. You'll face a life sentence or even death by lethal injection, an ironic penalty for you. But you're no hardened killer, are you? You're a professional physician and the proud Director of a medical institution, who maybe is a little too eager to help her patients, at any cost, right?'

Finally the penny dropped and Hammond said, 'You can tell your story, Margaret. That's better than the prospect of life imprisonment or a death sentence.'

For the first time in a long while she looked at Kappakas again. Apparently the inner fight was decided in favor of acknowledging her failure. 'I've always acted in good conscience, Detective. St. Luke's is a small, specialized clinic and has been deprived of funding due to the recent economic crisis. When I came to work here, raising funds was one of my tasks. Lately, not a single party has been willing to invest in developing cures for Alzheimer's. To be able to offer high-quality care, we found an agent prepared to supply cheaper medicines. I knew they were past their expiration dates, but I took the risk in the interest of our patients. I had no idea they were so bad that our patients would be poisoned by them.'

Kappakas noticed Santini had become a lot calmer as she defended herself. So he tried it again. 'This agent, is it Mr. Larkin?'

Santini nodded timidly. 'Yes,' she said softly.

Chapter 99

Kappakas chose not to dwell on the fact she had lied. 'How did you get into contact with Larkin?'

'Originally he only worked with Mark Peterson, Director of SocHom, who unfortunately died recently. He knew which residents were demented and could be referred to us. Maybe Larkin didn't want to do business with the clinic directly. Peterson strictly forbade me to approach Larkin myself. But after Mark died, I had to call Larkin anyway, however much he disliked it. I only wanted to know when a supply of meds was due again.'

'What kind of medicines did Peterson and Larkin offer you?'

'Dementia-inhibitors, diuretic and anti-rheumatic pills and some ordinary medicines. In the final stages of dementia, we always administer the drugs by injection, because we aren't sure the patients always swallow their solid pills, or aren't able to swallow them.'

Kappakas nodded. 'Yes, these are the medicines that are mentioned in the patients' file. How did the delivery and payment take place?'

'The deliveries were done through couriers, often first to Peterson, who then supplied us, and later through Larkin. The last time, a Mexican courier made his delivery directly at the clinic. I've never paid for them myself. Payments were always made by the Director of SocHom, Mark Peterson, and I reimbursed SocHom'

'Right. This Mr. Larkin. Where can we find him?'

'No idea. Really. He'll be somewhere in Naples. I don't have his address. Everything was done by phone, often in coded language. He always called me. The talks were short, maybe because he was afraid of being tapped.'

Kappakas thought for a moment. The name of Sykes, the undertaker, who'd suddenly ran away, went through his head. 'Where are the deceased patients buried or cremated?'

'At Crest Lawn. It's near the clinic. It's an old, somewhat desolate cemetery.'

'Earlier you said the deceased patients can be buried or cremated anywhere in the country…'

'Um…, yes, that's right. But we arrange the burial here when people have no relatives.

'And why no cremations?'

'Yes, that's odd. I never gave it a moment's thought. Maybe because of religious convictions? I can't give you a definite answer to that.'

'Who arranges preparation and burial? I mean, do you have a regular undertaker?'

'Yes, Sykes Funeral Home always takes care of it all.'

'Jim Sykes?'

She nodded. Kappakas was surprised Santini was so open now. Her earlier arrogance had given way to candid, thoughtful consideration. But then, the accusations were serious and she still had a long way to go.

'Doctor Santini, I have to say it surprises me that you are answering me so frankly and unhesitatingly. I've never seen you like this before.'

Santini was seemingly unimpressed by his words. However, an expert in facial expressions might have observed a slightly satisfied smile around her mouth.

'Now I get to a crucial point: as part of our investigation we exhumed the bodies of Mr. and Mrs. Eriksson.'

Santini's eyes opened wide with fear.

'They've been examined by a pathologist for poison in the stomach. However, the pathologist made a shocking discovery. The heart, liver, pancreas, lungs and certain other organs had been removed from both bodies.'

'Oh, my God!' Santini cried, putting a hand to her mouth. 'How terrible!' Shivers ran down Brett Hammond's spine.

Kappakas ignored the reaction. 'This is what we call illegal organ harvesting. What do you have to say about this?'

Santini's calmness had vanished and she began to tremble and stammer. Her lawyer was forced to take a stand against this allegation, which was in fact a direct insult. 'Inspector, how dare you accuse my client of such infamous and morbid behavior? I demand that you ask only questions and don't jump to conclusions.'

Kappakas quickly nodded to Hammond and humored him. 'Doctor Santini, are you in any way involved in the removal of organs or having them removed by others?'

'No! I've had absolutely nothing to do with that!' she insisted with some reproach in her tone.

'Seems clear enough to me. Larkin perhaps?'

'Larkin? You mean he did this to our deceased patients?'

'Is it possible?'

She rolled her eyes. 'Is it possible? Yes, anything is possible. I really don't know. I've never heard him talk about it or expected it.'

'You just said Larkin always phoned you. Do you happen to have his number?'

'Uh…, yes,' she answered unsurely.

'I'd like to have that number.'

'What do you want to do with it?'

'It may be useful in our investigation.'

Santini became suspicious. 'What's your plan, Detective? If you wish to go after Larkin, I want to have nothing to do with that. I only know him as an agent. I have no idea what other things he's involved in.'

'I promise you'll be kept out of it. At least, if you tell the truth. But I suspect you'd very much like to know if he's really in the illegal organ trade, right?'

'The mere thought horrifies me. Of course I want to know who violates our dead and uses them for some miserable business.'

Kappakas rubbed a hand across his chin. He waited a few moments and then said, 'Alright, you've made your point. There's one more question I'd like to ask. I came to Naples to find Elaine Iskander. Now this seems to be overshadowed by other suspicious circumstances inside and outside your clinic. This morning you accused George Broderick of the murder on Elaine Iskander. Can you prove that?'

Santini looked defiantly at Kappakas. 'Hmm…, yes, I think I can,' she answered hesitatingly, while swiftly looking at her lawyer. Hammond nodded reassuringly to indicate she could tell her story.

'He came to me totally upset, even crying, and said he'd killed Elaine. First I couldn't believe him, but that didn't last long, because I've never known Broderick to make sick jokes. He said he had caught her investigating the medicine boxes of medicines in the trash bins. Broderick thought she'd discovered the secret of the illegal drug deliveries, which he thought he had to cover up.'

It was as if a heavy weight had fallen of Dr. Margaret Santini's shoulders. She spoke extensively about Broderick's motives and the facts around the murder of her former employee. Oddly enough she didn't shy away from revealing her own role. She was clearly trying to minimize her sentence by giving full cooperation. 'I was completely at a loss what to do with the body, so I asked Sykes to come and collect it.'

'And did Sykes do that?' Kappakas asked.

'Yes, later that evening he came in his hearse and picked up the body at the backdoor. Two days later it was buried.'

'Are you absolutely sure?'

She thought for a moment. 'You mean; do I know if she was in the coffin?'

Kappakas nodded.

'No.'

Chapter 100

Ellis had only one question to ask; was it time to question George Broderick? It was Kappakas' mission, his commitment, his promise to John Iskander, to find out what happened to his daughter Elaine. Finding the answer to that question was the object of his original investigation. He'd asked Santini, and she'd disclosed a likely scenario. She denied having any responsibility for Elaine's death, but admitted to being an accomplice after-the-fact. One thing was sure now; a crime had been committed. If Iskander were still alive, by now she would have been spotted somewhere, or turned up at home or at work. Ellis thought now was the time to nail down the Iskander case. Santini had identified Broderick as Iskander's murderer. His confession might also be a breakthrough in the solution of the other suspicious matters.

After the questioning of Margaret Santini, Kappakas went to Matarazo's office to report to him. When he returned to the interrogation room, Ellis was waiting for him. She looked doubtfully at Kappakas. 'You know a lot about Santini now, but what exactly do you know about Broderick?'

'You're right. Not much, really. But now that's going to change, if I have anything to do with it. I requisitioned his gun and had it checked by the police lab. It may sound odd, but yesterday an eye-witness reported himself to Matarazo.'

Ellis frowned and shook her head.

'Yes, I was surprised too,' he continued. 'You'd never guess who this witness is.'

'Kappa, you know I don't like such riddles.'

'Of course. It's Don Atchison. From his room he saw Broderick walk outside. He didn't hear any gunshots, according to Matarazo, probably because Broderick used a silencer.'

'Do you trust Matarazo? If I were you, I'd speak with Atchison myself.'

'I trust him, and I think we may have been wrong when we pictured him as an evil genius. He seems to support this investigation; and as far as I know, he has no hidden agenda.'

'We'll see about that. I'm still skeptical. After all, in my profession, I must always distrust people until I'm satisfied with corroborating evidence or testimony.'

'Would you like some more water?'

'No, thanks…. When are we going to question Broderick?'

'In an hour. Matarazo will join me.'

'No; why?'

'We mustn't condemn the Chief. This is a case in his jurisdiction, and he must be involved in the case. Then he won't be able to butter his bread on both sides, so to speak, assuming he'd wanted to.'

She left it at that and changed the subject. 'Have you eaten already?'

'Haven't had time for it.'

'Like a sandwich?'

'Yes, good. And a pot of coffee, I really want coffee!'`

Chapter 101

When Kappakas entered the interrogation room, preparing himself to question George Broderick, Dick Matarazo was already there. 'You're late, Detective.'

'Blame it on your wonderful, well-stocked vending machines, Chief.'

'Was the coffee okay?'

'Okay? I took three cups. This is the best coffee I've ever tasted at a police station. In Jacksonville they make dark dishwater.'

Matarazo chuckled.

'Well Chief, I'd like to pay Larkin a visit. Do you have…?'

Matarazo interrupted him. 'When you say it like that, I suppose you mean you want to burst in on him and cause a ruckus?'

Kappakas smiled. 'Well, I'm more in favor of the soft approach. This is not Chicago or Detroit, is it? But seriously, do you happen to know where I can find him?'

Matarazo was on his guard now. 'Somewhere in an industrial park in Naples.'

'Yes, but do you know where exactly?'

Matarazo wasn't ready to say more now, and was much more interested in talking about Broderick. It was about time Kappakas was reminded, that as a guest of the Naples police force, he was subordinate to the Police Chief. The Chief would determine how and when action should be taken. Matarazo looked worried, as if he wanted to share a problem with his colleague.

'Detective; we know a lot about Larkin now, so it's time to act. But we also have an important suspect to question. If Broderick mentions incriminating facts about Larkin, we'll have even more information when we pay Larkin a visit. Then we'll go after him with full force.' He paused a moment, looking at his knuckles. 'Of course I know where he is, but remember I'm in charge of this case. I'm grateful for your help and everything you've done. But I need to decide when we go for it, and I need your cooperation, right? Be sure, I'll do anything necessary to clear up this dirty business once and for all.'

'Yes, I see. When have you planned the briefing for the raid?'

'As soon as we've finished with Broderick.'

'Fine, let them bring him in.'

Matarazo ordered a police officer to get Broderick from his cell.

Chapter 102

George Broderick looked tired. He trudged into the interrogation room and sat down in the wrong chair.

'Please sit over here, Mr. Broderick,' Matarazo said and showed him his place. The nurse dragged himself to the chair and looked around hazily. Matarazo and Kappakas were sitting in front of him. For security reasons a policeman was standing behind Broderick.

Matarazo began. 'Mr. Broderick, how do you like your cell? I can imagine you'd much rather be drugging patients with condemned medicines now, am I right?'

The nurse seemed unimpressed and kept silent.

'Why didn't you want a lawyer to assist you?'

He shrugged his shoulders. 'What difference does it make? You're going to condemn me anyway.'

'Well, actually, it makes a lot of difference. This interview is being recorded. Anything you say during an interrogation can be used against you in a court of law. You have a right to an attorney. If you can't afford one, the court will appoint one to represent you. Now, would you like to consult an attorney?'

Again Broderick shrugged indifferently.

'Right, Mr. Broderick, speak up. It's necessary to record your vocal agreement to waive your rights to counsel and your agreement that you are giving us answers under your own free will, okay?'

'Yes, okay.'

'Why did you kill Ms. Elaine Iskander?' Matarazo fired his first question. Kappakas tried to hide his surprise. He never would have used such an aggressive interrogation style. But here in Naples, Matarazo ran the show, so Kappakas had to play second fiddle during the questioning.

Broderick didn't even try to show any indignation. 'I'm not saying anything,' he said calmly.

'I can understand that. If I'd killed someone, I'd keep my mouth shut too.'

Broderick remained silent.

'Are you keeping quiet because you're ashamed of murdering her? Or do you think, I wish I had taken a lawyer; then I wouldn't be in a cold sweat now?'

Once again the male nurse shrugged his shoulders and showed no signs of being impressed.

'Well, Detective, it looks like one-way traffic today.' Matarazo looked confidentially at him.

'Okay,' Kappakas said. 'Then we'll have a quiet afternoon for once.'

Matarazo shook his head and looked concerned. 'That doesn't apply to our friend here. Your boss, Mr. Broderick, pointed you out as the murderer and she just said she will repeat her testimony under oath in court. You can play hide and seek as much as you like, but it won't make your sentence any lighter.'

'She's lying.'

'Well, you can talk after all. So, she's lying. I'll tell you something!' he said threateningly, slowly bending forward to intimidate Broderick. 'You are the one that's lying. We have a witness. He saw you the night of the murder.'

Broderick seemed shocked when a witness was mentioned. 'That's impossible! It was dark and...' He stopped abruptly and put a hand over his mouth.

Matarazo felt Broderick was about to break and pressed on. 'Yes? It was dark and you walked outside with the pistol and saw Elaine Iskander snooping around the garbage shed.'

Broderick began to shake his head. Matarazo proceeded, 'When you noticed she had packaging from the illegal medicines in her hands, you blew a fuse.'

'No..., no!' Broderick said loudly.

'You wanted to keep those illegal med's under cover at all costs. However, Elaine Iskander discovered the secret and had to be silenced, so you and Doctor Santini could go on doing your dirty medicine business.'

Broderick already had muttered objections a couple of times and was shifting around on his chair in agitation. The officer standing behind him watched closely in case he jumped up.

'Lies, all lies! I'm not saying another word.'

Matarazo turned to Kappakas. 'Detective, I think we should call Larkin.'

Suddenly Broderick's attitude changed and he stammered confusedly, 'Hey? Wh-wha-what?'

Matarazo ignored Broderick and continued his conversation with Kappakas. 'We could tell Larkin someone shot an innocent woman.'

Broderick's eyes widened and rolled around. He panicked.

'Yes, and I think Mr. Larkin won't like it. His position has been compromised by Iskander's death. He's going to take revenge.'

'Stop it! Shut up! I..., I...,' Broderick despaired.

Matarazo turned to his suspect again. 'Yes, Mr. Broderick? You want to say something?'

'I..., aah.... No! Don't tell Larkin! He'll kill me!'

Matarazo looked at Broderick in mock surprise. 'Now, why would he do that? You may have done him a favor. But, I can also imagine he has no use for you anymore.'

Broderick bowed his head, tears ran down his cheeks. He was about to make a confession. 'You know..., I love my work, the people and the clinic. I have a mission in life, helping others. She – I mean Ms. Iskander – didn't fit into my picture of the clinic. She discovered something that might harm St. Luke's objectives and reputation. I couldn't tolerate that. Yes, I followed her and ... killed her. There was no other way. She didn't respect the clinic's principles and she would have frustrated my work, my mission.' He paused. Then he looked at Matarazo and said, 'Sir, I killed Elaine Iskander.'

It was silent in the interrogation room. Behind the glass, Ellis had to swallow hard to release the tension that had built up in her as she watched and listened. Kappakas was curious to see what Matarazo would do next.

'George Broderick. Now that you've confessed to murdering Elaine Iskander, I want to know what you did with her body. Detective Kappakas is especially interested.'

Kappakas was grateful to Matarazo.

'Sykes Funerals picked her up. That's all I know, honestly.'

Kappakas and Matarazo looked at each other. Kappakas thought swift action was required. Matarazo sensed this too and said, 'Mr. Broderick, I'll have a clerk draft a written statement, repeating your confessions. It will be printed out for you to read and sign. Then you'll return to your cell, pending a hearing. The examining judge will decide if you'll be released on bail and when you must appear in court. I advise you to retain legal representation, a lawyer, or request that the court appoint one.'

Chapter 103

After Broderick had been taken to his cell, Kappakas said to Matarazo, 'You managed that pretty fast, Chief. My compliments.'

'Well, I think that in this case the interview tactics had to be adjusted.'

Is Matarazo also a psychologist? Kappakas wondered. 'Yes, I think he needs help to reconcile his personality with reality.'

'Listen; we have enough evidence to bring in Larkin. We must raid his place soon and round up his organization. But first I have to make a confession.'

Kappakas was all ears.

'We've been working on exposing Larkin's activities and dealings for a long time. Up to now I didn't have enough evidence to get him behind bars. I posed as a "crooked cop"; a cop who gives Larkin protection for money. You know of course what I mean. That's how he could do what he wanted, up to now. This bothers me a lot; he was able to continue his shady business without me lifting a finger to stop it, and that resulted in more victims. But I was in a tough spot. I needed good, strong evidence to clean things up in one swift action. We can run him in now for several serious criminal offenses. Sorry I couldn't tell you earlier. I wanted certainty before confiding in you. That's why I sent my men to keep an eye on you. I did it to convince Larkin he could trust me and I would protect him.'

Kappakas had calmly listened to the Chief's explanation and wasn't all that impressed by it. He conjured up a smile and said, 'Chief, we use methods like that in Jacksonville too. And I always gave you the benefit of the doubt. But I have a question: does Larkin fully trust you? I mean, is he playing you? Is he on to you?'

'Well, you never know. I'm sure he believes I'm really a crooked cop.'

Kappakas thought for a moment and said, 'I suggest we make a plan to capture and arrest him. His criminal activities must be stopped as soon as possible.'

Matarazo agreed and all afternoon the two men worked on a plan for Larkin's arrest.

Chapter 104

The twelve members of the arrest team were well aware of the seriousness of the operation. They had just been briefed about the planned arrest of Josh Larkin and his henchmen. The men and women were ready, practically straining at the leash to go do the job. The motivation to finally get a big criminal behind bars was stronger than the fear of risks involved in the action.

The energy released in the team was easy to explain. They really got wound up when Matarazo told them what sort of person Larkin was and what crimes Larkin & Co. were suspected of committing. While they listened, there was an unnatural silence, while most of the team's faces showed their disgust. That someone in peaceful and sunny Naples was capable of such things, was almost beyond the comprehension of the men and women in the force. The moment the Police Chief put his plan on the table, the tension in the team was released. Kappakas took stock of the situation and couldn't remember ever experiencing such enthusiasm among the police officers in Jacksonville. After Matarazo finished and the murmurs of the team died down, he stepped up to Kappakas, who was sitting in a corner of the room.

'They're ready to go for it, Detective. How about you? You look a little concerned.'

'I hope our plan works.'

'Come on. Don't be pessimistic. You know actions like these always involve risks. But as you see, our team is motivated. We're going to pull this off.'

'Yes. There seems to be a good plan,' Kappakas agreed. 'We've gone over the operation again and again. If everyone does what they're supposed to do, things shouldn't go wrong. But you never know; people make mistakes.'

Matarazo, in his heart of hearts, agreed. Mistakes could upset the plan.

Chapter 105

Ellis picked up her phone. She lay stretched out on her hotel bed after a long day of interrogations and a lot of waiting around. She was more than ever convinced she had a great story in her hands. Kappakas got permission to take her along in the police van, so she could follow the operation from close by, but out of the line of fire.

She hadn't heard Jake's voice for several days now. 'Hi, this is me. How are you doing?' she asked.

'Fine. I just finished my work.'

'Yes? Since when?'

'Yesterday; the job is done. But I've been offered another job.'

'Okay.'

'And how's Mike?'

'Mike's alright, I think. He left us a while ago when his girlfriend was threatened.'

'And old grumpy Kapkus, how's he?'

'You mean Kappakas. Oh, well, he's sweet, and a smart detective. I'll tell you all about it later.'

'How's the big story coming?'

'Good, I'm already working out my story and stuff like that.'

'Well, I think I get the picture. As usual I have to wait till your article is published. A secretive one, you are. But promise to give me a preview as soon as it's all over.'

'Yes, I will.'

They said goodbye and they hoped to see each other again soon. Ellis put down her phone and stared at the ceiling. Her thoughts didn't go back to Jake, but to Kappakas, who would have to break the bad news to Elaine's father. Probably John Iskander had already resigned himself to the likelihood that his daughter wouldn't come back. Slowly she was overcome by fatigue, which prevented her from thinking clearly any longer. She surrendered to it and fell asleep.

The following morning Ellis woke up invigorated. Although she'd had some bizarre dreams about gravediggers and body snatchers, she was sitting cheerfully at a table in the hotel breakfast room, thinking she was ready to witness the end of Naples' illegal medicine and organ trade. She had just poured herself an orange juice when her phone began to vibrate. She answered the call.

'This is Downtown Hospital. Do you have a moment, please? I'm going to put you through.'

'Yes, Dr. Gibson here. Am I speaking to Ellis Henning?'

'Yes, that's right.'

'I called to say that the patient was just picked up.'

Ellis didn't know what to make of this statement. 'Which patient?' she asked, surprised.

'Mrs. Atchison, Suzie Atchison. It seemed a good idea to call you.'

Suddenly, alarm bells started ringing in her head. 'Doctor, who picked her up?'

'One of the police officers; he said he had to take her back to the clinic at your request. You know what this is about, I assume?'

She began to stammer. 'Uh, y-yes of course. Thanks for your call.'

She jumped to her feet and rushed out of the breakfast room, while some of the guests watched curiously. On her way to the elevator she called Kappakas. He didn't answer.

'Hell,' she swore. In the elevator she tried to contact Kappakas again. When she heard his voice-mail, she left a quick message. 'Kappa. I was just called by Dr. Gibson at the hospital where Suzie Atchison was examined. He told me she'd been picked up by a police officer. I fear the worst. Call me back.'

After she'd stepped out of the elevator, she ran to her room. She grabbed a few things and left. She hoped Kappakas was having breakfast. She started her car and drove to the Ramada Hotel at high speed. She parked her car right in front of the entrance. Her phone rang.

'Kappa here; I'm in my room. See you in a minute.'

She ran into the lobby and gave her car keys to a receptionist. 'Police,' she lied. 'If my car is in the way, feel free to move it. I have to speak with someone here urgently.' Before the surprised receptionist could answer, Ellis disappeared into the elevator. When Kappakas opened the door of his room, Ellis rushed in.

'Kappa, they must have Suzie,' she gasped. 'Larkin has Suzie!'

Kappakas told her to take it easy and sit down. He poured her a cup of coffee and said, 'Tell me what that Doctor said exactly.'

She took a few large swigs and looked at him with concern. 'I was having breakfast when I got the call from Downtown Hospital. I was put through to Dr. Gibson, and he told me I had given the order to pick up Suzie. He said a police officer had come and was taking her to the clinic.'

'Alright; let's first call Downtown to check out this story. We can't be too careful.'

Ellis nodded. In her heart, she hoped there was no Dr. Gibson and someone had played a sick joke on her. But who? Kappakas phoned the hospital and after a few moments on hold, got Dr. Gibson on the line. 'Can you tell me what the policeman looked like, Doctor?'

'Well, yes, he was tall and broad-shouldered. He looked like a bar room bouncer to me. But the uniform fit him like a glove and he was very polite. I had no idea he could be an imposter. Did we make a mistake?'

'It can be tricky when a person poses as someone else. Did you ask for his ID?'

'Yes, definitely; that's policy here. Everyone must identify themselves.'

'Well, thank you for your phone call; now we can work on it.'

'I hope I haven't got Mrs. Atchison into trouble. That would be very bad.'

'Don't worry, Doctor. We've been on this for some time. Thanks for talking to me.'

Kappakas snapped his phone shut and gave Ellis a serious look. 'Larkin; almost for sure. It sounds like one of his guards picked up Suzie. And I'm afraid of what may happen to her. Come on, Ellis, we're calling Matarazo. The raid can't wait till this afternoon. We must do it now.'

Chapter 106

In the car Kappakas called Matarazo and told him about the phone call from the hospital. 'Suzie Atchison is one of Santini's patients. We prevented her from being taken to Larkin. In the hospital, poisonous substances were found in her stomach. She was just recovering from the effects of the drugs when they came to collect her. It looks like she's fallen into Larkin's hands after all. We should go after him at once.'

'I get your point, Detective. But I see no reason to raid him yet. We've planned the operation for this afternoon. Everyone is busy doing other things right now.'

'I hope you understand there's a life at stake here.'

'Yes, but we need to execute our plan. We know a lot of criminals, but we can't just arrest them all to prevent more casualties.'

'Chief, we know what Larkin can do to people. We're so close now. You don't want to have this on your conscience, do you?'

Matarazo laughed. 'That's pretty mean. You know we value every life, and if we can save someone, we do everything we….'

'Glad to hear that. I'm on my way now to check up on Larkin. I expect you and your team within half an hour. See you soon!'

'Detective, this is impossible! Don't do it. Wait!'

Kappakas had already terminated the conversation and decided not to drive to the police station. He drove into Davis Avenue in the direction of the industrial park.

'Aren't you going to the police station?' Ellis asked.

'No. I'm going to try and find Larkin's illegal business as fast as I can. That should force Matarazo to help Suzie. If he doesn't do it, we will, and he loses face.'

'So you know Larkin's whereabouts?'

'The other day I followed one of his guards. He drove into Prospect Avenue and then I lost him. We're going to explore that street and see if we can find him. We've got to do it.'

Near the corner of Prospect, Kappakas stopped and parked his car at a Steak & Ribs restaurant. 'Here, you need a vest if we go in. I also have a pepper spray for you. Keep your gun at hand. We must be prepared for resistance. I give Matarazo another fifteen minutes to come with his troops. If that doesn't happen, I'll go in. You stay in the car for the time being. Okay?'

'You're crazy! You're not going in alone. Why else are you giving me all this stuff?'

'You're not here in any official capacity. You're not authorized to enter a crime scene, and if things go wrong, nobody will forgive me.'

'As a matter of fact, I do have quite some experience with criminals and kidnappings, remember?'

'Yes, I know, but wait 'til Matarazo's here. Like I said, I give him another fifteen minutes. I'd blame myself if Suzie got hurt while we're here obediently waiting for the police to arrive.'

'Fine,' Ellis said. 'Let's go.'

Kappakas left the parking space and, after fifty yards turned to the right. They were now in Prospect Ave with its multitude of small and medium-sized companies. 'Larkin should be somewhere near the end of the avenue. At least that's where I last saw his bodyguard. You look to the right, I'll cover the left. Pay special attention to the type of company and the name.'

'How far do you think it is from here to his company?'

'Not sure. Crooks often stay in outdated, inconspicuous buildings, maybe a small warehouse or some kind of garage. Watch carefully.'

Kappakas slowly drove into the street and started to search. 'Look for area's with only a few parked cars. The so-called office is usually at the front.'

They passed several pleasure yacht and supply companies, and some workshops. 'Over there maybe?' Ellis asked.

'I don't think so. Looks too tidy. And look, a few fat Mercedes. Doesn't seem right. I know what kind of car the bodyguard was driving.'

'Tell me then.'

'A Cadillac. You'll recognize one easily.'

They approached Mangrove Business Center, which meant they had almost arrived at the end of the avenue. Kappakas suddenly saw a sign next to the road, which showed the faded letters, NAI. The area just inside the entrance was empty. Hidden behind the entrance fence, among a couple of trees and bushes, was a portable cabin, probably an office. Next to it were two pickup trucks. In the middle area, all kinds of car parts were lying around. About a hundred yards further in, there was a large shed. Near the shed, some containers were placed in the far corner, and a big car was parked there.

'Look, this is just the kind of area where criminals feel at home. It looks like the place where I last saw the Caddy. I think it's parked by the shed. Let's check it out.'

Kappakas steered his car through the open entrance and stopped near the office. He parked under a tree, just out of sight from the windows. 'I'm taking a look inside.'

Ellis gave the detective a surprised look. 'What are you going to do, Kappa? You said you'd wait fifteen minutes. It's dangerous to go in alone.'

'Ellis, I have no choice. I'm a policeman. My job is to catch the crooks and protect potential victims, whenever possible. Suzie Atchison may be inside. I don't know if I can rescue her, but doing nothing won't help her.' He nodded his head to emphasize he wouldn't be stopped.

'Well, be careful,' she said. 'When reinforcements come, I'll call you. Don't answer; just put your cell phone on vibrating alert.'

Kappakas got out of the car and cautiously walked to the small office. He tried to act as naturally as possible and purposely didn't look inside, as he walked to the front door. He looked for a doorbell or knocker, but there weren't any. He took hold of the handle, pushed it down and the door opened. Maybe people trusted each other around here? Kappakas entered a small hall into which a few doors opened. He wanted to announce himself, like a customer in a shop who discovers there's no one around.

'Hello! Is anyone there?' he called.

Kappakas waited a moment but heard nothing.

'Hello, Mr. Larkin, are you here?'

He opened one of the doors and looked into the room. It might be a lunch room. There was a bare wooden table, some chairs and a kitchenette. He looked around and saw a pile of brochures on a counter top. 'NAI – Naples Autoparts Imports' was printed on the cover of the brochures. Kappakas quickly skimmed through one, concluding he was in an actual car parts company. It might be a cover. He called out again to announce himself. Still no answer. Kappakas checked the other doors, and found a small office. Against the wall was a large desk with an armchair behind it. A few more chairs and a steel filing cabinet completed the furnishings. Kappakas gave up his search and walked out of the portable building. On the porch he looked across the back at the large grey shed. It could be used for storing auto parts, he thought.

A black Cadillac was parked in front of the shed. He'd been right after all. The car looked dirty and there were several large dents in the body. When Kappakas reached the shed's big steel sliding door, he could hear voices inside. He tried to understand what was said, but because of the solid construction of the shed, he could only hear dull murmuring. Back on the avenue a truck passed by. The bumps in the road caused the truck's cargo to make a racket. Kappakas took the opportunity to silently slide the heavy door open a little. What he hadn't counted on, however, was that the noise from the truck suddenly became more audible inside the shed.

Chapter 107

'Who's there?' a man shouted, alarmed by the sudden rattling noise. Kappakas froze for a second at the sound of the voice. From the back of the shed, a tall man appeared to size up the situation.

'Detective Kappakas. I'm looking for Mr. Larkin.'

The man came closer and Kappakas thought he recognized him. The build and the face of the very tall man more or less fit the description given him by the receptionist at the Ramada hotel. Hadn't he called himself Steve Zacker and said he had an appointment with me? Kappakas thought.

'What are you doing here, old man? You're not allowed to come here. Are you lost?' Sonny was now standing face to face with Kappakas and looked suspiciously at the detective, who showed his badge.

'Are you Steve or Sonny? You missed your appointment with me at the Ramada, right? Doesn't matter; just tell your boss I want to speak with him, now!'

Sonny's face reddened angrily. He shot a glance at the badge. 'Ah, you're that fucking cop,' he said and pulled a gun from inside his jacket. With his other hand he took out a walky-talky. 'Billy, come here. We have a visitor. You won't guess who.'

Billy arrived quickly.

'Frisk this dee-tek-tiff and take his gun.'

While Billy searched Kappakas, Sonny kept him covered.

'Guys, I'm not here for a fight; I just want to talk to your boss.'

Billy nodded to Sonny. 'Clean.'

'Come on.'

Both bodyguards kept Kappakas covered while they walked to a partitioned space at the back of the shed. Billy knocked on the door, then opened it and forced Kappakas inside. The room looked nothing like the space on the other side. Kappakas was in some kind of laboratory with bright lights, beige wall paneling, three cots and lots of equipment. It looked like some sort of outpatient clinic, but hidden in a desolate, dusty storage shed. At the back of the lab was a metal door with a wheel lock. Behind it a safe or cold storage might be hidden. Two men in white coats studied x-rays which were snapped onto a light box. Kappakas was still adjusting to the surprising situation, when Josh Larkin called him from behind.

'Well, well, isn't this the detective we've been looking for?'

Kappakas turned and looked at the man he'd been hunting for a long time. 'Are you Mr. Larkin?'

'Who else did you expect? 'Larkin sneered. 'What makes you think you can drop in - just like that?'

Kappakas didn't want to give the impression he felt uneasy. 'I won't beat around the bush. I've been informed you've kidnapped Mrs. Atchison from the hospital. I've come to pick her up.'

Larkin gave Kappakas a surprised look. 'You've come to pick up someone? Well, come along then.'

Billy pushed Kappakas to a modular wall which divided the room in two. When he walked behind the wall, he saw a bed with someone in it. Larkin stood beside the bed, looking grimly at the pale grey face of Suzie Atchison. 'Why do you want to take this woman with you? She's sleeping. I don't think we should wake her up.'

'You have no right to keep her. Why is she here?'

Larkin shrugged his shoulders and answered indifferently. 'Well, if you insist, we'll show you what we're going to do with her.'

He snapped his fingers and the two bodyguards took Kappakas to a different room, a sterile lab. The temperature in the room felt like that of a cold storage locker. The size was about twelve by sixteen feet. In the middle hung an opaque plastic curtain, through which the silhouettes of two men were visible. Larkin silently shoved half of the curtain aside. Kappakas saw the men do something with a body. They stood with their backs to Kappakas, so he couldn't quite make out what they were doing. He could see, however, that they wore surgical masks and latex gloves. On a table were various surgical instruments.

'What the hell is going on here!?' Kappakas demanded a little too loudly.

The two men, interrupted in their work, turned around. They looked at Larkin in surprise. They certainly could do without people looking over their shoulders. Larkin nodded and held up a hand to show they had nothing to fear.

'Gentlemen, this is Detective Kappakas. We've been looking for him for a while, and now that he's here of his own free will, we'll shed some light on our wonderful work for him. Go ahead, get back to your work.'

The two men, dressed like surgeons, again concerned themselves with the body on the operating table.

Larkin looked Kappakas straight in the eye. 'Detective; they're about to remove the vital organs of a young Mexican man. We can help a lot of people who urgently need a new heart, liver or some other organ. Without this opportunity, they would only have a short time to live.'

'I call this murder, Larkin. You're crazy. You won't get away with it, you know. We've figured out your gory business, and I've come to put an end to it.'

A nasty smile appeared on Larkin's face. Billy and Sonny's faces hardened and darkened even more.

'Did you hear that, guys? He wants to put an end to it.' Larkin got close to Kappakas and whispered into his ear, 'I think it's you we should finish off. You know too much. What a waste it would be if my clients must die because of a snooping, interfering cop.'

'You know this is criminal. If you stop now, you may get off with life in prison. If you continue, you'll probably be up for a death sentence.'

Larkin sighed and gave Kappakas a scornful look. 'You don't think I can do this work without connections in little old Naples, do you? There are others, friends of yours, who benefit from it too. Billy, cuff him.'

For the first time Kappakas felt frightened. It wasn't the handcuffs that scared him, but Larkin's remark about 'friends'. Did he mean Matarazo and his officers? Various possibilities ran through his mind. Larkin had a point when he said activities like these could take place in Naples, just like in big cities, Detroit or Miami. Miami? He tried to form a picture of Larkin. Was the man from Miami? Maybe things had got too hot for him there and he'd decided to move to Naples, where he met a public servant, who, for enough cash, wouldn't put any obstacles in his way. Or had he found a way to hide himself so well – also from Matarazo – he was able to carry on his macabre business undisturbed among legitimate companies on Prospect Avenue? Kappakas fought off the pain when Billy tightly cuffed his hands behind his back.

'Sorry, Kappakas, you may think you're a smart cop, but you won't get away from me,' Larkin said. He asked one of the men in white to give Kappakas an injection. The man took a needle and pushed it into a vial of liquid. Kappakas desperately hoped his vibrating alert would go off. The fifteen minutes were as good as over. He had to keep Larkin hanging on.

'What are you going to do, Larkin? Kill me and cut me open to sell my organs on the market? Is that what you call a "body parts trading" company?'

Larkin laughed scornfully. 'You know, Kappakas. I never understood policemen's lack of imagination. They really find it hard to understand real life, where people can take care of each other, and contribute to society's welfare.'

'You should have become a social worker, Larkin. But you're not. You're a ruthless criminal, who is quick to kill innocent people for money.'

'Say what you want. You're the one that's in the stand, and I'm your judge.'

Kappakas didn't reply to what Larkin said. 'Shall I name them? The people we know you killed for profit? Mrs. Warakomski, Mark Peterson, that Mexican over there, Mr. and Mrs. Eriksson. And, most disgusting of all, you ripped up Elaine Iskander's body. That's what you did, right? You cut her open and sold her organs to the highest bidder. You know Larkin, you have a twisted mind, that...'

Kappakas got a firm blow against the back of his head. Sonny wouldn't listen any longer and was ready to cut Kappakas into little pieces. Larkin raised his hand. 'Look, Kappakas, this is what happens when you bad-mouth our work. We don't like it.'

The white-garbed man stood behind Kappakas with a full syringe. He was going to stick it through the detective's sleeve when he heard a buzzing sound. Kappakas was dazed by the blow to his head and didn't notice his cell phone. The white coat warned Larkin, who signaled Billy to check what caused the sound. Billy searched Kappakas' pockets and found the phone. The buzzing had stopped. Billy handed it to Larkin.

'They still want to contact you, Kappakas. But you won't answer.' He opened the phone and saw the name Ellis Henning appear on the screen. A smile lit up his face. 'Well, well, look who we have here, little Miss Ellis Henning. Didn't Garcia get this woman out of Peterson's house? We could have used her. Is she warning you, or does she simply want to make contact, Kappakas?'

The detective slumped in his chair to reduce the pressure of the handcuffs on his wrists. He'd heard what Larkin said, and the call was the signal that police were here. It wouldn't be long before Matarazo released him from his painful position. Billy slapped his face. Pain seared through his right cheek.

'Come on, Greek; what's the meaning of that call?' Larkin snarled.

It's been a long time since anyone called me "Greek". Apparently

Larkin was losing his patience, feeling uneasy. In any case, the vibrating alert caused attention to shift away from the white coated man, who was still ready to stab Kappakas with a needle full of who-knows-what. But it was dangerous to play for more time, so he decided to raise the stakes. He wondered how Larkin would react. 'That's the sign Matarazo and his men are here.'

Chapter 108

Suddenly it was silent in the shed; everyone looked at each other for a few seconds before spontaneous laughter burst out. 'Ha, ha, Mr. Garlic Greek tries to be funny,' Larkin roared with laughter. Billy and Sonny too were enjoying themselves. 'Had you expected we were all going to hide now? Should we fear Captain Matarazo, all of a sudden, Naples' righteous police chief? When he comes in, Kappakas, we'll welcome him with open arms. And you may thank your girl, Ellis; she may have saved your life, but it's still...'

Larkin was interrupted by loud voices and footsteps at the shed's entrance. 'Here they are, your lifesavers,' he said with a nasty smile.

Seconds later, four members of the arrest team burst into the lab. They barked 'police!' and 'put your weapons down!' Kappakas also heard a woman's voice. They keep up with the times here, he thought. When the team had the situation under control, Dick Matarazo stepped through the door. It surprised Kappakas that Larkin and his men had quickly put back their weapons into their holsters. He got an odd feeling, one he'd experienced before.

'Dick, is it you?' Larkin asked pretending to be surprised. 'You scared the hell out of us.'

Dick? Of course, Matarazo's playing the crooked cop. At least, that's what he told me, Kappakas thought. Matarazo came over to Kappakas. 'What have they been doing to you, Detective? It was very unwise to act all on your own.'

'This is no time to worry about me. I caught Larkin dead to rights, kidnapping Mrs. Atchison from the hospital. If I hadn't taken immediate action, she would have been butchered like the young man behind that screen.'

Matarazo ordered three of his team members to come forward. The fourth member, who, judging by physical form was a woman, kept guarding the door. The arrest team wore helmets with face shields. Larkin hadn't said another word. He stood near Kappakas and watched everything closely. He regularly signaled to his bodyguards, mainly to indicate they should keep quiet. Billy's brain wasn't so sharp, and he took his boss's non-verbal cues as a plan of attack.

Suddenly Billy drew his pistol and aimed at one of the nearest police. The sound of the shot was deafening. He never had a chance to take cover when return fire hit him with lethal force. Billy was knocked back against the wall, crumpled to the floor and died almost instantly. The female team member lowered her arms, when she considered the danger was over. Matarazo and his men were shaken.

'Larkin, dammit. What is this? Have you lost control of your own people?'

Larkin pretended not to care. 'He couldn't handle the pressure, didn't understand. What are you going to do now, Matarazo, arrest me?'

Chief Matarazo ordered Larkin and Sonny to stand with their faces to the wall and their hands behind their backs.

'Chief, behind that wall are two other men in white coats,' Kappakas said, while the female team member helped him unlock his handcuffs. She whispered into his ear, 'I told you, I couldn't wait in the car for long.' With a jerk Kappakas turned his head to the side and saw Ellis wink at him through her face shield.

Matarazo walked to the middle of the room, a few yards from the partition. 'Come out with your hands up. And no tricks!'

Suddenly excited voices were heard from behind the wall, one of which dominated the other. Poor acoustics made it impossible to hear what the men said. As quickly as the commotion started, it stopped. Both men came out cautiously. The larger of the two walked closely behind the other, keeping a tight grip on his throat with his left arm while holding a pistol to his temple with his right hand. The smaller man's expression was fearful, and he looked around in panic.

'If you don't let me go, I shoot him,' the big man threatened, pushing the pistol firmly against the head of his victim.

'Alright, take it easy now!' Matarazo implored. 'No-one's leaving here. Don't do anything foolish - let go of that man.'

'No; I'm taking him with me and you stay here. It's Larkin you want, leave me out of it.'

That voice! A wave of dismay washed over Ellis. To breathe better, the big man pulled off his surgical mask.

'Sheldon? Is that you?' Ellis asked in amazement.

Rosenberg froze. He recognized her voice and panicked. He pressed the man even harder against him to make himself as unassailable as possible. 'Ellis? Are you Ellis Henning?'

Slowly she pushed up her face shield and stared into the bewildered face of Sheldon Rosenberg. She recovered quickly. 'Come on, Sheldon. It can't be that big a surprise. You know I was working on this case. But you, working for the other side, are a shock to me. You were one of my best friends.'

Rosenberg said contemptuously, 'Well, Ellis, you were always best in the class. You want to expose injustice and abuse. But you're naïve. You were fooled. I tried to mislead you with those medicine lists. Until you got help from that cop, I was able to do what I wanted, undisturbed.'

A self-satisfied smile appeared on Kappakas' face. Ellis didn't understand. She detested hidden agendas. She decided to stop liking Rosenberg. She was very disappointed and angry that he'd misled her for so long.

'Larkin, call off Rosenberg! You may have some influence on him. I don't want any more victims; one dead man is more than enough,' Matarazo said.

Rosenberg didn't give Larkin time to react. He began to sneer. 'Larkin? Hah, he's a cheap gangster boss, a money-grubber and a killer, of course. What I do is highly moral work, assigning the most vital parts of a human being to someone in distress. I deserve recognition and respect. But instead I'm hindered and suddenly surrounded by a horde of police. That smalltime gang boss over there is the killer.'

In the meantime, Rosenberg almost had reached the exit from the room. Everyone looked tensely as he made his way, knowing at least three firearms were aimed at him. Ellis put her hand in her pocket and pushed the sending signal of her beeper. Matarazo ordered his men not to shoot. It was especially Larkin he was after. Sometimes hard choices have to be made quickly under stress. If Rosenberg manages to get away, he'll soon be traced, he felt sure.

Kappakas considered the situation. Josh Larkin & Co had been overpowered all too easily and behaved – except for rebellious Billy. This was not what he expected from these criminals. He wondered how Matarazo would proceed, now that a lower-priority man demanded his attention. Larkin and Sonny were still standing with their faces to the wall and their hands cuffed behind their backs. They hadn't said anything. They felt weapons – probably Glocks – aimed at them. Larkin didn't much care for people, not even if they worked for him. Yet the whole situation made him a little more human. 'Sheldon, don't be a fool. We can solve this.'

'Is that all you can say? Thanks for the advice, Larkin, but I'm not taking it.'

Matarazo didn't want a shoot-out, so he let Rosenberg slowly edge back to the door. In the shed the back-up team could disarm and arrest him.

'Matarazo, do you have any more men walking around in here? You'd better tell me. I don't like bloodbaths very much.'

'Three men on look-out.'

'Three? Well, if I can handle two detectives and half an arrest team, I'll manage to get safely through the shed, don't you think?'

'It's your call.'

Rosenberg reached the room's exit and grabbed the door handle. He opened the door slightly and was able to see all the way to the shed's exit. He could not see the back of the shed. To do that, he would have to put his head around the door while dragging a man along at gunpoint. He felt cold steel against the nearly bald back of his head. The tension in his body instantly swirled away like water down a drain. Rosenberg sighed, lowered his gun and hung his head.

Chapter 109

'Easy now; throw your gun on the floor,' ordered the man, who held his weapon against Rosenberg's head. The surgeon hesitated. A fraction of a second later he realized he'd heard the man's voice before.

'I think I know you.'

'Throw your gun on the floor, now! I won't hesitate to put a bullet in your brain,' Mike firmly directed. His voice contained a lot of aggression and indignation, and it astonished Rosenberg. He dropped his gun and removed his arm from his colleague's throat. The latter jumped out of reach, and once at a safe distance from Rosenberg, he began to rail against his assailant. Rosenberg ignored him. Mike made sure Rosenberg couldn't move. Then two members of the arrest team moved in and cuffed him.

Mike stepped up to Rosenberg and looked straight at him. 'Maybe you're an even bigger bastard than Larkin. You're a sneaky character who fakes friendships. You hurt Ellis very deeply.'

Matarazo asked Mike to keep it short.

'One more thing, Rosenberg,' Mike said. 'Before you're locked up in your cell, maybe you should apologize to Ellis. That's the least you owe her.'

Rosenberg remained unmoved. He turned his head towards Ellis and gave her a hateful look. 'She can go to hell.'

Mike hit Rosenberg in the face.

'Enough! Men, take him away,' Matarazo ordered. Two officers marched Rosenberg out of the shed. Ellis looked shaken. Mike went to her side and put his hand on her shoulder. She nodded she was okay.

Meanwhile, Larkin and Sonny were also arrested and taken away. Larkin seemed meek as a lamb. What intrigued Kappakas most was that Larkin smiled when he passed Matarazo. He didn't like it. It all went too easy. Was Rosenberg used as a lightning rod? And where did Mike come from all of a sudden?

Clearly, he hadn't been in charge of these arrests, but he was glad it had gone so well. Ellis is a brave woman, he thought. And what that Rosenberg had done to her was downright nasty. But Kappakas was sure she would get over it.

After the crooks were taken away, Ellis went over to Suzie right away. She felt a pulse and found her still alive. Kappakas cast a glance behind the curtain and shivered. During his working life he'd seen many corpses, in all shapes and conditions: disfigured, headless or limbless. But this he'd never seen before. On a polished metal operating table was the lifeless body of a woman. Her entire chest and belly were cut open. Intestines had been removed, and her liver was lying next to the head. The table was drenched in blood. Kappakas felt his stomach turn. He left the sterile room coughing and gasping and sat down on a chair to recover. He only just managed to keep down the semi-digested food in his stomach.

'Kappa, you look white as a sheet,' Ellis said.

He pointed at the curtain. 'I strongly advise you not to go look in there,' he said.

Ellis decided to take Kappakas' advice to save herself from another emotional upset. Rosenberg's betrayal was more than enough for one day. 'No, thanks; I can guess,' she reacted grimly. Then she changed her tone of voice. 'Fortunately the arrests were made without too many incidents. One dead Billy, no struggling from Larkin, and we captured Rosenberg. So all in all, this is a successful operation, don't you think?'

Kappakas wasn't convinced. He waited for Matarazo, who was winding up things, making sure nothing was left to chance. The Police Chief called an ambulance to collect Suzie Atchison and take her back to St. Luke's. The Chief called his crime scene specialists to examine the corpses and take care of the evidence. Then he contacted an undertaker to transport Billy to the morgue. He would ask Larkin if Billy had any relatives to notify.. Matarazo had finished his phone calls and checked the shed from front to back, when he saw Kappakas waiting at the entrance.

'Well, Detective. We'll secure these premises as a crime scene for the specialists. The raid and arrests are done. You look tired and a little gloomy, if you ask me.'

'I'm not handcuffed and hit on the head every day, you know. But gloomy? No, just puzzled. It all went off smoothly. I hadn't expected this from Larkin. But maybe you know more, since you have a special relation with him.'

Matarazo shook his head. 'Come on, let's go to the station. It's not all what it seems.'

Kappakas wondered what Matarazo meant by that. It didn't feel right. Did the Naples' Police Chief play for higher stakes? Would his initial suspicions about Matarazo come true? He'd find out soon. He intended to ask for straight answers the moment the arrested men were in the interrogation rooms and charges had been brought.

Chapter 110

Ellis and Mike were waiting in Kappakas' car. Their faces showed mixed relief and fatigue.

'I was glad to see you again, Ellis. I'm sorry about what Rosenberg did to you,' Mike said.

'Lots of things are going through my mind. Everything Jake and I did together with Sheldon and Lisa, great things. It's unbelievable, almost a nightmare, that someone would demean himself and put his relationships and reputation at stake for money. I feel sorry for Lisa. If she doesn't know about Sheldon's sideline, his arrest will be a big shock. I'll call her as soon as we know the official charges.'

Mike listened attentively and didn't interrupt her. She paused for a second, staring through the car window.

'I still don't get why he drew our attention to those suspicious medicines. Maybe he had no choice. It seems like he has a split personality. What do you think?'

'Hmm…, maybe. I don't know him well enough to…'

He stopped talking when he saw Kappakas and Matarazo come out of the shed. They spoke a few words and then walked over to their cars. Ellis wanted to get out of the driver's seat for him, but Kappakas signaled she could stay where she was. 'I'll sit in the back. Just follow Matarazo.'

Ellis started the engine and they set off for the police station. In the rearview mirror she saw Kappakas' darkened face. 'What's on your mind, Kappa?'

First, he didn't react. The atmosphere in the car was a little tense. A photo and that woman behind the curtain, he thought. He swore inwardly. Then he muttered, 'It's not about what Larkin did to me. I've just been through something much more intense. I saw Elaine Iskander.'

Ellis startled. 'What? Where did you see her?' She momentarily lost control of the steering-wheel and nearly drove into the gutter.

'Careful! She was lying on an operating table behind the curtain. That's all I want to say about it for now. Anyway, we found her. That's important to her relatives. I'm going to inform John Iskander tonight.'

'Well, I wouldn't like to be in your shoes, Kappa,' Mike said. 'What a tremendous shock it must be for her family to hear how she ended.'

'Words aren't adequate to express what it will do to them,'

Kappakas said, looking out of the window. Then he realized Mike had reappeared on the stage. 'How did you get here all of a sudden, Mike? Have you two been concocting plans behind my back?' He gave Ellis a suspicious look.

'Jennifer thought I shouldn't leave you alone. When she was over the shock of that phone threat, I called Ellis and returned to Naples. We planned that if someone tried to escape from the shed while you were inside, Ellis would signal me with her beeper. Then I positioned myself behind the door. The rest you know.'

Kappakas growled. Everyone fell silent, lost in thought about what exactly had happened to Elaine Iskander. They were near the police station now.

'Are you going home tomorrow, Kappa?' Ellis interrupted the silence.

'I'm not sure.'

The cars stopped at the central police station. Matarazo was the first to get out of a vehicle. He walked to the patrol wagon with Larkin inside as the main guest.

'The most difficult part is still to come, I think,' Kappakas said with a mysterious look.

Ellis had switched off the engine and turned around. 'Kappa, what do you mean by that?'

'Oh, it's a personal matter.'

Ellis kept looking at him as if she was trying to force his thoughts to make a Wi-Fi connection with her mind. He made an apologetic gesture and decided to get out of the car. 'I'll tell you later, Ellis. When it's all behind us, we can look back.'

'I'm just curious.'

'Aren't most women?' he replied with a wink.

They saw Larkin, Sonny, Rosenberg and his helper escorted into the building through a back door for arrested suspects. Kappakas was the last to join the line and he beckoned Ellis with his hand.

'I think he means we can watch from behind the window,' she told Mike.

'Great, I'd like that.'

They went into the station and took the elevator to the third floor. Ellis noticed Mike no longer wore his 'Best Friends' ring.

'Have you and Jennifer broken up?' she asked casually, throwing Mike off balance.

'Why do you ask?'

She pointed to his right hand. 'It's not working out any longer? Was the distance too great?'

Women like to ask questions, want to know what's what, especially concerning relationships, Mike thought. 'What makes you think that? I don't wear my ring and you jump to all kinds of conclusions. I admit that distance is a problem for us, and I don't know her well enough yet. But she says she loves me. You know what? Jen even urged me to come back and help you. I already told you that. She thought I shouldn't let you down.'

Ellis listened to his words with some suspicion. 'Do you love her too?'

Mike hesitated before he answered. 'To be honest… let me put it this way: my feelings for Jen don't match hers for me. And that's really all I want to say about it.'

Ellis nodded, that was a "no." She looked at him approvingly, understanding his feelings, and dropped the subject.

The elevator doors opened and they walked into one of the interrogation rooms. On their way they met Kappakas, who told them Matarazo first wanted to question Larkin in room 3. The two other suspects were taken to cells. 'It'll take half an hour or so before he's shown in.'

'We'll enjoy ourselves,' Mike said, winking at Ellis.

Kappakas walked away from the two and, turning his head, laughed, 'I don't doubt it for a second.'

They watched Kappakas till he disappeared behind a revolving door. 'I think he's his old self again,' Mike said.

They were sitting in a waiting room by themselves, and in the distance they heard the sounds of shouting policemen and protesting suspects.

'I'm happy that he finally knows what happened to Elaine, as painful as the sight of her must have been,' Ellis said.

There was a short silence between them, and Mike suddenly realized she hardly ever talked about her relationship with Jake. He thought it was no more than fair to ask her about it. Casually and with a little cough, he asked, 'Umm…, how's Jake by the way?'

'I don't know,' she said shrugging her shoulders.

'You mean you haven't spoken to each other for a while.'

'No, I mean we don't really know each other. Jake is always away from home, sometimes for months. And even during our vacations together, someone else bumps into our hotel room and messes up my life. So when you ask me how Jake is doing, I can't tell you right now.' She kept looking calmly at him.

'I'm sorry. In any case, we have something in common,' he said teasingly.

She smiled. 'Maybe.'

A light blush appeared on her cheeks. Mike looked into her beautiful brown eyes. 'We've been through a lot together.'

He paused for a few seconds. 'I haven't told you this before, but to me you're a beautiful woman, and you do a lot of things that might make many women envious.'

'You picked a very romantic spot to tell me.'

Mike looked around and said with some bravura in his voice, 'Well, it could have been worse; we might have been in jail for burglary and theft.'

Ellis smiled. She put her hand on his and said, 'I like you a lot, Mike. But I think it's best just to stay friends for now.'

He put his hand on top of hers. 'That seems like a good idea.'

Sounds came down the corridor from the waiting room. They let go of each other's hands and saw Kappakas and Matarazo coming towards them.

'You can sit behind the glass now,' Matarazo said.

'How's Larkin?' Mike asked.

'He's calm, behaving very well. It'll change when he hears the charges,' Kappakas said, looking sideways at Matarazo. The latter didn't react and walked straight ahead to the interrogation room.

'I wonder how Larkin's lawyer will play it,' Ellis said.

Kappakas rubbed his chin. 'I don't know if he has what it takes to be able to do something for his client. Well, okay, we'll soon find out. See the both you later.'

They sat down on chairs behind the one-away glass. Kappakas entered when Matarazo spoke a few words with Larkin's lawyer.

'This is Mr. Ralph Ettinger,' Matarazo introduced Larkin's lawyer.

'Good afternoon, Mr. Ettinger,' Kappakas said.

'My client intends to do everything he can to demonstrate his innocence,' Ettinger said. He was considered one of the top criminal attorneys in the state. Kappakas gave Larkin a slightly surprised look.

'So Mr. Larkin thinks he's innocent. We'll see about that, won't we?'

Kappakas had agreed with Matarazo that he would interrogate Rosenberg later that day. First, Matarazo had the honor to make it hot for Larkin.

'Yes, the charges are quite damning,' Matarazo said. 'Murder of at least one person and possibly multiple counts, kidnapping of Mrs. Atchison, illegal organ removal and sale, illegal medicine trade.'

'My client denies any involvement in everything you accuse him of. You have no evidence that he has done any of the things you charge him with.'

Matarazo shrugged his shoulders. 'I think this is only the beginning of a series of crimes your client loaded on his back.'

Larkin appeared undisturbed and watched how Matarazo tried to give his lawyer a hard time. For the time being he seemed to have nothing to worry about. Ettinger emphasized once more he wanted to see proof.

'Fine, I'll give you proof, that incriminates your client, more than enough to indict and convict him.'

Chapter 111

Larkin still remained calm and left the fighting to both gamecocks. Suddenly Kappakas touched his head. 'Sorry, I have to get some aspirin. My head is starting to ache. Just go on without me, Chief, I'll be right back.' Rubbing his temples, Kappakas left the interrogation room. As soon as he had closed the door he joined Mike and Ellis.

'What's wrong?' Ellis asked.

'Nothing, I pretended to have a headache, so Matarazo would interrogate without me, at least for a few minutes.'

'Why's that?'

'It'll probably become clear. Just watch.'

Matarazo continued the questioning. Probably the Detective from Jacksonville is watching from behind the mirror with his friends to see how I'm doing, he thought. As Larkin had never been in trouble with the police, he didn't know people were watching and listening from another room. Ettinger had failed to warn his client about this.

'We can do business quickly,' Larkin said.

'What do you mean?' Matarazo asked.

Josh Larkin looked at Ettinger and expected him to agree with him. 'Isn't that so, Ettinger? We're going to make a deal.'

'If it's possible, I'm all for it. At least you two have something in common.' He looked at Matarazo and then at Larkin, who carefully hid his frustration about the arrest behind a smile, carved on his face.

'Aah, I think he'll let me go, Ettinger. Isn't that right, dirty cop?'

Everybody behind the glass, except Kappakas, was surprised by Larkin's remark. He'd been waiting for this and Larkin had just heated up things. His words continued to vibrate till Matarazo said something. 'Thanks for the compliment. I'm proud of holding a position in our community which allows me to expose criminals like you.'

He paused for a moment to see if Larkin got what he meant. Judging from his deadpan expression, this wasn't the case. 'Only our municipal criminal court judge and Florida's Attorney General know I sometimes do undercover work.' He watched Larkin closely. Two policemen were standing behind him to intervene in case the suspect became unruly. This reassured Matarazo; his next sentence would definitely open Larkin's eyes. 'Josh Larkin; for the past eight months, I posed as an interested business partner in Naples Autoparts Imports, which you manage and own. You paid me for protection, to look the other way and, if necessary, provide police support. All this was done within conditions regulated by law.'

Kappakas saw Larkin slowly change from a calm and assured man into an angry animal. Such tension he'd rarely experienced during any other interrogations. 'So, he was right, after all,' he said to himself.

Larkin stood up, bent forward, leaning with his hands on the table. The carved smile on his face changed into a fierce snarl as his criminal activities were being exposed. 'What are you saying now? Are you trying to set me up? You're a corrupt cop, Matarazo! You took my money. Aah, you're kidding, aren't you? Tell me you're kidding! You want more money!'

Matarazo said nothing, remained undisturbed and shaking his head slowly in disapproval.

'Hell, man, you cheated me!' Larkin shouted. 'You know what we do to traitors.' With his hand he sliced an imaginary line across his throat. Ettinger wanted to say something, but Larkin wouldn't let him. He leaned his upper body across the table and roared with anger. All his frustrations came out. 'You're a dirty rat, Matarazo!. You're a damned good actor. You betrayed me, but you haven't seen the last of me yet. I paid you. I guess you gave the money to your wife, so she could go shopping, you punk cop. Bastard!'

Matarazo signaled to the policemen to stand closer to Larkin. He wasn't sure what the man would do next. Larkin completely ignored his lawyer and continued his outburst. Matarazo had enough of it. He was brief. At any moment now the shit might hit the fan. 'Mr. Larkin, you're charged with murder, organ theft and sale, importing and selling illegal medicines, and kidnapping. Anything you say from now on can be used against you in a court of law. You have the right to remain silent, and you have the right to legal counsel, which you already have present...'

Suddenly Larkin stood straight and lashed out at Ettinger. 'You're a lousy lawyer. You've done nothing for me. Get me out of here, or else....'

The policemen grabbed Larkin by the shoulders and pushed him back into his chair. 'Keep your fucking hands off me!' he raged, but he had no choice.

Then Ettinger turned to Matarazo. 'Sir, I apologize for my client's behavior. I wasn't aware of your undercover operation, and I can no longer defend Mr. Larkin properly. I withdraw from the case so I will not do any further damage to Mr. Larkin's interests.'

Matarazo nodded. Ettinger rose from his chair and wanted to shake Larkin's hand, but he sat scowling in front of him. 'I regret this, Mr. Larkin, but I have no other choice.' Ettinger then excused himself and left the room. Matarazo gave Larkin a questioning look. 'We're done with you for now, Larkin. If you want, you may call another lawyer, or the judge will appoint one for you.'

'We'll see about that. First I want my money back, Matarazo. You took my dough, so don't think you'll get away with it when I tell it to the judge.'

'Do what you think you have to do. It's all within the law. Your money is deposited in a special account, controlled by the State Attorney General's office. I haven't used a penny for myself. If you're convicted, the money may be used to help compensate your victims. That's how it goes.'

Matarazo ordered the policemen to take Larkin to his cell. Remarkably, Larkin calmed down. He allowed himself to be handcuffed. At the door of the interrogation room, he turned around and gave Matarazo a nasty smile. 'You know, Dick, I'll be out in no time. You'll be very sorry.'

The officers pushed him out of the room, leaving Matarazo to his own thoughts. Dick? When Larkin gets personal all of a sudden, one must be extra-careful.

Chapter 112

Behind the one-way glass, spirits had risen high. In particular, Kappakas was pleasantly surprised by the interrogation's results. For a long time he'd given Matarazo the benefit of the doubt, although the Police Chief's behavior had raised significantly doubts. He looked apologetically at Mike and Ellis. 'Sorry, I couldn't share my suspicions of him with you. But I'm perplexed; everything went so smoothly. We should handle criminals this way more often. Interrogations would be a lot shorter.'

Kappakas gave a lengthy account of why he'd watched Matarazo so closely. 'The longer I thought about it, however, the more I realized the Police Chief's actions that worried me, might also be interpreted positively. I'm a little suspicious by nature. It's part of my job. Suspects often tell fairy tales, and it's very useful to have a lie-detection antenna in one's head.' He thanked Ellis and Mike for their active cooperation. 'I think my task is over. You were great in everything: your loyalty, doing difficult jobs, and even facing the risk of death. Quite an achievement! I could use you on my team of detectives. Great!'

They both shrugged their shoulders, embarrassed, and waved away the compliments. 'I think, we were lucky to be able to help you. It all comes down to a concurrence of circumstances, and we just couldn't stay out of things. I did it for my article, but also for you.'

'Thanks, Ellis. Yes, I was burning to expose Larkin. I wanted to prevent him from continuing his illegal medicine business. Don't forget Elaine Iskander discovered that. I did it for her too, and for her father.'

'Yeah, everyone has a special reason,' Mike said.

'What's going to happen to Larkin and Rosenberg now?' Ellis asked.

'They'll be brought up for a hearing in a day or two. Then they'll probably plead for release on bail. But first they have to find a lawyer.'

Mike suddenly got angry. 'Bail?! But then he'll be outside again. That criminal must stay in jail until his trial!' Ellis agreed.

'Yes, it's frustrating. But that's the legal system,' Kappakas explained. 'The prosecuting attorney will probably argue against the request for temporary release. But if the judge releases Larkin on bail, he's sure to set the bail high, though Larkin is the type who may try to leave the country.'

Mike shook his head. 'Can we speak to the prosecuting attorney?

We could tell him what kind of crook Larkin is.'

'The prosecutor will want to interview all of us who were involved to build his preliminary case, backing the charges. He'll likely argue against bail, considering Larkin's criminal activities and lack of a legitimate business or residential domicile in Florida. But then, the judge determines if he sets a bail or not. I'll see what I can do.'

Kappakas was thinking of John Iskander. He would inform him of everything he knew about his daughter. A difficult task lay ahead of him. John would want to know every last detail of the situation. The mere thought made him shiver. 'I've decided to stay for another couple of days. I want to be present when the judge determines if Rosenberg and Larkin are released on bail. Whatever the decision, after that I'm going back to my regular job.'

Ellis looked at Mike and asked what his plans were.

'I'm staying, of course. I want to be at the bail hearing. I can't wait.'

Mike also was curious about Ellis's plans. He looked at her, assuming she wouldn't let him down.

'Well, do I have a choice?' she reacted with mock-indignation. 'Not really; I'm staying too.'

Mike beamed at her, but not too conspicuously. Kappakas was about to go to his hotel. 'I'm entitled to some time off, I'd say, a little swimming, or fishing maybe. What are you going to do?'

They didn't know yet. Take a rest, maybe have something to eat and drink together. They said goodbye to Kappakas and wished for him to enjoy himself.

'As soon as I hear from Matarazo I'll let you know.' He walked down the corridor and took the elevator. Mike felt like having a drink and then a hearty meal. He asked Ellis how she felt about it.

She smiled and said, 'Sounds like a good idea. I'm famished. And we'll have the chance to have a quiet talk about everything we've experienced.'

Over the next few days, only one subject dominated the local newspapers: the arrest of Josh Larkin and his helper, surgeon Sheldon Rosenberg. Although the press soberly highlighted Rosenberg's morbid activities and left out the most sickening details, some readers took up their pens to ask the editors not to publish any more descriptions about the removal of body parts "because unstable people may read newspapers and get certain ideas – copy cats."

But the focus of attention was on Larkin's empire, because he was, after all, Rosenberg's boss and the brain behind the medicine smuggling, murders and organ trade. The residents of Naples hadn't read a story like that in their home newspaper – ever. They were shocked by the fact that a supposed businessman had set up shop in their beloved seaside resort and then committed such atrocious crimes.

In rapid succession the news bulletins on TV announced "Breaking News" or "News Alert" to keep people glued to the tube. Every detail about Larkin was spun out, hyped for greater effect and publicity. The Naples Sun Times sent reporters to Jacksonville to interview some of Kappakas' colleagues. The unorthodox detective was generally regarded as the driving force behind the arrests.

Dick Matarazo was complimented by various political figures, particularly the Mayor and Governor, because of his daring undercover operation to furnish proof of the crimes. He and Kappakas decided not to speak with the press, but the press simply attributed revelations to them surrounding the arrest at the industrial park.

True or not, the Napleonians devoured the stories and interviews. The names of Ellis Henning and Mike Garcia were featured only sporadically in the reports. Apparently the budgets of the news media were insufficient to do more digging into the backgrounds of these two friends of Detective Kappakas. The Naples Daily published a big story on the SocHom residential community and its deceased Director, Mark Peterson. The newspaper suggested that Peterson handed over demented elderly people to St. Luke's Clinic, where Dr. Margaret Santini was in charge, and who notified Larkin when a patient died. Then he would have the corpse picked up, delivered to his warehouse, and proceed with organ removal and sales.

A central figure in the article was Suzie Atchison, who'd barely escaped death and was saved by the heroic actions of Detective Kappakas. Many readers were moved when they read the interview with Suzie and her husband, Don. They were also very angry about what had been going on under their very noses.

All in all, the media published a stream of various, sometimes contradictory accounts with different people playing the leading part, but always with Josh Larkin as villainous linchpin. It was a great time for publishers and crime experts, and also for manufacturers of bumper stickers, which featured a grinning Kappakas cartoon. With a fishing rod, the detective held up killer shark Larkin. The heading was, "Kappa in Nappa". With the legend, "J'ville Cop Cleaned Our Waters".

When most people were starting to get tired of all the stories, a new event presented itself. After Larkin and Rosenberg had been indicted, the bail hearing would take place in five days.

Chapter 113

The morning was one like any other on the southwest coast of Florida. Naples was waking up and everyone gradually went about their usual business. The traffic calmly drove along the wide avenues, a road worker repaired a drain, and schoolchildren obediently walked in file behind their teacher. Fishermen removed canvas covers from their boats, vendors opened their beach kiosks, and a policeman parked his car along the roadside, where he waited for a chance to stop the first traffic offender. Ordinary things that happened on an ordinary weekday.

But it wouldn't be long before the everyday peaceful routine was over. Around the court house on Espinal Boulevard, all remained quiet at this early hour. The first court employees slowly trickled in to resume their work. Then police cars arrived and policemen started to cordon off the area. When cars from broadcasting stations drove up, some unsuspecting and unknowing bystanders realized something special was going to happen. For well-informed citizens – for who could now say he'd never heard of Larkin? – this was an important day in the judicial process for the notorious criminal.

Gradually the first people arrived who wanted to see everything close up. Among them were some clamorous demonstrators. They chanted and carried banners and sandwich boards, with the heartfelt cry, "Keep your dirty hands off people with dementia". On the lawns of the courthouse, a crowd of a hundred people gathered, while police kept them at a proper distance.

First Rosenberg's lawyer would argue the case for releasing his client on bail. Then it was show time for the biggest crook Naples had ever known. Black police SUVs with flashing lights approached the courthouse. The spectators ran to the cordon to get a close look at the two central figures. Heavily guarded, Rosenberg got out of the car in front. Loud jeering and chants of "butcher" filled the air. Photographers nearly clicked their cameras to pieces, and TV-reporters gave excited commentary about the arrival of the suspects. Rosenberg, who was handcuffed, was led inside immediately. A minute later, the door of the second SUV was opened. Armed officers guarded Larkin to prevent possible assault on his life.

Larkin wasn't very tall, so the spectators were barely able to see him. But that didn't stop them from raising the volume of their shouts and jeers. A young man, who had managed to sneak through the cordon, was hauled away. Only one or two people caught a glimpse of the "body parts dealer." The majority didn't see Larkin at all, but apparently nobody cared. After all they had come to express their disapproval. A reporter from the Daily said, with his hands over his ears, they'd succeeded.

An hour later, Dr. Sheldon Rosenberg was lead into the courtroom. Contrary to the noise outside, the mood inside was expectant and tense. About sixty people saw guards seat Rosenberg at the Defense table with his attorney. The bailiff asked all to rise, and Judge Harold J. Bustrum entered the courtroom and took his seat. The defense attorney and the prosecuting attorney stood before the judge. A request for release on bail is made during a procedural session, in which the question of guilt or presentation of evidence is not being dealt with. The judge decides if the suspect can be released, – temporarily – and with minimal flight risk or risk of injury to the public, before his case is up for trial, which may be months later.

Rosenberg's lawyer defended his request by stating his client was no longer a danger to society, as he had only been able to do what he did because Mr. Larkin had provided him with the work space, goods and devices. The prosecutor, however, contested this reasoning and asserted that Dr. Rosenberg should not be allowed his freedom to continue practicing his profession.

'Who can assure me he won't secretly remove a lung from a deceased patient in his hospital and sell it?'

The defense explained that Rosenberg had already been fired, so that risk was non-existent. The prosecutor persisted in his argument. 'Your Honor, it's evident the suspect, who has rationalized his morbid acts, has been willing to ruthlessly and emotionlessly cut up bodies on demand and is a great risk to society.' A shudder went through the observers. 'We can't look into his mind, but the danger is great the suspect will abuse his freedom. We must be one hundred percent sure he won't take any new victims. This is something the defense cannot guarantee.'

Statements and arguments continued between prosecutor and defense counsel, after which Judge Bustrum raised his hand and thanked both attorneys for the information. 'Dr. Rosenberg,' he began. Bustrum was a sturdy man, nearly six and a half feet tall. He radiated authority. Stern eyes looking over his glasses, part way down his angular nose accentuated his severity. He hadn't had a haircut in weeks and a shave might also have done him good. He coughed, cast a quick glance into the files in front of him and continued. 'Dr. Rosenberg, I intend to follow the prosecuting attorney's recommendation. Your request for release on bail is denied.'

The audience collectively expressed itself with a spontaneous release of breath. Outside the courtroom, the crowd burst out cheers, which could be heard from inside. Rosenberg looked at his lawyer, frightened. The latter shrugged his shoulders. At once, two guards positioned themselves next to Rosenberg and led him out of the room. People with banners embraced each other. The general feeling that the "Butcher of Naples" would stay behind bars, worked like balm to the soul. The news spread like wildfire, and the television stations mentioned the judge's somewhat unexpected decision. Many commentators had predicted Larkin would not be released on bail, but Rosenberg would. Judge Bustrum had already judged differently in Rosenberg, so everyone looked forward even more confidently to the hearing for the central figure in the case.

Nearly an hour after the judge sent Rosenberg back to his cell, Josh Larkin was brought into the courtroom. Again, the mood among the observers was one of intense interest. In general, it was thought that Larkin would not be released on bail. His crimes involved the employment of Rosenberg to do his dirty work. Although he hadn't cut into corpses himself, there seemed to be no extenuating circumstances to justify a different treatment from Rosenberg. The public strongly denounced Larkin's gangster-practices. But at the same time people were curious. Who is this man, doing business in our city, a man who thinks up and organizes these horrible crimes?

When Josh Larkin entered the courtroom everybody was quiet as a mouse. Finally they saw the man who had had such a great impact on life in Naples in the past few days. Some whispered he didn't look like a crime-boss at all, because he was so short and stout. He didn't live up to the over-sized evil image they had formed of him. On the other hand, there were also people who thought his posture was exactly right for an underworld chief.

Larkin had been wise enough to re-employ Jason Ettinger as his lawyer. They'd had a good talk with each other recently, with no gloves on. Larkin sat at the Defense table next to his lawyer, and the prosecutor was again at his table. Judge Bustrum took a good look at the man before opening the session with a hammer-blow, in contrast with the silence of everyone in the courtroom.

'Under discussion is the request for temporary release on bail of Mr. Joshua Marcus Larkin, living in Naples, Florida. I call on Mr. Ettinger to speak.'

'Thank you, Your Honor. My client requests, while awaiting his trial, to be released on bail. He wants to prepare his defense against the charges, and he can only do this in a safe and quiet environment. Furthermore it is clear that my client is no longer a danger to society, as his company has been completely dismantled and the buildings have been locked by the police under court order. As an ordinary citizen he wants to focus on what is to come.'

The murmur in the room was now clearly softer than an hour ago. The prosecuting attorney, Mr. Fitch, argued that the suspect was in charge of a criminal organization that had spread death and destruction in the community. 'The suspect was the leader who organized the activities that claimed many victims. He has given orders to murder people and…'

Bustrum interrupted him. 'Mr. Fitch, this is not a trial. I ask you to confine yourself to the question of why you think the suspect should not be released on bail.'

For a moment Fitch lost the thread of his argument, but recovered quickly and continued his plea. 'Your Honor, these are the reasons why I plead to reject the request for release on bail. Mr. Larkin is a notorious criminal who, once set free, has the resources and motivation to flee the country and resurrect his criminal organization.'

'But Your Honor,' Ettinger intervened. 'I only hear biased points of view from the prosecuting attorney, whereas his guilt hasn't been proven yet. I object to these….'

'Yes, yes, Mr. Ettinger, I can follow you,' Bustrum reacted annoyed and then gave the prosecutor a severe look. 'I warn you, Mr. Fitch, no prejudice, just facts.'

Prosecuting attorney Fitch decided to comply with the judge's directions and concluded his plea. 'I can only say, Your Honor, we reject bail for reasons of flight risk and of safety and peace in the community.'

'Well, that's finally a reason,' Bustrum said somewhat sarcastically. 'Mr. Ettinger, do you have anything to add?'

'Your Honor, I've already said what I had to say. I would only repeat myself.'

Chapter 114

Bustrum swept his hand across his face and thought for a moment. Then he turned to Larkin and said, 'I agree to release you on bail of five hundred thousand dollars. This session is closed.'

The hammer-blow resounded in the courtroom. The visitors looked at each other in amazement and despair. Nobody had counted on release. The public, the press and the experts, all had been wrong. Slowly the commotion built up and some people began to shout: "Jail for Larkin" and "We demand justice." Many people left the room upset and stopped reporters to express their dissatisfaction.

Larkin smiled at Ettinger. The lawyer kept a straight face and followed his client to the department where bail had to be deposited. The guards let him open his wallet. Larkin took out the bank check Ettinger had given him. He filled in the required amount, signed and gave the check to the clerk. The whole time Ettinger stood next to him and checked if all went well. The clerk called the bank to verify if the check was covered. It was confirmed, and then Ettinger asked the guards to release his client. Soon Larkin was standing outside on the steps of the courthouse with Ettinger at his side.

Dozens of demonstrators were waiting for him. Ettinger asked some guards to escort his client to his car. Before making their way through the crowd, Ettinger stopped and made a statement. 'The judge released my client on bail. We're happy about that, of course. I also want to say that release on bail is an important part of our legal system. I expect to see you later during the trial. I now ask you to let us through.'

Some hotheads tried to approach Larkin, but he was well protected. Press photographers pushed each other aside to take the best shots, and TV reporters shouted their questions, although they already knew Larkin wouldn't make any comments. When they were near Ettinger's car, the lawyer was hit on the back of his head by a well-aimed egg. He dove into the car, while a guard ducked Larkin into the backseat. Policemen cleared the way for Ettinger, so he could drive away fairly quickly. In his mirror he saw the policemen arrest the egg thrower.

'Dammit, Larkin, my new suit is done for. That's going to cost you.'

Larkin laughed. He looked with satanic pleasure at how people shook their fists and called him all sort of names. 'Just drive to my office. You worry about nothing. And thanks for your help. I knew you were good.'

Ettinger put on his professional hat again and informed Larkin about the requirements of his temporary release. 'It means you may not run, tempting though it may be. You must stay in Naples, and you're free to do as you like, except things that are against the law, of course.'

'Like committing crimes, you mean?'

'Forget it!'

'Then just say so.'

'Where can I drop you off?'

'Hotel Prospect,' he smiled.

Ettinger looked disapprovingly at him in his rearview mirror.

'Take it easy, I'm only going to pick up some stuff. Besides, my car is still there.'

Ettinger still looked suspiciously at his client. He had rented a suite for him in the Ramada. Returning to the crime scene was a bad idea. But as his lawyer, he couldn't reject his tenacious client's request. Ettinger slowly drove on. The windows at the back were covered with dark tint, so passing drivers were unable to see Larkin. This was a reassuring thought to Ettinger. He drove his car into Prospect Avenue. Larkin became grimly agitated, as he thought about what had happened to his company and facilities.

Ettinger stopped near the entrance of the former NAI premises. 'I'll send you the bill by the end of the week,' he said when Larkin got out of the car.

Larkin pretended not to hear his lawyer, and focused his attention on where his cover-up enterprise had been. When he arrived at the portable office cabin, he said thoughtlessly, 'Do as you like.'

Chapter 115

Kappakas had sent Mike and Ellis a text message proposing to have dinner in a good restaurant. They gladly agreed and met around seven in the cozy Bonefish Grill on 5th Avenue.

'Nice place,' Ellis said.

'Yes, it has a good reputation. I've eaten here before, and recommend the scampi, but the lobster is delicious too.'

'Do you happen to own shares in the restaurant?' Mike asked. They all laughed. After the waiter had taken their orders, Kappakas got serious.'

'Guys, I'm going home tomorrow. It's been a hectic day. My prediction came true: Larkin's out on bail and Rosenberg's in jail. The judge considered him a dangerous man, after all. My job is done. I'll return to testify at trial, but otherwise, I'll follow the news on TV. Once more, thanks for your help. Here's to your health.'

They raised their glasses.

'I'll miss you, Kappa,' Ellis said. 'We never saw you as a policeman, but as a friend, who fulfilled his promise to Elaine's father.'

'Now, don't get too sentimental, but I'm happy you feel that way.'

'Why are you leaving now?' Mike asked. 'The most important thing of all – the trials and your testimony– are still to come. Why don't you stay?'

'No, guys, it's not possible. It can take weeks, even months before the trials take place. And don't forget, I have work to do back in Jacksonville. I've already packed my bags.'

Mike felt a little disappointed, but knew that Kappakas was right.

'I suppose you two will stay around for a while?' asked Kappakas, who wasn't born yesterday.

Ellis and Mike looked at each other. 'Um…, don't know yet. It is exciting though; it may help me complete my articles; and maybe a book will follow. I don't know.'

Kappakas had a sly little smile on his face. 'It's not my business, but you both get along well, and I can imagine you'd want to extend your stay.'

He winked at Ellis, whose cheeks turned pink – and not from the wine. After eating the bass and lobster with relish, they talked for a little while about that peculiar Father D'Angelico, the frightened undertaker, Sykes, sweet Suzie Atchison, who barely escaped death, and of course Elaine Iskander. She was the reason why Kappakas came to Naples to investigate her disappearance, and then exposed a web of crime.

'How did her father take the news of her death,' Ellis asked.

'He was devastated. As a policeman I had to tell some of what Larkin had done to her. It was one the hardest thing I ever told anyone in my life. He cried, a long time, and said he wanted revenge. I feel deeply sorry for him and his family.'

'You're his friend, aren't you? It seems impossible to me to bring a friend such terrible news,' Mike said.

Kappakas rubbed his cheek. 'My experience is you can be honest with friends, but it certainly isn't easy. The close relationship helps us to face the truth together, though.'

Mike and Ellis nodded. It was time to go back to the hotel. Kappakas said he needed to sleep. They said goodbye and shook hands, hugged, and patted each other on the back. 'Go along now,' he said. 'I have to arrange something with the owner.'

They understood what he meant. Kappakas saw the two leave the Grill. He called the waiter and said he wanted to see the owner. The owner wasn't in, but Kappakas hoped the waiter would pass along his thanks for the delicious meals. The waiter promised to do it. Kappakas paid the bill and left the Bonefish Grill for the last time.

After taking a refreshing shower Kappakas took his suitcase and carefully packed his shirts, jackets, trousers, ties, socks and underwear. In the wheeled carry-on, he put his laptop, notepad and a few other small items. He put his plane ticket in his inside jacket pocket. Before checking out, he had a light breakfast. Kappakas thanked the helpful receptionist for his services. He looked around once more and left the hotel. He had the valet drive his rented car up to the entrance, and gave him a good tip.

His flight was scheduled early in the afternoon, so he had some time to detour from the direct route and pay a visit to Father D'Angelico. The priest's help had created a breakthrough in the Larkin investigation. He was lucky to find D'Angelico in the church. The priest was about to go to St. Luke's.

'Another death, Father?'

D'Angelico was in a hurry and first didn't seem to recognize the Detective. 'Ah, it's you. Sorry, but I'm still somewhat confused.'

'By what, may I ask?'

'Suzie Atchison died. I've just heard it. Oh, Mio Dio, I don't understand.'

For a moment, Kappakas was at a loss for words. Then he said, 'Well, Father, that's sad news indeed.'

'Absolutely. I must go to the clinic now, unless you... '

'No, no, by all means go. We may see each other at her funeral.'

Father D'Angelico already was gone and got into his old Ford. He quickly disappeared down the street. Kappakas returned to his car and thought. He was saddened by the bad news, although he wasn't really shocked. Suzie had been heavily demented and had passed through terrible ordeals lately. He had rescued her from Larkin's clutches, but apparently the stress had been too much for her. Kappakas considered the new situation and made up his mind.

An hour and a half later he returned his car at Southwest Florida International Airport in Fort Myers. Then he checked the status of his flight, went through security, and took a seat at his gate. It wasn't very busy in the terminal. Kappakas opened the newspaper he'd bought at the news stand just inside security. Maybe there was some news about the Larkin case, particularly since the bail hearing. As a policeman, he was also interested in court announcements. They were often about bankruptcies, but also businesses terminations by order of the judge, and convicts declared to be of unsound mind. One announcement caught his eye.

"By order of judge Scalutti the right of self-determination has, as of now, been deprived of Mr. J. Broderick, born August 12, 1982, living in Naples. It has been found the aforementioned person cannot be held fully responsible for his past and future actions."

Kappakas lowered the paper. This is the second surprise today, he thought. Broderick had, in fact, impaired control over his actions and behavior, both before the murder of Elaine and after. The man must have had a very difficult time during the many talks with psychiatrists and behavioral psychologists. Broderick will probably be detained in an institution under a court order. The man is too dangerous to society to move around freely. Kappakas sighed. He looked at the flight information display and saw his plane was due to depart in forty-five minutes. He closed his eyes and dozed off. He saw Suzie Atchison standing in front of him.

"You will come to my funeral, won't you, Detective? You saved my life. I'll never forget. I forgive everyone who has done bad things to Don and me."

Kappakas woke up with a start and anxiously looked at the clock. He saw the passengers were already being checked in at the boarding gate and some were walking through the gangway to the plane. He stood up, took his carry-on and lined up. Twenty minutes later the Southwest plane accelerated to more than a hundred and fifty miles an hour, then detached itself from the runway and headed for Jacksonville.

Chapter 116

Father Raymond D'Angelico shook hands with the Interim Director of St. Luke's, thanked him for taking care of preparations for Suzie Atchison's funeral, and left the clinic. He had just paid a visit to Suzie's husband, Don. D'Angelico informed him of the burial arrangements and asked him if he had wishes for the memorial service.

But D'Angelico doubted if his words got through to him. Don seemed preoccupied with the loss of his beloved wife and looked very sad. He had skipped two meals and was constantly looking out the window from a corner in the room. D'Angelico felt sorry for the man. He'd prayed with him and said he would be picked up for the service. Don nodded. When the priest wanted to leave the room, he saw him stand in front of the window, saying, 'The sword will defeat the enemy.'

D'Angelico stopped and turned around. He looked at Don and doubted if he should react to his words, but decided to leave the clinic. He had been told by the Interim Director that Dr. Santini had been arrested, for her use of illegal drugs on patients and because she had stronger ties with Larkin than was initially suspected. The Director had been unable to give him details about the arrest. D'Angelico hoped the new staff would wipe out the traces of the past and that St. Luke's would be a safe place again for people to convalesce and get specialized help for dementia.

When D'Angelico approached his church he saw a big black limo parked in front of the lawn. He paid no attention to it and entered the place of worship through a side door. In a few hours he would lead a mass here. There was enough time to make preparations and speak to the acolytes. They had mixed up the rituals during the previous mass, much to the amusement of the congregation. D'Angelico was an orthodox priest who honored the sacraments and church rites. One was a Roman Catholic or nothing, was his firm belief. Although the majority of his parishioners had a modern attitude and were averse to Rome, they loved their 'Father,' the parish priest. Many were proud of him when they read in the newspapers that D'Angelico had played a role in solving the Larkin case. So, many of them looked the other way whenever he made a small mistake, was dogmatic, or put the Pope on a pedestal, so to speak.

D'Angelico used to hear confessions before mass. Mostly, nobody was sitting in the confessional box and he would be out of it five minutes later. But it was his ecclesiastical duty to make his daily visits to the box. He opened the door and sat down on the wooden bench. He had put a cushion on it for comfort. Perfunctorily, he now opened the little curtain and actually saw a figure behind the perforated screen. For reasons of confidentiality confessants were allowed to confess their sins or tell their problems 'invisibly.' In principle, the priest didn't know who the person was who confessed that he or she had committed domestic violence, adultery or even murder.

'May God be with you. What can I do for you?'

D'Angelico heard some shuffling and snorting. He had to resist the temptation to look through the holes secretly.

'Actually, Father, I've come to warn you.'

In a reflex, D'Angelico raised his eyebrows, and deep furrows appeared in his brow. 'Just tell me, my friend; the Lord is with you.'

'Listen, you should keep quiet. If you're going to testify against Larkin, you'll be killed.'

It remained quiet in the box.

'Is that clear?'

D'Angelico was flabbergasted. He didn't dare look through the perforated partition to see who threatened him. 'Uh..., and who are you?' he asked hesitatingly.

'Doesn't matter, I've only come to warn you. When I leave this box you're going to stay inside for at least two minutes. If you come out sooner, you're dead.'

'Yes, yes, sure,' D'Angelico said with calm reserve.

The man left the confessional. His quick footsteps were clearly audible in the quiet church. After the sound faded away, D'Angelico opened the door. He saw the church was empty. He rushed to his room, took a glass of water, and sat down in his armchair. He trembled. Had the visitor only been a hired messenger, or was he one of Larkin's men?

The mass was about to begin, but D'Angelico felt incapable of leading the service. He called the auxiliary priest and told him what had just happened. The latter urged D'Angelico to take some rest and not to worry about the mass. The auxiliary priest promised to drop in after the mass, and together they would inform the police about the threat.

Chapter 117

Kappakas came into his department with an uneasy smile on his face. He was pleased to receive the applause and whistling of at least twenty police officers and staff. Everybody had followed his reported adventures in Naples with great interest and pride. He shook hands and got a big hug from a female colleague. Kappakas began to feel awkward, receiving so much acclaim. When he arrived at his glass 'cage', he shook his head. The glass was littered with the by now famous "Kappa in Nappa" stickers. On his desk was a beautiful box with a large bow on it. His voluptuous secretary, Julie Brock, nodded to him, indicating he had to open the package quickly.

'How did you get those stickers?'

'Never mind, just open the package,' Julie said impatiently.

Kappakas had experienced parties like this before, and he knew there was no escape from being the center of attention right now. 'A set of golf balls,' Kappakas said when he had unwrapped the present.

'Well, that's your hobby, isn't it? First-rate quality,' a colleague said.

Nearly all of them were standing in his little 'goldfish bowl'. That's what Kappakas called his windowed office in the homicide department of the Jacksonville police department.

'And now no more balls into the bushes, chief,' he heard someone call at the door. Everyone was laughing. Although he usually avoided attracting too much attention, this time he felt it was right his department had supported him in his work. He wanted to say something. Julie noticed it and she raised her shrill voice to call for attention. Some men snickered when Julie straightened her back and her ample bosom attracted their attention. 'Silence, please. The chief wants to say something.'

Kappakas got up and thanked Julie for silencing the crowd. 'The sexist gentlemen among us, please be quiet for a moment.'

He waited for them to straighten their faces. 'First of all, I'm glad to be back. For more than a month I've been walking around in Naples and met all kinds of people. I must say I've gained some completely new experiences in my police career. Particularly, Chief Matarazo's methods appealed to me. I guess by now you all know what happened down there, but still there's one thing I'd like to give some attention, and that's the fact that I haven't been able to give my friend, John Iskander, his daughter back. I had to tell him where and how I finally found her, and it was hard for me to bring him this awful news. Immediately before I left yesterday, I received the message that Suzie Atchison had died. You all know who she is from the newspapers.'

Some nodded their heads, others whispered 'yes.'

'Probably the stress had become too much for her. I intend to go back to attend her funeral. I'm doing this for personal reasons, and I'll take a day or two off for it. I also expect to testify at the trials of Larkin and Rosenberg; otherwise I'll follow them from here. Well, thanks again for your support and consideration. And special thanks are due to Pete Dykehouse for his help. Pete, you were an excellent contact man, I always had the feeling that I was in touch with you all here. Well, that's it then; let's get back to work.'

Still, the animated atmosphere returned. People laughed and chatted. Some patted Pete Dykehouse on the shoulder. Kappakas sat down in his imitation leather armchair and watched everyone slowly return to their desks or start to discuss preparations for some other arrest. Julie Brock was still near him and carried a number of files in her arms. 'Chief, could you read these later on?'

Kappakas gave Julie a tired look. 'Sorry, Julie, I still have to get reoriented. Even though I know this fishbowl like the back of my hand, I must get used to it all over again. Come back in fifteen minutes, okay?'

'Sure, chief.'

Kappakas leaned back in his chair and looked around him. From his position he could observe his whole department. He was working with great people, especially his secretary, Julie, he thought. The forty-eight-year-old unmarried mother had been his help and stay for over seventeen years. Some of his men showed a certain disrespect because of her figure or made jokes about it. He had called them to account about it once or twice. They said he shouldn't be so narrow-minded about it; it was just innocent banter. However, such behavior not only disrespected all the women in the office, but could result in legal complaints about discrimination in a 'hostile work environment.' So, he needed to give it serious attention.

Several times he'd made attempts to make his team into more of a 'family,' something that is common in fire-fighting units. Then the so-called funny remarks would disappear quickly, he thought, and colleagues would be more considerate of each other.

He got up and put the new golf balls into his drawer. He took the phone and dialed Dick Matarazo's number. 'Have you already been informed about Suzie Atchison's death?'

'Yes, Father D'Angelico told me. She probably died of natural causes. We're still investigating it. By the way, this morning he reported he'd been threatened.'

'He's been threatened? By whom?'

'An unknown man warned him during confession not to testify against Larkin. I take this very seriously, detective. We're going to put someone on guard at the church.'

'Do you think Larkin's behind this?'

'I'm not sure. It would be a stupid thing to do. Might also be one of Larkin's supporters, who thinks he's a great guy and who wants to scare Larkin's opponents. We rule out nothing.'

'In the newspaper I read Broderick has been declared of unsound mind. So that problem has been solved for the police. How about Santini? Is she cooperating?'

'We arrested her.'

'What for?'

'She has closer ties to Larkin than we first suspected. We're interrogating her tomorrow. And then, of course, there's her use of illegal medicines.'

'Wow, there's still a lot happening in this case, and now I'm not even around.'

Matarazo grinned. 'How is it to be working in Jacksonville again? Have you settled back in?'

'Everybody's been asking me that, and now you too.'

Matarazo laughed. Kappakas wanted to end the conversation, but changed his mind and asked, 'Chief; one more thing. I'm not comfortable with this threat against D'Angelico.'

Matarazo sighed. 'I understand, we're watching this closely. Maybe Santini can tell us something tomorrow. We're trying to get things under control. I know you have a special relationship with the priest. We're doing our best.'

When Kappakas had put down the phone, he got that strange, suspicious feeling again. Soon he would discover an unexpected truth.

Chapter 118

Don Atchison was looking in his bathroom mirror. With pouches under his eyes and a pale complexion, he looked haggard. He knew that if he combed his hair and shaved off his beard, he would look better. But Suzie's death had upset him very much and he didn't feel like caring for himself. Everyone gave him well-meant advice, but he wouldn't listen. All day long and sometimes even during the night he was thinking of Suzie. He missed her so much. Her sudden death had come as a great shock. He was convinced it was partly due to the stress and fear caused by her kidnapping from the hospital. He didn't want to speculate about what would have happened to Suzie if Detective Kappakas hadn't intervened. These thoughts would be too painful. How could life change course so dramatically?

What severe changes from the safe, carefree retirement residence at SocHom, to captivity in St. Luke's Clinic to treat Suzie's dementia, to her hospitalization, kidnapping, rescue and death. Don was scarcely able to comprehend that reality had been so hard and merciless. His grief developed into self-punishment. He ate little. His life seemed meaningless without Suzie. After the funeral he would take measures to alleviate his pain. That's what he had promised Suzie, and he would keep his word. Anyway, there was no longer a place for him at St. Luke's. Now that he was a widower, he was no longer allowed to make use of St. Luke's residential care. That was the policy laid down by the new Director. But Don didn't want to live alone at SocHom. At the clinic he knew the people and assistants. It was a small community and he had grown used to it. He walked back to his room and looked out of the window. The hearse was already in front of the entrance.

Don had asked Father D'Angelico to keep the interment as simple as possible. He had given him the names of those he would like to be with him at the grave. He put on a light jacket and from a drawer took some objects, which he put in the inside pocket. He was ready to go. Downstairs in the hall he met D'Angelico and also Detective Kappakas, Mike and Ellis. The St. Luke's Interim Director and Don's new counselor were there too. It was usual for representatives of the clinic to be present at deceased patients' funerals. Don accepted their condolences and waited for the undertaker to lead them all to the cars. Don preferred to follow the hearse in his own car, a little old Mazda, with the rest of the company behind him.

The hearse stopped near the entrance of the cemetery. Bearers lifted out the coffin. Don Atchison walked in front with Father D'Angelico at his side. The group went into the auditorium, and they were offered a cool drink, welcome refreshment, for the temperature had already risen noticeably. Don was quiet and stood in a corner of the hall. The others spoke softly with each other and looked at him now and then. The undertaker signaled the interment could start, and they all went out to the grave site.

Father D'Angelico offered a short meditation and spoke about Suzie Atchison's life. After a short prayer, the interment commenced. Don threw a white carnation on the coffin while it was slowly lowered into the ground. His lips trembled with grief.

'Goodbye, my dear Suzie,' Don mumbled. Tears filled his eyes and he shook all over. For safety's sake, Kappakas held his arm. After Suzie's coffin was in place, D'Angelico lead a prayer of thanks, committed Suzie to God's merciful care, and then asked everyone to stay a short while and have a light lunch, offered by the church.

'Funerals always make me hungry,' Mike whispered.

'Mike,' Ellis hissed. 'It's inappropriate to say that.'

Father D'Angelico asked everybody to sit down at a long table with sandwiches, donuts, pitchers of water, various soft drinks and coffee. Employees of the undertaker's and St. Luke's Clinic also joined the simple meal.

'In our parish it's the custom to have something to eat and drink after an interment,' D'Angelico began. 'Let's give thanks and pray for enlightenment of our souls and strengthening of our spirits.'

Mike and Ellis dutifully folded their hands but didn't close their eyes. No one else did, either. A Catholic habit, praying with eyes open, they heard later on. After the beautiful prayer, in which D'Angelico asked the Almighty to support Don in the difficult period ahead of him, he signaled to the cemetery's caretaker to fill the coffee cups. Although they were all still looking silently in front of them, Kappakas tried to break the sad atmosphere. 'Father, you have spoken very well. Not only have you given consolation to Don, but we can all draw strength from your words. I think you've lead Suzie's funeral in a modest and respectful way.'

There was a murmur of assent, and the atmosphere grew more relaxed. Soon everyone was talking pleasantly with each other, and now and then Ellis could even be heard laughing softly. Don, who was sitting next to D'Angelico, kept himself somewhat apart and enjoyed a sandwich. Finally, he had allowed himself to eat something. After finishing his meal, he excused himself to go to the bathroom. This gave Mike the opportunity to ask Kappakas what D'Angelico had experienced in the confessional. 'Kappa, do you know more about the threat against Father D'Angelico?'

Kappakas looked at Don's empty chair and said, 'Not much. I do know that Matarazo's working on it. He told me there's a police guard at the church. That's right, isn't it, Father?'

D'Angelico nodded and said he would probably be alright now. Ellis thought about what Kappakas had said earlier about Santini. 'This morning you told me that Santini is going to be brought in again today for questioning. Did they find evidence that she's involved in Larkin's crimes?'

Kappakas took a sip of his coffee and thought for a moment. 'Apparently, but remember she's a smart lady. I've personally experienced it. Maybe she had to own up. She must have known there was a connection between Sykes, the undertaker, and Larkin. By the way, I have some news about Sykes. The FBI is searching intensively for him now. You remember how he suddenly ran away.'

This last remark caused Ellis to point to the fact that Don was still absent. 'He's been gone for a while. You think he's alright?'

No one answered. Ellis said it wouldn't hurt to check the men's room.

'I'll go,' Mike said and left the hall.

Kappakas noticed the others had fallen silent and waited for Mike's return. 'He will tell us what's keeping Don so long,' he said, attempting to reassure everyone.

Suddenly the door of the reception room was thrown open. Mike ran in. 'He's not in the men's room. I've checked everywhere. I can't find him.'

Everyone reacted anxiously and started to talk in confusion. Kappakas raised his voice and said, 'Please everyone, stay calm. I'd like to ask the caretaker if there are any rooms where he may have gone. You know your way around here.'

The caretaker said Don could only be on the right side of the auditorium. 'There are several rooms, a prayer room and the mortuary. We should look there. It's no use looking on the left side; we would have seen him walk that way.'

Kappakas ordered Ellis, Mike and two undertakers to search the rooms off the right side of the hall. After a few minutes they all returned without finding Don. 'He's gone,' Kappakas concluded.

Suddenly Father D'Angelico put his hands over his mouth, his eyes nearly popping out of his head.

'Father, what's wrong?' Ellis asked in surprise.

'Oh, Mio Dio,' D'Angelico reacted frightened. 'When I was with him at the clinic he said something about a sword and striking down someone…'

He gave Kappakas a startled look. The Detective immediately understood what the priest meant. 'Don is going to try to find Larkin and take revenge.'

The bad news quickly passed among the group. Everyone looked astonished. Quickly Kappakas gave orders. 'Mike, you're with me. Ellis, take Father D'Angelico back to his parish, and the others, please return to your work.'

D'Angelico looked defeated. He shook his head. 'How could I have overlooked Don's remark? How stupid.'

Kappakas and Mike ran out of the building to their car, and noticed Don's Mazda was gone. Soon they were driving at high speed to the Naples' industrial park.

'Damn,' Kappakas swore. 'He has at least a fifteen-minute lead on us.'

The rush hour had already begun, so Kappakas had to decelerate or brake frequently to prevent collisions.

'What do you think, would he have a weapon?' Mike asked through the racing engine noise.

'I can't imagine. But he wasn't invited for coffee by Larkin; that's for sure.

Kappakas turned right and was now on Airport Pulling Road. There was a two-mile stretch of asphalt before him, leading straight to Prospect. This allowed him to accelerate to over eighty miles an hour, and hopefully he would be in time to upset Don's plan. At one crossing Kappakas had to stop for a red light, but he ignored most crossings, honking his horn and looking left and right to avoid any traffic.

'Mike, call Matarazo. We can't handle this on our own. We need local back-up.'

Mike tried to reach the police station, but the speeding car made it hard to press the right buttons. When he was finally connected, he said he urgently needed to speak with Chief Matarazo. The desk clerk told him he wasn't in and couldn't be reached by phone right away.

Dismayed, Mike looked at Kappakas. The latter tore the phone out of Mike's hands and shouted, 'Detective Kappakas here. We need him urgently. Where the hell is the Chief?'

'At the golf course, sir.'

Chapter 119

Don Atchison turned into Prospect Avenue and checked his note for the street number of Naples Autoparts Imports. He parked on the lot next to NAI. He locked the door and slowly walked to the office building. Although it was just half past four in the afternoon, the street was quiet. He felt weak, so the heat of the scorching sun made him gasp. Sweat poured from his body. But he didn't care about his discomfort. He had a mission to accomplish and nothing would stop him. He knew he shouldn't dawdle; he suspected pursuers would be close on his heels.

Don was standing in front of Larkin's office now. He took out his Ruger LCP automatic, a small but popular gun among women. He released the safety catch. The windows of the cabin were open. He heard noises; voices and music. Probably a TV, he thought. He heard sporadic laughter, which didn't come from the TV. He walked quietly to the door and tried to open it. The handle moved. In spite of his age, Don was still fairly limber. He opened the door slowly and cautiously eased himself in so the hinges wouldn't creak. He found himself in a small hallway where four doors opened from separate rooms. One of the doors was ajar. The noises came from behind this door.

Don held the Ruger straight in front of him and tried to look through the narrow opening. He saw a big armchair with a man and woman sharing the chair and watching TV. Their backs were to the door, so they didn't notice him. The TV program was an old sit-com. The man slumped in the chair and took some chips from a bowl on the end table, and then picked up a can of beer with his right hand. The other arm was around the woman's neck. She kissed the man on his cheek, softly making squeaks of delight. The man seemed mainly interested in the TV program. When the woman turned to kiss him, she could see the door where Don was watching through the narrow opening. She began to talk. 'Josh, darling, you will do that for me, won't you?'

Larkin; finally I've got you, Don thought, and he forcefully pushed the door open. It banged against a wooden wall. The woman screamed. Larkin was unable to say more than a startled 'What the f...!?'

Don was seven feet away from the couple and aimed his gun at Larkin. The woman, who was sitting half naked in the chair, screeched and fell to the floor for cover. Larkin had turned around and looked at the man who was pointing a Ruger at him. 'What the hell!?'

Larkin stopped talking abruptly when he saw the intruder take a step forward, aiming the pistol at his head.

'You there, on the floor, get out of here,' Don ordered.

The woman, in fact a girl less than twenty years old, was nearly in shock. She cried fearfully and just managed to grab her clothing from the floor before stumbling quickly past Don out of the room. Don wasn't distracted, keeping a close eye on Larkin.

'Who the hell are you? What do you want here?' Larkin barked.

Don looked sharply at the criminal, the murderer of his wife. Finally he had come face to face with his enemy. His eyes narrowed and betrayed his anger, focused on revenge. Larkin started to stand up, but Don stopped him.

'Don't move!' he ordered. The back of the armchair formed a barrier, which partly hid Larkin's body. Don wanted the crook to stay in an uncomfortably defenseless position. Larkin obeyed and saw the resentment in the intruder's eyes. The hand holding the pistol shook. Desperate, revengeful people are unpredictable and won't listen to reason, so Larkin's chances of survival were limited. If he wanted to get out in one piece, he had to start talking to the man and bring him to his senses. Don took a picture from his pocket. He tossed it at Larkin, and it fell to the floor next to the end table.

'Pick up that picture, carefully.'

With a false grin Larkin nodded, bent forward and picked up the photograph.

'Look at it.'

Larkin got angry and wanted to turn around, but changed his mind in time. 'What do you want from me, old man? Who are you? Are we going to look at photos, or are you going to tell me what you're here for?'

Don's gun hand began to tremble even more. 'Look at it, damn you! Look at the picture! Do you know who that is? You must know her.'

Larkin glanced at the photograph. He shook his head and tossed it on the table.

'That's my wife, and you killed her,' Don said, his voice breaking while he spoke. His eyes misted over. Emotion began to overpower him, and he was barely able to speak. Larkin very cautiously tried to take the Walther from his inside pocket.

'You've taken my sweet Suzie's life. You're a dirty crook, Larkin, a killer…'

Don started to tremble. Larkin saw tears clouding Don's sight. This was his chance to eliminate his opponent, before he became a victim himself.

'Oh, you're talking about the woman we picked up from the hospital?'

'Yeah! Kidnapped, you mean. She was my wife, dammit!'

Larkin conjured up a false smile. 'But I didn't kill her. Detective Kappakas, he's the one that took her away from here. She was still alive then. I'm not the person you're looking for.'

Larkin maneuvered his gun from his jacket and held it on the chair cushion by his leg. Without looking he released the safety catch. It was ready.

Don looked bitterly at Larkin. 'Suzie would still be alive, if you…'

Suddenly he heard a sound which definitely didn't come from the TV. Overwhelmed by feelings of sadness and loneliness, Don's mind was no longer clear when he turned his head towards the window from where he thought the sound had come.

Larkin saw his chance in a fraction of a second. He jumped from his chair, turning towards Don and raising his Walther. He pulled the trigger. One shot rang out, and another one. Larkin saw Don spin on his axis and grab his shoulder. Don's weapon crashed to the floor. Larkin grinned, but his expression changed to a grimace. He felt a sharp pain in his chest. A bloodstain appeared on his shirt, spreading across the fabric. Larkin staggered, the Walther still in his hand. He saw Don was trying to get up and leave the room. With a final effort he aimed his gun at Don, who was now standing with his back to him. More bullets were fired. The firepower hit hard. Larkin jerked backwards onto the end table, his impact breaking it to pieces.

Kappakas burst into the room with his gun at the ready. When he came closer he saw Larkin's Walther lying on the floor. Kappakas looked out of the window and signaled Mike to come on in. Don was squatting on the ground, holding his right shoulder, his face contorted in pain.

'Let me have a look,' Mike said and examined the wound. It looked like Don had been lucky. The bullet had hit his arm just above the biceps. He had been standing with his side turned towards Larkin, so his body was at its narrowest when he was shot. Kappakas carefully pulled up Don's arm where the bullet had entered and saw something he didn't like at all. The bullet had left the arm and penetrated the chest.

'This doesn't look good. Mike, call 911 and check if the police are already on their way.'

Blood gradually drained from Don's face and he closed his eyes. His body grew heavy in Kappakas' arms and he wanted to lie down.

'Don, listen, stay with me. Open your eyes. Come on, don't give up.'

While Kappakas kept talking to Don, his eyes caught Larkin's lifeless body. An investigation into this shoot-out should determine that Kappakas had fired at Larkin to protect Don. Mike picked up the office phone and called; '911 EMT's are on the way, and I hear police sirens in the distance.'

'Fine; Don is in bad shape. The bullet probably hit a lung. That's why he fainted. He needs oxygen, fast!'

Kappakas tried to keep Don awake, softly slapping his face and constantly talking to him. The ambulance appeared and EMT's immediately put Don on a ventilator and a drip too, then carefully maneuvered him onto a stretcher. The EMT's also checked Larkin and confirmed he was dead. Then the ambulance disappeared toward Naples Downtown Hospital at high speed with siren and flashing lights.

Two police cars arrived and a detective asked Kappakas what had happened. He searched the crime scene for empty cartridges on the floor and bullets in the walls. He told Kappakas to stay available for questioning to establish the facts and circumstances of the shooting.

'Yes, I know how it works, Detective. You have my full cooperation.'

Meanwhile, Mike had informed Ellis about the attempt on Don's life. She promised to get to the hospital as soon as possible. Kappakas turned to Mike. 'Come on, Mike, we're going to the hospital. I want to be there. That man doesn't deserve to die.'

Chapter 120

Father D'Angelico and Ellis arrived at the hospital too late to see Don Atchison. They met Kappakas and Mike in the main hall and discussed the new situation.

'We're waiting for the doctor attending Don. He promised to give us the results of his first examination as soon as possible,' Kappakas reported. They sat down in the waiting room and Mike got coffee for everyone. Not much was said and they all killed time checking their e-messages and news or reading magazines. D'Angelico was beginning to wonder about Don. 'We've been waiting more than an hour. Surely they must be able to give us a report by now?'

'Doctors want to be careful. When they inform folks about a patient's condition, the information must be reliable, even when cautioning about risks and uncertainties,' Ellis said. Right then, one of the doctors came out of the surgery. He walked to Kappakas with a neutral expression. Everyone grouped expectantly around the physician.

'I can tell you Mr. Atchison is out of danger. The bullet didn't penetrate the lung, because it was slowed down by the biceps of the upper arm. We expect he'll recover fully, after the use of his arm recovers from some temporary impairment. He'll likely need physical therapy for that.'

'That's good news, thank you Doctor,' Ellis said, visibly relieved. D'Angelico's eyes beamed. 'I always say: we Catholics are fighters; we want to enjoy life to the fullest.'

Kappakas smiled at the priest's aphorism and wondered if Don would enjoy life very much after Suzie's death. He turned to Mike. 'Mike, are you going with me to see Matarazo? I have a lot of explaining to do about the shooting and you're a reliable witness, so you can support me. They may also want to ask questions about your involvement.'

'Of course; I'm ready to go.'

They left, while Ellis stayed behind with the priest.

'Are they going to question Don later on, assuming he'll be back to normal?' D'Angelico asked.

Ellis thought for a moment. 'Yes, I'm sure. If he's capable of talking to the police, they'll want to know why he wanted to kill Larkin.'

'Yes, but he didn't get the chance. I don't know much about

criminal law, but I imagine Don's actions indirectly caused Larkin's death.'

Ellis smiled. 'Come on, let's not speculate now. I'm going back to my hotel. Are you staying here a little longer?'

'Yes, Ellis, I think so. Maybe I can be of some help to Don.'

Ellis left the hospital. While calmly steering her car through the traffic, her thoughts wandered off to Mike. Earlier that day she had agreed to his proposal to have dinner together in a good seafood restaurant after his visit to the police station. This was her chance to rope him into giving an interview about what happened in Larkin's office. His death should be a climactic point in her story about Larkin's criminal organization.

Mike had different plans, however, which should be the final episode of one of the most dangerous and exciting periods of his life.

Chapter 121

After four days, Don Atchison was released from hospital after treating his wounds and a little physical therapy. He had come through very well. Doctors had removed the bullet, which had lodged just an inch from his lung. He felt better and looked forward to being on his own. After ample consideration, he decided to return to SocHom, where a new Director had been appointed. Larkin's death helped him come to terms with Suzie's death, as least to some degree. In retrospect, Don was glad that he hadn't been the one to kill Larkin.

For that, Kappakas and Mike gave an account today before a special investigation unit of the police and the FBI. They were particularly interested in how Don Atchison had been able to slip away from the cemetery's auditorium. Mike's involvement and personal background were also topics of interest. The FBI agent was interested primarily in the interstate and cross-border trade in organs and illegal medicine. The FBI was still trying to trace Larkins' connections.

After an interrogation of more than two hours, the investigators concluded that Kappakas had acted to defend Don Atchison from the shooting attempt by Larkin. Although policemen are not permitted to use civilians in a raid, the FBI was convinced Mike wasn't merely an adventurer from Texas, but had actually been assisting with permission from Kappakas. The initial charge against him for his courier work for Larkin was also dismissed, as Mike had not known the contents of the packages he had carried. Mike provided whatever information he could about his connections in San Antonio.

Dick Matarazo, the highest ranking police officer involved in the arrest of Larkin, was praised by the Mayor, City Council and the Governor for his undercover role. Kappakas offered his apologies for his skeptical attitude towards the Police Chief. Matarazo said he understood; he'd been compelled to surround his actions with necessary secrecy, enough to raise suspicions.

'Larkin wasn't allowed, under any circumstances, to get the impression I just let you go your own way. He even proposed killing you. In fact, I had to assure him I wouldn't tolerate your continued presence and interference in my jurisdiction.'

'So you played it well. I actually doubted your good intentions, although I couldn't be sure you were on the take.'

Matarazo shrugged his shoulders. 'Well, Detective, it's a trick you can only play once. The media now has extensively covered my role. I'm glad it's all over. I can be myself again.'

Kappakas got up, making a move to leave. Matarazo stopped him. 'I have some news for you.'

'Is that so?'

'Early this morning, in a joint action of the Mexican and American authorities closed the pharmaceutical factory, Bioclon.'

'Really? That's very good news!'

'Sure. Several managers and employees involved in the illegal medicine racket were arrested.'

'Wow, things are moving fast now.'

'You can say that again. By the way, have you planned something for tonight?'

'Why's that? Are you asking me out?'

Matarazo laughed. 'The Governor wants to speak with you, if you have time, of course.'

'The Governor? Well, well. What does he want with me?'

'No idea. Maybe he wants to thank you for what you did for us here.'

'Ah, yes. I think I've got time for that. Where and when?'

'Here at the station. He's on a working visit in south Florida, and he wants to meet you.'

'That's fine. I've only seen him on TV a few times. I look forward to meeting the man in the flesh.'

'He expects you at six-thirty. Don't eat anything for now, Archie. I'll arrange something.'

'I'll be there.'

They said goodbye to each other, and Kappakas began to think about what he would say to the Governor.

Chapter 122

At 6:15 PM, Kappakas reported at the desk of the police station. He'd taken a short rest, showered and eaten a snack. He had no idea what Matarazo had meant by 'don't eat anything for now,' but he didn't want to disappoint him, so a snack was all, for the time being. Matarazo came down the stairs, wearing a different uniform.

'Hello Detective, the Governor is looking forward to meeting you.'

Kappakas looked somewhat surprised at the Chief. 'You look sharp. I don't recognize you, all dressed up like that. You make me feel underdressed now.'

'Don't exaggerate. You look fine, and shaven too. Just fine.'

'I had to. Make a bad impression on the Governor and I could get fired, just like that. He has enough influence.'

They both laughed and went upstairs to Matarazo's office.

'Have a seat,' Matarazo said, as they entered his office. Kappakas sat down in a leather chair and waited. The phone rang. Matarazo answered and told the caller he was on his way. 'The Governor is here. I'm going to bring him up.'

Kappakas nodded, took a magazine from the Florida Police Chiefs Association and began to leaf through it. He was surprised Matarazo hadn't met the Governor already. After all, he was the Governor's host. Apparently they don't care so much about decorum here in south-Florida, he thought. It wasn't long before a group of VIP's entered the building. Kappakas recognized the Governor's voice, as he greeted several police officers. Matarazo lead Governor Jack Morrow into his office and introduced him to Kappakas.

'Pleased to meet you. I was told you're from Jacksonville; is that right?'

'Yes, sir. But Naples was my second job recently.'

'Detective, I've heard a lot about you lately, and you've been in the news too. But first, I'd like to offer my condolences for the death of your friend's daughter.'

Kappakas nodded his head and appreciated Morrow for mentioning it.

'The main reason I'm here is to thank you on behalf of the people of Florida for your extraordinary police work. Without your effort, courage and cooperation with Chief Matarazo, we'd might still be chasing Larkin.' He gave Matarazo a roguish smile. 'Sorry, Dick.'

Matarazo took the Governor's remark well and said he'd done his best. He proudly patted Kappakas on the shoulder. Morrow produced a small box from his pocket. 'Therefore, I'm honored to present this medal, an award of merit for commendable service to the state.'

Kappakas was visibly surprised, his face colored slightly, a little embarrassed. Morrow hung the medal around his neck and shook Kappakas' hand. 'Congratulations. You're a fine example to others.'

Matarazo and his colleagues congratulated Kappakas. They were lined up at the door and Kappakas couldn't help thinking about the time when he'd won his judo black belt, the only one in his class at the police training academy. It had been an exceptional feat, and almost everyone on the campus had congratulated him. When everyone had seen the medal close up, they gathered around in Matarazo's office. The Chief wanted to make an announcement. 'Governor, Detective Kappakas, and guests, I request the pleasure of your company at an informal buffet.'

Kappakas enjoyed the food and drinks. He felt honored to have made a contribution to the safety of the citizens of Naples. That's what a cop's work is really all about: protecting the public by putting criminals out of business. Unfortunately, the central figure in his investigation had died prematurely and couldn't be tried. The fact Kappakas had helped break up a crime gang, made him feel good enough to forget any thoughts of retirement for now. Governor Morrow didn't stay long, but found time to go over recent events with Kappakas. Morrow showed a lively interest in the detective's methods and understood why Kappakas had been suspicious of Matarazo.

'We only set up undercover crooked cops in exceptional cases - and if we need the pay-off money!' Morrow laughed loudest of all. Then he left to return home, the Capitol in Tallahassee. Matarazo noticed the festive meal was coming to an end and sat down beside Kappakas. He poured himself another glass of wine.

'Want a glass, Detective?'

Kappakas gave him a mock-serious look. 'What are you doing to me, Chief?'

'You don't like it?'

'Oh, yes, an award like this would flatter anyone. Thanks again.'

'You're welcome.'

'There's something I'd like to ask you, though. In Jacksonville we never have parties like these, usually because there's no money for it. So I wonder who's paying?'

With a roguish smile Matarazo shrugged his shoulders and whispered, 'Don't tell anyone; it's some of Larkin's pay-off money.'

They both laughed. When Kappakas was on his way to his hotel half an hour later, he was thinking about the cordiality and friendship he'd received from the Naples' police force, and his award. It made him feel a little humble and very grateful. But he would never have met the Governor if it hadn't been for the support and effort of his friends Ellis and Mike. Waiting for a stoplight, he wondered how they were doing.

Chapter 123

'Would you like me to fill up your drinks, ma'am, sir?'
The waiter at Citrus Seafood Restaurant had done his best to make their evening special. He was hospitable, helpful, and unobtrusive; qualities many restaurant owners would appreciate. Waiters like George, who make their guests feel special, are real treasures.

'How about you?' Mike asked.

'No thanks, I've already had one too many, I'm afraid.'

'Half a glass for me, George.'

The waiter filled his glass and left their table to take orders from some new guests. Mike looked into Ellis's brown eyes. 'Well, how did you like the food?'

She put her elbows on the table and rested her dizzy head in her hands. 'It was a lovely dinner, Mike. Once again you found a great place, on the shore by the Gulf. I had no idea you were so romantic. You've also done your best to help me complete my story. All the loose ends are tied up now, I think. I really appreciate your help.'

He was barely able to suppress some nervous uncertainty. 'My pleasure,' he said, looking steadily into her eyes. He called George and asked for the check.

'We're so close to the beach; do you feel like walking along the water? I'm trying to be romantic, you know.'

She smiled and Mike was sure now. He liked her very much. She was pretty, intelligent, caring, and had an engaging personality. He appreciated her sense of adventure and commitment to justice. She looked at him, questioningly. She blushed slightly. 'Yes, I'd like that.'

Mike felt warm blood rush through his veins.

'But only if you keep me from falling. I've had a drop too much, I think.'

'Will do; shall we go?'

They left the restaurant and walked down the path to the beach. Once they reached a narrow strip of sand, Ellis took off her sandals. The water was dark and calm. The moonlight helped them spot any jelly fish that had washed ashore. There was a light breeze from the Gulf and now and then Ellis rubbed her bare arms. Mike put his jacket around her shoulders. She smiled gratefully. 'That's sweet.'

'You know, El, a few miles from here it all started. At the time I was spying on you from those dunes. Even then I thought you looked attractive.'

'Go away, Casanova.'

Mike smiled. He noticed Ellis almost stumbled when she stepped down wooden stairs. He caught her just in time. 'I promised to keep you from falling. Remember?'

They were standing opposite each other and Mike held her shoulders. He slowly bent forward. She held her breath. She wasn't sure if she would open her heart to him. He took her face into his hands and looked into her beautiful eyes. She turned her head away when his lips nearly touched hers. He waited and she felt his warm breath on her face. She couldn't resist her deeper feelings. They kissed.

Hand in hand they continued their walk along the tide line and thought about their future. Dozens of seagulls were tripping along with them across the wet sand. Somewhere in the distance they heard a police siren. They looked at each other and smiled.

Chapter 124

Six months later.

The hunt for undertaker Jim Sykes had been fruitless so far. As the days went by, the interest levels of the FBI and local police diminished. New cases came up, and the available budgets and manpower were limited. The authorities guessed Sykes would make a mistake sooner or later and get caught. His picture was everywhere: in gas stations, supermarkets, banks and of course government buildings. It was only a matter of time before Sykes would come out of his hiding place and be arrested.

The authorities had been more decisive with the trials of Sheldon Rosenberg and Margaret Santini. Within eight weeks after the request for bail had been rejected, Rosenberg was sentenced to twenty-eight years imprisonment during a tumultuous session. The members of the jury found him guilty of organ theft. He couldn't be charged with murder, so he escaped death with a long sentence, virtually for the rest of his life.

Dr. Margaret Santini was sentenced to seven years imprisonment. Her lawyer had made a reasonable case that she'd had no knowledge of what happened to the deceased patients of St. Luke's. She was blamed, however, for knowingly working with illegally imported and expired medicines. But no causal connection could be proven between the administering of the illegal medicines and the deaths of patients. Nevertheless, the jury found Santini had taken irresponsible risks, and now, between the four walls of her cell, she would have time to reflect on the undesirable consequences of her special treatment program. Her medical license was revoked.

As announced earlier, George Broderick was detained under an order for mental health assessment and treatment. His treatment, however, was problematic: the mental condition of the former male nurse and murderer of Elaine Iskander was more complex than initially believed. He would probably never be set free.

Mike Garcia and Ellis Henning continued their relationship and now lived together in Orlando. Mike found a job as a security guard. His new employer had been impressed by Mike's experience with the police during the Larkin affair.

Ellis wrote an extensive and suspenseful series of articles for her newspaper publisher about her adventures in Naples. From Random House Publishing she received an advance payment to write a book, which should be released in a few months, unless the editors slow it down.

Chapter 125

'It's in a great position, John, aim slightly to the left, you can't miss.'

John Iskander looked doubtfully at Archibald Kappakas. 'It's easy for you to say. You're way ahead with those new balls of yours.'

Kappakas shrugged his shoulders apologetically. His Cleveland 588 golf clubs, the expensive present from his department, had contributed a lot to his success in this friendly game. He had a stroke-lead which was almost impossible for his friend to make up on the remaining holes. Iskander aimed and tried to make his putt. It went straight to the hole, but curved away at the last moment, a bogey.

'Come on, my friend, let's get our gear together and have a drink.'

They drove back to the club house in the golf cart, where they enjoyed their beer. Iskander paid. The lounge was fairly crowded, mostly with golfers from one of the largest golf and country clubs in Jacksonville. The atmosphere was friendly and the alcohol flowed, either in celebration or consolation. Iskander stared into his glass and was thinking about the events which had dominated his life six months ago. With a serious expression he said, 'Arch, I'm considering visiting Elaine's grave. I really want to go there. I think it will help me get closure. Don't forget, she was our only child. We loved her very much.'

'I agree, John. I think it's wonderful, the relationship you had with Elaine.'

Iskander looked at Kappakas with tears in his eyes. 'Thanks. I really appreciate your help and concern for our family.'

Kappakas nodded and asked, 'I remember you said that you wanted revenge. How do you feel about that, now that Rosenberg's been convicted?'

'I never meant him, but Larkin. Without his money, facilities and warped mind, Rosenberg never would have been able to do it. Even though he's the one who cut up Elaine, Larkin was behind it all and provided the means for Rosenberg.'

Kappakas agreed. 'It would have been better for you if Larkin were still alive and could be convicted. Now he's escaped his trial. Do you hold a grudge about that?'

Iskander thought for a moment and shook his head. 'No, not really. Things don't always go the way you want. I've reconciled myself to it.'

They talked for a while longer and agreed to meet again after Iskander's trip to Naples.

John Iskander followed the directions on his GPS to the cemetery, where his daughter was buried. He'd decided to stay a night in Naples, so he wouldn't have to hurry to catch his return flight. He parked his rented car in the parking lot and got out. He looked at the cloudy sky, which stretched like a grey blanket above the peaceful cemetery. He entered the auditorium and asked the Grounds Supervisor where he could find his daughter's grave. He was given a plan with the route to the grave site.

Iskander found the path to Elaine's grave. When he was halfway down the path, he saw a tall, slim man sitting on his heels before a gravestone. Iskander didn't pay any further attention to it and only looked at the inscriptions on the gravestones. His heart began to beat faster when he found his daughter's tombstone. The man was a couple of yards away from him. Out of politeness Iskander greeted the man. 'Good afternoon.'

The man looked up. 'Hello,' he said, with a slight nod.

Iskander preferred to be alone, but had no choice but to adjust to this visitor, who was paying his respects to a deceased friend or loved one. The man saw that Iskander stood at Elaine's grave, putting some flowers in the holder.

'But that's Elaine Iskander's grave,' the man said. 'May I ask what your relationship is with her?'

Iskander wasn't in the mood to talk to a stranger right now. To be polite he answered the man. 'Well, Elaine is my daughter.'

The man's mouth fell open with surprise. He slowly rose to his feet and looked at Iskander with large, inquisitive eyes. 'So, you're Elaine's father.'

'Yes, I am,' he replied, but he had no idea why the man suddenly got so emotional.

The man stepped forward and wanted to shake Iskander's hand.

'Mr. Iskander, that's amazing. My name is Atchison, Don Atchison.'

Iskander was speechless for a moment, but then quickly extended his hand to Don. 'Hello, Mr. Atchison. Well, what do you know! I've heard so much about you and your wife.' Iskander sounded pleased, but subdued. Don nodded.

'Suzie is famous in Florida,' Don said with a touch of humor. The worst time of coping with his grief had passed, and he could handle his loss with a little more acceptance.

'It seems we have something in common, Mr. Atchison.'

Don was serious again, which showed Iskander that he'd touched on a sensitive point. Both men looked at the graves as their thoughts went out to their loved ones, who had both died unnatural deaths. Iskander broke the silence and they agreed to call each other by their first names.

'You know, Don, when Larkin came out on bail, I wanted revenge. I would have loved to strangle him with my own hands. In hind-sight, I'm glad I didn't get the chance.'

Don understood. 'I also wanted to kill him. I was that close,' indicating a narrow gap between thumb and forefinger. 'But I can't tell you how happy I am now that I didn't shoot the murdering scum.'

The men looked at each other with shared relief.

'We should see each other more often, Don. We could both benefit.'

'Good idea. Why don't we start right away?'

'What do you mean?'

'Come on, John, it looks like it's going to rain any minute. I'll show you my new house at SocHom. I have some gin left in the fridge. What do you say?'

Iskander agreed to Don's friendly offer. 'Well, friend, I think we have a lot of experiences to share.'

Don said goodbye to Suzie and promised to come back soon. Iskander stood in silence at his daughter's tombstone. He read her name, and memories came back to him: Elaine as a baby, a little girl, a teenager and young woman. He was overwhelmed by emotion. A lump rose in his throat. He took a handkerchief and wiped tears from his eyes. He looked at Don and said in a broken voice, 'Come on; let's go.'

As a token of support Don put his hand on Iskander's shoulder for a second. The two men walked down the cemetery with their heads bowed.

'Want to come back tonight?' Don asked.

Iskander shook his head. 'No, Don, I don't think so. I've read a lot about you and Suzie in the papers, but now I want to hear the complete story from your own lips.'

They both nodded in agreement.

Note of the Author:

"Only in my imagination, could Ellis Henning and Mike Garcia be part of law-enforcement raids and carry guns to capture the criminals. So please, don't take it too seriously, it's all a product of my fun-loving fantasy world.

Characters are fictional and any resemblance to real people, living or dead, is purely unintentional and coincidental. I apologize in advance if any characters or situations seem to be the result of bias based on gender, race or nationality, although there is, I admit, some stereotyping. No offense is intended."

Ray Vandenburg

Ray Vandenburg, born in 1947 in The Netherlands, is a retired Dutch journalist. In 2006, he started a private tours organization to offer sightseeing tours of Holland and Belgium to U.S. residents and others. Ray has a special interest in the political and social system of the USA. He likes to write mystery books set in Florida, and often visits the state and other parts of the country. Ray lives near Amsterdam with his wife, Tineke, and dachshund, Noushka.

www.ingramcontent.com/pod-product-compliance
Lightning Source LLC
Chambersburg PA
CBHW041025170626
46815CB00001B/1